"Levi, you startled me..."

Cadence swatted at his arm, appreciating the firm angles of his chest and shoulders.

Look at his face. She chastised herself for allowing her thoughts to dwell on the wide expanse of him and glanced up.

"Glad you didn't drop this," he said, holding out the bottle of newly shaken juice, a wide smile spread across his face.

Cadence couldn't stop herself from admiring his perfectly chiseled jawline.

"Thank you," she responded, reaching for the jar.

Levi pulled it back, just out of her reach. He leaned down, wrapping his fingers around the handle of the lantern she held, and took it from her. He set the dim source of light down on a tall wooden crate and hooked his arm around her waist, pulling her body in close to his—the bottle of cider at her back—and closed his eyes as his mouth descended on hers.

The feel of his strength, his grief, his desire, all poured into that kiss. She relaxed against him, her hands unwittingly sliding up his chest, around his neck, and into the dark waves of hair at his nape as she allowed herself to indulge in the pleasure his lips brought to hers. Her whole body suddenly felt alive and she didn't ever want the moment to end.

Nevertheless, Levi pulled away, staring down at her with eyes the color of warm honey pooled inside rings of chocolate. He brushed her lips and jaw with his thumb and smiled.

"I've been wanting to do that for a long time." He picked up the lantern and returned it to her hand with a pleased grin and skipped up the cellar steps, two at a time, to the kitchen with the cider still in his hand.

Cadence pressed her fingers to her lips, unsure her legs would still support her. "Mr. Redbourne," she said to herself, "you are full of surprises."

Also by KELLI ANN MORGAN

THE RANCHER
REDBOURNE SERIES BOOK ONE
COLE'S STORY

THE BOUNTY HUNTER
REDBOURNE SERIES BOOK TWO
RAFE'S STORY

THE BLACKSMITH
REDBOURNE SERIES BOOK THREE
ETHAN'S STORY

JONAH
DEARDON MINI-SERIES
BOOK ONE

Available from INSPIRE BOOKS

the Iron Horseman

REDBOURNE SERIES BOOK FOUR
LEVI'S STORY

KELLI ANN MORGAN

inspire books

Inspire Books
A Division of Inspire Creative Services
937 West 1350 North, Clinton, Utah 84015, USA

THE IRON HORSEMAN

An Inspire Book published by arrangement with the author

First Inspire Books paperback edition October, 2014

ISBN-13: 978-1-939049-15-5
ISBN-10: 1939049156

Printed in the United States of America

PRAISE FOR THE NOVELS OF AMAZON BESTSELLING AUTHOR

KELLI ANN MORGAN

"Excellent storyline and characters that had my full attention from start to finish…"

—*Kathy Hathaway*

"Excellent story. Well-drawn characters. The plot is full of shocking twists and turns you don't see coming. Ms. Morgan delivers a well-written read that is enjoyable to the end."

—*Rocky Palmer* on THE BLACKSMITH

"The Blacksmith is Kelli Ann Morgan's most romantic book yet. It has the perfect mix of fun, romance, and Old West adventure…"

—*Grant Morgan* on THE BLACKSMITH

"Strong characters and a compelling story make this an unforgettable trail ride…"
—*RaeAnne Thayne,*
USA TODAY bestselling author on THE RANCHER

"…stimulating and remarkably written…"
—*A. Eric* on THE BOUNTY HUNTER

ACKNOWLEDGEMENTS

After a lot of blood, sweat, and tears—literally—The Iron Horseman finally came to life because of the help of a select few individuals and productions...

To all those historians who have produced information and accounts from many different perspectives on the actual historical events that happened around the marriage of the rails in 1869 and to David at the Golden Spike National Historic Site and Museum for answering even my mundane questions.

To all my fans who have been extremely patient waiting for Levi's story. You drove me to produce a book I could be proud of, no matter how long it took.

To my incredible alpha reader, Grant, who's blunt honesty and never ending encouragement have made me a better writer.

To my amazing beta readers, Rocky and Kathy. There aren't words to express my gratitude for your hours of dedication to this project. You've made such a difference.

To my son whose creative imagination inspires me to always dig a little deeper and whose support never goes unnoticed. I love you, baby!

And, as always, to my husband who continually spends innumerable hours talking through plotlines, proofreading manuscripts, and providing the kind of encouragement that keeps me true to my characters and stories. Thank you, my love. I could not do this without you!

*To all of the teachers in my life
who have influenced my love for writing,
who have supported me in my publishing efforts,
and who have encouraged me to reach for the stars.*

the Iron Horseman

REDBOURNE SERIES BOOK FOUR
LEVI'S STORY

CHAPTER ONE

Kansas, Redbourne Ranch, Early April 1869

Clank.

Metal slammed against metal as the oversized horseshoe fell to the earth, encircling the iron post that had been pounded into the hard ground. Levi Redbourne shook his head as he watched his oldest brother toss his second horseshoe into the air.

Clank.

This time it had stuck in the ground and fell over to lean against the pole.

"How do you do that?" Levi asked incredulously, using a stick to mark Raine's newest score in the dirt. "I guess your duties as assistant deputy in town haven't taken enough of your time. You've been practicing while I was gone."

Raine laughed. "Maybe you shouldn't be gone so much."

Levi missed being on the ranch. He missed his family even more, but the work he was doing with the railroad meant something. He'd seen far too many people lose everything after the war, so when the opportunity arose that allowed him to offer a new start for many of them in towns across the West, he'd jumped at the chance.

"A small herd of wild horses broke through the fence in the north pasture," their father exclaimed as he dismounted his horse and started for the stable at a quick pace. Jameson was as healthy and spry as any of his seven sons.

Levi and Raine both followed.

"I think two of our mares may be in heat. If they couple with that blasted stallion leading the herd, no one will want the foals," their father said, grabbing an extra rifle. "Tag and Ethan are both out on a run with Marty and I need some help. It's getting late, so we need to hurry. Levi, go get Cole. He can work with Maverick tomorrow. Raine…"

Levi didn't hear the rest of his father's instructions to his brother as he headed out to the corral where Cole, his youngest brother, worked into the late hours of the evening with the newest addition to Redbourne Ranch—a beautiful black Arabian stallion. This horse was vastly different from the Morgans and Quarter Horses they generally bred, but Cole had fallen in love with the stallion at auction and their father had relented.

"There's trouble," Levi called out to his little brother.

Cole pulled the rope in that he'd been using to run Maverick around the corral. He led the horse from the large enclosure, closed the gate, and mounted bareback. "Well, let's go."

Levi shook his head. "Show off," he called after him as he ran to the stable where Apollo, his own grey and black mount, had already been brushed down, watered, and stalled for the night. He reached up onto the wall to retrieve the tack he'd returned there just over an hour ago.

It wasn't long before the four of them were ready to ride. Cole had left Maverick in the stable and now rode one of the broken Quarter Horses. Levi wished Tag were here. His brother was one of the most talented wranglers he'd ever seen.

He would have loved the challenge of pulling two mares away from the bunch of wild mustangs. He probably would have tried to convince their father to capture the stallion and then offer to break him. Levi was like Tag in a lot of ways, but getting a kick out of being bucked off a wild horse over and over was not one of them.

Jameson whistled loudly. Seamus, their giant black and white sheep dog, bounded around the corner of the barn barking and wagging his tail with anticipation. It was almost as if he instinctively knew what he was supposed to do.

When they reached the north pasture, it didn't take long to spot the downed fence. The top two boards had been broken completely in half with splintered pieces dangling from the side and one plank lying haphazardly on the ground. Raine and Levi jumped their horses over the downed fence, then dismounted. They made quick work of strapping it back together with a skein of wire Raine had thrown into his saddle bag. They would have to bring some new boards out here in the morning with the wagon to replace the broken planks and the fallen post.

"It looks like they've headed over toward the creek on Cooper's property," Jameson said, circling back around to the fence. "Cole, go let Mr. Cooper know that the mustangs are running wild on his land. He'll want to make sure to keep his horses corralled for the time being."

"Yes, sir," Cole said as he pulled toward the Cooper stead.

It was near dark when they were finally able to round up the missing mares, along with a few others they'd recognized from neighboring ranches. They would keep the other horses in their corral overnight and then deliver them back to their owners in the morning.

"You look like you could use a bed." Raine clapped Levi on the shoulder once their horses had been tended to for the night. Again.

"I could use a little something to eat first," Levi replied

with a tired smile. "I'm famished."

They all laughed when his belly gurgled in confirmation. As they rounded the house, soft tones from a guitar carried to Levi's ears. Hannah sat on the porch at their mother's feet and played while Leah hummed along.

It was expected of most girls that they learn to play the piano, but for the Redbourne family, it had been a requirement for all of them. Some had learned to play better than others, but they all could pluck out a tune.

However, a few of them had chosen to play additional instruments as well—Hannah loved the guitar, Ethan played the cello, Rafe the harmonica, and Raine had taken after his father on the fiddle. As if on cue, the three brothers joined in and started to sing as they each stepped up onto the porch. Levi sat on the railing, Raine leaned against the doorframe, and Cole joined Hannah on the floor. The ballad seemed to resonate against the semi-enclosed veranda and Leah Redbourne closed her eyes, a smile resting on her face as she listened to her children's music.

"It's been a while since we've all sung together. It's too bad that everyone couldn't be here," Raine said knowingly.

"Christmas. You'll all be home for Christmas, won't you?" their mother asked, sitting forward on her chair. "Levi?"

The holidays at Redbourne Ranch were something to experience, from the turkey run and archery tournaments to the traditional selecting of the tree and dancing. He loved Christmas at Redbourne Ranch, but he just couldn't promise anything. Not right now.

"I'll do my best, Mama," he said, stepping forward and kissing her on the top of her head.

She gripped his arm and looked up at him.

"I've missed you, son," she whispered.

"Me too," he whispered back.

"How about something with a little more spirit, sis?" Cole asked.

Immediately, Hannah started plunking out one of the rousing songs she'd written just last year—evoking loud laughter and a few slapped knees. This song spoke of a young girl with seven overprotective brothers who scared off all potential beaus.

"I've got warm natillas cooling on the counter." Lottie, the family's beloved Spanish cook, opened the door, enticing them inside with her delectable custards.

"Did I hear someone say 'natillas'?" Jameson came bounding up the steps and through the door before the others could scramble to their feet. "I guess they're all for me," he called back, laughter filling his voice.

When Levi arrived in the kitchen, there were small warm custards sitting in front of several chairs. He took a seat and waited for his father's cue before scooping into his.

"Heard the train's leaving on Monday," Jameson said without looking up from his treat.

Levi glanced at his mother who had stopped eating mid-spoonful. He'd worried about how he was going to tell her he was leaving. She had always supported him and his other siblings—even when they had a mind to do something that took them away from her. She and their father had let his brother Rafe spend a summer living amongst the Pawnee Indians when he was just eighteen. Will was across the ocean studying at Oxford University—although he was expected to graduate this fall. Ethan and Tag often ran herds between Texas, Colorado, and Wyoming and were gone for long stretches at a time. And it wouldn't be long before Cole joined them. Still, Levi hated seeing the sadness on his mother's face each time one of them left.

Leah swallowed. "Well, we need to make the best of the time we have together." She managed a smile.

"The decision has been made to join the rails at a place called Promontory Summit in Utah early next month," Levi volunteered the information before anyone could ask. "I have

to make stops in several towns along the way with much
needed supplies."

"I still don't understand why you want to give up ranching
for an iron horse," Cole said through a thick bite of the cream
delicacy.

"I'm not giving anything up. I have the opportunity to
build up communities instead of tear them down. Not
everyone was as lucky as us after the war. Many lost
everything—their families, their livelihoods, their homes. I
wish I could do more. The government stipends only go so far."

Raine looked down at his custard, an amused smile played
on his face.

"What?" Levi asked with a mock punch to his brother's
shoulder. "You know how I can do more?"

Raine looked up at him with a wide spread grin, but didn't
say anything, he just took another bite of his custard.

Levi looked around at the others at the table. All appeared
equally as confused.

His oldest brother stood to clear his dish and the distinct
clacking of his fancy new spurs triggered a thought—

My inheritance.

But that would require finding a wife and his job didn't
allow proper time for that. No wonder Raine was smirking
though. He'd already gotten his sizable inheritance when he
and Sarah had gotten married. Levi didn't know how much
exactly, but he knew it would be enough to make a difference.
He shook his head and pushed the idea from his mind.

"My work with the railroad is full of adventure. Besides,
I'm taking Apollo along in the livery car and I'll get plenty of
opportunities to ride."

A bride? the thought sneaked in again. The railroad would
be complete in a month's time. Maybe he'd entertain the
notion then. He and his brother exchanged a knowing look.

Done. He scooped the last bite of the natillas into his
mouth and nodded. *After the ceremony, at the completion of the rails,*

I'll start looking for a wife.

"He's a Redbourne," Jameson said, looking up at Levi, and pulling him from his thoughts, "he'll always be a horseman."

Raine clapped him on the shoulder with a chuckle. "The Iron Horseman."

Chicago, Late April 1869

"I'm not going to lie. It's a dangerous assignment."

Cadence Walker hadn't joined the Pinkertons to be safe. "I understand, Annie," she told her friend and recent mentor. "I can handle a little gold nail."

Annie looked at her with pursed lips and squinted eyes.

"And the double-crossing braggart," Cadence added with a dramatized lilt and an exaggerated roll of her eyes.

"Just as I suspected," Annie gloated, her hands perched firmly on her hips. "I told him you were too emotionally involved for this assign—"

"Oh, but I—"

Annie held up a hand. "I think losing Ms. Warne has affected his judgment, but…he seems to think you've got the perfect cover." She shook her head, pulled the hem of her dress from the floor, and crossed the room toward an oversized wardrobe.

Cadence forced the upturn of her mouth into solemn corners. She missed Ms. Warne too. After all, the young woman spy had been the one to introduce her to Allan Pinkerton. But, if Cadence had learned anything over the last couple of years, it was that people left. They died. And she had no say in the matter. Not even her father, another Pinkerton agent, knew of her involvement with the agency. If he ever found out…

She shivered. She didn't want to think about the consequences. She'd still lived at home with her mother to maintain a façade of normalcy, but her life was far from normal and now that her mother was gone, she just wanted to get away from the city. She wanted to live her life and now she didn't have to hide who she really was.

"You'll be needing some extra weaponry." Annie opened the closet to reveal a wall of strapped guns and daggers, and shelves full of concoctions from the apothecary along with the vessels used to transport them.

Cadence pulled her decorative single shot pocket pistol from her corset and laid it on the table, followed by a fine handled dagger from her boot and a pearl gripped six shooter from the folds of her skirt. She lifted her foot onto a wood-backed chair and raised her dress just enough to expose the derringer hidden in the garter a few inches above her knee. She pulled it and rested it alongside the others.

"I think I've got what I need," she said with a satisfied grin as she imagined the rifle that lay with her already packed luggage. "For now," she added.

"Don't be arrogant, Cade. It doesn't become you," Annie chastised, but shut the wardrobe nonetheless.

Cadence returned her weapons to the inner workings of her clothing and dropped her foot to the floor—ruffling the skirt layers to hang properly. "I wish you could come along," she said matter-of-factly.

Annie turned to look at her and simply smiled. "You'll do a fine job."

Annie Kramer had been working with the agency for a few years longer than Cadence, but something in her vigor and excitement for the job had changed as of late. Her eyes were dim and her demeanor short.

"Are you all right, Annie?" Cadence asked, suddenly concerned for her friend. She took a step forward, but Annie turned and reached for the door.

"Of course." She looked back at Cadence and smiled meekly. "I'm just a little tired is all."

Cadence mustered a smile, but although she couldn't place it, something was wrong. Then it hit her. Annie had worked with Sir, Mister, Doc, or whatever-he-liked-to-be-called Durant quite a few times in the past and she wondered why Mr. Pinkerton had not chosen the woman for this assignment. She was the obvious choice.

"There's something else," Annie said, handing Cadence a folded piece of paper. "An agent has been compromised. He sent word that he found something big, but we haven't heard from him in days." Annie took Cadence's hands in hers. "I'm sorry, Cade."

"I thought this was just a simple delivery and protection detail."

"Mr. Pinkerton is sending two male agents along with you. They'll apprise you on the way."

"Annie, I—"

"You mustn't keep them waiting." Her friend motioned out the door.

Cadence held her ground for only a moment, scrunching her eyes into slits and staring at the woman. Something was terribly wrong, but it didn't take long before she relented, grasping the material of her skirt and lifting it from the floor as she left the room.

The train would leave at eleven and she needed to be on it.

Wouldn't her father be surprised when she showed up at the homestead just outside of Bryan, new Wyoming Territory?

She smiled. *Surprised indeed.*

Once she climbed into the black carriage that would take her home, she opened the note. The name of the missing Pinkerton agent stared at her with bold clarity. Eamon Walker.

Her father.

CHAPTER TWO

Unofficial Wyoming Territory

The echoing sound of a lonesome train whistle sounded in the distance. Levi Redbourne's ears perked up and his head followed the sound. He set his bags up onto the platform, tossed two bits to the liveryman, and took Apollo's reins, securing him to the hitching post next to the station.

Finally.

Three towns along the railroad route had already met with untimely disasters—unexplained fires, missing livestock, and miles of broken fences. Normally, he would have just thought them coincidences, but something in Levi's gut told him otherwise. It was only those designated as rail towns that were being hit. Supplies and knowledge of farming and ranching were vital out here and part of his job was to ensure they would survive the harsh winters. Along with the provisions, each settlement needed to be equipped with at least a sheriff and deputy.

While Flat Plains had been spared any incidents thus far, Levi had worked with the townsfolk to assure that patrols kept watch during the evening hours—at least for now. He would be grateful once the railroad was finally completed and hoped that would see the end to the rabble-rousers that obviously didn't want that to happen.

Hissing steam released into the air as the train came into view. It moved even slower than usual and it seemed to be making an odd clunking sound.

"That can't be good," Levi said as he stroked Apollo's neck.

It took several more minutes, but the engine finally came sputtering to a rest in front of the station followed by Levi's sleeping compartment and a mixture of several other coaches including the dining car, a livery, and numerous supply cars.

Levi hopped up onto the loading platform, grabbed his first bag and tossed it up onto the landing of his compartment, then the other. He turned to see a few townsfolk who had gathered around and waved.

Thud. Thud.

Both of his bags had been thrown back down onto the platform at his feet and he looked up to see the conductor, a short man with a thick blond mustache and spectacles.

"I'm sorry, Mr. Redbourne," James said heartily, "but I am afraid the train won't be leaving 'til morning." He stopped at the foot of the stair and pulled a watch from his vest pocket. "There's a problem with the water injector pump. We'll need to have a new one crafted by the local blacksmith." He leaned closer to Levi. "There *is* a blacksmith in this little town, right?"

Levi pointed to the tent with a wooden sign that read, *Smithy*. Although, he wasn't sure the blacksmith, who was young and still new to the trade, would be up to the task. Too bad his brother Ethan couldn't be here. He'd have new parts molded in no time at all.

"Good," James said. "While the smithy is making the part, we'll have to refill the water tanks manually. Then, I figure the crew and our," he cleared his throat and sent a fleeting glance toward Levi, "passengers can disembark and have a stroll through…" he looked toward the main street, "…town."

"Passengers? This train was supposed to be comprised only of crew and supplies. No passengers. What happened?"

James shrugged. "One guess." He glanced out at the crowd that had gathered around the station.

Thomas Durant. It had to be. The man was the ingratiating Vice President of the Union Pacific Railroad and generally got whatever he wanted.

Levi closed his eyes. He was tired and the last thing he wanted was to entertain some hoity-toity businessmen from back East. At least the trip to River City would only last a few hours. He could simply greet them then retire to his compartment for the remainder of the trip. He imagined that James would take good care of them.

"I've already checked out of the hotel, so I'll just leave my bags in my compartment." Levi motioned to the coach with his sleeping quarters. The coach wasn't the same type of luxury sleeping compartment as was often afforded the train's important guests, but it was a place to sleep—small as it was.

James stood in front of the short metal staircase. "I'm sure the proprietor would be happy to give you back your room. It will be much more comfortable." The man's face twitched, his moustache scrunching up briefly toward his eyes. "I'm afraid we haven't had time to prepare it for you."

Levi eyed the man warily, but said nothing.

"If you'll excuse me, sir, I need to head back up to the tinder car to tell Festus where he can find the smithy or we may be here a lot longer than expected." James still stood in front of the sleeping car's entrance.

"You're up to something, James."

"I'm sure I don't know what you mean, sir."

"Okay, I'll play along." Levi glanced over at the hotel. "You'll know where to find me." He hopped down off the platform, grabbed his bags, and untied Apollo. "Come on, boy.

Back to the livery for a few hours, then we'll go for a ride." He led the horse to the stables and offered the liveryman another few coins for his trouble.

With this delay, he would have the time to help the men put the roof on the new permanent structure that would house the mercantile, the sheriff's office, a trading post, and a post office. It was almost complete and it was about time the General Store could be moved from the temporary tent into the building. The bank, Day's End Hotel and Restaurant, livery, and two saloons all stood of their own accord on the opposite side of the street, but all were joined with a well-constructed boardwalk.

As he made his way over to the store, it seemed awfully quiet and wondered where everyone had gone. A small group of young children dashed from the mercantile with sticks of hard candy protruding from their mouths.

"Need some more hands?" he asked the robust woman who ran the place as he stepped into the mercantile tent. "Seems the train's not leaving for a while."

"Ah, Mr. Redbourne. I'd heard that the train was delayed. What happened to your friend?"

"My friend?" Levi asked.

"The fella you was in here with earlier. Tall. Young." Mrs. Dowdry placed a large jar of confections down on the counter, then wiped her hands on her apron.

"I think you're mistaken me for someone else," Levi said with a laugh. "This is the first I've seen you today."

"Unless there is someone in this world who has your same smile and good looks..." She didn't finish, but cleared her throat.

It can't be. Unless...

"Nah," he said aloud.

"I'm sorry?" she asked.

"It's nothing."

"Well, I'm afraid there's nothing that can be done on the

new building without more nails. We're all just waiting on the
new blacksmith, bless his heart. Don't ask me how they let that
happen, but well, the smithy, he's a little..." The store's
proprietress looked as if she was searching for a polite way to
finish her statement. "...slow," she finally said with a gracious
smile. "A group of them are heading over to Emaline's for
some supper. Can I help with you with something?"

He shook his head.

Levi appreciated how the people here were always ready
and willing to help each other. It reminded him of home.
Stone Creek, his home town, had grown into quite a bustling
little community, but you could always count on the people
there. He loved that about small towns and got that same
feeling here in Flat Plains. Levi tapped on the counter and
turned to leave.

"Thank you, Mrs. Dowdry," he said as he ducked under
the tent flap and walked back out into the sunlight.

It pained him to admit, but Emaline Granger cooked
some of the best meals he'd had since being home at
Redbourne Ranch. His stomach agreed. It had been a few
hours since he'd eaten his breakfast of warm bread with
huckleberry jam and scrambled eggs. He mentally added 'good
cook' to his ongoing list of what he would appreciate in a wife.
He'd made up his mind to stop in at the restaurant and tell
Emaline, the proprietress, that he'd be staying the extra night
and ask for his room back.

The town had really pulled together this last week as they
worked on completing the building where the Day's End
Restaurant and Hotel had taken up residence. As he stepped
inside, Levi saw the pride Emaline had taken in adding the
finishing touches to her establishment. He hadn't really noticed
them before, but frilly purple curtains now adorned the
windows and lavender cloths draped the tables topped with
freshly picked wildflowers. And even though she only had two
of the beds to furnish seven bedrooms, she already had guests

bidding for accommodation.

"Did you forget something, Mr. Redbourne?" Emaline asked as she stepped from the kitchen with two plates of food in her hands. The young spinster stared at him with wide, expectant eyes. "I'm sorry I couldn't wait on you myself earlier. It seemed there was a problem with some of the furniture I ordered in from Chicago and well…" she closed her eyes with a slight shake of her head. "Never mind. Aren't you heading out today?"

"You did wait on me this morning, Emaline. At breakfast. Remember?"

"Of course," she said.

Levi nodded, satisfied.

"And again just a half hour ago."

The whole town seemed to have lost their minds.

"I'm just looking to get some supper, Em." He motioned to the group of men sitting around one of the larger tables in the room. "Fried chicken, if you've got any." Levi smiled.

Emaline's eyebrows furrowed together. "All right," she said slowly, the words drawn out as if she didn't quite understand. "I can't believe you're still hungry after all that roast and potatoes. It must cost a fortune to keep you fed," she said with a grin. "Just one moment and I'll have a fresh batch out."

Wouldn't he know if his brother was in town? It was too much of a coincidence. Tag was on a drive. Why would he be all the way out here in Flat Plains? Redbourne Ranch didn't have any contracts this far west. At least, not yet. Levi bent down and looked out the window. People bustled by as they went about their day, but he couldn't see anyone who remotely resembled any of his brothers. And it wasn't that big of a town.

She's mistaken.

Emaline delivered the plates still balancing in her arms to their proper tables and returned with a smile, all confusion gone from her lovely face. "I still have the rest of that cobbler, if you've changed your mind as well."

"I'll take some of your cobbler anytime," he said with a grin and a wink.

Emaline shook her head, but beamed up at him. "Please have a seat anywhere you like."

"Thanks." Levi took a step into the dining room. "Oh, Em? You don't by chance still have my room available, do you? Looks like the train's staying the night."

"Sorry. Just rented it out about a few minutes ago. To a pretty young thing too. You can have one of the others if you're interested. We can spread a pile of blankets on the floor." She grinned.

He was not going to sleep on the floor. "No, I'll be fine. Thank you. I think I'll spend the night on the train." He had a perfectly good sleeping compartment. He just needed to find out what James was hiding.

Levi took a seat next to the table of men who'd been working on the new structure. Mealtime was fairly uneventful, except for the fly that buzzed the sheriff's daughter's face, causing her to dump her soup into her lap. Levi felt a sense of relief when she excused herself to clean up as he would no longer have to listen to her endless chatter.

"So, how long do you think it will be before the train connects through California?" one of the farmers asked from across the aisle. The man's brothers had all headed West searching for gold and Levi knew how hard it was to be away from family.

Everyone's attention suddenly turned to and settled on Levi. He was sure they all had better things to do that sit around listening to him. "Next month," he said with an affirming nod. He took another bite of his mashed potatoes and ignored the stares still aimed in his direction.

Someone tugged on his shirt sleeve. He looked up to see Mrs. Cavanaugh, a portly little woman with a near white braid hanging down the side of her.

"Earl and I would love to have you stay with us for the night," the woman said, patting him on the forearm. "I know you've already checked out of your room here and since my son and his family won't be visiting for a few months, there will be plenty of room."

It sure would beat sleeping on the floor upstairs.

"That would be lovely, ma'am. Thank you."

The older woman beamed at him. "Supper'll be ready at seven," she said, squeezing his cheek. She reminded him of Lottie.

Levi used his napkin to dab at the corners of his mouth, set it atop his plate, and pushed himself away from the table. The woman's eyes followed him as he stood, her neck craned backward so far he thought she might tip over. He took a step back, bowed slightly with a tip of his hat, and smiled.

"I'll see you and Mr. Cavanaugh at seven." Levi stepped outside. The fresh air felt amazing. While the temperature had warmed considerably, there was still a light chill to the breeze.

He glanced over to the smithy where a dozen railroad workers had gathered around the fire. He suspected there wouldn't be any new nails today. The last few days had been spent mending fences, digging irrigation canals, and helping many of the farmers and ranchers construct outbuildings and corrals. A good horseback ride would do him some good before being cooped up in the boxcar on their way through River City and on into Laramie.

Levi headed toward the livery. It had been one of the first buildings to be erected in Flat Plains and still smelled of fresh cut wood mingled with varnish. The sound of an unfamiliar woman's voice caught Levi's attention and he scanned the oversized barn for her whereabouts. He couldn't see anyone. Not even the liveryman. He walked back to Apollo's stall and to his astonishment found the woman standing at the gate, palm open, feeding his horse an apple.

Her dark pecan-colored hair, unrestrained by a hat or

bonnet, fell softly about her shoulders. He'd gotten to know the people in town and for the life of him couldn't think as to how he'd missed the likes of her.

"Hmhmmmm." Levi cleared his throat and stepped forward. "Beautiful, isn't..."

The woman turned to face him.

"...he?" he finished.

Her eyes, darker than molasses and topped with thick, full lashes, burned into his mind. She was the most captivating creature he had ever seen. The soft blue of her dress made a stunning contrast against the nearly black tresses that hung loosely about her shoulders. Suddenly he felt at a loss for words.

"Here you are, Miss Walker." The liveryman appeared from a small room at the back carrying a saddle blanket and a heap of leather tack. He glanced up at Levi. "Mr. Redbourne?" He glanced toward Apollo and back to Levi. "I didn't think you'd mind. Miss Walker here wanted to take out one of the horses and she took an immediate liking to yours. I'm afraid she's set her sights set on him."

Levi glanced at the liveryman, sure his own mouth gaped open. He could hardly believe the man was truly indulging the idea of renting the woman *his* horse.

"I'm afraid the lady will have to select one of the others. Since the train isn't leaving until tomorrow, I'm heading out to the Cavanaugh place tonight and Apollo is how I'm going to get there."

The liveryman looked between the two, apparently unsure how to proceed.

The woman turned around and placed her elbows behind her, resting them on the stall's gate. "Mr. Redbourne?" she asked, seeming to clarify that she had addressed the correct person. "I was under the impression that the train leaving tomorrow is a supply train and isn't taking any regular passengers on this run."

Levi eyed her coolly.

How would she know that?

"Perceptive. It's not." He didn't feel like justifying himself—even to someone as beautiful as her. "Taking on any passengers, I mean." The train had become like a second home to him. Each of these scheduled supply trains always included his sleeping compartment. "I'm not a passenger. There will be another train on Thursday that will take you all the way to Ogden if you're interested."

Miss Walker raised an eyebrow and pushed herself away from the stall gate.

Levi swallowed hard. It was simple—she was beautiful.

Flat Plains had only been settled for a few months and he wondered how long she'd been living here. He didn't recall ever having seen her before. And he would remember the likes of her—though 'resplendent' was not on his list. He didn't know of any Walkers living around here. However, his good friend Eamon Walker, a Pinkerton for the railroad, was stationed farther west just outside of Bryan and he wondered if the man might have relatives who'd just moved to town.

"Mr. Gainey," the woman said, "I'm sure the chestnut mare over there will be just fine." Her smile added a touch of honey to her otherwise dark eyes. She brushed past Levi and followed the liveryman to the stall across the stable.

Had she really expected him to give up his horse when there were plenty of others here that didn't belong to one of the livery's patrons? He didn't even know the woman, but with eyes like hers, Levi imagined there was many a man who would do things out of character for her.

He shook his head—something that had become all too much of a habit lately—glad he would be on the train tomorrow, away from the very attractive distraction. *After the completion*, he reminded himself as he removed his tack from the saddle rack.

It didn't take long for Levi to get Apollo ready for his ride.

He led the gelding out into the street, unwittingly hoping for a glimpse of Miss Walker. It appeared that she'd already gone, so he mounted and turned toward the creek. He told himself it was part of his job to be interested in the newcomers, but something about her intrigued him.

As he rode, Levi admired the vast landscape surrounding him. Flat Plains had certainly been named correctly. There were a few sparse trees alongside the creek that meandered through a set of small hills. Although the mountains were visible, they were in the far distance from the new town.

CRACK!

A gunshot sliced the air in the distance and Levi urged his mount toward the sound. The Brickman farm wasn't too far from here. They'd had a lot of trouble over the past couple of weeks with coyotes and Levi hoped they hadn't returned. The young family's herd was small, but they couldn't afford to lose any of their cattle.

"Let's go, boy," he called out as he flicked the reins and squeezed his heels.

He hadn't gone far when he saw a flash of blue disappear down the side of the grassy bank. He slowed the horse as he cautiously approached the creek. Indian raids were not commonplace in this small town, but he needed to be careful. He reached down and pulled the rifle slung across the horse's side. He moved closer.

There, standing barefoot against the water's edge, Miss Walker hunched down, filling her canteen.

"Little cold out here to be going around without your shoes, isn't it?" he asked loudly.

She whipped around, pistol drawn.

"Whoa," Levi said, lifting his hands to where she could see them. "I didn't mean to frighten you." The little shooter she held was not known for its accuracy or distance, but Levi had no intention of testing its capabilities. Why would a woman out here need a little gun like that anyway? And where had she been keeping it? "A little jumpy, aren't you?"

She smiled up at him and released the pistol into a neutral position against her flat, lifted palm. "Sorry. A woman can never be too careful." She slid her weapon into the folds of her skirt.

"Where did your horse get off to?" Levi lifted his head and glanced across the flat landscape, but he couldn't see the chestnut mare. "Did she throw you?"

"Of course not," Miss Walker replied as she returned to her squatting position at the creek. She didn't elaborate.

Something had obviously scared the mare.

"It's quite the distance back into town. Can I offer you a ride?" It was the least he could do. Miss Walker looked up at him and bobbed her head. She took a long swig of the water, returned the cap to the canteen, and wiped her mouth.

"Thank you." She climbed back up the side of the grassy embankment without much of a struggle and it was then Levi noticed the dead snake a few feet from the woman's shoes.

He'd only heard one shot. There was something more to this Miss Walker than he'd originally thought. Too bad he wouldn't have time to uncover her secrets. Maybe he could come back in a few weeks and get to know her a little better.

'Brave.' Check.

Miss Walker sat down next to the trail and proceeded to replace her shoes. When she stood upright again, Levi dismounted and extended a hand to her.

"This is most chivalrous of you, Mr. Redbourne."

He lifted her up into his saddle with little effort and pulled himself up behind her. The heady scent of her hair filled his nostrils and he groaned inwardly. It had been a long time since a woman had had this kind of effect on him.

The train's delay just might prove to be worthwhile after all.

Levi Redbourne, or the Iron Horseman, as the men on the train had called him, just might have been the most beautiful man Cadence had ever laid eyes on. He was tall and refined and had wonderful taste in horses. The real kind—not steam locomotives.

She lay back against his lean form and reveled in the spicy scent of him. She had been pleased to learn that he would be accompanying her on the train toward Laramie. At least he would be someone to talk to, other than the two brutes Pinkerton had sent to accompany her. They hadn't been much for conversation.

In addition to finding her father, she had been charged with getting close enough to Mr. Thomas Durant that she could protect him with a close proximity. They were supposed to rendezvous at Bryan in two weeks, the same town where her father had gone missing, and she would accompany him the rest of the way into Promontory. She only hoped that she would be able to locate her father within that time. Time was running out and she couldn't let any man get in the way of her assignment. Handsome or not.

"So, tell me, Miss Walker," Mr. Redbourne's resonant voice sent a wave of gooseflesh down her arms, "which farm is yours? I haven't seen you around town before."

Good heavens, she thought, *he thinks I live in this tiny little town.*

"I don't live here," she said, trying to mask her disdain for small towns. "I arrived on the train and I don't plan on staying. I'll be heading out in the morning. Same as you."

He raised an eyebrow at her. "Now, how did you manage that?"

"Manage what?"

"As you mentioned earlier, that is a cargo train with supplies for the rail towns. No passengers, remember? How did you manage to get yourself on board?"

Cadence snorted airily. "My father works for the railroad. He has a place just outside of Bryan and I'm going out to meet him."

That is my cover after all. And it wasn't a lie.

Levi cleared his throat. "You," he said incredulously, "are little Cadie Walker?"

Cadence sat up straight in the saddle, away from the firmness and warmth of his chest. Only one man called her Cadie, and that was her father. She turned as far as she could in the saddle, but it was no use. She could not meet his eyes.

As if sensing her uneasiness, a deep, resonant laugh filled her ears. "Eamon speaks of you like you are a little girl."

"You know my father?" Her eyes opened wide in disbelief at her luck. Or lack of it.

She was surprised at her sudden enthusiasm to hear about her father. It had been years since she'd seen him. She just hoped she wasn't too late. His job as a Pinkerton for the railroad had taken him away from home for far too long. He'd tried to convince her mother to move west so they could be closer, but she'd insisted she and their two children stay in Chicago. Cadence felt like she barely knew her father anymore, but in that moment, she realized just how much she wanted to be reacquainted.

You sound like a little girl, she chastised herself inwardly. *Stop it.*

"Of course I know him. Eamon and I have worked very closely over the last year or so. He speaks very fondly of you." He snapped the reins on the horse with a slight jerk of his wrists. His arms felt good around her and a flush of heat spread in her cheeks at the thought. "Look," he said quietly, almost a whisper in her ear.

Cadence looked up to see her chestnut mare a few yards ahead of them, drinking from the stream. For a horse that had been bred out West, she sure had been jittery around that slithering critter.

Levi pulled his mount to a stop and helped Cadence down from the saddle before getting down himself. "Here, hold these, will you?" He handed Apollo's reins to her and took a few carefully placed steps toward the mare. She looked up at him and nickered softly. Levi reached out for her reins, which dangled on the ground and into the edge of the water, patting her neck and mumbling something Cadence couldn't hear. It didn't take long for him to coax the animal back to where she stood.

"Why don't you ride Apollo back and I'll take this old girl here." With a gentle nudge of her nose into Levi's face, it seemed the 'old girl' approved. Levi laughed—a great sound.

"Why do they call you the Iron Horseman?" she asked. "It seems you are anything but iron-like with horses, so I assume it has something to do with your job since I've heard steam locomotives referred to as iron horses."

Her question evoked a wide smile in his tanned features and a loud guffaw erupted as he tossed his head backward with obvious amusement. Cadence's heart did a little flip-flop inside of her chest. She couldn't remember ever having seen a man with teeth so white or a smile that lit up such a beautiful face so fully. She felt the heat rise in her cheeks again at the thought.

Still chuckling, Levi collected himself enough to look at her. "I'm afraid, my lady," he said with a slight bow, "that is a story for another day." He pulled himself up onto the mare. "We should get back."

Cadence climbed up into the saddle on his horse and clicked her tongue. "I'll race you back," she called over her shoulder as she quickly urged Apollo into motion.

"Oh, no you don't," she heard Levi call from behind her.

Cadence couldn't help the wave of giggles that erupted from the pit of her belly as blood rushed through her body, leaving a tingling sensation in its wake. Apollo was powerful. No wonder Levi had chosen him.

The wind whipped through her loose hair and she scolded herself for leaving her hat back at the livery. It would take a long time to get a brush through her hair tonight, but right now, it didn't matter. She was having more fun than she'd had in a long time.

The sound of Levi's whistles and hollering had quieted. Cadence dared a glance behind her only to find that he was nowhere to be seen. A slight twinge of worry crept into her thoughts and she considered turning around until she saw Levi to her far right galloping up the middle of the street from the other direction toward the livery. She quickly inched her already bunched dress up a little higher on her legs to give her more room, leaned down closer to the saddle horn, and squeezed her knees into the impressive gelding's flanks. With the livery focused in her sights, she raced toward the building with reckless determination.

As she approached the livery's front gate, Levi whizzed past her and she watched with amazement as he dismounted at a run directly in front of the livery while the horse was still moving. Too late, Cadence realized she was running out of road. She pulled herself up with a tightening of the reins, but the sudden change caused Apollo to rear.

Within seconds, she found herself flying backward. She closed her eyes until she landed fully on her hind end. Thump.

Ouch.

She opened one eye and then the other. Levi raced toward her, all playfulness erased from his handsome features. She'd been lucky she hadn't killed herself.

"You were lucky you didn't kill yourself," Levi breathed her thoughts as he reached down and scooped her up from the ground.

A smile played with Cadence's mouth.

"Are you all right?" he asked quietly, his brows crumpled together and his face stoic.

Cadence was strangely touched by his concern, then she remembered why it had happened in the first place.

"You ride with the circus or something? I couldn't take my eyes off you." Heat flooded her cheeks and she wanted to crawl into a hole. "I mean…" What could she say? "You can, um, put me down now, Mr. Redbourne. I am not hurt. Well, my pride maybe, but I am fine."

Levi laughed as he set her back on her feet. "It was just a little trick I learned from my cousin, Lucas."

"Is he as addlepated as you evidently are?"

"I'm not sure anyone is, really. Well, maybe one person."

"Oh, yeah? And who might that be?"

"That," a resonant voice from behind them boomed, "would be me."

Cadence turned around to find an exact replica of Levi Redbourne approaching from the direction of the hotel along with another man equal in height and stature, but with a shade lighter hair.

"Tag," Levi breathed out with a grin. Without looking back at her, he made the distance between him and his double in a few short strides and they embraced.

Curious.

CHAPTER THREE

Levi shouldn't have dismissed the idea of his brother being in town so readily. He'd just chalked it up to wishful thinking. But, folks had been acting strange toward him all morning. The firm grip his brother had on him felt wonderful. It had been way too long. When Tag released him, he pulled Cole into a tight hug. It was so good to see them both.

"Hey, baby brother," he said to Cole, "I'm surprised they could pull you away from that stallion long enough to get you out this direction."

"He's done," Cole beamed. "It didn't take long. I rode him here."

Levi hadn't seen him in the livery.

"He's out running the pasture behind the stables."

Levi couldn't help the grin that broke across his face. He pulled Cole in again for another hug and lifted him off the ground. He couldn't have been more proud.

"You're a natural."

"You can put me down now," Cole said through short gasps for air. "I want to meet your lady friend."

Cadence. He'd nearly forgotten. How was that even

possible?

Levi realized the scene he was making. Three Redbourne-grown men already gained enough attention, they didn't need anymore.

"And who, might I ask, is that lovely woman you had all wrapped up in your arms over there, Levi?" Tag motioned with his chin toward Cadence, but didn't wait for an answer. He walked over to where the young beauty was still brushing the dirt from her backside as she led Apollo toward the stables.

Levi's neck grew warm.

Where are your manners? he could hear his mother saying and quickly pushed the devilish thoughts from his head.

Keep it in check, Redbourne.

He caught up to Tag.

"This is little Cadie Walker," Levi said as they approached the livery door. "My friend Eamon's daughter. You remember? The railroad Pinkerton I brought home for a visit last summer?"

Miss Walker flashed him a look full of daggers.

"You're Cadie?" Cole extended his hand to hers and pulled it up to his lips. Levi rolled his eyes. It was odd to see his baby brother, now a man, trying to impress a girl. Besides, Cole was all show. He hadn't even been home to meet Eamon. He'd been in Silver Falls, Colorado visiting his best friend.

"My name is *Cadence*," she said coolly, looking at Levi, "and yes, Eamon Walker is my father. You are obviously some relation of Mr. Redbourne here." She motioned with her head, but did not look at him. "Twins."

Tag laughed. "We," he swooped his arm in front of him and took a bow, "are *Mr. Redbourne's* brothers, ma'am. Cole and Taggart."

"It is my pleasure to meet your acquaintance." She dipped her head in a slight bow, her hand still in Cole's. Levi had to fight the urge to swipe it away. Not that it should matter to him any. Still, he couldn't help the relief that washed over him when she slid her fingers from his brother's grasp.

"So, what is Eamon's daughter doing in a little town way out here with the likes of you?" Tag elbowed Levi in the gut, then directed his attention to Cadence. "I thought you were supposed to be living back East somewhere."

"Chicago, actually. I am moving out here to be closer to my father and to help him run the homestead."

"Wait, Eamon is giving up the agency?" Tag asked.

"He purchased some land in Bryan," Levi informed them, "where he's building a homestead. I think he wants to have a place to hang his hat. He won't be a Pinkerton forever." Levi still didn't understand his friend's reasoning. Eamon had a home in Chicago where his wife, son, and until recently Cadence still resided. Although his wife had made it perfectly clear that she had no intention of moving west.

Cadence shrugged. "He thinks I'll find a husband out here where the odds are better than ten to one."

Levi felt the color drain from his face.

"Don't worry, Mr. Redbourne," she placed a hand on his chest, "I have no interest in my father's plans...except for the homestead, of course." She smiled. "Chicago was stifling—especially under my mother's constant watch." She turned to his brothers. "I've only just met Mr. Redbourne this afternoon when he...rescued me from a runaway horse."

Tag and Will both nodded knowingly. Levi groaned. He would never hear the end of this.

"What a lucky day for us," Cole said with that dimpled grin that always seemed to charm the ladies.

"Will you be riding the train with us to Bryan?" Cadence asked Tag, ignoring Cole's attempt.

"'Fraid not. We've got work to do," Tag answered.

"What *are* you fellas doing all the way out here?" Levi managed to ask, still reeling from the events of the last five minutes.

"We heard you were causing some kind of trouble out here and thought we'd drop by to lend a hand." Cole laughed as he clapped Levi on the shoulder with a chuckle.

Levi turned to Tag.

"Business," Tag said matter-of-factly. "Dad bought a new stud for the ranch from a breeder in Cheyenne. So, we drove a small herd of cattle up to one of our buyers, but the horse won't be ready until tomorrow morning. A Mr. Dowdry saw us as we rode back into town. He stopped me." Tag smiled. "It didn't take long before we realized he thought I was you. When we explained, he told us you'd given him a second chance with a new life as the owner of the mercantile here in Flat Plains. He told us he believed you'd be around 'til Thursday."

"Since we can't pick up the stallion until tomorrow, we decided it would be worth the extra trip for the chance to catch up with you," Cole cut in. "This one," he ruffled Tag's hair, "just isn't the same without you around." Their younger brother was as tall as them, seemingly still growing, and he wouldn't let either of them forget it. "He really has become such a bore."

Tag hit Cole's arm with the back of his hand.

"I can't remember the last time he made me laugh," Cole said with a hint of amusement. "You really have to consider coming home. It's just not the same there without you—not nearly enough shenanigans to be had."

"I should be home for Christmas." Once the transcontinental line was complete, Levi imagined it wouldn't be long before he would be able to start visiting home more often. The journey across country would only take a few days. He glanced at his brothers, genuinely glad to see them. "Have you had any supper?" Levi asked with a grin. "Miss Emaline makes a wonderful fried chicken plate."

"We picked up some of her vittles an hour or so ago."

"Of course you did." He remembered Ms. Emaline's confusion.

"I think we've mixed up quite a few people in this little

town of yours too." Tag glanced around the main street and Levi's gaze followed. A small group of townsfolk stared and murmured amongst each other.

"Well, I'll be." Mrs. Cavanaugh bustled over the boardwalk and down onto the street, pushing her way through the small crowd. "I knew it. I wasn't seeing things after all, Levi. There *are* two of you."

Levi laughed heartily.

"Mrs. Cavanaugh, this is my brother, Tag."

"I'm older," Tag said with a smirk.

"By three minutes," Levi retorted.

"That's all I needed." Tag loved the fact that he'd had a head start.

This time it was Mrs. Cavanaugh's turn to laugh. "I'm making up some hot potato soup and rib cutlets tonight for supper. You'll both come, won't you?"

Tag and Cole stood up straight.

"Yes, ma'am," the brother's answered in unison. Levi could imagine each of them licking their lips at the idea of a home-cooked meal after a few days on the trail.

"It'll be good to have boys in the house. If only for the night." Seemingly satisfied, Mrs. Cavanaugh turned to leave when she caught sight of Cadence. Levi thought the older woman must have recognized her because she threw her hands in the air and rushed to the spot where Miss Walker still stood.

"My heavens. Aren't you just the prettiest little thing? Did you arrive in town with these men, my dear? Which one of these strapping young cowboys belongs to you?"

Levi contained a chuckle at the worried look on Mrs. Cavanaugh's face. A woman of Miss Walker's age would not be traveling alongside two grown men without a chaperone unless she was married to one of them or related.

Cadence looked back and forth between the Redbourne brothers and Mrs. Cavanaugh.

"Cade Walker, ma'am. I'm afraid I'm just here for the

night as I arrived on the supply train."

Visible relief washed over the older woman. "Where ya headed, darlin'?"

"Bryan area. My father has a place there."

Levi was sure by the barely contained exasperation on Cadence's face that she was tired of explaining herself to others.

"Levi here is leaving on the train tomorrow," Mrs. Cavanaugh nodded knowingly. "I see you two have already been acquainted."

The woman would have him married to any girl who could smile right if he wasn't careful.

"Well, where is your traveling companion, dear?" Mrs. Cavanaugh asked.

Miss Walker smiled kindly at the older woman. "It's not too much farther to Bryan. I'm on my own." She placed a hand on Mrs. Cavanaugh's. "But don't you worry. It's fine," she cooed. "My father is a Pinkerton. He taught me well. I can take care of myself."

Levi didn't doubt that. An image of the dead snake back by the river flashed through his mind and he smiled to himself. If it had been Hannah, his baby sister, all seven Redbourne brothers and their father would have been called out to handle the situation and she would have been bit long before they'd gotten there.

"I'm sure you are a very capable young woman," Mrs. Cavanaugh told her. "Do you have a place to stay tonight?"

"Yes, ma'am. I've arranged for a room at the Day's End Hotel."

"You're a smart little gal, aren't you? Well, you'll be joining us for supper as well, you hear?" Mrs. Cavanaugh patted Miss Walker's hand and let go with a curt nod of the head. "Levi knows where we live," she said as she turned and walked back across the street and disappeared into the small crowd.

"We haven't been this spoiled in a long time," Cole said as he stepped up next to Levi.

They all chuckled in agreement.

"Well," Cadence said, her hands on her hips, "I guess I'll see you fellas tonight." She brushed past them and stepped up onto the boardwalk, heading toward the Day's End.

"Do you think mama would approve?" Cole asked, pointing with his chin toward the retreating Miss Walker, a wry grin gracing his features.

Levi slugged him playfully in the side. "Not for the likes of you. Besides, I thought you were going to go to school overseas."

"For her, university could wait. Or, I could just marry her and take her with me."

"Like hell." Levi realized he'd spoken the words aloud.

All three of them laughed.

"Fire!" someone yelled from down the street.

Levi looked up to see swirls of black smoke rising from the newest building in the town's square. The bank.

There was no mistaking the acrid scent of pinewood burning. Shouts rang down the street. The few men in town ran down the dusty road past Cadence and toward the hotel. She glanced back at the livery, where she'd left the Redbournes, but to her dismay they were already gone.

"Seems there's a fire at the bank," a newly familiar, deep, resonant voice sounded behind Cadence and sent a chill gliding down her arms and over her skin. A reluctant smile touched her lips as Levi grabbed a hold of her hand and pulled her with him down the boardwalk. When they reached the Day's End, he let go of her hand and pulled open the door.

"Stay here. I'm going to see what's going on," he said before turning on his heel to leave. "I'll be right back."

Stay here? She tried not to take offense as she realized he was actually trying to protect her. A fire in an empty new building didn't sound coincidental and the only way she would be able to help would be to see it for herself. Cadence pushed open the door and marched down the rest of the boardwalk toward all the commotion.

The tall rectangular building was in flames and several men and women lined the street passing buckets down the row to the burning bank. For such a small town, they were surprisingly adept. Levi and his brothers were beating at the flames licking the sections of the boardwalk, and Cadence found herself staring, not knowing what else to do. It was an uncomfortable feeling.

A woman ran down the wooden walkway carrying several heavy blankets. She shoved one into Cadence's hands. "We could use every hand," the woman said before joining the others beating on the blaze.

Cadence bunched up the thick woolen covering and ran forward swinging the cloth, slamming it down on the flames closest to her.

"My bank." A thin, balding man with wired spectacles wiped at his dripping forehead with a rag. He stood next to her, looking up at the flames, exasperation lining his soot-stained face.

A loud cracking noise came from the building.

"Everyone back away," someone shouted.

"What happened here?" Cadence asked the obvious owner of the bank with a grunt as she beat at another plank.

The man looked down at her as if noticing her standing there for the first time. He didn't grace her with a response, but dropped his hands and merged into the small crowd that had stopped in their spots, holding buckets.

"I'm 'fraid there is nothin' more we can do, Ezra," a man said from the far end of the building. "We'll just have to let it burn."

Cadence froze. *Let it burn?*

When the banker recovered from the shock of the man's words, he hung his head.

"Look on the bright side, Ezra, at least you didn't have the whole town's money inside." Another man stepped forward and patted the banker on the back.

"We'll get it rebuilt in no time," yet another called out.

Cadence was touched by the deep sense of community, but it seemed that no one cared about the real issue here. How had the fire started and why was nobody looking for the answers.

"Ezra," Levi walked up to the small group of men and Cadence's heart did a little dance in her chest, "I'm sorry to disturb you, but this doesn't look like an accident. Can you tell me what happened here?"

Handsome *and* smart. Nice combination.

Cadence tried to remind herself that this little town was not her responsibility, but she'd been trained too well to ignore the signs. Someone had started a fire in the new bank, but why? There was no money to steal, they'd said it was practically empty, so, what would anyone have to gain?

It is none of your concern, Cadence Walker. You have a job to do and you best stay focused on that. Her mental tirade warred with her desire for justice.

"Look out!" a woman's voice screamed from the street.

Cadence looked up in time to see the sign atop the pent roof slide off the collapsing structure toward her. She tried to jump out of the way, but the scorched wood reached her with alarming speed, its weight knocking her face-down onto the street.

Pain welcomed her into its fierce embrace as scorching heat burned through the flesh of her leg above her boot and gravel burrowed deep into her cheek.

Get up! She demanded of herself.

With all the strength she could muster, she kicked the

board from her legs and managed to turn herself over onto her bottom only to see that the hem of her dress was on fire. Before she could clear the hair from her face enough to see what she was doing, Levi was there. He gathered the material of her dress and expertly beat it against the rest of the folds to extinguish the flames. Without a word, he scooped her up into his arms and ran with her toward the tent that currently served as the mercantile.

With a protest on the tip of her tongue, Levi dumped her into the horse's trough where half a tub of water still remained. It splashed up onto her throbbing face and soaked her now displaced coiffeur.

Horrified, Cadence opened her mouth to tell Levi Redbourne exactly what she thought of this plan, but realized that the cool water felt wonderful against the burns on her skin. The stench of burned flesh lingered in the air and she wondered if he'd been hurt during his act of misplaced chivalry.

"Sit," Levi commanded, as if she were some sort of dog.

"Is that how you always treat a lady? How dare you speak to me that way?"

"This wouldn't have happened had you listened to me. I thought I told you to stay put." Levi ran his hands through his hair, wet with perspiration.

"You, Mr. Redbourne, are not responsible for me. I can take care of myself."

"I can see that." Sarcasm dripped from every word.

Cadence pounded her hands against the flat surface of the water surrounding her. If he only knew the extent of her capabilities.

Time to change tactics.

"Mr. Redbourne, I am sorry," she said in a voice so sticky Cadence thought she might be ill. "I'm afraid that I am not accustomed to taking orders from anyone. Especially perfect strangers." A wet tendril fell down onto her face and dripped down her chin. She lifted the sodden lock and pushed it aside only to have it fall once again in front of her eyes. "But you seem like you're only trying to help."

Levi took a deep breath, then turned, without a word, and disappeared into the mercantile tent. It was only a matter of seconds before he returned with a cloth and a bottle that looked as if it contained some sort of salve. He dipped the rag in the clear substance and reached up to her now throbbing cheek. The cool cloth touched her skin and she sucked in a startled breath. It stung.

Oh, quit being a baby.

CHAPTER FOUR

Cadence Walker was stronger than that. She would not allow him see her wince again, but when he pulled the knife from his belt, she was unsure whether she would be able to maintain the tough façade.

"And just what do you think you are going to do with that?" Cadence eyed the weapon with apprehension—not that she really thought he would try to harm her in any way. Unwittingly she reached down to her boot and felt for the dagger she kept there.

"There are a couple pieces of gravel embedded in your cheek—"

"And you're going to cut them out? I don't think so." She started to stand, but he pressed down on her shoulder, keeping her in the increasingly cold water.

"I'm not going to cut them out," he said with a shake of his head. "I'm just going to coax them out with the flat side of the blade."

As if that sounded any better. She watched him as he poured some of the clear liquid over his knife, unable to take her eyes off his face. He was gentler than she'd expected him to be.

Levi avoided her gaze as he quietly worked on his task.

"Shouldn't a doctor be doing this?"

"Shhh," he chided.

Cadence closed her eyes to the pain that emanated from her face. She was sure she looked a sight.

"There. Now that wasn't so bad, was it?"

Gooseflesh cascaded down her body. The chill from the water and the light breeze added to her discomfort.

"Now, let me see that leg." Levi held out his hand like he expected her to swing her legs out of the trough on display for the whole town.

"Levi?" one of his brothers called from a distance, but she wasn't sure which one. "She all right?"

"She'll be fine," he yelled back over his shoulder. "She's quite capable," he said more to himself than to his brother.

Cadence wanted to smack the irritatingly smug twitch that touched the corners of his beautiful mouth. Not that she'd noticed.

She *was* capable. However, every smart woman liked to be taken care of once in a while. If she had to be stuck in a small town like Flat Plains for the night, at least it was in the company of a very…capable man.

"Well?" Levi asked.

"Well, what?" she asked back.

"Your leg."

Heat flooded Cadence's otherwise cool cheeks.

Of course.

She hesitated a moment longer, then decided she'd save her strength for another battle. She turned so she could lean against the backside of the trough and lifted the injured leg from the water—sopping skirt and all.

Levi's fingers touched her bare skin as he pulled back the folds of her dress to the area just above her knee where the burning sign had left its mark. Cadence was grateful it hadn't been the other leg, where she'd strapped her favorite blade. Luckily, the water hadn't been deep enough to get to her revolver, but she worried about the pistol secured at her thigh. She didn't know how she would explain her weapons if he were to find them.

"Just stay put, would you?" Levi said as he stood.

"But..." she tried to protest.

He reached down and lifted her chin with his finger. It took her a moment before she could meet his eyes.

"Trust me," was all he said before he turned and walked back toward the bank.

What was wrong with her? She was Cadence Walker, a Pinkerton for heaven's sake. Her emotions were all too real for the charade she played. Her nerves were normally as thick as steel, but for some reason, she felt like the helpless female where Levi Redbourne was concerned. That just wasn't acceptable. It was time to get herself together.

Cadence stood up in the trough and shook the excess water from her hands. Luckily the watering trench was stationed near a hitching post and fence. She steadied herself against the wood for support and climbed out of the oversized tub. Her feet hit the ground with a thud. The bottoms of her skirt squished into the dust, immediately sullying the hem. She raised her hands into the air. Her dress clung to the curve of her body as it hung heavy with the excess weight of the water.

"Ooooo," she grunted. The wet dress skimmed her blistered skin and Cadence gritted her teeth against the sudden pain.

The Day's End was just a couple of doors down. Luckily, she had a change of clothes, but doubted that this dress would be dry before she had to be on the train when it left in the morning.

The town seemed oddly quiet now as many onlookers watched in awe as the embers of the bank still smoldered with light wisps of pale gray smoke—the flames still licking at the scorched wood. Something was definitely going on in this town. Fires didn't just start on their own in brand new buildings. From what Cadence could tell, there wasn't a doctor, and from the looks of it, there wasn't a sheriff either. These people needed help. The train would be leaving in the morning and that didn't give her much time.

"Howdy, Sheriff," the liveryman called from across the way.

Cadence turned to see a tall, burly man with a bright shiny badge pinned to his chest making his way toward the rubble.

So much for detective work. He can take care of it.

She marched to the hotel, her hem and feet now covered in mud, and stopped at the front door. She highly doubted that Ms. Emaline would appreciate her making tracks through the restaurant, but her leg ached and her face throbbed. She just needed a clean rag and the water basin from her room.

A twinge of guilt settled in Cadence's gut as she thought of Levi. He had tried to take care of her, but admittedly, she was as stubborn as her father. She sat down on the wooden bench just outside the door and made quick work of removing her boots. After squeezing the excess water from the bottom of her dress, she gathered the base of her skirt up into her arms, careful to expose nothing above the knee, and with one hand full with her boots and the other the folds of her dress, she pushed her way into the restaurant. A few dozen eyes spun to greet her.

Of course, it would be dinner time. She nodded her apologies, quickly made her way to the staircase, and headed up to her room. This place needed a separate entrance. Maybe she'd suggest that to Miss Emaline the next time she saw the woman.

Her room was simple. Yellow roses adorned the curtains over the quaint little window on the far side of the room and the bed covering had the same coloring. It was nice, and right now, the warmth of the room felt like heaven. Careful not to get mud on any of the furnishings, Cadence lifted her dress up over her head and wadded it up—hem first. She considered making her way back down to the creek where she'd killed the snake, but thought better of it. A clean rag sat on the vanity and a fresh pitcher of water graced the table. She'd make do.

Luckily, the room had wooden floors. Cadence was careful to avoid the rug until she was able to clean the mud from the sides of her boots. She placed them, upside down, next to the vanity and proceeded to wipe down her legs. She winced when she reached the spot on the side of her calf where a few small blisters dotted the reddened skin just above the section that had been protected by the top of her boot. The area seemed to grow hotter by the minute. She remembered how nice the cold water of the trough had felt. She rung the dirty water from the rag into the basin and proceeded to douse the cloth with fresh water from the pitcher.

The cool rag felt nice against her skin.

Knock. Knock.

"Hello, dear, it's Emaline. Is everything okay?" the proprietress asked through the door. "I saw you sneak in and it looked as if you might need some help. "

Cadence stood up and walked over to answer the door before realizing she had not yet donned another dress.

"Just a minute," she called, pulling a lavender skirt from her trunk along with a white collared blouse. It was her favorite combination and she wanted to look nice for dinner tonight. As soon as she finished the last button on her shirt, she swung the door wide.

Miss Emaline's eyes grew wide and she stepped back away from the door, apparently startled. "Is everything all right?" She reached a hand up toward Cadence's face, but pulled it away as if she'd crossed some line of impropriety. "What...what happened?"

"Sorry." Cadence hadn't intended to scare the woman. "Everything is grand," she said.

"But, your cheek. Did someone hurt you?"

"No, it's nothing. Really," she said when the woman looked as if she didn't believe her. "I just took an embarrassing little spill on the road."

Emaline looked down at her feet.

"The room is lovely." Cadence wanted to put the woman at ease.

Emaline looked up at her again, a smile alight on her features.

Cadence glanced over at the table where the wash basin sat filled with filthy water. "Is there somewhere I might be able to dispose of the water?"

Emaline looked at her with scrunched eyebrows. "Would you like me to refill your pitcher?"

"That won't be necessary. Sorry about the floors. I hope I didn't dirty them too badly."

"Nothing a mop can't handle." She smiled. "You can just toss the bath water out the window into the alley. I've got some shrubbery growing down there. A little muddy water won't hurt them."

Cadence nodded.

"Well, then. Will you be joining us for supper?" Emaline asked.

Cadence cleared her throat. "Mrs. Cavanaugh has invited me to join her and her husband for supper this evening. I hope that's all right."

"Of course, dear. Bessie is a wonderful cook. I'm sure you will have a lovely time. Is there anything else I can get you in the meantime?"

Cadence looked around the room. She couldn't think of a single thing at the moment. "I wish I had time for a hot bath, but I think that will have to wait until I get to my father's ranch."

Emaline smiled and nodded. "The creek is still a little cold yet for a...swim."

Both women laughed.

"Thank you for your generosity, but I think I have everything I need." A drop of water fell onto Cadence's cheek."

Her hair.

Emaline had turned to walk away.

"Actually, Ms. Emaline, do you think you might help me with this mess?" She held up a damp lock of hair.

The hotel owner's face lit up. "I would love to. It is such a beautiful dark color."

"Thank you." Cadence stepped away from the door to allow Emaline to enter.

"I wish you were staying longer. There aren't many people our age in this town—not yet anyway."

For the first time, Cadence looked really hard at the woman. Her hands were work-roughened and her eyes puffy from being tired, but Emaline was indeed a young woman. It was not appropriate to ask a woman her age, but at this moment, Cadence really wanted to know.

"You've really accomplished a lot here. There aren't many women courageous enough to brave life in the West."

"And yet, here *you* are," Emaline said as she led Cadence over to the vanity.

"I admire you. Can't be easy running this place out here in the middle of…"

"Nowhere?" The woman filled in for her. "I'm one of the lucky ones."

Cadence folded her lips together. "Do you have help? A partner?"

"A husband, you mean?" Emaline clarified with a smile as she collected the brush from the dresser.

Cadence remained quiet.

"I'm afraid I've not yet been married. When Mr. Redbourne came to Boston and offered me the opportunity to start a new life here in Flat Plains I thought he was mad."

Cadence sat up a little taller on the bench at the mention

of the Redbournes.

"But when I realized that I could either cook and clean for the family I was attending for a mere room and board or I could have my own place and cook and clean for profit, I chose Flat Plains."

"Why did Mr. Redbourne offer...?" Cadence knew her words were coming out wrong.

"Why would Mr. Redbourne offer such a thing to a lowly servant girl?"

"I'm sorry. That's not what I meant. You are lovely. Truly."

"It's all right," Emaline said, collecting some of Cadence's hair into her hands and brushing through the wet locks. "Levi said that he needed people who weren't afraid of a little hard work to help settle some of these towns in the West. He said there were three men or more for every woman out here, and he was right." Emaline looked at her through the mirror with raised eyebrows and a sneaky little grin.

"Is there someone special here?"

"Mr. Redbourne was right," Emaline stated, pulling tighter on Cadence's head. "There are a lot more men than women out here, but not all of them are the marrying kind."

"But you have your eye on someone. I can tell."

"Jeb Richards," Emaline whispered with a nervous giggle. "He has a daughter just a year or two younger than me, but he is a good man. Have you met him?"

"Can't say as I have." Cadence hadn't met many of the townsfolk in this little place. She'd only been here the better half of a day, but there were some names and faces that came readily to mind. Jeb Richards wasn't one of them.

"He's the sheriff here," Emaline clarified.

"Ahhh," Cadence noted. She'd seen him a little earlier and had wanted to catch up with him to discuss the fire.

Emaline worked through Cadence's damp hair. She set the brush down on the bed and proceeded to work with her fingers, tugging and twisting. Cadence suspected that the woman was braiding her hair, which would be nice and simple for tonight.

"Thank you for helping me."

"How'd it get all wet anyhow?" Emaline asked without reservation.

"Your beloved Mr. Redbourne tossed me in the trough."

Emaline gasped. "He what?"

"The burning sign from the bank landed on my leg," Cadence said.

The woman gasped again. "It didn't. Are you all right?"

"I guess he thought soaking me in the horse's drinking trench and embarrassing me in front of the entire town would be the quickest and best way to cool it off."

Only a moment of silence passed between them before they both burst into laughter.

"He is handsome, isn't he?" Emaline said after a short time.

"Who?" Cadence asked, but she knew exactly to whom Emaline referred.

"Mr. Redbourne, of course. And did you know he's got six brothers ta boot?"

Seven Redbourne men? What would the world do?

"Yes. Mr. Redbourne is handsome. If you like strong jawlines and perfectly shaped lips."

Emaline guffawed loudly. "You do like him."

"Did I just say that out loud?"

Emaline finished with the braid and dropped it around the side of her neck and let it fall down in front of her. Cadence reached up, running her hand down the copious length of it.

"Well, you're right. And he's kind, and smart, and from what I've seen, still unattached."

Cadence's heart made a little skip.

Emaline stood up. "I like you, Miss Walker."

"Cade, please."

"Cade," Emaline affirmed as she took a step toward the

door. "All right, I've got to see to the supper crowd, but we'll talk before you leave tomorrow."

Cadence nodded with a painful smile and reached out, grabbing her new friend by the hand. "Thank you."

Emaline gave her shoulders a little squeeze and then closed the door behind her.

Cade reached up to the cuts on her face and winced. She turned back to glance into the mirror. A light blue and purple tinge had started to show just beneath the surface of her skin below her eye.

What a story that'll make.

Clouds glazed over the sun, casting a shadow in her room. Cadence glanced at the clock on the vanity. It was time to go. She looked down at her bare feet and then to the closet where her soaked dress boots lay. Luckily, she'd grabbed an extra pair from the bag she'd left on the train. They were older and worn, but she didn't imagine the Cavanaughs or their guests would be looking at her feet.

Cadence hoped that the liveryman would still be willing to rent her another horse after her not so graceful dismount that had landed her on her backside. She bent over to retrieve her dry boots and grimaced. Her rear end ached, her face still throbbed, and her blistered leg stung. What could she say? Levi Redbourne had quite the effect on her. He'd turned her into a perfect fool in just one day.

The thought of seeing him again caused a hollow sensation to develop in the pit of her stomach and she quickly donned her boots—stained and all. As she went to leave the room, she realized she still had not thrown out that basin of muddy water, so she sauntered to the other side of the room and lifted the window that opened into the alley. The basin was heavier than she'd expected and it sloshed a little onto the wooden floor of the bedroom. Grateful she hadn't spilled any on her favorite white blouse, she reached the window. With a slight jerk of her hand, Cadence tossed the muddied contents down into the flowers growing below.

"What in tarnation?" she heard a familiar voice bellow from below.

She stuck her head out the window and had to stifle a giggle when she caught sight of Levi staring up at her, muddy water dripping down his perfectly carved face.

"Of course," he said, wiping his hair out of his eyes. He shook his hands free of the water, shook his head, and strode out onto the main street, grumbling.

"Whoops."

Splash.

An onslaught of dirty water emptied down on him like rain in a storm. Thickened liquid coursed through his too-long hair and down his face. He reached up to his cheek to wipe away the little rivulets that coursed down his face and pulled away a finger-full of dirt.

"What in tarnation?" He looked up.

Cadence Walker's head poked out from an open window two stories high.

"Of course," he said, wanting to wring her little neck. Had she intended her target or had it just been happenstance?

Levi flicked his hands at the air, dirty water splattering onto the buildings surrounding him, and he headed out into the street. He'd simply come into the alleyway to admire the wooden planters Emaline had filled with brightly colored wildflowers and other green foliage. He'd recognized the flowers as the same ones they grew along the creek.

After reminding himself multiple times over the last quarter of an hour that he wasn't trying to locate Cadie Walker, he'd finally decided to join his brothers at the livery to get the horses to take out to the Cavanaughs place. She'd just disappeared while he'd been trying to help her. If Cadence didn't want his help, well then who was he to force it on her?

'Frustrating as hell' would not make it on his list. It didn't matter that her mouth haunted his every thought, or that her laugh still tickled his ears.

When he reached the stables, he saw Apollo grazing in the corral alongside a dozen other horses—including Maverick. Apollo hung his head over the fence. Levi rubbed the gelding's neck and handed him the apple he'd purchased in the mercantile tent.

"Women," he said through gritted teeth. "They're enough to drive a man mad."

"Having trouble there, are ya Levi?" the liveryman asked from the chair in front of the window—his feet propped up while munching on some fruit of his own. When he looked up at Levi, he sat up straight and tossed his core into a can. "Well, why're ye soaking wet?"

"Miss Walker." Levi didn't care to elaborate.

The Irish stable owner tsked, then chuckled. "Women'll do that to ya."

Levi had a mixture of feelings for the woman. She was beautiful, there was no doubt, but there was something more about her. She irritated the hell out of him, but in an endearing sort of way. He was mad.

"Do you have somewhere I could clean up a bit?"

"Through there," the liveryman pointed to the door to the room behind his chair, "you'll find some towels. The pump is out back near the trough." He chuckled again. "I guess that's what happens when you dump a perty lass into the horse's drink." He full out laughed as he leaned backward against his chair and picked up a pipe.

Levi guessed he probably hadn't thought through his actions with Miss Walker well enough, but the woman had been on fire. He'd only done what any man would have done.

Right? he asked himself. The trough had simply been the closest water available. He blew out a breath. Maybe he had just been trying to teach her a lesson for not doing what he'd told her to do and staying put, but he'd thought it harmless enough. Apparently, he'd been wrong.

Loud laughter echoed in the livery as Cole and Tag walked in through the gate.

"What happened to you? Little Cadie Walker dump *you* into a trough?" Tag mocked.

Levi didn't answer. He growled and headed for the towels.

"Impossible." Cole's mouth dropped to a gape. "It really was her? What happened?" he asked, following him inside the livery.

Levi didn't feel like talking about it. He just wanted to dry off and forget about the woman. He grabbed one of the cloths and headed out back to the water spout. A few good pumps and water sprang from the faucet. He dipped his hands into its cool freshness and splashed it against his skin. How had he gotten into a mood?

Enough.

When he lifted his head, Cole and Tag each held out towels for him to wipe his face and hands. He looked at them as they tried to contain the chuckles that threatened.

"Okay, I guess I deserved it," he said with a gritty edge to his voice. He snatched the towel from Cole's extended hand. One was not enough. He needed to change. At least his shirt.

Admitting he'd been wrong was not something he'd had to do very often—not that she hadn't needed water on that leg—but dumping her in the trough was probably not the right way to go about it. He couldn't help it. She got under his skin and that hadn't happened in a long time.

"You have some way to wash your clothes in that fancy train car of yours?" Cole asked, jerking his head toward the station.

"It'll keep," Levi responded, throwing the towels back at his brothers.

"What does that mean?" Tag asked.

"It means I'll have them washed once we get to River City." The next town on the route had few more hills than Flat Plains, but he guessed the name had been contrived from wishful thinking as there was no big river to speak of. However, he knew a few of the women there who would be happy to help him out. He had to admit, he'd been spoiled by the many townsfolk in each of these communities—many of whom were grateful for the fresh start he'd offered.

"We? Once *we* get to River City?" Cole raised an eyebrow.

"Ah, come on," Levi said as he headed inside. "It's getting dark. The Cavanaughs will be waiting on us."

"Shouldn't we go collect Miss Walker?" Cole asked.

His little brother, like all of the Redbourne men, loved women. But at his young age, he hadn't had much experience with them and Levi figured that wasn't from lack of trying.

"Yeah," Tag chimed in, "Mrs. Cavanaugh invited her. I'd hate to see the little lady ride out all alone when she could keep us company along the way."

"Speak of the devil," the liveryman said, jumping up from the chair and exhaling a breath of smoke. He'd obviously been listening to their conversation. "Why, Miss Walker. This lovely mare will be accompanying ye on the train tomorrow, heading for Laramie. I thought ye might want to take her out to your supper invitation with Mrs. Cavanaugh."

It wasn't the same mare she'd taken out earlier in the day, though the horse had similar coloring. A darker, almost mahogany color, but similar.

"Thank you, Mr. Gainey," she said without taking her eyes off of Levi. "Mr. Redbourne," she started, her lips folding together and then apart before finishing, "may I have a word?"

"Whooooaaaa," Cole chuckled.

Tag whistled low.

"Shut up."

CHAPTER FIVE

Cadence bit her lip. She had no idea what to expect or exactly what she would say when Mr. Redbourne reached her, but her mother had always taught her that she couldn't just ignore her mistakes. Her heart beat faster every step Levi took toward her. How could he look so handsome, even now, with wet hair and a recently mud-stained shirt?

The memory of being tossed in the cold water trough flashed through her mind. She remembered how he'd commanded her about like a dog, and suddenly, she no longer wanted to apologize.

"Yes?" Levi inquired when he reached her.

"Are you ready? I thought you and your strapping brothers might escort me on the ride out to the Cavanaughs."

He just stared at her for a moment, like he'd expected her to say something different. Then, with a knowing glean in his eye, the corners of his mouth turned upward.

"Ma'am," he said, bowing slightly with his hand in front of him. He winked before turning on his heel and walking toward the stall where Apollo had been housed. "My brothers don't bite, you know. You could have said that in front of them." He lifted a black Stetson from the post and pushed it down firmly on his head. "Let's go," he said, leading Apollo outside.

"Aren't you going to change your shirt?" she called after him, leading her own mare out into the street.

"Yes, ma'am." He pulled a white garment from the saddle bags of his horse.

Cadence didn't know what to say. Surely, he was not going to change his shirt right here. In front of her. And the whole town. She turned away from him.

He laughed.

After a moment, she dared a glance over her shoulder. There he stood wearing a blue shirt, almost identical to his brother's. She looked around for Tag, but didn't see him.

"Looking for someone," Levi said in her ear. How had he gotten behind her so quickly?

Cadence whipped around. Levi towered over her, adorned in a fine white linen shirt. She felt her brows crease together in the center of her forehead.

They all laughed.

Tag, who'd been standing next to Apollo in the blue shirt, handed the reins to Levi.

"That's unnerving," she said matter-of-factly.

"That was nothing compared to their usual antics," Cole told her, admiration lining his voice. It wasn't hard to tell that he looked up to his older brothers.

Cadence could only imagine the havoc they would cause if they had a mind to. Levi quickly hitched his horse and hers to the empty cart that had been leaning on the ground in front of the stable.

"We'll ride," Cole said when Levi motioned to the back of the buckboard. He and Tag pulled out ahead of them astride their horses.

The drive to the Cavanaugh's place was fairly uneventful and filled with conversation. Cadence wondered if the

Redbournes were ever at a loss for words. Although Levi hadn't spoken a lot, he seemed to be in good spirits. She was glad. While the dumped water hadn't been intentional, it had given Cadence a sweet sense of satisfaction—retribution at being tossed into the trough.

"Well, come on in. Come on in." Mrs. Cavanaugh met them at the front gate. Even from here, Cadence could smell the delicious aroma of cooking meat. Beef had only been allowed as a delicacy more than anything at home, as fresh meat was not as widely available in Chicago as it was out here. She was grateful for the invitation to eat with the Redbournes at the Cavanaugh's table.

Cadence wanted to jump down off the wagon, but thought better of it as Levi came around to offer her his hand. She placed her hands on his shoulders and he lifted her by the waist and set her on the ground in front of him.

"Thank you," she said with a smile as she turned for the front porch.

"Lawsy sakes, child. What on earth happened to your face?" The short woman hovered her fingers just above the cuts on Cadence's face.

"It's nothing, Mrs. Cavanaugh. Really." She hoped the wounds would heal quickly as she had already grown tired of having to explain.

As if sensing her irritation, the older woman dropped her hands into her apron. "Let's get you inside. Supper is already on the table." Mrs. Cavanaugh placed her palm against Cadence's back and guided her into a chair at the beautifully decorated table.

"It looks lovely." Cadence was reminded of the parties she used to attend as the table was set quite formally. And the food smelled so good.

The men joined them shortly. Mrs. Cavanaugh nearly pushed Levi into the chair directly across from Cadence. It amazed her how easily such a small woman could command these large men.

Mr. Cavanaugh offered grace.

"You heard the bank burned to the ground earlier?" Levi asked after he'd finished chewing a bite of meat.

"News travels fast out here," Mr. Cavanaugh replied.

"Such a shame too. Ezra just had his new vault installed. He was so proud of that building." Mrs. Cavanaugh slurped up a spoonful of soup. "Who could have done such a thing?"

"I still don't understand why it was more important to get that bank built, than to complete the building for the General Store." Mr. Cavanaugh cut off another piece of beef. "But, you sure picked some good folks, Levi. This is beautiful country. God's country."

Silence.

This territory had seemed more like a barren wasteland to Cadence than God's country, but she figured that these folks would find beauty anywhere. Maybe she'd just been too preoccupied with thoughts of her father and her assignment than to actually appreciate the differences the landscape had to offer.

"Miss Walker here was trying to help put out the fire and the bank sign tumbled down right on top of her," Levi said before taking another bite of his food.

"You must have been awfully scared, my dear." Mrs. Cavanaugh placed a hand over Cadence's.

"She's real lucky to have nothing more than a few small burns on her leg and those cuts on her face. It could have been a lot worse."

Why did he have to mention it? She just wanted to change the subject. Mrs. Cavanaugh did it for her.

"So, Miss Walker, did Levi recruit you too?" The question seemed simple enough, but Cadence wasn't sure how to respond.

"Recruited?" Cadence asked. "I've only just met these gentlemen. My father is the one who recruited me to the West.

"It's okay, dear," Mrs. Cavanaugh patted her on the shoulder. "Not everyone gets chosen special like us, isn't that right Earl?"

"Now, Bessie," her husband warned, but in a gentle sort of way. "The girl is certainly made of the stuff it takes to make it out in these parts. Leave her be."

"Where did you say your family is from, my dear?"

Cadence wasn't sure where this conversation was leading, but alarm bells starting going off in her head. "Chicago originally, though my father travels a lot with the railroad and has purchased land just outside of Bryan for a new homestead."

"Oh, my. How terribly exciting. Are you heading to Bryan then to be with your pa?"

"Why all the questions, Bess? Let the girl eat her supper." Mr. Cavanaugh looked up from his food to wink at Cadence.

"A body can be interested, can't she?" Bessie stared at Cadence, apparently still awaiting a reply.

Cadence swallowed the warm mouthful of soup she'd taken. "Yes." She unfolded her napkin and dabbed at the corners of her mouth. "There wasn't much left for me in Chicago…" Suddenly, her reasons for leaving swelled to the surface and she didn't want to talk about it anymore. She hadn't thought of Daniel once today.

Everyone stopped what they were doing and looked at her expectantly.

Cadence sucked in a short breath and smiled. "So, I am going to Bryan to find my father an—"

"You mean he's not expecting you?" Mrs. Cavanaugh opened her mouth in what Cadence thought was an attempt at mock horror. "And no chaperone," she tsked. "You're traveling all alone out here where anything can happen and no one knows where you are?"

Suddenly, the older woman didn't seem so endearing.

"I know where she is," Levi chimed in, earning him an uncertain look from tonight's hostess.

Cadence offered him a grateful smile, then turned to Bessie. "Of course he knows I'm coming," she lied. "I just meant that I've never been there before and I'll have to find the ranch once I get there."

"Good." Bessie harrumphed. "Every woman, especially one as pretty as you, needs a good man around to help her. You look real hearty, like you got a lot of good child-bearing years on you, dear. Don't you think so, Levi?"

All three Redbournes coughed. Levi nearly choked on his food.

Cadence bit her lip to stop herself from smiling.

"Sorry?" he said, asking for clarification after downing near a full cup of his drink.

Cadence wasn't looking for a man. Daniel had been everything she'd ever wanted and the thought of being married to someone other than him was something she'd not allowed herself to entertain in the three years since her love had been killed.

"I was just saying that Miss Walker seems like she would make a good wife."

It took a moment for Levi to recover. "I'm sure she would indeed." He scooped another spoonful of the delectable potato soup into his mouth, but did not take his eyes off Cadence.

If only they knew. She could cook and clean with the best of them. She'd also been known to knit a scarf or two and darn socks—though she preferred to do things that took her away from mundane chores. As she finished her supper, Cadence glanced down the hallway and noticed the most intricate and brilliantly colored pieced quilt she'd ever seen.

"Mrs. Cavanaugh," she exclaimed as she pushed herself away from the table, "is this your work?" She reached up and, without actually touching the cloth, ran her fingers over the stitching. In her life before joining the Pinkertons, Cadence had participated in many domestic undertakings. She'd held tea parties, quilted, and—

Thump! Thump! Thump!

"I wonder who that could be at this time of night." Mr. Cavanaugh stood up from the table to answer the door. "Are you expecting anyone else, my dear?"

Mrs. Cavanaugh shook her head as she joined Cadence next to the hung quilt.

"Evenin', Sheriff."

"I'm sorry for the intrusion, Earl, but I have a matter to discuss with your guests." Sheriff Richards pushed in through the small doorway and glanced over the room, from each of the Redbournes to her. "Would y'all mind stepping outside for a moment?"

Cadence looked at the man from head to toe.

So, that's Emaline's fella.

"Awww, Jeb." Mrs. Cavanaugh, a good foot shorter than the sheriff, stepped in front of everyone and placed her hand on the Mr. Richards' chest. "I'm sure whatever it is can wait until morning. But, you're welcome to come in and sit a spell."

"'Fraid not tonight, Bess. From what I understand, Levi's leaving on the train tomorrow and I need a word."

"It's all right, Bessie," Levi stepped up next to the woman and put his arm around her shoulder. "We'll be right back." Levi motioned for his brothers to follow. When his eyes met Cadence's, they locked momentarily, and he winked. Again.

All three Redbournes walked out the door. Cadence moved to follow. She was itching to know about the fire, but Bessie placed a hand on her arm to stop her retreat. A moment later, Levi poked his head back in.

"He wants you too."

Cadence exchanged looks with Mrs. Cavanaugh who nodded her approval and moved her hand to Cadence's back and gently pushed her toward the door.

"I'm sure it's fine, dear. Levi will take good care of you."

It was Cadence's turn to cough. Why did everyone seem to think she needed a man to take care of her? Her mother,

Annie, and now Mrs. Cavanaugh.

She stepped into the cool evening air and wrapped her arms around herself.

The sheriff scratched his cheek and ran his tongue over his teeth, making a squeaking noise as he sucked in.

Cadence smiled to herself when she thought of how sweet Emaline was on the man. She could see how his easy manner and modest good looks would attract the lovely spinster.

"Levi, as you probably suspected, it looks like the blaze at the bank was no accident. Someone started that fire and I want to know why. I know you vetted every one of the people living around here and I thought you might have some idea where to start. Is there anybody here you might suspect of being capable of doing such a thing?"

Levi scrubbed his face with his hands. "There's been a lot of growth in this town since I brought people in, Sheriff. Of those, there isn't a single person I wouldn't trust with my life. Why would anyone here want to see the bank destroyed? It'll be an important foundation for this town."

"That's what we're trying to find out."

"Miss Walker," the sheriff turned his attentions to her, "I noticed you standing near the bank when the train first arrived this morning, and—"

"Surely, you don't think I had something to do with it?" she asked him point blank.

"I certainly do not, but," he scratched his head, "we was wondering, that well, with your pa being a Pinkerton and all, I expect you got some of his smarts and thought you might have seen something suspicious while you were acquainting yourself with our little town. What do you think? Did ya?" he asked.

Cadence thought for a good long while before answering. She was just grateful she hadn't become a suspect. After all, she'd only been in town one day. Of course, Taggert and Cole had only been here as long as she had, and a number of the railroad crew had all arrived at the same time on the same train.

"I don't think your culprit lives in Flat Plains."

She'd expected them to laugh. Most people didn't take well to women with ideas—especially about the law. They didn't.

"What do you mean?"

"Well, everyone living here has a vested interest in seeing this little town succeed. I think the answer lies in who doesn't want to see it succeed. I would start by talking to anyone new in town—including me, the Redbournes here, and the crew who arrived this morning."

"Nicely said," Levi commented.

Cadence couldn't help being pleased by his words.

"Wasn't me," Cole said.

"Don't look at me." Tag raised his hands in the air.

"Well, everybody is pretty new here, though I have seen a few unfamiliar faces over the last couple of days. So, who is new to town?"

"Obviously, it wasn't any of us," Cadence said, offering the Redbourne brothers a little smile—which still hurt her face. She had to stop doing that until the cuts and bruises on her cheek and below her eye healed. "But there are plenty of people who arrived with the train—from the engineer and conductor to the boys keeping the engine fueled." She didn't mention her discreet traveling companions who had opted to stay back on the train.

"I guess we've got a little work to do, deputy," the sheriff spoke over his shoulder.

Cadence tilted her head until she saw the shadow of the dark figure behind Sheriff Richards. The short man stepped into view, but with the fading light, it was still hard to see him fully.

"This here is my new deputy, Mathias Horn. He's helping me out with this investigation."

Each of the men shook hands, but he simply nodded in Cadence's direction.

"There's a few of 'em staying at Emaline's place," Deputy Horn spoke. "Some of the others holed up in tents behind the station, and the rest, I heard, stayed on the train. The way I figure it, if it was somebody from the railroad, they'll be headed out in the morning. Why don't we just wait and see."

Even in the low light, Cadence could see the sheriff's jaw clench. The younger man, it would appear, still had a lot to learn about keeping the law.

"Thank you all for your time." The sheriff tipped his hat. "Ma'am. I'm sorry to have interrupted your supper."

Levi stepped forward and placed a hand on the sheriff's shoulder. "Let us know if there is anything else you need."

"Your little lady here has been a lot of help. You should keep her around," he said, tipping his hat before mounting his horse.

Not him too.

Once the sheriff and his deputy left, they headed back into the house.

"Why would somebody from the train want to start a fire in a new bank in this newly sprouted town?" Her curiosity was getting the better of her. She couldn't help it. She wanted to know what had happened.

"That's exactly what I intend to find out." Levi glanced at Cadence.

Was that admiration she saw in his eyes?

Her heart flipped over in her chest.

This might be a problem.

"I'll be right in," Levi told the others. He wanted to sit out in the fresh cool air and think.

Cadence stopped at the door before heading back into the house. When she caught his gaze, their eyes locked for a few unspoken moments, then she disappeared inside.

Miss Walker was as smart as a whip. With the tidbit of information she'd been given, she'd made a solid assumption. When the sheriff had asked about the townsfolk, Levi had gone over each of their interviews in his head. Not one would be capable of doing such a thing. He thought of all the new people he'd met over the last week, including the green deputy. People had been moving in from back East since the day Flat Plains built their first permanent structure after the railroad had moved on.

Levi sighed heavily as he ran his fingers through his hair. Union Pacific officials had received some threats over the last couple of months, but had deemed them harmless. Now, given the incidents over the past few weeks, it seemed the rumors were true. Someone was out to sabotage the railroad and he needed to be prepared. There were plenty of Pinkertons on their payroll. He suspected Eamon would be first in line to get to the bottom of the trouble, but his friend was in Bryan.

Levi leaned against the fence and glanced out across the flat prairie. The waning sun splashed bright pinks and orange hues across the cloud-filled sky. Detective or not, something bothered him about the whole situation, he just couldn't put his finger on it.

Why the bank?

They were lucky no one had been seriously injured or killed.

"Levi," Tag practically yelled.

Levi had been so caught up in his thoughts he hadn't heard his brother calling. "Sorry. Were you speaking to me?"

"Miss Walker has a room in town. We believed seeing her home safely would be the correct thing to do, but didn't think it appropriate to have you escort her without a chaperone."

Eamon would kill him if anything happened to his daughter on his watch.

"And you two are the chaperones?" Levi asked with an air of disbelief.

"I told your brothers there was no need, but they are insisting on escorting me back. It's only a couple of miles. Really, I will be fine."

"Miss Walker, if you think for one moment that our mama raised a bunch of hooligans, well..."

"You'd be right," Tag chimed in with a chuckle. "But, she taught us manners too. You'll have an escort back to town one way or another."

"Well, *gentlemen*," she emphasized, "I would be happy for the company. Thank you."

Levi and his brothers headed to the stable to retrieve their horses.

"I guess there is some adventure in what you do, big brother," Cole acknowledged as he opened Mav's gate. "But I still don't know how you can travel from town to town without a place of your own to hang your hat."

"Maybe you should join me at the marriage of the rails in Utah." Levi finished hitching the horses to the front of the wagon.

"There is so much I could say about that statement." Tag led his mount out into the yard.

"One ride on the train with me, kid brother, and I'll have you convinced."

"Ha!" Cole snorted. "One Iron Horseman in the family is plenty."

Levi laughed as he climbed up onto the high buckboard seat.

"Now, you'll come back and see us again, won't you, dear?" Mrs. Cavanaugh was saying as he pulled up in front of the door. She squeezed Cadence tight.

Levi hadn't missed the edge that had seemed to accompany Bessie's questions and comments all night. He'd been surprised at her unusual bite and hoped the woman was just being protective and not a busy body. Cadence had seemed to handle her with poise and grace.

"It would be my pleasure," Cadence said with a polite smile. "And thank you for showing me your quilts. You are very talented."

Levi couldn't tell for sure in this light, but he thought Bessie's cheeks looked even rosier than before. She was pleased. He jumped down off the wagon seat and ran around to help Cadence up. After saying his goodbyes to the Cavanaughs, he joined Cadence in the wagon and they pulled out behind his brothers.

Only the sound of crickets' songs disturbed the otherwise quiet of the ride back into town. The silence that passed between Cadence and him seemed comfortable somehow. While the lantern secured between the horses kept the newly worn dirt path beneath them lit, the waning moon offered enough light for Levi to see Cadence's pensive expression.

"How long has it been since you've seen your father?" Levi asked.

She was quiet for some time before responding.

"My father has been a Pinkerton for as long as I can remember. He's been working with the railroad since I turned fifteen. I guess it's been a while." Her voice was quiet, almost reverent as she spoke. "He's been asking me to come out here for ages, but my mother forbade it."

"What changed her mind?"

"She died."

Silence.

He didn't know what he'd expected her to say, but that wasn't it.

Levi remembered what it had been like around the ranch when Sarah, Raine's wife, died. He'd seen what it had done to his oldest brother. What it had done to his whole family. He'd seen plenty of death and loss during the war. It hadn't been pretty, and the memories still surfaced occasionally. It had taken years to learn to control the terror and sorrow, but Levi had been determined to go forward and do something positive.

By working for the railroad he could help people make a new start and find hope again.

"I'm so sorry to hear that." Levi said quietly. He wondered if Eamon knew. He couldn't imagine what her life had been like—growing up with only one brother, barely knowing her father, and then losing her mother.

"Thank you."

Silence.

"What is it like having a twin?" Cadence turned to look at him, the moonlight adding soft blue highlights to her hair.

He chuckled, thinking of a thousand different ways he could respond to that question. He and Tag had been inseparable growing up.

"Let's just say there was never a dull moment around Redbourne Ranch."

"Troublemakers, huh?" she asked, a smile in her voice.

"Something like that."

When they reached town, there was only a small glimmer of light coming from the livery door. Levi climbed down, walked around to the other side, and held up his hand for Cadence. Her foot caught on the metal step and she toppled awkwardly into him. His heart beat a little faster, but he wasn't sure if it was simply from trying to catch her or if it was from the warm feel of her against him.

She looked up.

"Here you are." Levi set her on the ground.

Cadence's fingers lingered on his chest before she pushed herself away from him and over to where his brothers were tying their horses to a hitching post.

"It was very nice to meet you, Mr. Cole Redbourne," Cadence nodded at his younger brother, "and Mr. Taggert Redbourne." She extended her hand to them.

"The pleasure was all ours," Cole said, stepping forward, clasping her hand in his, and bringing it up to his lips.

Levi laughed.

He pushed Cole away and kicked the air behind him as he followed Tag toward the livery with the wagon. Levi walked Cadence across the street to the door of the hotel. She stepped up onto the boardwalk and looked back at him.

"You did well with the sheriff tonight," he said, kicking at the dirt. "I think you'd get along well with my oldest brother, Raine. He's a deputy in Stone Creek where we're from. And Rafe. He's a bounty hunter. I know they'd like you."

"I'm sure I would." She placed a hand on the door knob. "Especially, if they are anything like you, Mr. Redbourne."

Levi didn't know what to say.

Cadence released the door handle and stepped to the edge of the boardwalk, just inches away from him, and leaned down to place a kiss on his cheek. He closed his eyes. She smelled like honeysuckle and he couldn't help but wonder if she tasted like it too.

"Thank you for all of your help today. You are quite the gentleman." Her words were quiet. She turned quickly and disappeared through the door.

How was he going to get any sleep now?

CHAPTER SIX

Cadence closed the door to her bedroom and leaned up against it. Her chest heaved from her hasty flight up the stairs. She'd kissed him on the cheek. What had she been thinking? He wasn't her assignment and allowing him to be a distraction would be dangerous. He was the kind of distraction that led to a permanent arrangement and she wasn't ready to go down that road again. Not yet. But he smelled so good. Looked so good. How was she supposed to avoid him over the next few days of being confined on a train with him?

He knows my father.

She pushed away from the door and quickly changed out of her skirt and blouse into a comfortable night shirt. She reasoned that maybe she'd met Levi for a reason. Maybe he could help her find her father. Or maybe one of his brothers could. He'd mentioned two of their names, but right now she couldn't remember them. She thought hard about their conversation, but had been thinking more about watching his lips move than the actual words that had come out of them.

Stop this, Cadence, she chastised. She needed to focus on getting to her father and all of the sudden, morning didn't seem soon enough. She needed to get to Bryan and the sooner, the better.

Beams from the morning's soft light spilled through the partially opened curtains in Cadence's room. It hadn't taken as long as she'd thought it would to get to sleep. Although she couldn't remember her dreams, she felt light and carefree. They must have been good.

The train whistle blew.

What time is it?

Cadence threw the covers off her and jumped out of the bed. She couldn't be late or she'd never hear the end of it. It had already taken some coercing to get her and the other detectives on the non-passenger train to begin with and she didn't want to find out what would happen if she missed it.

A few moments later, she was dressed in her new earth-colored skirt and pink blouse. Her everyday boots had dried enough to travel, so she tossed the others, along with her wadded up dress from yesterday morning into her trunk and glanced around one last time at the room. She was ready.

When she got down to the street, the Redbourne's were waiting just outside the hotel.

Cadence breathed out slowly. She hadn't missed it.

"Allow me," Cole said as he scooped up her trunk and slung it up over his shoulder and onto his back.

"Thank you," she said, amused by the youngest Redbourne brother's over exuberance.

"We thought we would escort you to the train—though I believed you would have been down here long before us." Levi smiled teasingly.

Stop that, she wanted to tell him. He had to know what that smile was doing to her resolve.

Cadence watched as a dozen or so men loaded livestock

and horses, including Apollo and the mare she'd ridden from the livery, into the supply cars at the back of the train along with a few head of cattle and sheep.

"All aboard!" the conductor sang from the platform next to the train.

"I guess that's us," Levi said as he turned to his brothers. "It appears the blacksmith was able to figure out how to make a new part for the pump." He looked around. "I haven't seen the sheriff yet this morning and I'd like to speak with him before we leave."

"Levi," Sheriff Richards called as if on cue. He ran toward them. "Mrs. Olson recalled seeing a stranger hanging around the bank yesterday, but couldn't tell us for sure if it was someone she recognized, just that he was thin with suspenders and an odd twill hat. We talked to the group of men staying in those tents last night, but no one seemed to know anything. If whoever started that fire is on that train with you, then you best be careful. No tellin' what he'll do next."

"Thanks, Sheriff," Levi said, extending his hand. "You're doing a fine job here. I wish I could stay and help, but my duties take me elsewhere. I know I'm leaving this town in good hands."

Sheriff Richards nodded. "Thank you," he said, then stepped back into the small crowd that had started to gather there.

Cole set Cadence's trunk down on the platform and pulled Levi into a big hug. "It's never the same without you, brother."

Levi clapped him on the back. "I've missed you too."

Tag raised a hand toward Levi and they clasped each other by the forearm before Levi pulled his twin into his embrace. Cadence couldn't be sure, but she thought she saw him wipe away a tear before breaking their hold.

"Until next time."

"Goodbye, Miss Cadie Walker," Tag teased. "We hope to cross your path again someday. Make sure you take care of this rascal, you hear?"

"Yes, sir," she said with a salute. "And it's Cade."

They all laughed and Cadence smiled. She waved as Taggert and Cole untied their horses from the hitching post in front of the station and mounted.

"Shall we?" Levi asked, picking her up by the waist and setting her on the platform. His hands felt good. Warm.

Many of the townsfolk Cadence recognized had joined them at the station and were waiving their well-wishes. She knew they were there for Levi, but they greeted her as well.

"Last call," the conductor boomed.

Levi picked up a large traveling case and slung his satchel over his neck, then grabbed the handle of her trunk.

"Better board," he said, pointing with his chin. He looked so handsome in his big black hat that Cadence had a hard time looking away as she walked until her shin smacked into the large open metal steps.

"Ouch." Heat flooded her face. Not again. He was going to think she was a complete imbecile. No one would believe she was a capable and highly skilled Pinkerton now, if her life depended on it.

"What is it with you anyway?"

Cadence wanted to offer some witty retort, but thought twice about it. She could be the smooth Cade Walker that Mr. Pinkerton had chosen to do this job, regardless of the man accompanying her. The commemorative golden nail was tucked safely in her trunk and it would only be a matter of days before she reached Bryan and she could find out what had happened to her father.

Levi would be stopping in River City for a few days and then on into Laramie, but maybe she could persuade him to help her with her cause first. Once she found Detective Eamon Walker, she would meet up with Mr. Durant and would escort him the rest of the way to the meeting of the rails. Everything would be back on schedule.

It wouldn't be long before the transcontinental railroad would be complete and her mission would be over. Then, and only then, could she entertain the idea of actually falling for one Mr. Levi Redbourne.

Once the makeshift station of Flat Plains was nothing but a speck, Levi climbed up the metal stairs and into the only passenger compartment on this five-box train. He'd not really thought much about it before, believing Mr. Durant to have something to do with it, but now he wondered how Miss Walker had been able to secure passage on a supply train or why Mr. Durant would have wanted it. He wasn't at all sure that Eamon knew his daughter was attempting to join him at his place in Bryan. After all, the railroad Pinkertons did not generally stay in one place for long—at least they wouldn't until the route was complete.

Durant was the only one with the pull to get her on the train and he realized there may just be more to her story than he'd first believed.

What aren't you telling me, Miss Walker?

Levi shook his head.

Sleep had eluded him over the last few days—especially last night with thoughts of Cadence invading every precious moment of silence—and he wanted to crawl into the bed in his quarters and get some sleep before they arrived in River City.

However, he glanced over the car and realized there were two men he didn't recognize sitting in various seats along the compartment. They weren't crew, so they had to be more of the passengers James had warned him about. Then it dawned on him. The men must be the Pinkerton agents assigned to this run.

Something wasn't right and he casually slid his fingers across the cool steel holstered at his belt. He needed to be alert.

With a possible arsonist on board, he would feel better if Cadence stayed close to him. He looked down at his bewitching traveling companion who'd sat down in one of the benches and was looking out the window.

Luckily, this train had been mostly stocked with supplies and some livestock, but despite the two conspicuous strangers in the seats, there were no additional passengers to please or entertain. He breathed a heavy sigh of relief and moved to the seats on the opposite side of Cadence and dropped their luggage on one of the benches since they wouldn't fit on the overhead racks.

They sat together in a comfortable silence. Levi studied her face while she watched the scenery outside as it slipped past at a steady speed. Her features were soft, almost glowing, and her mouth naturally turned in an upward direction.

This was going to be a long train ride if all he did was sit and stare at the prettiest girl in town like a school boy.

"You must spend a lot of time on this train, Mr. Redbourne." Cadence spoke, but did not turn away from the window.

Levi thought for a minute. "This country is growing and I want to be a part of it."

"Do you ever miss your family?"

"Every day. But seeing people like Bessie and Earl Cavanaugh have a good home to live in or someone like Emaline to be able to open a restaurant and hotel of her own, makes it worth the sacrifice. Besides, it won't be forever."

"What do you plan on doing when the railroad is complete? From what I understand it isn't too far away."

"As a matter of fact, we're hoping the route will be completed within the next couple of weeks. Promontory Summit, Utah. We got word not too long ago."

"Will you be there?" She turned to look at him for the first time since boarding the train.

"Yes," he affirmed.

She smiled and a few more moments of silence passed between them. Their conversation seemed so easy and light, but Levi couldn't shake the feeling that she was hiding something. Cadence turned her body to face him and with her hands in her lap leaned forward.

"Do you know Mr. Thomas Durant?"

Levi squinted his eyes at her.

She does know the doctor. Not that the swindler practiced any type of medicine anymore. Levi suspected he just liked having a title. He didn't care much for the man.

"Yes, I've worked with him over the past couple of years. How do you? Know him, I mean."

"Know him? Oh, I've never met the man, but I've heard that he is quite brilliant when it comes to business matters."

Levi couldn't explain it, but he was disappointed. He didn't know whether it was because the Vice President of the Union Pacific had pulled the wool over such pretty eyes or because she could be taken in so easily. He'd expected more.

"He knows how to make a buck, if that's what you're asking." Levi could not hide the distain in his voice.

President Lincoln, God rest his soul, had been clear in his vision to unite the country and Levi would do everything in his power to live up to that dream. The railroad could have been finished months, maybe even years before now, but Thomas Durant had seen fit to lengthen the route and stall enough that he would be able to capitalize on the funds the government offered for each finished mile of track.

"You don't like him," Cadence stated matter-of-factly.

"Are you hungry?" Levi wanted to change the subject. Talk of Durant made him angry and he didn't want to be angry.

"Famished," she responded with a grin.

"Wait here," he told her as he stood up and steadied himself to the movement of the train.

She nodded lightly.

Levi made his way to the dining car. There would be no

one there running the bar as he and Miss Walker, and the two
well-dressed gentlemen, he suspected to be Pinkertons, in the
other car were the only passengers, but he'd become well
acquainted over the last few years on where the foodstuffs
were kept. He opened the cupboard behind the bar and pulled
out a large wheel of cheese and one of the chunks of bread
that he suspected had been purchased in town just before
they'd left. There was a spot of jerky hanging on one end of
the cupboard.

"That'll do," he said to himself, barely above a whisper.

When he returned to the passenger car, Miss Walker sat
on the opposite side of the row—where he'd been sitting
before. She closed her trunk with a snap and smiled up at him.

Suspicion peeked its head, but he shoved it back down.

I'm sure she was just freshening up, he thought. *Maybe she didn't
want me to see her unmentionables.* He quickly dismissed any idea of
impropriety and handed her the bread.

Cadence sat up a little taller in the chair and peered over
his arm.

"Is that cheese?" she asked, then bit her bottom lip. "I
love cheese."

Levi smiled. *A woman after my own heart.* Cheese was one of
his favorite foods.

Miss Walker pulled a handkerchief from the pocket of her
skirt and laid it across her lap.

He broke the bread into four smaller pieces and set them
down on the back of his satchel. He pulled his knife from his
boot and quickly sliced off a few chunks of the cheese.

"Ah, Mr. Redbourne," the conductor said as he stepped
into the car and closed the door behind him, "I see that you
have met our lovely Miss Walker." He turned his attention to
Cadence. "Miss Walker, I hope you are comfortable and have
everything you need." He eyed the bread and cheese Levi had
acquired from the dining car. "That little town sure had a lot to
offer. Unlike some of the other places we've seen along this

route."

"Some of the farmers in Flat Plains," Levi handed the conductor the newest slice of cheese he'd cut from the wheel, "or more likely their wives, are quite ingenuitive," he confirmed. "Thanks, James."

The man shook his head to the cheese.

"We'll make sure to save you some." Levi grinned as he took a sumptuous bite of the creamy treat. He'd tried for the past few months to get the man to smile, but the conductor simply bowed curtly.

"That would be appreciated, sir."

The wheel of cheese was bigger than his head, and there were three more just like it in the next car over. It would certainly be enough to feed the whole crew. For the next few days anyway.

The car jerked and wheels screeched. Levi and James both extended their arms to gain some sort of balance and to brace themselves against the sudden shift in motion. The train was slowing to a stop, but it was too early. They weren't supposed to reach the next town for hours yet.

Levi glanced over at Cadence whose hands were white from gripping the side of her seat, but the expression on her face was calm as if she'd learned to mask her fears. He stepped to the back of her seat and lightly touched her shoulder.

She turned and looked up at him, her eyes fixing on his expectantly.

"I'm sure everything is all right, Miss Walker. Please stay here." He nodded and turned to leave, but quickly remembered all too clearly her disregard for following directions. "Miss Walker," he cleared his throat, "I would very much appreciate it if you would remain seated while I go speak with the engineer." He worked hard at keeping the sarcasm from his voice. Maybe she'd respond in kind to a sickeningly sweet approach.

"I'll be right here," she responded, to Levi's relief.

It took only a few minutes to discover the problem.

"It's been a long time since I run over cattle, Mr. Redbourne," the train's engineer explained. "I know the cowcatcher is supposed to protect the train, but I figure we can't be too careful."

A small herd of buffalo had been grazing along the tracks, but luckily, none of them had been directly in their path.

Levi clapped the engineer on the shoulder. "You're a mighty fine driver, Buck."

"Thank you, sir."

"Now, let's try to get to River City in one piece."

"Yes, sir."

"Glad to have you on board too, Festus," he said to the man charged with managing the blaze that kept the engine running properly.

A man of few words, the fireman grunted his approval and wiped the sweat from his brow with a heavily soiled rag.

Levi climbed back through the compartments and opened the door to the passenger car.

"A herd of buffalo seemed to—" He looked up to see Cadence surrounded by a few of the young men in the crew that he recognized.

Levi groaned. He walked stealthily up behind one of the men.

"Train's moving again. I'll bet you boys have somewhere you need to be."

They all looked up with wide eyes.

"Yes, sir, Mr. Redbourne," one of them said, his ears turning a dark shade of red.

"It's all right. Just get a move on or this train is going to make a few more stops ahead of time."

The kid he addressed tipped the brim of his cap and the crewmen scrambled.

"You must be accustomed to men fawning all over you wherever you go," he said as he sat down next to her.

She didn't answer. She didn't have to. The smile that graced her strong, yet very feminine features said it all. The good Lord blessed a lot of women with pretty looks or intelligence or some other talent, but it had been a long time since he'd met one, outside of his own family, that had so many all combined. He liked it. He liked her.

"You play?" he asked as he pulled an old checkerboard from one of the closed overhead compartments.

"I've learned a few things from my father. Have you? Learned anything from my father?"

Levi smiled, one eye arched at her obvious challenge. He was delighted to discover that Cadence knew how to play.

"A thing or two."

They both laughed.

The rest of the afternoon was spent in light conversation. By the time the sun had nearly reached the horizon, Levi was tuckered. Besides the one bunkered sleeping car for the crew, there was only one other compartment with a place to sleep on the train. His. There were two bunk-style beds in the room, but it was simply not proper for an unmarried man and woman to share the same sleeping quarters.

Although, he argued with himself, *sleeping here on the benches would be the same and much less comfortable.*

He looked over at Cadence, whose eyelids drooped heavy with fatigue. She'd leaned her head against the glass as she watched the shadows pass outside. It had been a long day—a long couple of days—but he guessed it was worse for her. Wyoming was a far cry from Chicago. He could only imagine the trepidation, or maybe even an odd sense of excitement, that must be her constant companion as she ventured west to start a life in the untamed wilds of the new Wyoming Territory.

"Come on," he said as he reached forward and touched her shoulder.

She turned to look at him with a faint smile. "Where are we going?"

Levi removed a lantern off one of the hooks hanging at the edge of the car and lit the wick. He reached down and enveloped Cadence's hand in his, and heaved her tired form up from the leather bench toward his sleeping compartment.

"To get some sleep."

CHAPTER SEVEN

Cadence blinked a few times.

Certainly, she'd heard him incorrectly.

"Wait," she said, pulling her hand from the warm comfort of his. "My things." She couldn't just leave her trunk sitting out here in the passenger car with the physical portion of her assignment inside. She glanced quickly at the two men who had both adjusted themselves for sleep on their respective benches. By their closed eyes and even breathing, most would believe them already asleep, but she knew better. She'd used the trick before. While she knew she should feel safe with the two Pinkerton escorts keeping watch, she'd never met either of them before the day they'd boarded the train and didn't want to take any chances.

"They'll be fine here until morning." Levi said.

Cadence glanced at the sleeping men.

"Your things," he clarified.

As one of the detectives snored in what Cadence thought was a feigned sleep, Levi eyed the man, then shot a glance at the other and seemed to change his mind. He stepped past her, hoisted her trunk up onto his back and held it with one hand, then held out the lantern to her.

"Will you hold this?"

She took it from him, holding it up against the fading light seeping in through the small windows. Levi reached down, slid her free hand into his, and led the way down the familiar narrow hallway.

"Where are we going?" she asked again.

"To my quarters," he replied without looking back at her.

Cadence reviewed in her mind the location of each of her weapons.

Levi guided her to the compartment where she'd spent her nights on the train before the train had stopped in Flat Plains. Heat filled her neck and face when she realized she'd been sleeping in *his* room. She wondered if he knew, or if he would even care.

Levi let go of her hand, set her trunk on the floor at his feet, and opened the door to the sleeping compartment. He motioned for her to go inside.

Cadence hesitated only a moment before stepping over the threshold and spun around to face him. "Thank you," she said, leaning against one side of the doorframe and draping her arm across to rest against the other.

He ducked under her arm and into the confined room. Cadence felt for her pistol and wrapped her fingers around the cool handle as she turned around to watch him. Levi opened a cupboard above the bed and pulled out a quilt and pillow. He stopped short when he glanced over at the small table in the cramped corner of the room.

Her large pink hat, along with her hairbrush and a few pins, were still laid out in plain view. She smiled her unease.

Levi cleared his throat.

"I hope you have a pleasant night," he said with a gentlemanly nod of his head and stepped past her, his arm gently brushing against hers as he moved back out into the hallway.

"Goodnight," Cadence whispered before closing the door. She released her grip on the pistol and exhaled a giggle.

Breathe, she reminded herself. Deep down, she'd believed Levi to be a gentleman, but a lady could never be too sure when traveling alone—especially this far west where traveling alone literally meant no one else. She quickly undid her skirt and pulled the blouse over her head.

A thud against the bottom of the wall startled her. It came from just outside the room. She grabbed the blanket from the bed and shoved it up against her chest. She pulled her pistol and opened the door to peer outside. Levi tossed and turned about on the floor, apparently trying to find a comfortable position to sleep. She quickly set the gun on the table.

"What on earth are you doing?" she asked with wonder. How a man his size could fit in a hall that small was something to consider.

Levi glanced up at her, still holding the pillow at his ear.

Cadence couldn't help the giggle that spilled out into the air.

"I'm sorry, Mr. Redbourne. I seem to have taken your bed." The words sounded more brazen than she'd intended. "I mean, I hate for you to sleep on the ground. In the hall. Isn't there somewhere else you'd rather be?"

Levi raised an eyebrow.

Shut up, Cadence Walker! she commanded. Maybe she could start over. She slammed the door shut, took another deep breath, and counted to three.

His deep, rich laugh penetrated the door and she could feel the heat stain her ears and face. When she mustered the courage to peek out again, Levi sat with his back against the wall, knees bent, and he leaned against the doorframe with his pillow.

"Go to sleep," Levi said huskily, without looking up.

She waited a moment. "Goodnight," she said as she quietly closed the door behind her.

How am I supposed to get any sleep now?

Levi awoke with a jolt as the locomotive's wheels squealed against the tracks.

"Not again," he muttered under his breath, scrunching his eyes as if he could will them to stay closed and force sleep. His back hurt, his legs cramped, and he'd scarce slept a wink, but he could not make himself wake fully to the day. Even through closed lids, the light of morning penetrated the darkness through the window in the door at the far end of the compartment.

The train shook, a soft rumble in the background of his restless sleep.

Thwak!

Levi's body slammed against the opposite wall of the hallway. His eyes flew open. Metal bars, knobs, or other objects jarred into his ribs and his bad knee knocked against something hard, causing a shock of pain to shoot through his entire leg. His blanket and pillow danced midair as he tumbled with the contents of the car. The assault lasted no more than a few seconds, but finally, he gained enough wits about him to thrust his hands forward in an attempt to brace himself between the walls. The moment he felt like he'd gained enough of a footing to avoid further injury, the force of another impact threw him again, this time into the door handle of his sleeping compartment, which jammed mightily into his ribcage and sucked his breath from his lungs.

It stopped with a final lurch and he dropped to the ground. Everything around him was filled with absolute silence lasting mere moments before distant calls of alarm sounded outside. Levi gingerly pried himself from the wall, which in all the mayhem had become the floor.

Cadence.

His thoughts immediately turned to the woman on the other side of the door. There was no telling how much damage had been done or what dangers still remained for them if they remained inside. He cautiously eased his way up onto his knees, though one still smarted from a blow, and managed to crawl back to the door of the sleeping compartment. He twisted the handle and it fell open with ease.

"Miss Walker?" he called inside as he peered down into the small room. The mattresses from the bunks lay askew. Blankets and bedding had been tossed everywhere in disarray, but he couldn't see her. "Cadence!" he boomed loudly this time.

"I'm here," a muffled call penetrated the chaos of the layers of pillows and bedcovers. Her head appeared from somewhere inside the mess.

Levi turned onto his back and placed his hand over his chest. Pain emanated from his legs and side. He'd been lucky he hadn't hit his head. He tried to sit, but the pain in his side made it hurt to breathe.

"Are you all right?" he asked through forced breaths as he pushed himself over and up onto his aching knees.

"I'd be better if someone would lend me a hand," she said, an edge of sarcasm lining her voice.

He reached down into the room and pulled her from the bedlam.

"What happened?" she asked, her eyes searching his.

"I don't know." Levi dusted his hands on his pants. "But we need to get out of here." He stood up as best he could, but with the car on its side, he had to hunch down. Until he knew the train car no longer posed a threat, he needed to get them outside. They could be dangling off a ledge for all he knew as the floor angled awkwardly. "Come on." He took a hold of her hand and started forward.

Cadence pulled back, letting her fingers slip through his hold on her. She looked down at her attire, a thin nightshift, and threw a hand up to her chest. She dropped down onto her belly and reached into the room.

"We don't have time. We'll come back for it later. I don't know how long these walls will hold our weight," he held out his hand again. "They weren't meant for this kind of support."

"I will not leave this train in my night clothes, Mr. Redbourne," she said lying flat on her belly. Cadence reached down into the hole and with only a moment's struggle, retrieved some clothing. From the coloring, Levi guessed it was her outfit from the previous day.

He knew he should look away.

Needed to look away.

It took every ounce of strength to do so and he forced himself to think about what had just happened. The train had derailed—that much was for certain. Most of the windows had been blacked out, but light still shone in from the far end of what had become a metal cage. If they could make it to the back of the car, they'd be able to pull themselves from the wreckage and he would be better able to assess the situation.

"You're out of time." Levi dropped to his haunches, grabbed ahold of Cadence, and slung her over his shoulder, careful to avoid hitting her head on the overly low ceiling. The effort was rewarded with a sharp stabbing pain to his side. He ground his teeth together and headed toward the only light coming into the car.

"Put me down this instant. I am perfectly capable of getting out of this place on my own." She kicked him in the ribs and he nearly dropped her. Once he could take another breath, he plopped her down onto her rear end with a thud. The unstable floor groaned in protest.

"Anybody down there," a voice called from outside.

James.

"We're here!" Levi called up to the conductor, whose head appeared through the upturned door. He held out his hand to help Cadence up from the floor, but she was already on her feet, yanking on her purple skirt from yesterday. "We're leaving. Now!" he barked the order.

She shoved past him, a pair of women's laced boots tied together and strung over her shoulder.

Clever.

Cadence wedged a bare foot against the angled wall and with her arm braced against the side of the door, pulled herself out.

Levi followed.

When he reached the surface, he scanned the wreckage and his gut lurched at the destruction that greeted him. The sheer force of their velocity had plunged their compartment deeply into the hillside. Couplings on several of the train cars had been torn apart and coaches had been strewn across the countryside like scattered feed for chickens.

Levi climbed over the awkward railing and upturned staircase and jumped the short distance to the ground. Cadence followed his lead around the stairs, but her skirt caught on a protruding piece of iron. He reached up, released the cloth, then placed his hands at her sides to lift her down. His hand slipped off her hip and she fell against him, her forehead butting against his chin.

Blast it all!

At least he was able to keep his boots planted on the earth and he didn't drop the woman.

Cadence reached up and brushed a dark lock from her face. "Ouch."

"Sorry about that. Are you all right?"

She was so close to him, Levi could scarcely breathe—it didn't help that his whole body ached from the tumble.

"Excuse me," she said without looking at him. "I'm quite all right. If you could just put me down…"

"Oh, yes. Of course."

Once her feet were secured solidly on the ground, she took a small step backward.

Levi cleared his throat. There were pressing matters that needed his attention. He would deal with his growing attraction toward Miss Walker soon enough.

"James," Levi called out to the conductor as he ran toward a groaning man, "what happened here?" Levi asked, fearing escalation between the railroad and the natives. He threw his hands through his hair and briefly closed his eyes to the all too vivid memories of battle.

The conductor shrugged, his arm bleeding through a tear in his shirt sleeve. "It looks like we hit a barricade. You there," James called to one of the seemingly uninjured crewmen, "take this man over to that tree. We'll need to collect all of the wounded together." He turned to Levi as he started toward the engine. "I'm heading up to the front. I don't know what we hit, but Buck should be able to tell us what happened and there's bound to be more injuries up there."

James was as close to a medic as they had on board. Those who'd suffered injuries would be better in his hands than any other here.

Levi looked down to where a man leaned against an uprooted railroad tie, a bone protruding grotesquely from his leg. Suddenly, the magnitude of what had just happened hit him and he dropped his hands to his knees, gasping for air.

The distant noise of cannon fire echoed in Levi's ears, penetrating that moment where memories collide with reality. It was out of place, but Levi ducked out of instinct. He shook his hung head, desperately trying to rid his mind of the painful battle where he'd lost so many good men.

"Mr. Redbourne?" Someone called to him from a distant place.

The rhythmic thumping of Levi's heart blocked out all other sound. His breathing increased and he began to pant heavily as he watched in his mind's eye as soldiers under his command fell one by one to the earth, soot-stained and weary. Dead.

"Mr. Redbourne?" The voice grew louder.

He clenched his fists, willing the vivid recollections of his past to vanish.

It's not real.

As his sight regained focus, a woman's dark brown eyes snared his, drawing him back to the present. Her lips repeating his name over and over.

Snap out of it, Redbourne.

Levi held Cadence's searching eyes, his vision clear. She was scared. He grabbed her shoulders. "Are you all right?" he asked urgently.

She took a deep breath. "No. Are you?"

"Why don't you go sit down over ther—" he glanced around, realizing that there was nowhere for her to go that would remove her from the devastation that surrounded them. Mounds of rubble and debris, splintered off from the train, extended across the tracks and down both sides with shocking devastation. The first few cars appeared to have taken the brunt of the damage. One of the supply coaches, the livery car, and the caboose were still coupled together and sat only at a slight angle off the tracks.

Through the haze, he could see horses, cows, and sheep littering the countryside, running amuck in the background. It had been wise for someone to let the animals out to prevent further damage. It looked as if the remainder of the train might tip over at any minute.

"I don't want to sit, Mr. Redbourne," she said. "I can help. Let me."

Levi nodded. "Go find James. He headed up to the locomotive to check on Buck, the engineer."

Cadence ran straightway toward the head of the train.

Levi's stomach turned at the acrid stench of burned flesh. Smoke burned his nostrils and stung his eyes. He wiped the back of his hand across his face to clear the haze-induced tears. Bodies lay prostrate amidst the ruin of supplies that had been scattered from the lead cars. Battered and bloody, those men who were able carried the others to the shade of the cluster of trees where James worked to bandage the vast amount of injuries caused by the wreck.

A deep, agonizing moan caught Levi's attention and he rushed to the side of a man whose hand extended into the air, reaching out for something. Someone. He took the man's hand in his and knelt down beside him.

"Mr. Redbourne?" It was the kid who'd been talking to Cadence in the dining car. "Am I going to die?"

Levi ignored the bleeding gash at the side of the young man's head and the heavy soot streaked across his face and clothes, and bit back his fear for the boy's sake.

"Not if James has anything to say about it," he said in a voice he hoped portrayed a level of reassurance. "What's your name, kid?"

He didn't respond.

Levi closed his eyes briefly and opened them again, relieved when the youngster swallowed and squeezed his hand, however weakly.

"Barrow, sir," he choked out gruffly. "My name is Barrow."

"Well, Barrow, how did you come to be on this adventure with the railroad?" Levi had to keep him talking.

"My family...," he swallowed again, "needed the extra mon..." his speech slowed and Levi's stomach knotted as the boy's eyelids drifted shut.

"Barrow," Levi shook the kid lightly on his shoulders and his eyes twitched as if trying to open them.

"Tell them...," he licked his lips. The kid tried to sit up, straining against his own skin.

Levi looked up. His eyes locked on Cadence who had joined James in the shade with the other patients. "Water?" he called out to anyone who would listen. "Does anyone have water?" He looked back down at Barrow.

"Tell them," he grunted as he collapsed back against the

dirt, "where…to send my pay."

Levi could feel the boy's strength draining from his near lifeless form.

"Hang on, kid. You can tell them yourself." He couldn't stop the single tear that escaped his tired eyes and trailed down the side of his face. He felt helpless—something he'd only felt a few times before, mostly during the war—and he didn't like it one bit.

Barrow needed something to drink. Levi looked around again. Everyone was busy attending to others. It was up to him. He hadn't wanted to move the kid, but there was no other choice. He wished, not for the first time, that he'd paid more attention when his brother, Rafe, had gone on about medical treatments, trying to educate his family about medicine and the discoveries he'd learned in med school.

Levi stood up.

"Don't go," Barrow said with strained breath.

Levi reached down and pulled the youth into his arms. He needed to get him to the shade, to where James attended the others. When he looked to the small cluster of trees, Cadence was no longer standing there. He scanned the disheveled yard and with each step, his worry grew.

Steam blew a storm of smoke from the engine chimney. Levi's breathing sped up as it became more labored. He tripped over a large wooden plank protruding from the ground, but was able to keep himself upright with his substantial load. He stepped more quickly, working to avoid the massive amounts of debris that cluttered the ground in front of them.

"Where is Cadence?" he asked with desperation as he reached the tree and laid Barrow gently on the ground in the tall grasses growing there.

"She went to retrieve some water from one of the barrels in the tender car," James nodded to an upturned car that had all but splintered apart and Levi wondered if the barrel would still be intact.

"How many have we lost?" Levi asked.

The conductor pushed his spectacles up higher on his nose, stopping only long enough to give him an update. "I'm not sure. I've only made it this far down the cars. Most of the men I've encountered are bruised and battered. But Buck is hurt real bad. He's burned pretty seriously on his face, arms, and back. His leg looks mangled. I doubt he'll ever walk again. I'm headed back that way now." He held up a piece of material that Levi recognized as curtains from the dining car.

"Where is he?" Levi asked, his heart hurting for the man he called friend.

The conductor nodded his head toward the east side of the tracks and turned to go.

"James, stop. I'll bring him to you. You're needed here." Levi motioned to the kid.

"Mr. Redbourne," James's voice was quiet. His face twitched slightly as if his thick mustache had tickled his nose. "I'll join you."

"But…" Levi looked down at the short conductor who'd been working tirelessly to patch up those who'd been hurt in the wreck. James shook his head and looked at the ground.

It took a moment, but understanding suddenly worked its way through Levi's mind. His gaze darted to the spot where he'd laid the kid. The color had drained from his face, now ashen against the dried streaks of dark red blood.

James stood and reached a hand up to Levi's shoulder. "He's gone, my friend," he said with a pat before turning to go find Buck, his limp highly noticeable. "Oh, and Levi," he added, turning back toward him, "the lad makes four so far." James tsked, then hurried off toward the hissing steam engine as fast as his injured leg would allow.

Levi's stomach clenched as if he'd just been kicked in the gut. He glanced over at the other man lying next to Barrow and realized he too was dead. Images of dead soldiers, both friend and foe, flashed through his head. He needed to sit down. Whoever was responsible for this…

He didn't want to think about that right now.

Levi spotted Cadence nearby speaking with the man who'd broken his leg. Levi recognized him as one of the other passengers on the car—a possible Pinkerton. He squinted his eyes against the brightness of the rising sun. The man handed Cadence a leather tube that resembled a carrying case for maps, which she promptly strung over her head and across one shoulder.

She did know the man. But why lie about it? Curious.

Moments later, she disappeared behind the tender car and reemerged holding a wooden bucket tightly against her bosom he guessed was full of water. The engine rattled back and forth, then started to violently shake, steam hissing from the chimney. Cadence's current path cut directly in front of the upturned engine that Levi feared might blow at any moment.

"Run!" he screamed as he bolted forward toward her.

CHAPTER EIGHT

She can't hear me!

Giant puffs of smoke erupted in a cloud above the engine.

"Cadie, get down!" Levi yelled again, running as fast as he could. He threw himself on top of her, shoving her to the ground. He covered her head, and his, with his arms as best he could.

BOOM!

Waves of heat rushed above him, caressing his back with its scorching warmth. Just as Levi lifted his head, flames shot wildly from the engine and a shower of coal and small chunks of wood fell to the ground. It appeared that everyone else had been clear of the explosion.

"Mr. Redbourne," Cadence said quietly from beneath him.

He looked down at her.

"I...I can't breathe." Her face was flushed a light red.

Levi pushed himself off the ground and into a standing position. "I beg your pardon, ma'am," he said, extending his hand to her.

Her bosom heaved with the much needed air. She clapped her hand against his, allowing him to pull her from the ground.

"Well," she cleared her throat and dusted off her dress, "I'm afraid we'll have to go collect some more water." She lifted the now empty bucket from the ground, scanning the area as if searching for something else. Without missing a beat, she discreetly picked up the tube he must have knocked off of her when they fell and she headed back toward the tender car.

"Nothing to worry about. Our locomotive just blew up. All in a day's work," Levi muttered under his breath as she retreated.

"Is everybody all right over here?" James hobbled to his side.

"Nothing more to add to your load today, James."

Cadence returned in just a few moments and handed the full bucket to the newly appointed medic.

"Thank you, Miss Walker." James nodded as he took the bucket from her. "Mr. Redbourne."

Levi spotted a small group of half a dozen horses running just on the other side of the tracks along the rail line and he whistled when the familiar gray came into view. "Come on, boy," he called for his horse. When Apollo saw him, he neighed and pranced before changing direction toward them, leaving the others behind. Levi scrubbed at his muzzle. "You all right, boy?"

Apollo lifted his head and nickered as if telling him everything that had gone wrong with the day.

"There are still three men unaccounted for," James reported as he turned back toward the suffering engineer.

Levi lifted his brows as he ran his hands across Apollo's flanks and neck. "I'll take a look around," he said, leading Apollo away from the conductor and groaning engineer.

Together, he and Cadence made their way back toward the sleeping car. She'd thought she might be able to gather some of her things and he'd agreed to help. He didn't miss the way that she kept touching the tube slung across her back, as if reassuring herself it was still there and he briefly wondered at the contents of the long, slender cylinder.

"Are those the three?" Cadence stopped, leaning up against Levi and pointing to three men walking in a line toward them, guns raised. They pulled two horses along behind them.

Levi's hand shot to his hip, but he'd taken off his holster when he'd tried to get comfortable last night, attempting to sleep in the hallway.

Damn.

"Well, if it isn't Mr. Redbourne, the Iron Horseman himself, I presume," one of the armed men taunted.

"Am I supposed to know you?" Levi asked, one eyebrow raised—his voice a low threatening tone. The nickname for him had caught on a little too well. He took a step in front of Cadence.

"Naw, I suppose not. But I'm very interested in getting to know the perty little lady yer protectin' there, Redbourne."

Levi pushed Cadence farther behind him. "What are you boys looking for?"

"Well, you see," the man in the middle turned and spat into the dirt, "word has it that there is something mighty valuable in your cargo."

Levi didn't recall having seen any of these men on board.

"What kind of valuables are you looking for? You realize this is a supply run? There are just grains and wares back there, I'm afraid." Levi jutted his chin toward the damaged cargo hold. But he had dealt with too many ruffians to believe they would go to all this trouble for something that simple.

"We come looking for something that traitor, Abraham Lincoln himself, had commissioned for the railroad."

Levi flexed his jaw.

Traitor? How could anyone say that? This man was the obvious traitor to the newly combined union.

"And, why would such a valuable be on *my* train?" Levi's hands balled into fists, his fingers itching for a trigger.

"Yer a Yank, ain't ya? I heard you knew the *Pres-i-dent*

personally." The man spat into the dirt again. "You got what I came for?"

"Yes, I knew the President. He was a great and noble man. Decent and caring. You would do well not to defame his good name again."

The man guffawed. "And just what is you gonna to do to stop me?" He cocked his gun and took a step toward them.

Levi glanced from one man to the next. They looked like they would enjoy a good round of fisticuffs. But now, he had Cadence to think about. Eamon would kill him if anything happened to his daughter.

"We're not looking for any trouble, so you can have whatever you want, but there is nothing on this train that…fits your description."

"We'll just see about that. And don't worry about looking for your Pinkerton, Redbourne. We took care of him first," the man said with a wry grin.

Cadence gasped.

Levi glanced over toward the man who'd spoken earlier with Cadence. He lay motionless on the ground, his arm and head strung across a small crate at an awkward angle. Dead. From here, it looked like they'd broken his neck.

His jaw flexed again.

"Clive," one of the other riders whined. "Let's just get on with it. Stop playing around."

"You two," Clive motioned to those with him, "go gather the others. I'll be waiting right here."

The two ruffians mounted the horses behind them and with pistols in hand, they rode to opposite ends of the train. Levi couldn't think of how he could warn James, but the conductor was a smart man and he knew how to handle himself. He hoped that was enough.

"Now," Clive said as he took another step toward them, spinning his gun, a lecherous smile tainting his face, "why don't you introduce me to the lady, Redbourne?"

Levi's stomach turned when the vile man licked his lips.

Cadence took a step behind him.

Clive seemed pretty steady with that gun, each spin completely controlled, but one little distraction could turn the tides in an instant to their favor. Levi had already noted several places where he and Cadence could take cover.

The man took another step closer and Levi slapped Apollo's rump. Before Clive realized what was happening, the gelding reared at their attacker, throwing him off balance to the ground and Levi shoved Cadence behind the railing of an overturned train car.

It took only moments for Clive to recover from the brief shock. When he came up, gun waving around, ready to shoot the first living thing he saw, Levi already stood above him, fists raised. He quickly disarmed the man, but didn't have time enough to collect the piece before he took a blow to his jaw. He stumbled backward and fell onto the earth.

Splitting pain shot up his face and into his ear. He looked up. Clive pulled a large steel blade from his belt and with murderous intent gleaming in his eyes, started toward him. Levi pushed himself up as far as he could, his hands still behind him, and he crawled backward, trying to gain his footing as his heels slid against the dirt.

"You're not such a big fella now, is ya, Redbourne? And I'd be willing to bet you isn't made of iron."

Levi's hand hit up against something smooth and hard. He wrapped his fingers around a cool steel bar and, without hesitation, shot up off the ground, ready to swing. The man grinned wickedly, then lunged at him. He was too close for the bar to do any good, except maybe deflect the blade away from his body.

CRACK!

Clive's eyes grew wide with surprise and blood pooled in his mouth, oozing out of the corners as he dropped onto his knees and fell forward. Levi rolled out of the way.

What the hell?

Levi scanned the immediate vicinity, unable to see from where the shot had originated. He looked back to make sure Cadence was all right. She'd stepped out from behind the railing of the train car, a gun in her hand with smoke swirling a light grey cloud around her.

Couldn't be. Could it?

Cadence stood out in the open, gun drawn, staring at the fallen form of the man she'd just shot. They'd told her she would always remember her first kill with perfect clarity, but for her, every shot that had hit its mark haunted her. She knew she'd never forget the look of shock and resignation that had cursed Clive's features just before he'd landed, face-down in the dirt. Scoundrel or not, his blood was on her hands.

"He was going to kill you," she whispered aloud without looking at Levi. She knew he would have questions, but there was no time to explain or commiserate. The other two riders would have heard the shot and would be back at any moment.

"Cadence?" He scrambled to his feet, collected Clive's gun from the ground, and reached toward her. "Are you all right?"

"Let's go," she said, this time meeting Levi's eyes head on. Her jaw flexed. There was no time to explain or consider the ramifications she'd experience later. They had to get to the others. Too many people had died today and they needed to act before any more followed.

Cadence pulled her gun up to her shoulder and hunched low behind the cars and debris. Levi was right behind her, following closely. They ran along the overturned rail cars, stopping only at the large gaping spaces that had once been wooden cargo holds. She kept ahead of him, peeking around the cars in anticipation of the enemy, not wanting to provide Levi the chance to talk to her.

Once they reached the engine, Cadence looked around the sunken chunk of metal. The conductor knelt in the grass next to the older gentleman lying prostrate on the ground. Clive's partner sat astride his horse, gun aimed at a small group of men, some looked to be gravely injured, that had been gathered together. It was strange that one weasel-like culprit with a gun could bend the others so easily to his will.

The longer they waited to get the men back their guns, they ran the risk of the other rider discovering his dead friend and alerting this one. She moved to stand up, but Levi set his hand on her shoulder. He crouched up close to her and whispered in her ear.

"Give me a minute to get over there." He pointed to the cowcatcher that now sat cockeyed from the front of the engine. "He'll be outnumbered, and outgunned."

Was that appreciation in his voice?

She'd expected him to try to stop her. To think her a simple female.

"Hear that gunshot fellas? Sounds like one of ya already got outta hand." The man waved his gun, but didn't take his eyes off the men he guarded. "My guess is Clive shot your *Iron Horseman* dead in his boots and is 'bout to take up with that little piece of tart back there."

Cadence lifted her skirt just enough to pull the pistol she tended to sleep with. "Your guess'd be wrong." She said in a loud voice, standing up straight, her revolver in one hand, her pistol in the other, both pointed directly at the man's chest.

As the man shifted his stance to change his aim, Levi stepped out from behind the iron shield around the other corner of the devastated engine train in front of the tinder car. "I wouldn't," he announced loudly.

Levi urged the man to drop his weapon with a curt flick of his gunned hand. The ruffian complied.

"That's a smart man," Levi said. "Now, why don't you climb down off of that horse there, real easy like?"

The crewmen scrambled to collect the weapons they'd thrown on the ground at their attacker's request.

"Where's Clive?" the tinny sound of the man's worried voice grated on Cadence's nerves.

Two of the men grabbed a hold of him and proceeded to tie him up to the railing on one of the overturned coaches.

Cadence met Levi's gaze and he nodded as if he understood what she needed to do. They couldn't celebrate yet. There was still one armed man looking for trouble at the other end of the train.

He was about to find it.

Cadence briefly spoke to a few of the others, who surprisingly gave her their full support, and together, five of them—including her and Levi—walked openly toward the caboose in a solid wall of gun power. It didn't take long to reach the caboose. From a short distance, the bandit recognized defeat. He turned his horse toward the field and high-tailed it for the trees.

"Should we go after him?" one of the crewmen asked, appearing a little disappointed that they hadn't had their showdown.

"Let him be. If he knows what's good for him, he'll steer clear of us from now on."

The rest of the crew ran toward them and everyone started speaking at once.

A long, full whistle carried across the air. Levi stepped into the rustling crowd. He encouraged all of them to join together at the head of the train.

When they reached James, he knelt next to Buck, but looked grim. The engineer was alive. Barely.

"There are a half-dozen horses running around here somewhere." The men rallied around while Levi laid out their options. "Buck's in a real bad way and unless we can get him to a doctor fast, we're going to lose him."

Apollo and two Quarter Horses had stayed close, but the

others would take some time to collect—time Buck didn't have.

"Listen," Levi said, standing up at the head of the group, "we've lost four of our own today."

"Five," James interjected. "We lost another crewman."

Levi looked at him, then with a flex of his jaw, back to the rest of the crew. "Five," he corrected. "Words can't express the depth of our grieving, but we are not done. These braggarts have not gotten the best of us. We are alive and we will fight."

"Here, here," a man yelled from the group. Others echoed the sentiment.

"It's time to rally together and press forward."

"What do you want us to do, Levi?" another man yelled.

"You," Levi pointed to a small group of men standing in front of the tinder, "we need two of you to take those two horses and round up as many of the others as possible. We'll need to gather the livestock, but because we only have three horses to divide among us, you'll need to bring them back as soon as possible. The rest of you will have to work on foot for now." He looked at the two men holding Clive's captured accomplice. "You two, there is a territory Marshal residing in Cheyenne to whom you can deliver that man. Explain what's happened, then send word to Grenville Dodge at the Union Pacific. You can leave as soon as these men return with the horses."

They nodded.

Cadence watched with amazement as Levi reined everyone in and gave them directions. He united them with his words and organized them so they wouldn't get restless. A born leader, the crew looked up to him.

The last of the men would be stationed at the wreckage with weapons to deter looting until relief could be sent from River City while they waited for another train.

"And finally," Levi announced, "Miss Walker and I will

take Buck into River City where there is a prominent doctor in town."

Two men left immediately on horseback to try to round up the six to dozen or so head that had scattered after the train derailed, leaving one horse for her and Levi. They fashioned together a make-shift travois or logging sled for Buck and secured it to Apollo.

"I've patched him up as good as I can, Mr. Redbourne. He's lost a lot of blood and I'm worried that he's broken a few ribs as well as fractured his leg." James shook Levi's hand. "He's a good man. God speed."

Levi nodded. He spoke to a few of the others before joining her at the horse.

Cadence couldn't help but to stare at the dead bodies that now lay in a line beneath the only cluster of trees for what looked like miles. The two Pinkerton agents who'd been traveling with her discretely were among them, along with the fireman, whose face was so badly burned he was almost unrecognizable, the young Barrow, another crewman, and Clive. She turned away. Death only served as a reminder that getting close to people was dangerous—a risk she'd been unwilling to take since Daniel. She surveyed the wreckage again as Mr. Redbourne made his way toward her. It all seemed so unreal. Like a bad dream from which she had yet to awaken.

"It's still early yet," Levi said as he helped Cadence up into the saddle. "I figure we're only a couple hours ride from River City, but with him," Levi motioned to the injured man lying in the travois behind the horse, "we'll have to take it slow. I'm hoping we can make it before nightfall." He climbed up behind her with a pained groan. She imagined he was more hurt that he let on.

Cadence didn't generally consider herself to be a stupid girl, but right now, she felt like the child at the back of the school house with the word 'dunce' written on the tall pointed hat. She and Levi would be riding into River City *on the same horse*. How could she have been so thick? It didn't help that he was the most beautiful man she'd ever seen, and in her line of work, that was a lot of men. She readjusted the leather tube slung across her back to rest in front of her so it wouldn't get damaged.

Levi clicked his tongue, urging the gelding forward. Cadence couldn't very well sit up straight in the saddle not touching him for hours. If they were going to be traveling for a long while, she might as well enjoy the feel of his strong chest behind her and his arms around her. She relaxed back into his chest. There was no sense fighting it.

They'd only been traveling a short while when Levi shifted in the saddle.

"So, you want to tell me what happened back there?"

Cadence wasn't sure how to respond. She wasn't sure what she could say. It was obvious that she'd blown her cover with most, if not all, the men back there. There was no use pretending.

She sat up a little straighter "I shot a man," she said. "What more is there to say?"

"You looked quite comfortable with that revolver you carried." He spoke as if he shared her secret. "Did your pa just teach you well or is there something more to the story?"

"Does it matter?"

"Not really, I suppose. But you're holding up pretty well. My mama and baby sister are strong women, but I can't imagine they'd be holding up half so well."

"Are you suggesting that I have no conscience, Mr. Redbourne?"

"Not at all, just wondered if you wanted to talk about it."

How could she answer that without telling him the truth? She couldn't, so she didn't answer at all. Cadence reached down and slipped her hand into the pocket of her dress. The pouch with the diamond tipped golden spike had been securely tucked there. If Clive's friends or anyone else wanted it, they'd have to find it first.

"You handled yourself very well out there. You'd give my brothers a run for their money."

From the way he'd spoken about his brothers, a sense of pride welled up inside of her.

"Thank you, by the way. I don't think I said that yet."

Cadence bit her lip.

Buck groaned.

"Maybe we should stop and get him some water," she said, determined to change the subject. They'd been following a small creek for quite a while.

Levi pulled on the reins and the horse came to a stop near the edge of the little winding river. He unstrapped the canteens from his saddle bag and bent down onto his haunches with a slight grunt to fill the container.

Cadence slid off the horse's back. Her legs felt wobbly, like Annie's huckleberry jam looked every time she pulled it out to spread on her biscuits back home. As she walked to stretch out her legs, a burning pain accompanied the unsteady feel and she better understood Levi's reaction to the exertion. It didn't help that the burn on her leg still throbbed every time her skirt brushed over it.

The terrain they were following was not as flat and plain as the quite appropriately named Flat Plains—which made it harder to traverse with their passenger. Dark clouds quickly rolled in overhead and the temperature of the air dropped considerably. Cadence rubbed her hands across her lightly covered arms and shoulders.

"We need to get a move on," Levi said as he held the canteen up for Buck to drink. "It won't be long before that storm reaches us."

Cadence stood next to the mount and waited for Levi to join her. Something about him put her at ease. She couldn't explain it.

"Miss Walker?" Levi said warmly. "Look at me."

She looked up into pools of warm honey and realized she could get lost in those eyes.

"I figure we have another hour or so," he told her as he examined the cuts beneath her eye. "Buck is still losing a lot of blood, but he's awake." He pulled away and suddenly she felt cold. "Are you all right?"

Truth was, she was tired, but she couldn't think of a better way to fall asleep than in Levi Redbourne's arms.

"Let's go."

CHAPTER NINE

The time on the trail gave Levi time to process everything that had just happened. It all seemed a part of some horrifying illusion. Those responsible for the derailment would pay. Clive already had. With his life.

Levi couldn't help but admire the strength of the woman who'd fallen asleep in his arms. She'd shown courage today in a very difficult situation. She'd acted decisively—something hard to come by in most of the women he'd met. He'd been blessed with strong women in his family, which had spoiled him for many of the ladies who'd offered him their attentions.

Cadence Walker was different. She was smart and funny and very influential on those around her. Levi wasn't at all surprised Pinkerton had hired her on to be one of his revered lady detectives. Yes. He knew. He'd been around Eamon enough to know how a Pinkerton acted and reacted or didn't act at all in any given situation. He wondered if his friend knew.

She's a lot like her father, he mused.

A soft moan escaped Cadence's lips and she tilted her head so that it fit perfectly in the curve of Levi's neck. He could get used to this.

The small town of River City came into view as they passed through a large thicket of sweet-smelling pine trees. He guessed it would only be another quarter hour before they arrived.

Plop. A lone droplet of water caressed his cheek and rolled downward.

Levi drank in the scent of rain as he glanced up to the heavens.

"Please, God," he whispered into the sky, "please let it wait just a few minutes more."

By the time they finally reached the small settlement, gusts of wind had the town in a flurry. There were only a few completed buildings on Main Street—a mercantile, a livery, and blacksmith shop. Most people had been working on getting their homes built—then their businesses would follow.

The church and hotel were nearly complete, but the rest of the town's businesses were still a series of tents. People littered the street, tying down the edges of their make-shift edifices with strong rope and iron stakes. Boards were being hammered into place over the windows at the general store and the Ferrier.

No one paid them much attention as they rode down the street. Luckily, on his last trip to town, he'd met the doctor at his home, just a few minutes to the north.

"Hang on, Buck," he called out, but his words seemed to be carried away on the wind.

They pulled up in front of a quaint little wooden house, painted gray with planters of wildflowers growing in the windowsills. The young sapling at the edge of the property leaned to the north with the force from the storm. Levi dismounted and ran up the few short steps to the door and knocked loudly.

A few moments passed before the kind doctor answered his door.

"Why, Levi," the greying doctor pulled his shirt collar up

around his neck, "what are you doing out in weather like this? Come in and get yourself warm. Margar—"

"Please, Doc," Levi pointed to the sled holding his friend.

"Well, why didn't you say something?" he said with only a moment's hesitation. He grabbed a coat of the hook next to the door and steered Levi forward.

Cadence slid down off Apollo's back and joined them. Levi was grateful for his wide arm span as he was able to take up both sides of the top end of the travois. The doc and Cadence each held a side at the bottom and carefully, they carried Buck into the house.

"Oh, my," the doctor's wife exclaimed when she saw them set the stretcher on the porch as it was too big to fit through the doorframe.

"In here," Doc directed.

Levi gathered Buck into his arms and gingerly carried him into a small room at the back of the living area. He laid the man down on the tall table in the center of the space and backed away so the doctor could examine the patient.

Buck reached out and touched his arm, the faint motion seeming to drain him of energy.

"Tell them it wasn't my fault, Levi," he whispered. His hand fell.

"Buck, don't talk like that. Doc Gordon is real good. You'll be—"

"Margaret will have some hot lemonade." The doctor turned him around and with a light push, ushered him out of the room toward the kitchen where Cadence was waiting patiently.

"Excuse me, ma'am." He glanced at Cadence, then to Mrs. Gordon. "I have to go see to my horse. May I use your barn?"

"Of course, dear. There's some fresh hay in the loft. Help yourself. I'm just fixing up your wife a nice glass of hot lemonade to warm the soul. I'll have one waiting for you when you return."

Did she just say 'wife?' That might be a little hard to explain.
"Oh, we're not...um..."

"Oh, no," Mrs. Gordon placed a hand over her mouth. "Is *that* man," she pointed to the doctor's room, "your husband?"

Cadence looked at Levi, pleading for rescue. It was just like him to tempt fate. He'd decided to wait until the railroad was complete before looking for a wife, and here, fate brought the woman to him. He smiled.

"What she means to say, Mrs. Gordon, is that we are courting. We have not yet married.

Cadence relaxed visibly. "Yes, that is what I meant to say."

Mrs. Gordon clapped her hands together. "A wedding. Does your family live here in town, dear? You must introduce us." She muttered something more, but Levi couldn't hear her as she turned into the kitchen, presumably for the lemonade.

Mrs. Gordon would assume that Cadence's family was here, since it was highly improper for an unmarried woman to be accompanying her betrothed on a trip away from home. He would have to be careful on how he presented things in the future. He smiled and reached his hand up to tip his hat only to realize it wasn't there.

Cadence giggled.

Levi liked the sound of her laugh. It made him feel warm inside like hot buttered bread on a cold afternoon. Apollo waited patiently by the front gate, despite the increasing storm. The rain had yet to fall and Levi recognized his ingratitude.

"Thank you, Lord," he said quietly. He led Apollo into the barn, removed his saddle, brushed him down, and shoveled some hay into his stall. Luckily, the doctor had planned on expanding and had more than one stall in his barn. "You did well, Apollo. Get some rest and we'll see you in a few hours."

Levi stepped back into the doc's house to find Cadence sitting on the couch sipping her hot lemonade with Mrs. Gordon.

"You have chosen quite a lovely woman, Levi." She motioned for him to sit down on the couch next to Miss Walker. "She was just telling me about her life in Chicago. You must be so proud."

Levi half-smiled. In all their conversations, she had yet to have told him any details about her life in Chicago. "She should tell you more. She really is quite a fascinating woman."

Cadence turned to look at him over her shoulder and squinted her eyes in speculation.

Dong. Dong. Dong.

"That will be my cornbread muffins. I set the clock so it would strike when they would be done. You two just sit still and I will have them out in a moment." She set her teacup down on the table in front of the couch and excused herself from the room.

"So, are you going to tell me about Chicago?"

"I don't know what she was talking about really. I lived just a plain ordinary life there."

Levi raised a brow.

Doc Gordon opened the door from his office room, wiping his hands on a rag, his features looking grim.

Levi stood, a sudden knot of worry twisting inside his gut. Cadence stood and slipped her hand into his as if it was the most natural thing in the world. He squeezed.

"I'm sorry, Levi." Doc shook his head. "There was nothing more I could do for your friend. The damage was just too extensive. I'm afraid he's passed."

A weight dropped inside Levi's gut and irrefutable anger welled up inside of him. If only he'd been more vigilant.

How could I have let this happen?

Buck had a wife and three grown children. This news would be devastating to all of them. He continued to stand there, staring at the doc.

Who could do such a horrible thing?

Seven men had needlessly lost their lives today and for

what? His hands balled into fists at the injustice of it. He wanted to scream. To hit something. To let it out, but he couldn't lose control. Especially not here. Especially not in front of Cadence.

Mrs. Gordon walked into the room holding a plate full of muffins and stopped at the doorway. "Oh, dear," she said quietly. She quickly moved to set her confections down on the table.

"Thanks, Doc." Levi cleared his throat. "I know you did everything you could." He glanced at Cadence and then to Mrs. Gordon. "If you'll all excuse me for a moment, I think I forgot to close the barn door." If he could just get some air to clear his thoughts, he would be all right.

"Levi," Cadence placed a hand on his forearm.

It was too much. He turned to Mrs. Gordon. "Ma'am," he said with a curt nod, then strode to the door.

Cadence followed. "Levi," she said again, her hands at her sides.

He whipped around to face her, his eyes threatening tears that he didn't want her or anyone to see. More than anything he just wanted to pull her into his arms, to find comfort in her touch. She didn't give him the chance. She threaded her arms beneath his and nestled her body against him. The knot in his throat grew. He fought to keep his emotions in check.

"You, Mr. Redbourne, did everything you could too," Cadence whispered against him.

He squeezed her tighter against him. "I liked it better when you called me Levi," he said quietly.

"Levi," she said his name again.

He pulled away from her enough to see the compassion in her face. She too had had an exhausting day, but she still looked beautiful. *Please, God, keep her safe and we will find who did this and bring them to justice.*

"Hmhmmmm," Doc cleared his throat. "We probably should take Mr...uh..."

"Buchanan," Levi provided, looking up again at the doc.

"Buchanan into town," the doc finished. "Since I'm guessing he has no family here, the undertaker can make arrangements for his burial. He lives in the small house right behind the funeral tent."

Mrs. Gordon rushed forward. "You and Harold can head into town. Why don't you leave your betrothed here with me?"

"But," Cadence interjected, "I need to—" What could she say?

"Betrothed, Levi?" Doc asked, his confusion apparent. "When did this happen? I thought..."

Levi cleared his throat and the doctor stopped his comment.

"Mrs. Gordon's right," he said quietly. "It's been a long day. If the sheriff wants to speak with you, I'll bring him back with us." Levi brushed a strand of hair from her face.

"Might as well go on and kiss her," Mrs. Gordon said. "It might make you feel better."

Levi knit his brows together and then realized his arms were still wrapped around Miss Walker.

Cadence looked up at him. She didn't pull away, but he couldn't bring himself to do it. If he was going to kiss Miss Walker, he didn't want it to be because of grief or because someone had goaded him into it. He released her.

"We should go."

"We should go?" Cadence repeated Levi's words, still reeling over them near an hour after they'd left. She pounded at the dough Mrs. Gordon had put in front of her. They were finishing up the last details of a late supper—since they'd taken the doctor away from his peaceful evening.

Several lanterns lit the whitewashed kitchen and Cadence was grateful for the light. She pounded the dough again. It had been a long time since she'd done any work in the kitchen. At home, her mother had done most of the cooking after Daniel had passed away. It had been three years and her friends and family still treated her like a delicate twig that would snap with the slightest pressure. It had served her well as a cover, but the façade had grown old. At least now she didn't have to pretend with her mother.

"Now, we'll just break off pieces like this," Mrs. Gordon tore off a chunk of the dough, "and roll it flat." She accomplished the task in a few short seconds. "And then, we'll wrap the chicken, a hearty spoonful of gravy, and the vegetables, sealing off the ends like this." She held up her example for display before setting it neatly into the pan of hot oil on her stove.

Cadence followed suit. However, she was careful not to make a splash when she placed her concoction into the pot. Her mind drifted back to Levi. She scarcely wanted to admit the disappointment she'd felt when he had not elected to kiss her. Her time with him was running short. It wouldn't be long before they reached Bryan. She'd managed to push her worry for the missing Pinkerton to the back of her mind. She didn't want to think about the possibility she may have lost her father too.

He's too stubborn to die, she reminded herself. *He'll be fine.*

Once she was in Bryan she would find her father, assess the threat, and then proceed with the rest of her assignment. Thomas Durant had received several threats detailing what would happen to the railroad and all those who supported it, if he followed through with his intention to meet the Central Pacific in completion of the Transcontinental Railroad. While a Pinkerton was generally visible on every train, Mr. Pinkerton had wanted someone who would be able to get close to Durant and protect him from within. Someone unexpected.

Her.

Everything she'd heard about Thomas Durant was

unpleasant. Even though Annie had tried to deny it, she'd not ended her assignment on good terms with the man. Still, Mr. Pinkerton would not have entrusted Cadence with an assignment of this magnitude if it wasn't important.

"You find out what or who is threatening the railroad, and stop them," he'd told her. "The joining of the rails is an important step in uniting this great nation." Those had been the last words she'd heard from Allan before leaving Chicago, and she was determined to make certain nothing would prevent that from happening.

"I'm sure they will be back at any moment, dear," Mrs. Gordon said, patting her on the shoulder. "You looked like you were quite far away just then." She placed the plate of chicken dumplings down in the center of the gingham covered table. "Is everything all right?"

Cadence smiled and nodded.

"Would you mind going down into the cellar, dear, and retrieving a bottle of cider?"

Cadence cleared her throat and nodded. She picked up one of the lanterns from a hook near the back door and walked out into the pantry where the brisk evening air seeped under the door. The cellar steps were taller than she'd expected and she nearly tripped over her dress as she descended. The door at the bottom of the stairs opened easily and Cadence held up the light to reveal a room of shelves full of bottled goods—each carefully marked with the name of the item and the date it had been sealed. Mrs. Gordon would have gotten along well with her mother.

It only took a moment to locate the bottles labeled 'cider.' They were large enough that Cadence guessed they would only need one. She tucked it into her arm and turned to go back up the stairs, but someone blocked her way. She jumped back, the jar slipping from her hold, but she didn't hear it crash.

"Levi, you startled me." She swatted at his arm, appreciating the firm angles of his chest and shoulders.

Look at his face. She chastised herself for allowing her thoughts to dwell on the wide expanse of him and glanced up.

"Glad you didn't drop this," he said, holding out the bottle of newly shaken juice, a wide smile spread across his face.

Cadence couldn't stop herself from admiring his perfectly chiseled jawline.

"Thank you," she responded, reaching for the jar.

Levi pulled it back, just out of her reach. He leaned down, wrapping his fingers around the handle of the lantern she held, and took it from her. He set the dim source of light down on a tall wooden crate and hooked his arm around her waist, pulling her body in close to his—the bottle of cider at her back—and closed his eyes as his mouth descended on hers.

The feel of his strength, his grief, his desire, all poured into that kiss. She relaxed against him, her hands unwittingly sliding up his chest, around his neck, and into the dark waves of hair at his nape as she allowed herself to indulge in the pleasure his lips brought to hers. Her whole body suddenly felt alive and she didn't ever want the moment to end.

Nevertheless, Levi pulled away, staring down at her with eyes the color of warm honey pooled inside rings of chocolate. He brushed her lips and jaw with his thumb and smiled.

"I've been wanting to do that for a long time." He picked up the lantern and returned it to her hand with a pleased grin and skipped up the cellar steps, two at a time, to the kitchen with the cider still in his hand.

Cadence pressed her fingers to her lips, unsure her legs would still support her. "Mr. Redbourne," she said to herself, "you are full of surprises." She smiled and climbed out of the cellar.

When she stepped back into the kitchen, she placed the lantern on the table for some additional light. Levi stood up and pulled out the chair next to him. She sat down, unable to help the happy curve to her lips, and filled her plate.

"The Gordon's have invited us to stay," Levi said, breaking off a piece of one of the chicken-filled dumplings.

Mrs. Gordon smacked his hand away. "You'll be staying in separate rooms, of course." The woman eyed him with warning.

Levi put his hands in the air. "My mama would have my hide if I was anything but a proper gentleman."

The meal was delicious.

Cadence had never experienced filled dumplings before. They were delightful. She guessed everyone else felt the same as the entire basket of twelve dumplings had disappeared. She stood up and started collecting the empty dishes.

"Allow me." Levi pushed his chair back and reached for the plate she held. When his fingers grazed hers, Cadence sucked a quick intake of breath, and she met his gaze with a smile.

"The sheriff?" she asked quietly. She'd been waiting all night for the uncomfortable conversation a visit from the local lawman would create.

Levi shook his head, then turned to Mrs. Gordon. "You both have slaved over this wonderful meal. It seems only fitting that Doc and I do the dishes."

Cadence allowed the apprehension to drain out of her.

Mrs. Gordon patted her husband gently on the shoulder a few times. Cadence guessed she approved of Mr. Redbourne's actions. Begrudgingly at first, Doc Gordon stood up and began to help Levi clear the table.

"Never look a gift horse in the mouth, my boy," Doc Gordon said.

"Are you calling me a horse, Harold Gordon?" Mrs. Gordon called as the men turned to leave.

"Only in the best sense, my love," he replied, leaning over to kiss his wife lovingly smack on the lips.

Cadence smiled at the sweet exchange.

As Levi and Doc headed into the kitchen, she decided the

men were lucky a pump had been installed next to the sink. It wasn't that easy in most places.

"That man of yours is really something, isn't he?" The look of utter delight on the woman's face told Cadence that she wasn't accustomed to having someone else do the chores.

"He is something all right." Cadence watched with appreciation as Levi demonstrated how to wash a dish for the doctor. It seemed for all of his talents with medicine, housework just didn't come natural to Doc.

Cadence's chest heaved lightly with a silent laugh.

One adventure after another.

Bryan. Thoughts of her father pushed their way to the surface and she fought to keep calm. The longer it took for them to get back on the train, the longer her father was out there somewhere, possibly hurt or...

There was nothing she could do to help him right now, but a good night's rest would go a long way in keeping her alert and ready when the time came. They'd be on their way in the morning. Hopefully, a train could pick them up in town and they would once again be on their way.

Levi looked back at her and winked. If she didn't know any better, she would say they were the most in love and believable couple she had ever seen. This was a part she could play.

Heaven help her—it felt good.

Levi awoke before the sun. They would have a lot to do today. He needed to gather as many men as he could to ride out to the wreck and salvage all of the goods that had not been lost when the train derailed. His men would need some relief—especially if word about the derailment had gotten out or coyotes had come around to call. He imagined they were ready for a good hot meal and a place to sleep.

Levi sat up, picking a stray piece of straw from his hair.

Apollo nickered quietly.

The barn was as good a place as any, he'd figured, to get a night's rest. It sure beat sleeping in a train corridor and being tossed about like a ragdoll. At least Mrs. Gordon had given him a bedroll with a couple of blankets and a pillow. It had taken some time, but eventually he'd gotten some good sleep.

Levi pushed aside the blankets and stood up. He folded the bedding and tossed it below before climbing down the ladder from the hayloft.

A sliver of light shone through the barn doors. Levi welcomed the warmth of the sun's rays as he stepped outside to stretch. The morning smelled like rain, but the clouds had mostly dispersed and the ground was damp, but there were no puddles on the ground. It must have been a very light shower.

Levi loved mornings for a much different reason now than when he was a child. He glanced behind him up at the high door to the loft. How many times had he and Tag scared the dickens out of one of his poor unsuspecting siblings? Too many to count.

He remembered one time in particular when his baby sister, Hannah, had gone out to the barn to milk the cow and had sat down on the stool—unsuspectingly sitting on the cow pie that had awaited her. Or the time he and Tag had completely dismantled the family's outhouse one morning before church on Sunday and had left it sitting in a neatly organized heap at the foot of the front porch stairs. They'd taken their father's wrath on that one and they'd been assigned latrine duty for two full weeks, Levi remembered with a smirk. The look on their father's face when he'd discovered the missing structure had been worth it.

It was a long time ago. Levi chuckled. Those days seemed all too distant.

"You're up mighty early."

Levi spun around to see Mrs. Gordon with her basket,

heading toward the chicken coop. He glanced up onto the wrap around porch where Miss Walker had just emerged from the house, pulling her hair up into a tie as she ran down the stairs.

"Now, Mrs. Gordon, you just get your pretty little self back into the house. Miss Walker and I will take care of your eggs. It's the least we can do for your hospitality."

"Oh, I couldn't," she said with a pleased grin on her face. "It's been such a pleasure to have the two of you under our humble roof. It's a shame you'll have to be leaving us so soon."

Cadence hurried past them into the chicken coop. "Who needs a basket when you've got a perfectly capable apron." She paused a second, turned around, and scooped up the bottom of the apron she wore into a bowl-like shape. He could only guess she'd borrowed it from the kitchen.

Levi extended his hand for the basket. "You're not going to let her have the advantage, are you now, Mrs. Gordon? See," he said, standing up straight and waving his arms in front of him, "no apron."

Mrs. Gordon laughed heartily. "Why, I've never been so spoiled in all my life." She handed over the basket. "You'd better git. She's already a half-dozen eggs ahead.

Levi grabbed the basket and ran toward the coop. "Oh, no you don't."

Cadence giggled, but he could see the concentration on her face as she worked to keep her bundle of eggs steady within the confines of the material at her waist. If she collected too many more, she wouldn't be able to carry them into the house without breaking them.

"Sorry, Redbourne, I'm afraid I've gotten the rest." She smiled haughtily at him as she ducked out of the coop and walked with care toward the house. "I beat you," she called back.

Levi laughed heartily. Sure enough, she'd been able to collect all but four eggs. She continued to amaze him.

The Gordon's were kind enough to offer for Cadence to stay with them while Levi rode around to the surrounding farms and into town to band together enough men and wagons to head out to the wreck and collect the supplies, but she would hear nothing of it. She seemed to have a keen desire to go back to the train. Most women would dread the long ride, but Cadence Walker was not most women.

She'd claimed to be headed to Bryan to be with her father and start up a life there, but if Levi's hunch was correct, he couldn't help but wonder what kind of mission the woman was on or what else she was up to. He'd have to keep his eye on her. Something he didn't think would be too difficult.

CHAPTER TEN

"Well, I think that's the last of it."

Huge lodge poles extended bulkily from the wagon at the back of the line. Levi didn't know if he'd ever seen James, the conductor, break a sweat before. He certainly didn't think he'd even ever seen the man without his hat.

"Nice work." Levi clapped James on the shoulder.

They'd been able to round up a total of eight wagons, mostly from the surrounding farms, to help transport the cargo. They'd been traveling back and forth between the train and town all day. It went much faster this time.

Wagons full of grain, tools, cloth, and other building supplies had been loaded to the hilt, emptied in town, and refilled again. While there were two armed men for every load, Levi had kept all of the buckboards together to diminish the chance of a raid on the route. This was the last trip and Levi was hopeful they'd make it without incident.

"Only a few more things to be loaded and we'll be on our way," Levi said casually to the couple of men still here from the small rail crew.

Levi glanced over to the make-shift corral where he'd

housed Apollo with the other horses from the train. The wrangler had been able to round up all but two of the horses. All other livestock had been gathered, driven into town with the first load, and corralled in the large pasture behind the livery.

"Any trouble last night? Coyotes?" he asked the men.

"No, sir. We think two of the horses are running with a wild herd that ran near here last night, but they didn't bother us."

A wild herd? Levi thought of home and smiled. He looked down the line to see Cadence climb out of the coach that housed his sleeping compartment, with the help of four or five of the men standing above the door.

What was she up to?

"How long before you think Dodge will have a crew out to patch the tracks?"

"Depends. Has there been any word from the others?" Levi asked.

James shook his head.

"If they were able to deliver their message, then I know Gren will have another crew here before nightfall," Levi said dismissively as he continued to watch as a man raised his hands and clasped them around Cadence's waist, helping her down from the top of the side-turned train car. Her laughter floated on the air and Levi felt his insides grind.

You don't have a claim on the woman, Redbourne.

He looked away, rubbed his hands together, and scanned the remainder of the goods to be loaded. A few barrels of salted meat, nails, and flour had been set upright and stacked. Butter churns and crates of milk tins still awaited pickup. Amazed that only a limited number of the barrels and crates had been damaged in the wreck, Levi motioned for one of the wagons to back up to the stacked goods.

"This is the last one, boys. Let's get her loaded quickly and we can be on our way," Levi called out to the few men who'd scattered about the wreckage, but were still within earshot. He picked up one of the crates of milk tins and headed for the back of the wagon.

Laughter.

He glanced up to see Cadence smiling brightly at one of the young cowboys from town.

CRASH!

Everything went quiet and all eyes turned on him.

"Ouch," Levi growled.

He'd run into the back of the wagon and dropped the crate on his foot. At least the crate hadn't broken apart, but he wasn't so sure about his pride. He caught Cadence's eyes. She smiled warmly.

Are you all right? she mouthed at him.

He nodded gruffly.

Something warm filled Levi's belly and he reached down for the now splintered crate. It looked like there was plenty of straw and packing on the inside that he didn't think there would be any damage to the milk tins either.

"You should keep your eyes on your destination, Redbourne," one of the men said with a laugh as he clapped his new friend on the shoulder.

He locked eyes with Cadence again as she made her way toward him.

"Maybe I am," he whispered under his breath. "Maybe I am."

"Race you," Cadence called as she passed Levi, already at a gallop.

They'd just crossed the Overland Bridge and only had another ten minutes until they reached town.

"Come on, boy," she heard Levi urge his mount. "We can catch her."

She leaned forward in the saddle and looked straight ahead—sure the mare she rode could feel her excitement. It had seemed that over the last couple of days she had turned everything with Levi into a competition. It was fun that way, and helped avoid the dangers of getting too close.

She jumped over a rock, but when the horse landed, something was off. She felt as if her saddle was sliding, rubbing back and forth across the horse's back. Immediately, she pulled on the reins. It wasn't enough. The saddle had come completely loose, the strap now flapping around with each step. She was going down either way, but this time she wanted a little dignity. Rather than fall on her rump and embarrass herself like she had earlier, she let go of the reins, swung a leg over the back of the mare—not an easy feat in this blasted skirt, and did her best to jump away.

The ground came a lot faster than she'd expected and the planned roll turned into something of a thud and scrape followed by another thud.

Not as graceful as she'd hoped.

Her hands stung from where she'd tried to catch herself. Multiple cuts and scratches once again bloodied her hands. Her shoulder had hit the ground pretty hard, but she'd learned over the years to walk it off. Her mount now pranced around her excitedly in circles, but she hadn't bolted. For that, Cadence was grateful.

People were going to start to think she was an abused woman.

She pulled herself up off the ground. She'd been worse off, but to add insult to injury, her saddle sore legs protested every step. Cadence finally reached her saddle and heaved it up to have a look. It was still fully intact.

"You and horses just don't seem to mix," Levi said, an edge of concern lacing his voice. "Are you all right?" he asked as he stepped in front of her horse and calmed the mare down enough to collect her reins. He walked the horse over to where

Cadence stood.

"Everything okay?" A big, red-headed burly man asked as he pulled the first wagon in the little wagon train to a stop.

"Elvin, can your boy maybe ride the mare back to the livery?"

The youngster jumped down off the wagon seat and was at Levi's side in moments. The youth seemed very anxious to be on horseback instead of riding along in the wagon.

Levi handed him the mare's reins.

"You're quite a man already I see. You can saddle a horse I expect?" Levi asked.

"Yes, sir," the youth said proudly.

Levi took the saddle from Cadence, handed it to the kid—who strained slightly under its weight—and placed her face between his hands, lifting her chin enough so he could look at her face.

"Wasn't me. Or the horse," she said, finding it a little difficult to speak with her chin cupped in Levi's hands. She reached up, wrapped her hand around his wrist, and tugged lightly.

"Sorry," he said and quickly released her. But the moment he saw the streaks of blood on his cuff, he grabbed her wrists and lifted them, palms up.

Scrapes lined the fleshy part of her hands.

"Haven't we already done this twice before?" Levi asked.

Cadence couldn't tell whether he was teasing or annoyed, but she kept a keen eye on the kid as he attempted to saddle the mare.

She hadn't had a chance to inspect the straps and worried that they might be damaged.

"Wait," she said as the kid was about to climb up into the stirrups.

Levi looked at her, his brows knit together. She felt the cinch and visually inspected it along with the rest of the straps and pieces on the saddle tack. Everything looked perfectly in order.

"I wasn't joshing with you when I said that it wasn't my fault, or the horse's. I made sure the saddle was nice and tight right before we left the wreckage site. Someone had to have messed with the buckle when we stopped for water at the creek's edge. It's the only time I was away from her."

"That's a pretty serious accusation, Miss Walker," Levi said. "Did you see someone near the mare?"

She hadn't seen anything suspicious, but it was the only explanation. She knew she'd secured the tack properly.

Levi walked around the mare and inspected the tack on his own.

"Give this to the liveryman," he told the boy, apparently satisfied that the saddle was fit for riding. He reached into his pocket and pulled out a small pouch. Coins jingled inside and Levi removed four bits and placed it in the young boy's hand. "And this is for you." He retrieved another dime and the boy grinned with excitement.

"Now, git." He helped the boy up into the saddle and lightly tapped the mare's flank. The kid's father was quick to get the wagon back on the road and moving again.

Levi's horse, Apollo, appeared to be content and not nearly as restless as Cadence felt.

"I believe you," Levi whispered as he moved to retrieve something from his saddle bags.

When he returned, he scooped her hands back up into his.

Cadence couldn't tell from his expression if he was upset with her. She tried several tricks to get him to meet her eyes. To smile.

"Good thing for you my mama taught us to always keep this with us." He held up a bottle that looked like it had been filled with a white poultice of some sort. "Probably because we've all gotten ourselves into this exact type of trouble. A lot." He smiled.

Finally.

"You must miss her." She wanted to know more about him.

"Of course. But my work here is important." The boyish almost-grin she'd seen mere moments ago seemed to melt away with her pain.

Levi applied generous amounts of the white substance on her hand. She winced as the cool liquid stung her torn flesh. He pulled a neatly folded handkerchief from his bag and gently worked to clean the area. He was quiet for the next few minutes as he tore the cloth into strips and wrapped them around her hands, tying the last bit into a knot.

"It's not much, but it will have to do until we get back to Doc's."

She didn't know what to say. It was nice for the Gordon's to give them a place to sleep and all, but she was itching to get back on the road. As much as she'd tried to curtail her anxiety over her father, she had to be careful not to obsess over him and her assignment. However, as much as she liked being around Mr. Redbourne, her father and her job had to come first. Maybe when this mission was over...

Stop. It's not the time to even think about such things.

Levi turned to put the bottle of liquid away. Cadence reached out and placed a hand on his forearm and he stopped. As much as she reveled in the feel of his strong flesh, she let go.

"Thank you."

He nodded and closed the leather satchel.

"Levi?" she called his name.

"Hmmmm?"

"Why do you believe me?"

"Why would you make it up? To save face? Somehow, that doesn't seem like something you would do." He lifted her up and sat her sidesaddle. "Give me a look at that leg."

She knew he just wanted to see her burns. "What makes you think so?"

"Well, you're a Pinkerton, aren't you? The Pinkertons I know wouldn't lie about something like that. The burn looks like it's healing nicely."

How did he know?

Cadence stood there with an open mouth and scrunched eyes. Had he known all along? Did her father know? There were too many questions swirling through her mind, but for some reason, anger was the emotion that bubbled to the surface.

What was she supposed to say?

"A Pinkerton?" she scoffed.

"Don't play that game with me. I've known your father way too long. I think I've earned more respect than for you to deny it." He climbed up onto the horse and lifted her enough that he could slide into the saddle with her on his lap. The long leather case she carried knocked him in the chin.

"Sorry," she said, moving it back in front of her.

His jaw pulsed and he raised an eyebrow, but did not speak.

"How long have you known?" she asked quietly.

"Doesn't matter. What does matter is that we find out who would want you hurt. Would anyone here recognize you as the law?"

"Who would believe it?"

"I did." He nudged Apollo forward and they started back to town.

Cadence thought back through the day at all of the stranger's faces she had encountered. None of them had seemed familiar, but there were few out there somewhere who would recognize her as a Pinkerton. Her assignments had been mostly in Chicago and farther east. She was good at her job. Mr. Pinkerton had oft told her as such. And most situations she'd been able to assist with had never required her to reveal her identity, but there had been an occasion or two where it couldn't have been helped.

Her trunk. The thought of her luggage sunk a pit deep in her gut. If someone here was indeed after her and knew that her trunk was among the other supplies they'd collected, they might find more than what they bargained for—clothing and her letters from Daniel weren't the only things they'd find. The trunk was full of weapons and enough money to turn any man's head. Not to mention an envelope full of property deeds to land across the line.

"I don't think so. Only a small handful of people have been privy to my status as detective. My mother never knew and I don't think my father even knows."

Levi lifted an eyebrow, but did not say a word.

"You should tell him," Levi whispered. "He would be proud of you."

She leaned her head against his shoulder and smiled against him.

I hope so.

When they reached town, there were two men on horseback waiting outside the livery. Levi helped Cadence as she slid down and then dismounted.

"You have something for me?" Levi asked the men, handing the reins to the liveryman. "Thanks."

The thinner of the men dismounted and handed a telegram to Levi, who quickly opened the piece of paper and read the contents. He nodded and said something to the man that Cadence couldn't quite hear, but the men both headed into the livery.

"What is it?" Cadence asked, curiosity claiming the better of her as she followed.

"Another threat has been made against Thomas Durant and the railroad. And the Central Pacific is gaining on us. The race just got serious."

"Another threat?"

"No specifics, but we'll need to keep an eye out. It looks like the CP plans on making it to Promontory Summit in Utah by the seventh. Just in the nick of time. The celebration is already scheduled for the eighth."

"Wait, May eighth?"

Levi nodded, still glancing at the note as if rereading it. He was preoccupied with something else in the notification.

"Why? Does the meeting of the rails interest you?" Levi asked distantly.

"Maybe."

She had even less time than she'd expected. The train would get her to Bryan in a day or two at the most and she hoped to be able to find her father within a reasonably short time. Then, she could make it to end of track within the week—if all went according to plan. That should give her plenty of time to stop whatever shenanigans were being planned to destroy the ceremony and celebration.

"I've been summoned," Levi said without looking at her. He folded the paper, but crumpled it as he tucked it into his pocket, muttering something under his breath. "As if I wouldn't be there anyway, the man has the gall to summon me," he said to himself more than to her. "I'll be heading there sooner than expected I guess. With or without the train."

"What do you mean, without the train? There has to be a train. I need to get to Bryan as quickly as possible. That train is coming. Right?"

"Right," Levi answered affirmatively. "Just not exactly sure when. With all the threats against the line, we have to be careful until it is finished." He tipped an imaginary hat, then looked up at her, all playful expression gone from his face. "What aren't you telling me?" He eyed her speculatively.

"I just really want to see my father." And that was the truth.

He must have believed her because Levi nodded and turned and walked toward the mercantile.

By the time the last of the supplies finally arrived in town, Cadence wondered just how long it would take for the railroad crew to make the necessary repairs to the track. She didn't plan on staying in River City any longer than she needed to. Clive and his brutes had damaged a good chunk of the line, and by their conversation earlier, she guessed their motives had been an attempt to thwart the meeting of the rails.

Clive had been looking for a trinket forged by the President. He hadn't gotten it. She reached into her pocket for the large golden spike she still carried. If anyone knew what it was or its significance to the newly unified nation, she could jeopardize the whole mission.

Suddenly, she wished she'd brought the cylinder along with her, but hoped it would be safer at the Gordon's place. Cadence scanned the street looking for the wagon that had carried her belongings into town. She had to get to that trunk before anyone else.

Levi emerged from the shop with a new hat shadowing his already dark features. For a moment, Cadence entertained the idea of paying Mr. Redbourne to escort her by horseback through Laramie and on to Bryan, but she was in no hurry to spend days on end in a saddle. She was already sore from the few trips they had taken back to the wreckage.

She would never admit it to him, but she was drained. Every part of her lower body seemed to burn sore with exhaustion. Her hands and face still stung with scrapes and cuts. She looked around. This town offered no relief. A good hot bath sounded like heaven. Cadence just wanted to be able to put her feet up on a forward moving train and be on her way, but if it was going to take any longer, she would have to find another way.

"Here you are, Miss Walker," a bearded farmer who had been driving the third wagon in the train handed her the trunk. "Not a scratch," he said with a wink.

"Thank you," she smiled genuinely as he placed the trunk at her feet.

Whew.

Levi shook his head. "Your clothes? Really?"

"A girl needs to look her best."

His eyes nearly rolled to the back of his head as he pulled a saddle from a hitching post next to the jailhouse—construction in progress. This town was just way too small for her liking.

"Stealing saddles now?" She couldn't help but ask.

"Nah. The liveryman left it there for me while he gives Apollo a good brushing. I need to take this out to the tanner. I noticed one of the straps is wearing thin and I don't want to end up falling on my backside, now do I?" He walked toward a rather small tent with an unusually acidic smell coming from inside—though she suspected that the man standing in the gated area around the back was the tanner.

"Scamp," she called playfully after him.

Cadence needed to get to Laramie. Annie would have coded instructions at the telegraph office there and time was running out. The end of the railroad line entertained Mr. Durant and several other very important men that would be making the decisions that could make or break the railroad. Without so much as a telegraph office, Cadence felt cut off from the world. Maybe she wasn't cut out for this sort of life after all. Her father would be very disappointed if she told him she'd changed her mind about considering a permanent move.

"Thank you, sir. I'll be back in a little while," Levi said as he walked back around to the front of the tanner's tent.

Clank. Smack. Bump. Giant lodge poles spilled out of the back of the now broken and obviously overloaded wagon bed at the edge of the small town.

"Clear way," a man yelled, his hand cupped around his mouth. Several of the menfolk scattered to avoid the rolling logs.

"Excuse me," Levi said as he turned and ran toward the chaos. Luckily, the ground they were on was fairly level and the logs wouldn't get too far. She figured they should all look on the bright side of things. It had certainly been the easiest way to unload the wood—despite the damage to the wagon. Any wainwright worth his salt would be able to repair the broken box without much thought. That was, if they had a wainwright in this tiny place.

"Yoohoo. Miss Walker." Mrs. Gordon waved her hands in an attempt to gain Cadence's attention. Three other women, all pristinely dressed in high-fashion crinoline skirts, waddled hurriedly behind her.

"Mrs. Gordon, it's so nice to see you."

"We are having an evening tea at Matilda's tonight and we thought you may want to invite your mother and join us. We are very anxious to meet the Walker family, you know."

Cadence tried to think back as to why Mrs. Gordon would believe that her mother would be living in River City. Their engagement. She had to think fast.

She smiled. "How wonderful for you to have invited us, but you see," she looked around, trying to think of anything that would get her out of this mess. "The truth is, Mrs. Gordon, Mr. Redbourne and I are not getting married. Anymore," she added. She didn't want the woman to think any less of Levi. "We agreed it was for the best since he will be traveling so much with the railroad and my father is waiting for me to join him at the ranch he's building for me in Bryan."

"You mean the Walkers will not be settling down here in our…fair city? I had just assumed…" Mrs. Gordon's face said it all. She was saddened at the news.

"So, a young woman of your age is traveling out there alone?"

"Well, not alone exactly."

"With a man?" The woman with a yellow feathered atrocity atop her head tsked. She turned to the lady next to her. "Well, we certainly don't need Walkers around our children if they have such an obvious lack of mores. We should be glad she'll be moving on." She raised her nose in the air, turned toward the framed building that would become the church, and stomped away. Her friend with the purpled azalea broach followed.

"She's the minister's wife. Thinks she's better than everybody else. Don't pay her any mind, dear." Mrs. Gordon patted her on the hand. "I'll be sad to see you go. We were hoping to get a few youngsters around here. I hear that Laramie is full of young people. River City won't amount to much if it's just us old fogeys to make a go of it."

"You don't give yourself enough credit, Mrs. Gordon. You're as spry as they come. Besides, you've got Mr. Cardon and Mr. Faulk over there. They are both young strapping gentlemen." Cadence thought about the young cowboys who had unwittingly helped her retrieve her trunk from Levi's quarters on the overturned train car. In her opinion, they would both make quite suitable matches for someone.

"Yes, but I'm afraid there are no young ladies for them to court." Mrs. Gordon looked at her with wide, hopeful eyes. "Do you have any friends, Miss Walker, who might be interested in coming to River City?"

"Isn't that part of Levi's job? We should tell him this town needs more young women. They seem to follow him like hogs at mealtime." At least that's what she'd expect for a man that handsome

Mrs. Gordon laughed and snorted, which caused her to laugh some more. "We'll talk to Mr. Redbourne. And, my dear, I wouldn't be too sure about not marrying the man. I've seen how he looks at you."

Cadence laughed too. She scanned the area where the logs had tumbled free and watched as Levi helped lift one of the last timbers into place. Her mouth went dry when he looked up at her, sweat glistening in the waning sun, and wiped his forehead.

Suddenly, she was feeling quite hungry. Was it suppertime?

CHAPTER ELEVEN

Summoned?

Of course he wanted to be at the meeting of the rails. It was the culmination of all the blood, sweat, and tears that he and so many others had put into seeing the nation whole. But to be summoned by the likes of Thomas Durant was no honor.

Levi picked up the barrel of foodstuffs he'd procured from the mercantile tent and slid it all the way to the back corner of the wagon he'd purchased from the preacher. The man's wife's eyes had grown large when she realized how much Levi had been willing to pay. She'd muttered something about the Lord providing. He made a mental note to 'provide' the good preacher with a new carriage when the celebrations were complete.

The minister had to be a saint to deal with such an ungodly woman. He'd had to swallow his laughter when she'd walked into the soon-to-be church with what looked like a ring of a dozen canaries strapped to the top of her head.

Levi chuckled at the memory.

"What are you doing out here, son?" Doc Gordon stood in the open doorway to the barn.

He shoved a half-dozen quilts into the back, next to the barrel. He'd procured the beautifully crafted blankets from a sweet little old widow living at the edge of town. Her husband had just passed away since coming to River City and her talents with a needle was the only thing that would now provide any income. He hadn't really needed six, but after seeing the poor circumstances she faced, he'd decided to purchase all that she had completed.

"I'm afraid my business takes me elsewhere over the next couple of weeks, but I'll be back. There is still a lot of work to be done to get this town ready for the next winter."

"Miss Walker heading out with you?"

"I'm sure her pa is anxious to see her, as you can imagine."

Levi picked up the trunk that Cadence had been so keen to retrieve from the wreckage and tossed it in the back alongside his own luggage. One of the hinges broke loose, spilling hues of pink, gold, and white lace through the slight crack in the partially opened luggage.

He closed his eyes.

Women.

"You leaving at first light?"

"Yes, sir." Levi reached into his pocket, pulled out a folded leather packet, and handed it to the doc.

"What's this?"

"It's the deed to a parcel of land on Main Street. I figured you'd want a place of your own in town and that would make it easier on folks who need you."

"Levi, I can't accept this." Doc handed the documents back to him.

"Sorry, Doc. It's a done deal." Levi shut the back of the buckboard. "This town needs you."

"But…"

"Now, Doc, wasn't it you who told me I shouldn't look a gift horse in the mouth?"

He opened his mouth with the beginnings of a protest and

then appeared to think better of it. "So I did." He hung his head. "Thank you, Levi."

CRASH!

Both men rushed out into the yard where Mrs. Gordon swatted at a big black dog with her broom. It looked as if he'd knocked over a portion of the chicken coop. The birds balked with excitement and feathers flew about the yard.

"Haaaartrold," she squealed.

"Better run. Seems the Mrs. isn't taking too kindly to the new member of our family." He started for the house, then turned. "Sure you won't wait for the train? One usually comes round here every week."

"Believe me, Doc, I'd much rather take the train than travel cross-country in a wagon with a woman packing pink and yellow frilly things."

They both laughed.

"Oh, Levi, there've been a lot of raids around these parts for the past few weeks. Mostly bandits and rustlers looking for an easy score. Best be careful if you're planning on traveling with just one wagon."

"Noted. We'll be fine. We've got a couple of guns between us and I've seen firsthand how good Miss Walker is with a revolver. But thanks for the warning. We'll be careful."

Levi wondered about Clive's partner, the one who'd gotten away. It would be one thing if the three of them had been working alone, but there had been something in Clive's words that led Levi to believe that they had only been part of a bigger plan to bring down the railroad—especially in light of the newest threats. If that was the case, he and Miss Walker would need to be extra vigilant.

The new sheriff of River City had arrived only a day or so before them and while he'd helped transport the cargo from the train, Levi had yet to sit down with and welcome the man to town. He figured he should probably acquaint him with some of the unique problems that came with running a small town like River City. In particular, he wanted to discuss the saddle Cadence was using when it came loose. He didn't know if they'd intentionally meant to hurt Cadence or just to slow down the transport, but either way, someone in this town was looking for trouble.

"What's this I hear that you are leaving tomorrow morning?" Cadence burst through the doors in a huff. "Please tell me that you are taking me with you. I can't wait in this place for another week. I need to get going."

"Don't you think it's time that you tell me what it is exactly that you are doing? I'm guessing the plan isn't to meet up with Eamon in Bryan and learn how to run the ranch."

"Of course I'm going to Bryan."

"I don't buy it."

Cadence took a breath and when she spoke again her voice was as warm as honey on a summer's day. "Mr. Redbourne. Levi," she corrected," will you take me with you to Laramie?"

He didn't answer.

"Please."

With a voice like that it was no wonder she had the attention of every man within hearing distance. Compiled with her sultry dark hair, darker eyes, and curves that befit the most tempting woman, she was downright dangerous. Not to mention her wit and abilities with a gun.

Stop it.

Cadence took a step closer and Levi took a step back.

"Whoa, woman. What are you doing?"

When she caught a glimpse of her trunk in the back of the wagon, her smile fell.

"What happened?" she asked, a hint of accusation lacing her tone.

"The latch broke apart when I tossed it in." There was no use making more of it than it was.

She stepped onto the foot rail at the front of the

buckboard and climbed up and then over the seat. After fiddling with the broken fastening to no avail, she spun it and harrumphed.

Levi handed her the rope he'd intended on using to secure the luggage.

"Thanks," Cadence said and made quick work of the task.

When she was finished, she looped the remaining rope on her arm, stepped over a few of the smaller crates on the wagon floor, and walked to the back edge. Levi reached up to help. She stepped up onto the wood and he lifted her down.

"Why, Mr. Redbourne, you are such a gentleman." She stepped away from him and tossed the rope onto a nail on the side of the barn. "Thank you," she looked back at the trunk, "for not trying to leave me here."

She was a little spitfire to be certain. Levi wasn't sure whether he wanted to strangle her or to kiss her, but he'd now have a few days to decide.

The ground rumbled in low tones. Levi opened his eyes with a jolt. Only one thing made that sound. He sat up and reached for his gun. Wild horses ran along the stream only a few yards from the area where they'd made camp.

"Cadence," he whispered, though he wasn't sure why. "Cadence," he called a little louder this time.

She peeked out of the rounded covering he'd built over the back of the buckboard.

Levi pointed at the horses and Cadence disappeared inside the wagon. She emerged a moment later, dressed and holding a rifle.

"Where did they come from?" she asked as soon as she got within hearing distance. She sidled up next to him as he crouched behind a boulder that protruded from the ground. They had chosen this place for camp because it had provided some cover with the trees and rock formations.

"They're abundant out here, but most are impossible to tame. I doubt they even realize we're here."

"What are they doing?" she asked, her eyes revealing her curiosity.

"Running." He couldn't help himself.

She smacked him on the arm with the back of her hand.

Apollo snorted and Levi glanced over to where the horses had been tethered for the night. The brown Quarter Horse that he'd purchased from the liveryman neighed loudly and pawed at the ground. Levi was surprised to see that he remained steady amongst the thunderous chaos. He would be a good wrangling horse. Tag would like him.

It didn't take long before the wild horses had changed direction and headed toward the hills away from them.

Cadence leaned against the boulder and slid down onto her rump. "I don't know how people do this for a living."

"What?" Levi asked with scrunched brows.

"Ranching."

"This isn't ranching. At Redbourne Ranch, we get a lot of people bringing us horses to tame—some wild, some just young. Other horses we breed to combine the best traits for different needs or tasks. Not every horse is meant for heavy lifting, or running long distances, or even everyday riding. The goal is to have horses that can stand up to unusual situations. This," he pointed to the distant horses, their hooves pounding against the ground in methodic rhythm, "is what wranglers are for."

"Your brother, Taggert, is a wrangler, isn't he?"

Levi was surprised she would have picked up on that.

"That's something Tag loves to do, but our mama isn't so excited about the idea." Levi thought about the last time Tag had come home with a broken rib after being knocked off his horse. He'd tried to explain that he'd just been grateful he'd been able to get back up before the mustangs had trampled him, but that hadn't helped his plight much.

"I can see why. Those horses are powerful."

"You're not kidding." Levi walked over to the wagon and climbed into the back. He'd cleared a place for Cadence to sleep, but the area was still cramped. He smiled at the crumpled quilts that had gotten some use during the night and quickly had to change the direction of his thoughts.

The food barrel was at the back of the wagon. He wanted to make up some food before getting back on the road. By his estimation, Laramie would only be another day or two. They could stay at his cousin Noah's place for the night and then head out for Bryan. At this pace, he had every reason to believe he could make it to Promontory Summit with plenty of time to spare.

When he returned to their little camp, Cadence already had a fire going. She continued to impress him. For someone who certainly didn't like small towns or the country, she sure seemed to know her way around. He'd thought being a lady Pinkerton was all about gleaning secrets from high-society women about their husbands' undertakings, but he was learning that there was more to Cadence than being a spy.

He placed the metal supports over the fire and topped it with an iron skillet full of salted meat and fresh cracked eggs the Gordon's had given them. Once they had a good breakfast in their bellies, they could get back on the road and be on their way.

Snap!

Levi froze.

"What's wrong?" Cadence asked, her gun already drawn.

"Shhhhh." He placed a hand over Cadence's mouth.

Snap! Another branch to his left. It was not far off. The smell of food must have brought an animal there. He glanced around and squinted into the sparse trees to see if he could locate the coyote. Nothing.

He reached down for his gun, now holstered at his side.

A deer and her fawn stepped out from the brush. Levi heaved a sigh of relief and fell back against the boulder. A breathy chuckle accompanied a sigh. The sound startled the deer, and they scampered away.

Cadence laughed too. Visible relief added color to her otherwise perfect features. She scooped food onto two tin plates and handed one to Levi. "I never thanked you for the wagon. I know that you could have chosen to make the trip on horseback. I wanted you to know how much I appreciate the gesture."

He loved that Cadence spoke what was on her mind. She didn't play many of the foolish games other women played. She told it straight. Even if her job required her to deal in secrets, Levi trusted her. Something that hadn't come easily since the war.

'Trust.' Check.

It had been days since he'd thought about his mental list for qualities in a bride, but he smiled, knowing the list didn't really matter. He could never marry just to gain his inheritance. When the time was right, he would marry for love.

One drop, then two. Rain fell in a light blanket across the plains. Cadence was grateful for the wrapper Levi had built to cover the back of the wagon, but still, she felt guilty he was sitting out on the wagon bench getting wet. It had started as a mere drizzle and slowly the rhythm of the droplets on the tight canvas cover became faster and more methodical. She couldn't believe the lengths that Levi had gone to in order to assure her as much comfort as possible on their long trip across the territory. They'd been careful to stick to the trail as much as possible.

Water dripped from the brim of Levi's new hat. It wasn't as cold as Cadence had expected the rain to be. She slid the beautifully decorated quilt from her shoulders and stepped to the front of the wagon and, using one of the crates as a step, climbed over the seat.

"What are you doing?" Levi asked with concern.

"I'll take a turn," she said, holding out her hand for the reins.

"What kind of man do you think my mama raised?" he asked, holding firm to the leather straps.

Well, if all she could do was keep him company out here in the rain, then she would do that. Night would soon be approaching and as she looked out over the vast countryside, she couldn't help but appreciate the beauty of the earth through the drizzle. The greens of the grasses and sage seemed muted, almost smoky, under the darkening clouds and she wanted to appreciate the color. Summer, she imagined, would turn the landscape prairie brown. With the mountainside as a backdrop, the plains looked like a painter's masterpiece with its trees in silhouette and sparse hills and dales.

Flash!

Lightning split the sky in several cracks following by a loud, booming thunder.

Cadence snuggled up against Levi and weaved her arm through his and held tight. It felt good.

"Why don't you go on back inside?" He turned and looked down at her.

"Because I'd rather be out here…with you."

He didn't say anything more, but the corners of his mouth turned upward. They drove until the sun was so low in the sky that they could barely see the trail in front of them. Levi pulled up alongside the backside of a ridge where the land seemed to break apart to provide some semblance of a shelter for them.

"We'll have to stop here for the night. I imagine we'll be in Laramie early tomorrow." He jumped down off the wagon. "Now, get back inside before you catch your death."

Instead, Cadence climbed down off the wagon, walked

around to the back and pulled out the first of four stones they had been using to secure the wagon. She lifted up her skirt, not sure why she bothered as the hem was already black from travel, and placed the rock beneath the first wheel. She repeated the steps until all four rocks were in place.

"Do you never do what you're told?"

Cadence jumped. She hadn't heard him step up behind her.

"If it makes sense," she called back as he rounded the buckboard to get to the hitch on the other side. "Which it didn't. Why should you have to do it all?"

The air now held a crisp chill and Cadence rubbed her arms briskly against the cold. The rain had let up for the moment, so with nothing more for her to do outside, she climbed up into the back and slid open the knots she'd tied in the ropes that held her trunk closed.

They'd both catch their deaths if they stayed in their wet clothing. She pulled out a dry night shift and quickly proceeded to undress. There was nowhere to hang her soaked dress without getting everything else wet, so she draped it over the back of the seat until she could pull on her clean night dress. The material felt warm against her skin and she was grateful for the covering.

There wasn't a lot of cargo in the back of the wagon, but the items were bulky and awkward. Cadence tried to push a few of the barrels and crates to the side in order to make room for Levi, but some of them just wouldn't budge.

The flap between the back of the wagon and the driver's seat blew open and a sharp gust of wind slapped against her face. It gave her an idea. She pulled her wet dress from the seat and, trying to keep it as far away from her dry clothes as possible, hung it up outside the flap in front of the make-shift door to help block the wind.

"I'll just need some—" Levi climbed up onto the wagon and threw back the back covering.

Cadence gasped and whipped around to face him. He'd

startled her.

"Sorry," he said and disappeared.

The cold night wind swirled about Levi's body as he strode away from the wagon. It was exactly what he needed. He'd worried about where he would sleep until the rain had stopped. When he climbed up onto the back of the wagon, he'd expected to find his bag with some dry clothes and a bedroll, but what he'd found instead was an angel in her night gown. Air had caught in his lungs and he'd found it very hard to breathe.

Levi inhaled deeply of the freshly cleansed air, impervious to the biting wind that threatened to seep deep into his already chilled bones. If he stayed out here, he was likely to be frozen by morning. That wouldn't be good for either of them.

He wished he'd thought to bring the buckskin trousers that went with the buckskin coat his brother, Rafe, had made for him during his time with the Pawnee. At least then he could have stayed mostly warm out here. He considered trying to hang the coat above him, but it just wouldn't be large enough to make a difference.

What should I do, Lord?

A drop of water touched the tip of his nose followed by another on his cheek. In moments, the rain had started again. There was no choice. He had to get into the wagon. Before he opened the flap this time, he knocked on the wood of the gate.

"Cadence," he called, "it's a little wet out here. Do you think you might show a man a little mercy?"

"Well, come in and get yourself dried off," Cadence said in a no-nonsense sort of way. "And as long as you don't snore, you can stay."

Levi could hear the smile in her words. He shook his head and climbed inside. It was already warmer without the breeze whisking through his too long hair, but his clothes still held a chill. He avoided her eyes as he delved into his bag for something dry to put on. Once he'd grabbed a fresh shirt and his cotton pants, he glanced around the very small space.

"I'm not going to look if that's what you're worried about," she said, holding the blankets up around her.

What did you expect, Redbourne?

Still, he waved his hand at the air, motioning for her to turn her back to him and she complied with exaggerated motions as she pulled more of the blankets up around her curvy form and faced the opposite direction.

"I'm glad you're not a complete idiot," she said. "It would have been just plain irresponsible to try sleeping outside in this."

He nearly stumbled on top of her as getting his wet pants off was more of a chore than he'd expected. Even still, he'd never dressed so quickly in his life. When he was done, he threw his wet things at the top of the wagon bed behind one of the barrels, and cleared his throat.

"Thank you. I honestly wasn't looking forward to freezing to death beneath the wagon."

The light was just about gone, but Cadence shifted beneath the blankets and turned around to face him, her hand curled beneath her head, her hair spilling wildly across the blankets. "What exactly do you do for the railroad, Levi?" she asked as if she'd been waiting for the answer for a long time.

"I'm an engineer," he said quietly as he pulled back the blanket to see that she'd folded all of the quilts into two separate and quite comfortable looking bedrolls. "But not the kind that drives the locomotives."

He could feel her eyes on him, coaxing him to go on.

"See, the railroad claims land where they plan on building stations and then they sell those lots to people wanting to build a life for themselves out West." He turned onto his back. "Because the towns along the railway have had a reputation of being Hell on Wheels towns, lawless and rowdy, we wanted to make sure that these towns had every chance of survival. So, one of my responsibilities is to recruit good couples and families to found the towns. We give them a stipend as long as they stay for a contracted amount of time and then we provide a good deal of supplies and I help them build up their homes and businesses to help them get star—"

A soft rumbling noise interrupted his lengthy job description and he turned to look at Cadence—though near impossible to see her face in the full darkness of night. She was asleep.

He closed his eyes, grateful to be warm. "Goodnight, Miss Walker," he whispered as he snuggled farther down into the depths of the make-shift bed.

CHAPTER TWELVE

Cadence and Levi pulled into the growing town of Laramie while the sun shone brightly at the highest point in the sky. Cadence had never been so happy to see clusters of buildings and houses dotting the landscape.

"Noah's ranch is on the far edge of town. I figure we'll head there first." Levi motioned ahead with a flick of his wrist.

People bustled about their morning. A small group of women stood in front of the General Store and a gaggle of young boys sat on the boardwalk just outside of the barber shop with their chins resting on their fists. A boy emerged from the building with a wide grin and a short cut. A man inspected the child's cut and sent him off across the street to an open field where several others kicked around a ball.

"Next," a rotund man with a stern look on his face called from the doorway and one of the seated youth jumped up and ran inside.

Levi waved as he passed and the expression on the barber's face lightened significantly. He'd been here before.

When Levi had said the far edge of town, she'd thought maybe the end of the street, but they left Main Street behind with nary a glance. When they finally reached a spread, set apart with a large wooden archway, she hardly dared hope that they'd arrived.

The homestead was one of the biggest homes Cadence had seen in quite some time. As they passed through the arch, a woman stepped out of the house, drying her hands in her apron, then waved.

"Why, if it isn't Levi Redbourne himself," the woman said with a grin.

Levi jumped down from the wagon, picked her up, and spun her around.

She giggled.

"Where's that husband of yours?" Levi asked once he set her down.

"I'm afraid he's out repairing a fence in the north field. I don't expect him for another hour or so." The woman looked up at Cadence. "Who's your friend, Levi?" she asked, taking a step toward the wagon.

"Kate, this is Cadence Walker." He quickly made his way to the wagon and raised his hands to help her down.

Cadence placed her hands on his shoulders and allowed him to lift her to the ground.

"You remember my friend Eamon?"

"Of course," Kate said with a smile.

"She's his daughter," Levi said proudly.

"And your...friend?" Kate asked, taking a step toward her.

Levi cleared his throat.

"Welcome," Kate said as she threw her arms around Cadence.

She hadn't expected such a warm welcome, but was pleased by the sudden display of affection.

"Levi told me you and your husband ran a ranch, but I must admit, I didn't expect a place this size." Cadence looked around, unsure of where the property started and ended.

Kate laughed, her voice warm and pleasant. "The property

extends as far as the eye can see." She squeezed Cadence around the waist and they began walking toward the house. "This was my father's homestead, God rest his soul," Kate continued. "When Noah and I married, we purchased a larger plot of land to accommodate..." she stopped and looked at Cadence. "You know what? We'll talk about all of that once you are settled and have some warm vittles in your belly. You must be famished."

At the mention of food, Cadence's stomach churned. "That would be lovely," she said with a grateful smile.

"Fannie, our cook, was just about to put some potatoes in to cook," Kate said. "I'll have her add a few more." She let go and took a step toward the house before turning and looking back at Levi.

"Why don't you set yourself up in the bunkhouse and I'll make up a room for Miss Walker."

"Sure thing, Kate. Thank you."

Kate disappeared inside the house and Cadence didn't know whether or not she should follow.

"She doesn't bite," Levi said in her ear as he carried her trunk on his shoulders and passed her on his way into the house.

Cadence followed.

The inside of the house was even more wondrous than the outside. It seemed very open. The ceilings were so high she imagined Levi's brother Tag could stand on his shoulders and still not be able to touch the roof. The smell of stewing meat wafted through the air and her stomach protested again. They'd had some fruit jerky for breakfast, but that had worn off hours ago. It had been days since she'd had real food and suddenly, her mouth started to water.

"Just finished some fresh biscuits," Kate said as she entered the enormous kitchen. "Have some to tide you over until the food is ready." She held out a basket of steaming biscuits and Cadence reached in, enclosing the warmth in her palm.

"And she makes a wonderful preserve too," Levi said between bites.

He must've been hungry also.

After Kate had spoken with her cook, she motioned for Cadence to follow. They walked into a large room with a big bed situated between two tall windows, each adorned with white curtains with small yellow roses. Sunlight hit the wooden floors, giving the room a warm look and feel.

"I'll trust you'll be comfortable in here," Kate said with a smile. "Fresh linens are in the wardrobe and the water closet is just through there."

Water closet?

"I can have Virg fill a tub for you if you'd like a bath."

Cadence felt like she had died and gone to heaven. Her eyes must have shown her wonder because Kate giggled.

"Noah spoils me," she said as if whispering a secret. "I'll have Fannie put on some water to boil. In the meantime, why don't you get yourself settled and I'll be back to check on you in a bit?"

Levi walked up to the doorway. He exchanged a look with Kate before stepping past her and into the room. He swung the trunk down onto the bed and smiled.

"Nice place, isn't it?"

"It is lovely." She slid the ropes from her luggage and opened it. "They have a water closet. Inside," she said, careful not to let her voice carry. Even in Chicago, indoor plumbing was not widely available. "She's preparing me a bath."

Levi laughed. "Well, I'd better leave you to it." He tipped the brim of his hat before walking out the door.

Cadence had never expected to be this excited over a bath, but after her travels, it had seemed an eternity since she'd been able to bathe properly and she welcomed the idea.

She opened the wardrobe to find a handful of bath sheets, towels, and linens for the bed.

This had to be heaven.

"So, tell me everything," Kate said as she leaned across the table toward Levi.

"There's not much to tell," he replied, shoving another bit of biscuit into his mouth. It seemed to melt on his tongue and he had to concentrate on not closing his eyes in delight.

"You are riding in a covered wagon across the state of Wyoming with a woman who would put any to shame with her gorgeous dark hair and eyes. She seems quite taken with you, and there is nothing to tell?" She snatched the basket of biscuits out from beneath his reach. "I have hot apple pie and candied pecans," she coaxed.

"Why aren't you out with Noah anyway? I was quite surprised to see you here at the house...cooking of all things." The last time he'd been in town, Kate had been the last one he would have expected to see in the kitchen. She'd been working her father's ranch since he'd been killed and seemed to have no interest in womanly affairs.

"Don't you try to change the subject, Levi Redbourne."

He shrugged. "So, she's beautiful," he said without raising his eyes to meet Kate's.

"Yes."

"And smart."

"Yes."

"And you should see her with a gun. I saw her kill a man, right in front of me."

"Abusive husband?" Kate asked knowingly. "It's hard to miss those cuts and bruises healing on her face."

"What? No. To save my life."

"Now, you're just teasing me."

"No, I swear. You'll like her. She reminds me a lot of...well, you."

Color flooded Kate's cheeks at his appraisal.

"She killed a man? What happened? Is she all right?" Kate asked, concern etching her brows.

"It's a long story, Kate."

"Good thing we've got plenty of time," a deep voice called from the doorway.

Levi turned around. Noah Deardon, his cousin on his mother's side, hung his hat from the hook above the cabinet and made up the distance between them in a few short strides. Levi pushed his chair back and greeted him with a firm embrace.

"Apollo seems to be working out for you," Noah said as he clapped Levi on the back. He stepped away with a grin.

"What can I say?" Levi said with a shrug.

"That I know you well enough to choose the perfect horse." Noah removed his hat and bent down toward his wife. "How is the most beautiful woman in the world on this fine afternoon?" he asked, leaning down and kissing her, cradling her head in his hat.

Levi looked away—more out of a sense of privacy than embarrassment. He was not a stranger to affection. His parents had often kissed each other or teased playfully around the children. He was just happy to see his cousin settled down and happy.

"Happy." Kate echoed Levi's thoughts with a giggle. "And excited to see her hard-working husband home to fill his belly." She turned to Levi. "I haven't forgotten our conversation," she said with a playful swat to his shoulder. "I can't wait to hear this long story of yours."

Levi exaggerated a loud groan.

She laughed again.

"So, what story are you going to recount?" Noah asked, pulling out a chair, flipping it backward, and straddling his legs around it. He rested his arms against the back and stared at Levi.

"Kate, do you think that I could get—" Cadence stopped short in the doorway when she caught sight of his cousin.

Noah slapped Levi's shoulder with the back of his hand, his eyes unfaltering from the beauty now standing in his kitchen.

Cadence's eyes flitted between Levi and Noah. "I'm sorry. I thought you were talking to Kate," she said to Levi. She looked at Noah with a smile that made Levi's heart skip a beat. "Where are my manners?" She stepped toward them and extended her hand."

Noah was already on his feet.

"You must be Mr. Deardon, Kate's husband."

"It's Noah, ma'am. And yes, I belong to Kate. I mean," he cleared his throat, "Kate's my wife." He took her hand. "And who," he looked down at Levi, "might you be?" He returned his gaze to a smiling Cadence.

"I am the one for whom they are filling the tub." She lifted her chin in the direction to where Virg carried two steaming buckets of water through the hall.

Noah nodded with a grin. "You with this scalawag?" he asked.

"Why yes, that *scalawag* is accompanying me to Bryan."

"What ya headed there for? Heard it's drying up and people are moving on to Green River."

Cadence opened her mouth to speak.

"Noah Deardon, can't you see our guest is waiting for a bath. Leave her be. You can talk with her once she's had a chance to wash off the trail." Kate returned to the kitchen and ushered Cadence into the other room, but Cadence turned back and smiled at Levi with a little wave before she left.

Levi's belly flipped inside.

"If it's about that one, it's going to be some story," Noah said as he tossed his hat onto the table and returned to his position on the chair. "Can't wait to hear all about it. She's a beauty. Still doesn't hold a candle to my Katie," he said with a decisive nod, "but pretty all the same. Where'd you meet her?"

Levi smiled. Katie and Cadie—though Cadence didn't much appreciate her father's nickname for her.

"She's Eamon's daughter."

Noah whistled. "Does Walker know you're gallivanting across the prairie with his daughter?"

"Not exactly."

Noah burst out with a loud guffaw. "I reckon I wouldn't want to be you when he finds out."

"It's not like that, Noah. She'd have headed out to Bryan to meet him all on her own if I hadn't agreed to accompany her. And somehow, I didn't like the idea of a young woman out here on the trails alone." He took some time to explain what had happened with the train.

"So, it's a chivalrous thing you're doing here then. Doesn't have anything to do with her undeniable charms?" Noah's smile reached his eyes.

Levi knew his cousin was just harassing him. "She's beautiful, I'll give you that. But, I don't know. There's more to it than that."

Noah's playful smile turned to one of interest.

"Oh, no you don't go telling the story without me." Kate reemerged from the other room. She stood on her tip toes trying to reach something from one of the higher shelves.

"Allow me." Noah was at his wife's side in a moment.

Kate looked up at him and Levi saw the unmistakable love in her eyes. Not wanting to intrude on another moment, Levi took the last biscuit from the basket and broke it apart. It was still warm. Noah set a bowl down in front of him and passed out an additional three—one for Kate, Cadence, and him.

"Fannie found a bundle of recipes your mother gave Noah and I when we were married," Kate said. "I believe this is one of Lottie's favorites. Lottie, that is her name?"

Levi's stomach growled. He hadn't had Lottie's stew in ages and the thought had his mouth watering. He nodded.

"Lottie is an amazing cook."

"Fannie too," Kate beamed.

"The tub is filled, ma'am. Will there be anything else you need from me?" A slightly flushed Virg stepped into the kitchen with a tip of his hat.

"Thank you," Kate said. "The meat gravy will be ready shortly, Virg. Make sure to come back on up and have a smothered potato."

"That's very kind, Mrs. Deardon."

Levi knew the man wasn't going to get out of it.

The time passed quickly as Levi recounted the events of the past few days to his cousin and his bride. He could hardly believe half of them himself.

"Well, I think she's very brave," Kate said, standing up from the table.

Fannie, their cook, removed a dozen or so potatoes from the oven and tossed them onto the table top. The food smelled heavenly.

"Wouldn't expect any less from Eamon's kin," Noah said.

"Noah! Kate!" A tall man with a blue neckerchief threw open the door to the kitchen scanning the large room. His eyes fixed on theirs. "You two might want to get out here. Bertha is having some trouble with her calf."

The air grew heavy as Noah grabbed his hat from the table. Kate wiped her hands on her skirt and headed to the wardrobe in the hall. Levi guessed that's where she kept her linens.

"Make yourself useful, Redbourne," Kate called as she tossed him a few towels and rushed past him and out the door after Noah.

Levi followed. He stopped at the threshold and looked back toward the room Cadence was in.

She'll find us soon enough, he decided and took a step out the door. He'd not gotten two steps before the nagging feeling in his gut told him to at least let her know where they'd be so as not to worry her. So, he secured the towels under one arm, opened the door, and strode quickly to Cadence's room and knocked on the door.

"Miss Walker?" He paused a moment, but didn't hear anything. "Miss Walker, we'll be out in the corral if you'd like to join us. One of the heifers is having a hard time calving. But don't worry, we won't be far and I'll be back to check on you soon."

"Levi, we need those towels. And your hands!" Kate called in, desperation lining her voice.

Bertha was one of the last cows to calf and she was Kate's favorite. He'd heard Noah warn her against becoming attached to the cow, but she'd obviously not listened.

He looked at the door. Still no response.

"Coming."

Cadence let the air out of her lungs in a rush. She held the bath sheet closed in front of her and stepped out from behind the wardrobe—Levi's retreating form still visible.

"That was close," she said under her breath as she quickly tip-toed into the room the Deardon's had been so kind to offer for the night, and closed the door.

Another deep breath.

"Idiot," she chastised herself when she looked at the beautiful blue dress Kate had laid out for her on the bed alongside a small bundle complete with a corset, chemise, and bloomers. Kate had been gracious enough to offer some of her clothes while Cadence's were washed and dried before they headed back out on the road.

Her excitement about the hot bath had meddled with her thinking enough that she'd forgotten to take the clean underthings and dress with her into the water closet. The warm bubbles had felt so good against her skin that she'd not thought about the problem until she emerged from the soak and had stared at the dress she'd been wearing for three days.

Cadence closed her eyes at the idea of Levi Redbourne discovering her in such an undressed state and immediately heat flooded her face and neck. She quickly pushed the thought aside and donned the clean garments. The fresh scent of the clothing filled her nostrils.

Before long, she found herself walking about the ranch in search of Levi and her newfound friends. It seemed oddly quiet, but she guessed there wasn't much to do during the day around the homestead. She'd heard stories of working out in the fields, but didn't have much experience with animals other than an occasional horse and her mother's cats. The light breeze sent gooseflesh down her arms and she rubbed them briskly.

"Hello!' she called loudly. Levi had said they would be out in the corral, but the property seemed to have endless outbuildings, each appearing to have its own corral.

"We're out here," a voice called from one of the buildings ahead of her and she quickly found her way out back.

Kate knelt on the ground, uncomfortably close to the mama cow, and Noah stood behind her with one towel draped over his shoulder and another, wet and bloodied, in his hands. Levi stood at the head, rubbing the heifer's face and neck, speaking to her in a soothing tone. He looked up and motioned for her to join him.

Cadence looked down at the clean dress and hesitated, but only for a moment. It wouldn't have lasted long anyway— being clean.

Levi pulled a short stool in front of him and held open his arm. Cadence moved in front of him, her back supported by the firm expanse of his chest. He felt warm and a new wave of gooseflesh descended down her arms. She mimicked Levi's motions, petting and doing what she could to reassure the mama.

"You're a natural," Levi whispered in her ear. "Been around cattle before?"

She shook her head, not trusting herself to speak.

A lowing moan brought Cadence's hand back to the cow's neck and she stroked the animal in quick, short movements. Levi placed his hand over hers and slowed her down until her hand gently glided down and back.

"We're almost there. This one is just stubborn enough to live," Kate said, meeting Cadence's eyes with a wink.

"It's very dangerous for a calf to come out backward," Levi said quietly behind her. "Kate had to reach in and turn it around so both of them didn't die,"

Cadence looked up at Kate, whose look of pure determination crinkled her brow, but did nothing to scar the woman's perfect features. She didn't miss the way Noah beamed at her. Cadence smiled.

The mama cow howled for a short moment.

"Here it comes," Kate said.

Cadence glanced up ahead and watched as the front legs and head emerged. She wasn't sure whether to be sick or awed. When Kate quickly took ahold of the calf's legs, wrapped a rope around them just above the hoof, and started to pull, Cadence sucked in a breath. She'd never seen anything quite like it before. Noah grabbed onto the legs and Kate moved closer, grabbing the calf just above its midsection, her hands slipping against the slick mucus covering the babe. With another pull, it slid out onto the ground.

"It's out," Noah yelled with excitement as he used his towel to pull a thin white layer off of the new calf and wiped it down. "No broken bones. The mouth and nose are clear, but it's not moving." His voice turned to one of concern.

The mama cow made a quick attempt to pull herself to her feet, but Cadence guessed she was just too tired.

"Place him where Bertha can see him." Kate wiped her nose on her shoulder. The anxious look on her face worried

Cadence and she wondered what they would do if the calf didn't survive.

Levi helped Cadence to her feet and they stepped away from the obviously tired mama.

Noah scooped the baby calf up in his arms and placed him at the mother's head. Bertha tried again to pull herself to her feet and, this time, she was successful. She began to lick the babe's face and body, nudging her newborn with her nose.

It seemed as if everyone was holding their breath— Cadence certainly was—as it fell dead silent. Another few moments passed. Still nothing.

Noah dropped his head and Levi placed his hands on Cadence's shoulders. Kate's jaw flexed, but still she watched. After another minute or so, the babe lifted its head, but it dropped back down.

Noah laughed. Kate heaved a relieved sigh and stood up to join them, leaning forward, her eyes unwavering from the calf. Within moments, the little one started stretching its legs and tossing about, trying to pull itself into a standing position. After several attempts of pushing off its front legs and falling on its face, the calf finally stood upright. Wobbly, but upright.

Cadence laughed and relaxed against Levi, who wrapped his arms around her. She liked being in his arms.

"I think they are going to be fine," Kate breathed with satisfaction.

Noah placed an arm around his wife. "You did it, you know." He smiled down at her. "Now, I think that we're the ones who need the bath." He looked up and winked at Cadence.

The men in this family were certainly bold, but heaven help her, she liked it. If only she wasn't so worried about her father and she didn't have a job to do, she would consider staying here forever.

Cadence could feel the lines of worry crinkle her brow. She didn't want to ruin such a special moment, but somehow thoughts of the man she'd scarcely seen over the last few years worked their way into her memories and she realized just how much she missed her father.

Please, God, let him be all right.

She determined that there was nothing she would be able to do until morning. But she would send two telegrams at first light—or as soon as the telegraph operator opened his doors—one to Annie to tell her about their delays, and a second to Bryan with hopes of reaching her father.

Tomorrow.

For now, she just laid her head back against Levi, not wanting this feeling to end.

CHAPTER THIRTEEN

"Are you sure you can't stay any longer?" Kate asked as Levi threw a bag into the back of the buckboard.

Levi threw his arms around his cousin-in-law. "Thank you for letting us stay, but I'm afraid we've already been here longer than we should have. I'm supposed to be in Utah in a week and I won't make it if I laze around here any longer."

"Laze around here? Three mended fences, a new wing on the chicken coop, and the water wheel. And you laze around here? I know that the milliner is thrilled that you and Noah were able to help him get a new water wheel up and running. His business depends on it. We really need to hire more men to help Noah out around our place. I don't know when he's going to realize he can't do it all alone."

"I'm afraid he already knows. He just didn't want his bride to find out." Noah joined them at the wagon. He smiled at his wife and nodded at Levi. "I don't know how we've been able to do so much. Kate's right. I guess it's time we hired on a few more hands."

"I'm glad to see that you are settling in well here," Levi said, reaching out a hand to his cousin. A splash of blue crossed the corner of his eye and he looked up to see Cadence step out of the house and onto the porch. The morning breeze blew her dark locks away from her face, her skin pink and glowing.

"Be careful," Noah warned. "Bryan has had its fair share of trouble."

"When the officials at the railroad decided to move the division point for the rails to Bryan, Green River suffered," Levi told him. "I think fear of losing their homes has driven some of the people to do desperate things, but I don't think there'll be too much more trouble—especially if Black's Fork is drying up like you said and people are moving back to Green River."

Levi thought it was probably just a matter of time before the railroad relocated back to the original town that had been selected for the route. They had the better water source in the valley. When Durant was no longer in charge, someone with a clear head would see the best route for the line—not just the amount of money they could make selling residential lots in a newly founded town.

"I hope you're right. Miss Walker," Noah said as Cadence approached, "you look lovely as ever. Are you sure you want to make the rest of the trip with this stranger here?"

"Honestly, he's not so much a stranger anymore. He's more like...family."

"You mean like a big brother," Noah nudged, a grin spread wide across his face.

"Something like that," Cadence said with a playful smirk, taking a step closer to Levi.

Levi's gut wrenched. He didn't want to be a big brother to Cadence. He had enough siblings to watch over.

"We'd better get on the road. Hopefully, by the time we reach Bryan, we'll be able to find your father and then we can catch the train to the end of track." Levi thought about it for a moment. "I'll," he corrected, "be able to catch the train to the end of track."

"I hate to see you go, but I'm sure Eamon is anxious to see you, Miss Walker." Kate pulled Cadence in for a brief hug.

She nodded. "It's been a long time."

"Well, you've made good time. If I keep training horses like Apollo, I may have to go into the family business." Noah laughed. So did Levi.

"It looks like running a cattle ranch is taking up enough of your time. I can't imagine Kate would appreciate you being gone even longer hours."

"Who said anything about me? Kate's just as good," he glanced at his wife, "if not better at training them than I am."

She beamed up at him. "Come on, Noah. They know they are welcome anytime. We need to let them go."

"Yes, ma'am," he said, stepping away from the wagon.

"Thank you again for letting us stay here," Levi said, opening his arms to his cousin. "Kate," he said with a smile, "keep this one in line."

"Will do."

Woo. Woo. The call of the train greeted Levi's perked ears with relief.

"The train," he said with more excitement than he'd intended. "I knew he'd send another quickly."

Levi closed his eyes. *We probably should have stayed put*, he thought. But Miss Walker had been too anxious and he couldn't very well have let her set out in a wagon on her own.

Instead of traveling alone with Miss Walker for another few days, he hoped that now, they'd be able to catch the train in Laramie.

Cadence pushed the curtain aside to peer out the window as the train pulled into the large roundhouse in the oddly bustling town of Bryan. She was pleased to see that this town had some semblance of civilization with multiple restaurants, hotels, and a telegraph office. Several buildings lined both sides of the main street including shops of various sorts and a concert hall.

It was comparable to Laramie, but she appreciated that this little town had some varying landscape with steep hills dotted with green as well as the buttes and mesas with their red and orange hues she'd grown accustomed to seeing on her trip though this territory.

Levi leaned over the seat and glanced out the same window. He smelled good and looked even better. Cadence liked being near him.

"It's a beautiful day," he said as he looked up at the sky full of billowy clouds. "Your father's place is just a couple of miles east of here." He pushed away from the seat and stood upright. "If we can get the wagon unloaded from the stock car and are able to purchase a few supplies, we'll make it there before nightfall."

Suddenly, Cadence felt a weight settle in her stomach. She pulled from her pocket the response telegram Annie had waiting for her at the Laramie telegraph office. *Another threat on railroad celebration. STOP. Find Det. Walker and get to Durant.*

Questions flooded her mind and she fought to calm them. First and foremost she had to know if her father was still alive. That thought alone made the idea of protecting Durant from an unseen assassin not seem quite so formidable. A Pinkerton always remained calm and in control. She could not let her nerves show.

"Are you ready?" Levi asked as the train came to a stop. He strung his satchel over his shoulder, threw her trunk onto his back, and picked up his suitcase.

Cadence shoved the note back into her pocket. She couldn't shake the butterflies that suddenly felt like they would escape her belly through her throat. She quickly gathered her other belongings and headed to the end of the passenger car. It was not like her to get nervous, but something about her father discovering her profession made her…anxious.

Feel it on the inside, but don't show it on the outside. She shook her head, smoothed her dress, and plastered a smile on her face as she made her way to the end of the car.

How Levi had been able to squeeze through the small doorway was surprising enough with his height and stature, but with the load he'd carried it was simply baffling. When she reached the spot where he'd disappeared, she looked down the stairs and onto the platform. He'd already set down the luggage and stood, hand extended, ready to help her down.

She slid her hand into his, reveling in the warmth and comfort his touch provided. It had been a long time since she'd been able to let down her guard, trust, and feel at ease with anyone—especially a man.

"Why, thank you, kind sir."

"Anything for you, ma'am." He held her eyes until her feet were firmly planted on the ground.

She wasn't sure if he was playing the part or if there was a hint of truth to those words, but, heaven help her, she hoped for the latter.

One of the crewmen placed the remainder of their luggage down next to the trunk and other bags that stood erect in a pile next to Levi.

"You joining us at end of track, Mr. Redbourne?" he asked Levi as he hopped back up onto the bottom metal step of the train. "We have just six days. Think we'll make it?"

"It's going to be a close one, but yes, I wouldn't miss it," Levi affirmed.

Six days?

Cadence swallowed. That didn't leave her much time to locate her father and get to Thomas Durant. She needed to send word back to Annie and let her know she had arrived in Bryan and would write again once she found Agent Eamon Walker.

"Welcome to Bryan," a portly man with a black vest and pocket watch greeted her as he passed.

She smiled and dipped her head in acknowledgement.

"Wait," she called to him. "Do you know Eamon Walker? He's a Pinkerton. Owns a ranch not far from here." She was hopeful that she'd be able to locate him quickly.

"Can't say as I do. I'm afraid I'm new to town myself and haven't had time to meet up with many folks yet."

"Oh, well, that's all right. I'm sure you'll enjoy your time here." Cadence looked out over the mixture of buildings and business tents that lined the main street through town.

"Miss Walker? Will you be all right to stay here while I go get the horses?" Levi asked, pulling her from her observations.

"Yes, of course."

He waited as if he didn't quite believe her.

Cadence knew what most men wanted in a woman. She'd been highly trained on how to be that woman, but something was different with Levi. She didn't need to play a part with him. She didn't have to be someone she wasn't, but for her, that's where the problem lay. She was always playing a part—with her mother, at work—there was never a time when she was just…Cadence Walker. She wasn't sure she even knew exactly who that was anymore.

"Well, we won't get out to my father's ranch without them."

Levi threw his head back and laughed. "There she is."

Cadence smiled begrudgingly.

Metal groaned as the side wall to the closest supply car was opened. Cadence took a step backward. Two men stood on either side, lowering the steel door carefully with a rope pulley system. By the time the buckboard had been unloaded, Levi returned with the horses and proceeded to hitch the team while Cadence lifted their belongings and tossed them into the back. She was relieved to see that the ropes Levi had used to secure her trunk had held together nicely.

"Surely some of the people of this town will know my father. He's been working on and building the homestead for over a year. I know he's gone a lot with the railroad, but..." she stopped herself mid-sentence. She was rambling.

"Why does it matter if they know him or not? I know where he lives. You'd know if he was on assignment, right? We'll be out to see him in about an hour or so."

Cadence bit her lip.

"Can we just go a little faster, please?"

"What's the rush? I understand you're anxious to see Eamon and all, but we'll be there soon enough. There's no need to push the horses."

He didn't feel the same urgency she felt because she'd never told him. Part of being a detective meant knowing when to divulge information and when to keep it safe. Levi needed to know the truth, but she wasn't sure she was ready to tell him.

"Out with it."

"Out with what?" She tried to appear unperturbed.

"You've been sitting on the edge of that seat stewing over something. So, out with it."

"Mr. Redbourne."

He looked at her with a raised brow.

"Levi," she corrected. She breathed deeply and exhaled.

He glanced over at her, his eyebrows lifted expectantly.

"My father...is missing."

"What do you mean, he's missing? How do you know?"

Cadence played with the cylinder rope across her chest. "I've known since I left Chicago."

"Whoa." Levi pulled the wagon to a stop and looked at her.

"We received word from a Pinkerton agent that he'd been compromised and injured. That was the last anyone had heard from him. When they selected me for this mission, it was because the missing agent was my father."

"So, what is this mission of yours exactly?" Levi asked, pointing to the tube across her back.

"It's sealed. I have no idea what's inside," she said honestly. She reached into her pocket. "But, I have to deliver this to Mr. Durant before the last spike is driven connecting the East to the West." She handed the cloth-wrapped package to Levi.

He pulled back the material to reveal the diamond tipped gold spike and turned it over to reveal an engraving. "A country united," Levi read. "President Abraham Lincoln." He looked up at her. "It's his signature. But how?"

"It is to be one of five, the last spike that will fulfill the dream of a united nation. Only a select trusted few even know of its existence."

Levi stroked the letters with reverence.

"Somehow, President Lincoln must have known that he wouldn't live to see his vision realized and had it forged on the day the Transcontinental Railroad commenced." Cadence looked down at her hands. "But, that's not all." She tucked a stray lock of hair behind her ear. "Threats from an unknown source have been made on Thomas Durant and anyone involved with seeing the completion through. We think there may be an attack at the ceremonial celebration that will prohibit the ability to drive the last spike and complete the line."

"I knew about the threats on the railroad, but why didn't you tell me any of this before?" Levi asked, quietly folding the cloth back over the spike and returning it to her.

"I'm telling you now."

Levi picked up the reins and gave them a good slap. "We'll I guess we'd better find your pa."

As they pulled onto the main street, a tall wooden gallows stood ominously looming over the town. Cadence shuddered. In her few short years as a Pinkerton, she had not been unfortunate enough to witness a hanging, thank the Lord. A strangely ill-omened feeling seemed to have settled over the people here. While the street was busy with folks bustling about and wagons being filled, it was oddly quiet, and Cadence wondered if some poor soul had already lost his life today. In her line of work, she knew it shouldn't bother her, but it did.

Clive's face, as he fell to the earth with a hole in his chest, invaded her memories and she closed her eyes willing it to go away. Bottom line was, she'd killed him. And no matter how much she'd tried to justify it in her mind, a man was still dead because of her. She'd managed to suppress the incident this long. She would just have to lose herself in her work for a few more weeks. She knew she'd have to face the consequences at some point, but there was no time for them now. She needed to get to her father.

"There's Eddie," Levi said, pulling the wagon to a halt.

"Who's Eddie?" She called after him as he jumped down in front of a man in a blue plaid shirt and scruffy beard.

"Your dad's foreman," he replied over his shoulder.

Cadence climbed down from the seat and rushed over to where the two men were already deep in conversation.

"Who put him there, Eddie?" Levi raised his voice—something that Cadence had yet to hear. He didn't wait for an answer. "I found your father," he said as he started across the street.

"I'll take care of your rig," the foreman called after him.

Cadence leapt down from the boardwalk and ran after Levi. "Where is he?"

Levi didn't stop. He marched up onto the wood planks in front of the sheriff's office and stormed inside.

"Where's Walker?" he demanded.

Cadence stepped into the doorframe to see a man scramble from behind a desk to get to his feet.

"Now, don't you come barging in here, Redbourne, like you know anything about what's been going on." The man, Cadence guessed a deputy, righted himself and stood up in front of Levi, barely reaching his shoulders. He took a step backward, but did not lose the firm, focused expression on his face.

"Levi?" A familiar, but weak and scratchy voice called from the corner of the office.

Cadence stepped farther into the room.

"Daddy?"

CHAPTER FOURTEEN

Levi lifted the scrawny deputy up by the collar of his shirt. "Explain, Merle," he said as calmly as he could. "Fast."

"He killed the sheriff, Levi. What was we supposed to do?"

Levi growled, but he let the little fella down.

Killed the sheriff?

"Daddy?" Cadence questioned as she rushed to the bars separating her and her father.

Eamon Walker was a Pinkerton. And a damn good one. Something was off here. Levi could feel it in his gut.

"What happened?" she asked, dropping down to the floor

"Did you ever consider there might have been a reason?" Levi asked.

"I know what I saw, and that man killed the sheriff."

"Levi!" Cadence's voice filled with alarm. "He's hurt."

Levi clenched his jaw.

Eamon clutched his side, his shirt stained with dark reds and browns.

Levi reached up and pulled the steel ring of keys from the hook on the wall.

"I can't let you do that." The deputy had drawn his gun

and pointed it directly at Levi who raised his hands into the air.

"I'm not going to break him out. He's bleeding. Or don't you care about doing what's right anymore?"

"Leave them be, Merle. This is between you," Eamon coughed, "and me. Neither Redbourne nor my daughter have anything to do with this."

"Why hasn't he seen a doctor?" Levi demanded, his hands still raised.

"Ain't one," the deputy responded matter-of-factly.

"How is there not a doctor in a town this size?"

"We had one up until last week. He got thrown from his horse and broke his neck. No more are moving in either. Since Black's Fork started drying up last winter, people have been relocating to Green River."

"Look at him," Levi motioned toward Eamon. "He needs help."

"We tried to help. Got the bullet out and everything, but how would I know what else to do for him? Besides, what's the point? He's just going to hang for what he done." Merle looked apprehensive and Levi wondered if it was the deputy talking or a certain rancher who hadn't been too keen on Eamon starting up his own spread.

"What happened, deputy?" Levi asked. "Why did Eamon kill the sheriff? Was anyone else there?"

The deputy didn't say anything.

"Come on, Merle. Eamon is your friend."

"He *was* my friend," Merle corrected. "Now, unless you want to join him in that cell, I suggest you hand those keys back on over to me."

Levi had an idea. "What happened?" he asked again, slowly moving his hand with the keys closer to the deputy as if returning them. "Last time I saw the two of you together you were laughing over the poor hired hand out at the ranch who'd stepped in a bucket and couldn't get his foot out."

Merle snorted a laugh. "That was something, wasn't it,

Walker?" He stopped mid-laugh, a serious expression returning to his face.

Drop the keys.

Before Levi could stop her, Cadence slipped between him and the deputy, his gun aimed at her chest. Levi wanted to strangle her. She'd thwarted his plan. Pinkerton or not, at the wrong end of the gun was no place for a lady.

'Merle, was it?" she asked, her voice as sweet and smooth as honey. "Surely, you wouldn't begrudge me a short visit with my father." She took a step toward the deputy and his gun.

Levi tensed. "Cadence," he called in quiet tones below his breath. It didn't appear that Merle was playing any games and the last thing they needed was for her to get herself killed.

"Cadie, honey, you need to get on out of here." Eamon dragged himself up off the mattress he'd been resting on with a grunt. He reached forward to grab ahold of one of the bars to steady himself.

Levi instinctively moved toward him, but there wasn't much he could do from outside the cell.

"I plan on it," she said, though her eyes did not waver from Merle's.

Levi glanced around the small room. He had to get Cadence out of there, out of harm's way. He would never be able to forgive himself if something happened to her. But he wasn't all that sure that she was the one needing protection. He knew she was armed and he was well aware she knew how to use her weapons.

He jingled the keys, then tossed them onto the ground in front of Eamon.

"Now, what did ya go and do that for?" Merle asked, leaning to one side far enough to see the keys. "Maybe you should step back, Miss Walker. I'd hate for you to get hurt."

Cadence shot him a look that could freeze hell.

"Merle," Eamon coughed again, "I'm warning you."

"A girl needs her pa, Merle, don't you think?" Cadence

tucked a stray piece of hair behind her ear and smiled up at the
deputy, pulling his attention back to her.

No wonder so many men fawned all over her. She was
remarkable.

"You wouldn't deny a girl the opportunity to say goodbye
to her father, would you, Merle?" Cadence reached up to his
shirt collar and rubbed it between her fingers.

"Of course not." Merle cleared his throat.

"Are you going to shoot me, deputy?" she asked, a hint of
a smile playing with her mouth.

Merle dropped the gun to his side and holstered it. "I
guess it'll be all right." He turned to Levi. "But just the girl. Do
I have your word, Redbourne?"

Levi nodded. He bent down to retrieve the keys and
quickly slid them into the lock.

"Thank you," she told Merle with a pat to his chest. She
rushed inside. "Daddy?"

Eamon turned his back to the bars and, as if his legs could
no longer keep him standing, he slid down to the floor.

"Daddy?" Cadence called, a tear streaking a path down her
cheek. She laid her head down against his chest just below the
shoulder.

Eamon kissed the top of her head.

Lying there, Cadence looked almost vulnerable.

"Now, let's take a look at that wound," she said, lifting her
head and mustering a smile.

Levi looked over at Merle who stood so close Levi could
overpower him without much effort. However, he needed to
think about how Raine or Rafe, his law keeping brothers,
would handle this situation. With Merle as the only law left in
this town, he had to make the man see reason. And in order to
do that, he had to find out what had happened.

Cadence pulled back her father's shirt. Angry red swells
surrounded a black gouge in the side of his abdomen where
Levi guessed he'd been shot. Another inch and the bullet

would have missed him completely, but left unattended it had become infected.

"Who did this?" Levi asked.

It took a moment for Merle to meet his eyes. He glanced up at Levi, looked down at a rock on the floor, and kicked it across the room before glancing back up. "The sheriff."

"Levi," Cadence spoke without looking up, "we've got to find a doctor. What about James?"

Levi shook his head. The train had already left.

She cradled Eamon's cheek with her hand then turned to meet his eyes. "He's burning up. Help me get him back onto the bed."

Levi looked at Merle, who nodded. He rushed into the cell and lifted Eamon's weak body.

"Wait." Cadence stepped out of the cell and grabbed a folded blanket from a shelf in the open closet next to the deputy's desk. She opened it, shook it out, and laid it across the filthy thin mattress.

Levi placed Eamon carefully on the bed. "It's good to see you, old man."

"Levi, did you bring my little Cadie here?" Eamon's voice was low and scratchy. He sounded so frail, unlike the man Levi had grown to know and love.

"I came with her, but she has a mind of her own."

Eamon laughed between coughs. "She's like her mother that way. Stubborn."

"I think she's more like her father than you know."

Eamon coughed again.

"You need to rest. Just hold on, my friend. We'll find help."

Merle stared at them all. He seemed conflicted. Levi didn't care what the man said, you didn't just stop caring about a friend because it was your duty—perceived or not. He couldn't shake the feeling that this whole mess boiled down to Adwell—greedy rabble-rouser.

"This isn't over," Levi said. He clipped the deputy on the

shoulder, threw open the door, and ran out into the dirt road.

Masses of people filled the street, bustling about tending to their business. The town had grown amply since he'd last been here. He stopped an older man with graying hair heading into the gunsmith shop.

"Excuse me, sir. I'm looking for a doctor. Do you know of anyone here who might be able to help?"

"'Fraid not, son. Is everything all right?"

"No," Levi said with a wave as he turned back onto the street, stopping a variety of people.

He knew he probably looked like he'd gone mad. His manners were lacking and he'd started to sweat, but he had to find someone who would know what to do. It seemed this town hadn't grown enough to include anyone in the medical profession. He stepped up onto the boardwalk in front of the mercantile, pulled off his hat, and ran a hand through his hair.

Then, he turned back to the advertisement in the store window.

PHYSICIAN NEEDED. See inside for details.

He marched into the store, pulled the paper down from the window, and slammed it onto the counter in front of Mrs. Turner, the shopkeeper.

"Has anyone inquired about this?" He stared at her, trying to keep the desperation from his voice.

"Had a fella in here just the other day," she said, prying the announcement from Levi's crumpled fingers. "But I gotta tell ya, Mr. Redbourne, he stank of spirits. Told him to get out and come back when he'd had time to sober up. Haven't seen him since."

"Do you remember his name?" At least it was something.

"Melvin maybe." She looked up to the corner of the building as if trying to recall. "Or Alvin."

"Do you know how I might find this Melvin-Alvin person?"

"I'd imagine any of the saloons in town." She shrugged.

"Come to think of it," she snapped her fingers, "you ought to check the Sagebrush. He said something about a Gloria and I think that that singer woman, Gloria Martin, is coming to perform on stage at the Sagebrush tonight." She rounded the corner of the counter and pulled another flyer from the window and handed it to Levi.

He didn't have time to wait until tonight. If this drunkard knew anything about medicine, he just might be Eamon's only chance.

"Thank you kindly, ma'am." He tipped his hat, his manners apparently returning, and headed out toward the Sagebrush. He hoped for Eamon's sake that Mrs. Turner was right about the saloon. There were more than a dozen of the watering holes in this place. It would take him too long to check all of them by himself.

When Levi stepped up in front of the Sagebrush, he stopped and took a deep breath. He was not a fan of these places. He'd seen too many men ruin their lives wasting their money and their time gambling away their farms, their horses, and losing their families to drink and unwholesome women. If Merle was right about the town drying up, he figured the saloons would probably be the last to go.

Levi stepped through the barroom doors, which swung back and forth behind him. His boot heels echoed across the worn pitted floor. The musty stench of liquor and smoke burned his nostrils. The place went quiet for a moment and a mass of heads turned in his direction. He scanned the room.

"I'm looking for Melvin," he said while he had their attention.

With that, everyone turned back to their own business. A man with a white shirt and bowtie sat down at a player piano and started with a lively tune. The sound of coins flipping across a table and drinks sliding down the bar brought back memories he'd sooner forget.

At least it hadn't been his own vices that had taken him

into places like this.

Maybe Melvin isn't the right name.

"How can I help you, darlin'?" A woman in a bright orange dress placed her hand on Levi's forearm. "Can I get you something to wet that beautiful mouth of yours?" She reached for a glass with a quarter full of amber liquid at the bottom and held it out to him.

"You know Alvin?"

"Sorry, sugar. Why ya lookin'?"

"I thought he might know something about doctoring."

The woman wagged a finger in front of him. "You must mean Elvin. He's always talking about how these spirits are good for disinfecting cuts and such. You'll find him over there." She pointed to a man slung across the bar wearing a particularly fancy, but disheveled suit with a deep burgundy shirt and a silver brocade vest, empty glass in hand.

"Thank you for your time, ma'am."

"Come back and visit anytime." She winked.

Levi walked up to the stranger and patted him with both hands on the shoulders.

"Come on, friend. It's time to go."

Elvin looked up at Levi, his eyes red and glassy. "Where we goin'?" he asked, his tongue and mouth moving in odd directions.

The man was younger than Levi had expected him to be. They were probably near the same age and he questioned whether or not the man had any qualifications. Still, he was the only person who'd even had a hint of experience. Levi placed the supposed doc's arm up over his own head and lifted.

"I think I'll stay and have another drink."

"Not today, I'm afraid. Someone needs you."

"Well, why didn't ya say so?" Elvin's head bobbed around as he tried to look at Levi. "You seem like a nice fella." His eyes squinted as if trying to focus. "You look awfully familiar. Do I know you?"

"Not yet."

"Hang in there, Daddy. Mr. Redbourne went to get help."

In all her life, Cadence had never seen her father look so...weak. Heat emanated from his body and every time he moved, he groaned in pain. Becoming a Pinkerton had been her way of helping people, but right now she felt helpless. She knew how to patch up a cut or two, but this was something completely different. For the first time in a long time she didn't know what to do.

"What in the..." The deputy flung open the door.

Splash.

Cadence stood up to see what commotion on the street had captured the officer's attention. Levi stood next to a barrel filled with water, holding and dunking the head of an unkempt man. Cadence pushed her way past the stunned deputy.

"Levi, what are you doing?" she asked, her hand hovering over her heart.

"This," Levi pulled the young man up by the hair, "is the only chance your father has."

She stared at him, then turned and glanced back into the small little jail cell where she could still see her father huddled on the bed. She jumped down onto the street next to them.

"How is *this* going to give my father a chance?"

"He's a doctor." Levi swung the drunkard around to face him. "There is a man in there who needs your help, Elvin," he said hunching down as if trying to get the man to look him in the eye.

He's...the doctor?

The man ran his shaky hands through his wet, dark hair. "I can't. Look at me."

"You have to. A man's life depends on it." Levi helped Elvin up onto the boardwalk and gave him a little push into the jailhouse. He turned to Cadence. "He'll need some supplies. I'll just be a minute."

Elvin took another wobbly step toward the cell and caught himself on the metal bars of the still open door. "I can do this," he said as if trying to convince himself. When he looked at his patient, the look on his face sobered quickly.

"Eamon? What have you gone and done to yourself?"

Eamon smiled weakly. "I seem to have gotten myself shot. The other one didn't make it out so good."

"Daddy, really." Cadence darted a look at the deputy who didn't seem to have heard the comment. She was just grateful that he was allowing this man, Elvin, to at least look at her father. She stepped closer, the pungent stench of spirits piercing the air.

Elvin turned to Cadence. "I'm going to need a bottle of liquor."

"Mr…Elvin. I hardly think that now is the time for spirits."

"Not for me. For him," Elvin responded with a gesture toward her father. "For the wound," he clarified. "We're going to have to reopen it."

"I'll get it," the deputy volunteered, much to Cadence's surprise.

"Thank you," she mouthed to him.

The three of them sat there in awkward silence until Cadence couldn't stand it anymore.

"So, Elvin, where did you study medicine?"

He sat up straight and attempted to straighten his askew cravat. "Harvard Medical School. Back East."

Cadence wasn't sure what she had thought he would say, but that was not it.

"I graduated top of my class."

He didn't seem much older than she.

"And when was that exactly."

Elvin pulled a gold-crested pocket watch from his vest and clicked it open. He closed one eye and looked up toward the ceiling. "I'd imagine it's been a couple a years now."

Nothing like a straight answer.

When Levi returned with a satchel over his shoulder and a crate of supplies in his arms, Cadence breathed a sigh of relief. He stepped through the doorway and she couldn't help but notice the chiseled cut of his arms. Levi set the crate down on the floor next to Elvin and pulled the strap of the satchel over his head and set it on the end of the mattress in the cell. When he opened it, he pulled out the bottle of the white substance he'd used on her cuts and handed it to the doc.

"Hey," Elvin said holding up Levi's poultice, "I've seen something like this before."

The deputy returned holding up a bottle little more than half full. "Will brandy do?" he asked. He stood behind Cadence and held it out.

Elvin took it and his hands started to shake. He stared at the bottle, then swiped the back of his hand across his mouth.

Cadence placed both of her hands over his and they stopped trembling. "You can do this." She looked at her father. "You have to do this." She pulled her knife from the strap on her leg and placed it in her palm extending it out to him.

Levi laid her father down flat on the bed, then stepped from the room to grab the deputy's wooden backed chair. He lifted it over their heads and turned it backward at her father's feet and straddled it.

The young doc took a deep breath and gently picked up the blade by the leather wrapped handle. With a strong exhalation he removed the top from the liquor bottle and poured a generous amount over Eamon's abdomen, then handed the drink up to his patient.

Her father declined with a slow shake of his head. "Never did care for the stuff."

He was getting weaker, his lids now barely able to stay open. Cadence took hold of his hand and squeezed.

"I love you, Daddy," she whispered, fighting to keep the

tears that threatened at bay.

"Hold tight, Walker. We'll have you feeling better in no time." Levi winked at Cadence and a calm reassurance washed over her.

"Thank you," she whispered.

Thank you.

CHAPTER FIFTEEN

Levi awoke to the sun penetrating the bright blue curtains adorning the windows of his room. It had been a long night, but sleep had eluded him for most of it. It had taken a while, but he'd finally been able to convince the deputy to allow him to bring Eamon over to the hotel to sleep in a real bed.

He glanced over to the older man, at last resting peacefully, then glanced at the man sleeping in the chair next to the bed. Despite Elvin's condition, it had appeared as if he'd done all he could.

Every muscle in Levi's body begged for more sleep, but he dragged himself from the warmth of the patchwork quilt he'd lain beneath and placed his bare feet flat on the cold floor. The nippy air raised the hairs on his arms. He rubbed his hands together and shook himself free of the chill.

After he'd pulled on his trousers and boots, he grabbed his shirt and vest from the end of the bed and strung his arms through the sleeves. Not wanting to wake the others, he carefully made his way across the room and opened the door. Cadence sat with her head leaning up against the frame, a soft snore buzzing against the otherwise quiet of the morning.

Levi dropped down onto his haunches. She looked so innocent, so beautiful, lying there with a peaceful expression on her face. He chuckled a little thinking about how the feisty woman would respond if he called her innocent or peaceful.

She was going to wake up with a crick in her neck if she stayed there. He reached underneath her legs and lifted her up into his arms.

Cadence stirred.

"Morning, sunshine," he said with a smile.

She turned and looked up at him, wiping the sleep from her eyes. "You can put me down, Redbourne."

Levi dropped his arm holding her feet and they fell to the ground. Her fingers touched the bare skin of his chest, leaving a tingling sensation in their wake, and he cursed himself for not having buttoned up his shirt before. Her palm flattened against him and instinctively he covered her hand with his. She looked up at him, her eyes filled with the catch lights from the morning rays.

Damn, she is beautiful.

"Cade, I..." He bent down to whisper in her ear, what could he say that wouldn't make him sound like a fool?

Without warning, Cadence raised up onto her toes, placed her hand against his cheek, and kissed him. When she pulled back, her thumb dawdled against his mouth and she smiled, biting her bottom lip.

"My father?" she asked quietly.

"Sleeping." Levi cleared his throat, fighting the urge to touch his mouth, surprised at the sensations that lingered there.

Cadence was quiet for a moment. She folded her lips together.

"Good. We've only got five days before we have to make it to Promontory Summit. I figure that gives us little more than twenty-four hours to find out what happened here and why the town wants to hang my father."

"Maybe we should get some breakfast before we start

pulling apart this already dying town for clues?"

"But—"

"Come on. I'll race you down the stairs." Levi dodged past her and started to run.

Cadence's giggle followed him all the way to the dining room where several other patrons already sat eating scrambled eggs, biscuits, and salty ham.

The incredible smells coming from the kitchen triggered Levi's mouth to water. He realized it had been nearly twenty-four hours since he or Cadence had had anything real to eat.

"You must be hungry," he said, guilt filling his empty belly.

"Famished," she replied. "It smells so good."

There was an empty table at the edge of the room just beneath the window.

"Come on." He motioned for her to follow him.

When they reached the window, he pulled out a chair for her, then joined her at the table.

"Where is he?" The front door to the dining area of the hotel swung open and two large men, dressed in heavy canvas slickers, burst into the room, guns drawn.

Guests scrambled to their feet and backed up against the far wall.

Cadence's hand shot to her hip where Levi guessed she had a gun hidden in the folds of her skirt. They exchanged a glance. She nodded. Her back was to them, but she had an instinct when it came to trouble.

Levi stood up from the table. "Can I help you gentlemen?"

They both turned their guns on him. "You Redbourne?" the man with the long scraggly hair asked, his eyes squinted as he moved toward them.

"Who's asking?"

"Merle said we'd be able to find you here. Said that you convinced him to let that scalawag Walker out of his cell." The man took another step toward them.

Cadence carefully pulled the gun from her dress and

placed it on the table, her fingers still around the grip and on the trigger.

Levi moved to the side of the table, his hip at her shoulder. "I did. The man was dying. It seemed the right thing to do."

The man holstered his gun and stepped forward with his hand extended.

"Name's Deputy U.S. Marshal Keaton Stevens. I'm a friend of your brother's."

Levi shook the man's hand. "I thought for a minute there that we were going to have an issue." He noted out of the corner of his eye how Cadence quickly returned her weapon to its hiding place before anyone saw.

The patrons in the dining room all started moving back to their tables, muttering amongst themselves.

"My friend Jake and I came as soon as we got word that the people of this town were planning on hanging a Pinkerton."

"Are you here to stop it?" Cadence ground back her seat against the floor and stood up next to Levi to face the Marshals.

Both men removed their hats.

"We're here to see that he gets a fair trial," Marshal Stevens said. "You know him?"

Cadence looked up at Levi and then back at him. "He's my father."

"Ah." The Marshal looked down at the hat he twisted in his hands. "Well, I figure we should go check in on the patient. What room?" he asked Levi.

"Which brother?" Levi asked. "You said you're a friend of my brother's. Which brother?"

Stevens laughed loudly. "You're just like him. Always suspicious. Rafe. I know Rafe Redbourne. When the deputy across the way told us that the prisoner had been taken from his cell to sleep in a cozy bed by a big fella named Redbourne, I knew it couldn't be a coincidence. It appears respect and...unconventional run in the family."

Levi smiled. "You *do* know my brother."

Stevens and Jake both chuckled.

Thank you, Lord.

"Now, I don't know what y'all are doin' around here, but your scarin' my guests," a thin little dark-haired woman with streaks of gray bustled in between the men. "Either sit yourselves down and eat something or turn around and get out of my hotel."

Levi had to admit, the woman had guts.

"Excuse us, ma'am. We're just here to call on one of your...guests and we'll be on our way."

With the Marshals in town, Levi saw the light to an otherwise dreary situation. He doubted that Eamon would be awake enough to talk to them right now, but at least he would have a fair chance. Levi nodded toward the stairs where he and Cadence had raced.

"Second door on the left."

Cadence moved to go with them, but Levi stopped her with a hand in the crook of her arm. "You need to trust them."

"Trust them? How do I trust men I just met?" Her chin lifted defiantly.

"You trusted me."

Cadence opened her mouth to respond, but somehow it appeared as if the words had left her because she shut it again. She jerked her arm from his grasp and marched out the door the lawmen had come in through.

Guess we're not eating. He dropped his shoulders, closed his eyes briefly, and shook his head with a slight movement. *Where could she possibly be going?*

Levi threw some coins down on the table and started after her. When he reached the street, a splash of purple disappeared into the mercantile. He dodged around a few people and slipped into the store behind a display of fresh goods.

"I'd like to purchase a hammer," Cadence told the clerk

on the other side of the counter.

The man nodded, placing a stub of a pencil behind his ear. He turned around and pulled the tool from a bin attached to the wall.

"Do you have anything a little bigger?" she asked when he placed the instrument down on the bar in front of her.

What was she doing?

"I have a sledge. But you, little lady, would have a hard time lifting the thing."

"I'll take it." She placed a bill on the counter.

Levi stepped out from behind the display of wooden crates and joined her.

"A sledge?" he asked with a quiet voice, working to keep a chuckle at bay.

"Somebody's got to tear that thing down," she turned to look at the gallows haunting the street, "before someone gets hurt."

Levi wouldn't put it past her. He could only imagine the reaction she'd get at the first blow and determined she would not be purchasing a sledge today.

The clerk returned with the heavy hammer and set it onto the counter with a thud.

"The lady's changed her mind," Levi said, guiding Cadence away from the weapon.

"No I haven't," she called back over her shoulder. She stopped moving and attempted to twist away from him.

The last thing Levi needed was for her to get the townsfolk, who were already determined to hang her father, all riled up.

"Levi," she said, her jaw tight in her resolve, "I'm warning you."

Her judgment had obviously been clouded with emotion.

Levi reached down and scooped her up and over his shoulder. He tipped his hat at the clerk, whose shoulders raised lightly with a chuckle before pulling his pencil from his ear and returning to the paper he'd been studying when they'd walked in.

"Levi Redbourne! You let me down this instant!"

As they neared the stables, the liveryman dumped a fresh bucket of water into the horse's water trough.

"Don't you dare," Cadence cautioned, the slight quiver in her voice masked with firm resolve.

Levi fought the urge to a repeat performance. He pulled her from his shoulder and set her down next to the drinking trench.

Cadence punched him in the shoulder.

Ow.

"Cadence," he lifted her chin to look at him, "do you really think tearing down those blasted gallows will stop a determined lot from seeing a hanging?" He threw a hand through his hair. "You're not going to do your father any favors if the town sees you as a mad woman on a mission."

She looked away, smoothing her skirt.

"You're right," she said with a huff. "But that doesn't mean I have to like it. I need to start thinking like a Pinkerton and not like his emotionally distraught daughter."

You said it, Levi thought with a smirk. He raised a brow.

"There's not much time." Cadence started walking back toward the hotel. "I still have a job to do. Let's get my father taken care of and then I have to get to end of track. There's more at stake than we can afford." She pulled open the door and disappeared inside.

"She's quite the spitfire, isn't she?"

Levi spun around to see his brother, Rafe, leaning against the fenced corral, his booted feet crossed at the ankles and his arms crossed over his chest.

"Rafe?" Levi said incredulously.

His brother's broad grin widened as he pushed himself away from the railing and made up the two steps between them. They gripped each other in a firm embrace, then stepped apart.

"What are you doing here? How did you know where to find me?"

"Honestly, I had no idea you were here. I thought you were headed out to end of track. I've been following a couple of thugs for a few days now and they led me here."

Alarm bells went off in Levi's head.

"Thugs?"

"There's a five hundred dollar bounty on the one impersonating a friend of mine, a Marshal. And another hundred on his quiet friend."

Levi shot a glance at the restaurant door. *Cadence.* Levi spun around and darted for the hotel door.

"What is it, Levi?" Rafe called after him.

"Upstairs," he said over his shoulder in a gruff whisper. He feared speaking any louder for fear of backing the men into doing something drastic.

Rafe was only one step behind him as they sprinted through the dining area and up the staircase. When they reached the top of the stairs, Rafe's gun was drawn. Levi reached beneath his vest to the holstered pistol he kept at his side and pulled it free. He stepped onto the other side of the door to the room where Cadence had slept and stretched for the handle. He twisted it open, but the room was empty. Levi pointed at his room, where Eamon and the doc had slept. The door was shut and a few muffled voices carried through the hall.

Rafe nodded and led the way down toward the room. Levi leaned up against the wall outside the door. He'd told Cadence to trust them and now she was in danger. When he got that pretend Marshal in his hands, he'd take an ounce of trust out of his hide.

"You hell-cat!" The muffled voice coming from the room bit out the words with striking clarity.

That's it!

Levi didn't wait for Rafe's signal. He threw the door open and barged inside, gun pointed. To his surprise, Eamon was sitting up on the bed holding his side while the two brutes Rafe had apparently been chasing sat back to back on the floor, their hands tied with something that looked like the green ties from the flowered curtains. Elvin was standing behind the chair, his eyes and nose still a little red.

"Took you long enough," Cadence said, standing up straight and tucking her revolver back into the folds of her skirt. She rushed to the side of the bed and placed her hand on her father's cheek.

"Are you all right, Daddy?"

Eamon put his hand over his daughters and nodded.

Levi returned his pistol to his holster. Relief flooded him at seeing she was safe. That Eamon was safe.

Rafe also slid his guns to their holsters. He dropped down onto his haunches in front of the new prisoners. "Didn't your mama ever teach you not to mess with a beautiful woman?"

Levi glanced down at his brother who was now staring up at Cadence. He'd seen that look in Rafe's eyes before.

Rafe stood up and moved toward the Walkers.

"Oh, no. I don't think so," Levi said, grabbing his brother by the arm and pulling him backward. "Cadence," he said from a safe distance, "this is my brother, Rafe."

"Ah, the doctor turned bounty hunter?"

Levi smiled. He hadn't realized he'd talked so much about his family with her. She'd listened. And remembered. Impressive.

"Why, yes, ma'am," Rafe said in that sultry voice that had always made women swoon. "And you are?"

"Cade Walker."

"Well, Miss Walker, it is a pleasure to meet you. And might I say that this," he pointed to the men on the floor, but didn't take his eyes off Cadence, "is very…impressive." He stepped around Levi and held out his hand to her. She slid her hand into his.

"The pleasure is all mine," Cadence said with a smile that widened the pit in Levi's stomach. He needed to stop introducing her to all of his brothers.

"Now don't be getting too cozy with my daughter there, Redbourne." Eamon eased himself to the edge of the bed and swung his legs over the side.

Rafe laughed, dropping Cadence's hand. "Good to see you too, old man."

"Cadie," Eamon said, turning his attention to his daughter.

Cadence glanced at Levi then back at Eamon. As much as she fought it, Levi could see that she was pleased at her father's use of the familiar name. She moved to sit next to him on the bed.

"Do you want to explain to me what just happened, little girl?" He said, wrapping his arm around her shoulder and giving a light squeeze.

"Ah, Daddy, I'm not such a little girl anymore."

Too true, Levi thought, heat suddenly creeping up his neck.

Cadence sounded so sweet and innocent, not unlike Hannah, his own little sister, when she was talking to their mother.

"So," he said, coughing a little, "how long have you been working with the agency?"

Cadence's mouth fell open. She seemed at a loss for words—which was odd for her. "How…how did you know?"

Eamon leaned over with a groan, holding his side, and placed a kiss on his daughter's forehead. "Honey, it didn't take a detective to see that you know your way around a gun. Not just any woman could have gotten the upper hand on two armed men with only an injured man and a drunk for support. You've got reflexes like…" he winced in pain, "your pa."

"Stop right there," Rafe pulled his gun, pointed at the so-called Marshal Stevens, and cocked the hammer. The man's hand had gotten loose from the bindings and he was working to remove the rest.

"Nice improvising," Rafe told Cadence, nodding his head in approval. He removed cuffs from his belt and clicked them in place. It was hard to miss the scowl on the imposter's face, but the man tried to conceal it with a forced smile.

"Come on, Redbourne. You've had your laugh, now let us go."

"Let you go?" Cadence jumped up off the bed and crouched down to face the man. "Let you go?"

"Cadie," Eamon reached for her.

"It's all right, Daddy." She brushed her hand in a broad stroke across the air. "If I hadn't come up to the room when I had…" she glanced away and stood up straight without finishing her thought. "We need to get them over to the jailhouse."

"We'll just stand you up." Rafe grabbed a hold of the fake Marshal's shoulders and lifted both men awkwardly from the ground.

The first man stumbled enough to allow his friend to pull something from the back of his boot. A glint of metal in the beams of light coming in from the window caught Levi's attention.

"Knife!" he yelled as he shot forward, shoving Cadence out of harm's way.

Hot, searing pain stung Levi's shoulder. The blade had sliced across his arm. He and Cadence landed on the ground with a thud. He raised himself up enough to look at her briefly. "Sorry," he said quickly before he pushed himself away from her and off the floor. He spun around.

The second man, the quiet one, had somehow gotten loose from his bindings and held the knife, blood casing the blade, his stance crouched and ready for a fight. He lunged toward Rafe, but his brother was too fast for him, and with a simple move all Redbournes had all learned as children, he had the man's arm twisted up behind him. With a little coaxing, the knife fell to the ground and Rafe kicked it away.

In the ruckus, the pretend lawman lowered his head and shoulders, his hands still bound behind him, and started toward Rafe, who'd yet to draw his gun. Levi took a single step forward and landed a well-timed punch to the side of the man's head sending him sprawling into the dresser in front of the window.

"I'll take these boys down and get them locked up." Rafe had finished securing new bindings on the quiet one and held them while reaching down to pull the other to his feet. "I'm guessing there is a sheriff somewhere around here."

"Just ask for Merle. He's the deputy." Eamon moved to stand up, but staggered backward onto the bed. "Damn bullet."

"Detective Walker?" Elvin said quietly, nearly hidden behind the curtains. Levi had almost forgotten the doc was even there.

"Yes?" both Cadence and Eamon responded together. They shared a chuckle.

"Eamon," the doc clarified. "I don't think you are in any condition to get up just yet."

Eamon leaned back against the wall and Cadence lifted his feet up onto the bed.

"You still need to rest, Daddy."

"We need to talk, Cadie girl."

"We will." She smiled at her father and placed a kiss against his forehead.

"All right, no more fiddling around," Rafe said, yanking good and tight on the culprits' bindings. "Don't make me shoot you."

"I'd listen to him if I were you." Elvin stepped out from behind the chair.

"Vinnie?" Rafe obviously recognized the doc. He turned to Levi. "Watch them."

Levi pulled his gun and leaned back against the wall.

"Vinnie Harper!" Rafe extended his arm and gripped

Elvin at the forearm.

"How are you, Redbourne?"

Rafe clapped the doc on the shoulder. "It *is* you. I never expected to find Mr. Valedictorian in a little town this far out West. I thought you were taking up residency at the hospital in Boston. How are Shelly and baby George?"

Elvin's face turned solemn and he began to wring his hands. "Cholera." He dropped his head. "Took them both."

That explains a lot, Levi thought.

"Vinnie, I'm so sorry," Rafe said. "Come on. I'll buy you some supper and we can catch up. I just need to get these fellas down to the jailhouse." He pulled out his gun and motioned to the door. "Let's go," he said to the bound men.

A slip of paper fell down onto the floor and Rafe bent down to retrieve it. "What's this?" He looked at it, then handed the telegram to Levi.

Pink in Bryan STOP Stop him before completion STOP

"Before completion of what?" Rafe asked.

Levi looked at Cadence. "The railroad." He passed the message to her.

"We have to get to end of track," she said after reading the brief missive. She stood up and walked over to the men Rafe had escorted to the door. "What's going to happen at completion?"

"Shoulda known you was a Pink. Heard them lady detectives'll do anything for information." He licked his lips. "What ya going to do for me, wench?"

Levi started forward, but Rafe raised his arm and held him back.

Cadence took a step closer until she was mere inches from the man. Levi's jaw flexed as she placed a hand on the brute's overcoat and smiled. She gripped a hold of his collar and pulled him down gently, her lips moving slowly toward his ear.

Levi couldn't bring himself to just sit back and watch someone else on the receiving end of her kiss.

With no warning, Cadence raised her knee hard and slammed it into the man's groin. He doubled over in agony.

"You b—"

Levi pushed past Rafe and cold-cocked the thug before he could get the vulgar word from his lips. "That's no way to talk to a lady."

The dolt dropped to the ground with a groan, but no further utterance escaped his mouth.

Levi stepped toward Cadence. He lifted his uninjured arm toward her. She slipped her shoulder beneath his and snuggled into him.

"Why, I do believe you saved my life and defended my honor. A true gentleman of gentlemen," she said, looking up at him with wide, smiling eyes. Then, her expression turned serious and she turned to face him. "Thank you."

CHAPTER SIXTEEN

Rafe pulled the needle and thread through the skin just below Levi's shoulder as he stitched up the wound. "She's sweet on you, you know."

Cadence stepped into the room at the abandoned doctor's office with a fresh bucket of water and some clean rags. "He speaks the truth," she said with a grin as she approached the table where Rafe was working on Levi's cut arm. "She *is* sweet on you."

Levi sat up straight, earning him a smack on the back of the head from his brother.

"The only pretty face you should be looking at right now is mine."

Cadence couldn't help but snicker. "Do all of you Redbournes have such pretty faces to look at?" She set the water down, but made the mistake of glancing at Levi. His bared chest looked as if it had been carved from warm-colored stone. She forced her gaze upward, fearing she'd already crossed the line of propriety—something she hadn't concerned herself with in a long time. That scared her a little.

Levi smiled at her. A light seemed to fill her insides and

she felt the corners of her mouth turn upward. She couldn't help herself. Just being near Levi made her feel safe. Protected. Loved.

"Ma'am," Rafe said in greeting with a nod and a mischievous smirk as he continued his work.

Cadence recognized the same white poultice that Levi had used on the wounds on her face and leg. Rafe slathered it over his brother's stitches and tied a bandage around his arm.

"How are you holding up?" Levi's question was simple enough, but she wasn't sure how to answer. The last few weeks had taken a lot out of her and tonight she'd almost lost her father. She refused to let him see her weakness, but chose instead to channel her fears, her guilt, into being strong.

"Good. I'm just trying to figure out how to be in two places at once."

She didn't want to leave her father until she knew he would be safe, but she still had a job to do and time was running out. Eamon was in no condition to travel, but she couldn't leave him here unprotected.

"Levi told me that you have an assignment to complete before the Transcontinental is completed." Rafe washed his instruments over the sink with the water she'd hauled in and wiped them down with a fresh towel.

Levi slid down off the table.

Cadence swallowed. Hard.

He picked up his shirt and examined the cut sleeve. "Waste of a perfectly good shirt."

They all laughed.

"I have to get to end of track, but how can I leave my father here with the whole town wanting to see him hanged?"

"They are not going to hang Eamon. You have my word," Levi said, meeting her eyes with square certainty. "Besides, I think once we pay a visit to a certain rancher named Adwell, your father's problems with the law will go away."

Cadence believed him. From her experience, Levi

Redbourne was a man of his word.

"I've already sent word to the Marshals," Rafe said, "I suspect Keat is already on his way. The real Keaton Stevens." He placed his tools in a squat black bag. "I'll stay."

There was something about these Redbournes that made her trust them. Before she could stop herself, she sprang into Rafe's unsuspecting arms. "Thank you."

"Hmhmmm." Levi cleared his throat.

Cadence looked up at him sheepishly. His expression was almost sour and his jaw flexed. Was he jealous? She glanced up at Rafe and quickly took a few steps back. "Excuse me."

"I don't mind," Rafe said with a laugh. "But, by the looks of him," he pointed to Levi, "he might."

"Jealous?" Levi snorted. "Of a scalawag like you? He wadded up his shirt, stuffed it into a large brown satchel, and retrieved a fresh folded shirt from the end of the table. "Not likely." He shoved his arms through the sleeves and pulled his vest from the back of the chair.

Cadence held her breath.

Levi winked.

She exhaled.

He reached down and took her hand into his. "Come on. We need to go talk to Eamon. Maybe he'll have some idea why those brutes were sent to kill him."

As Levi led them out the door and into the street, Cadence bit her lip. She liked the feel of her hand in his. Maybe too much. She had to force herself to stop thinking about Levi. It wasn't like her to lose focus.

When they got back to the hotel, her father was sleeping. Cadence hated to wake him, but they would be leaving on the next train and didn't have much time. They needed answers. *She* needed answers.

Cadence walked into the room. Elvin sat on the chair next to the bed, his hands fisted and curled against his bowed head. He hadn't left her father's side. She stepped forward and placed a hand on the doc's shoulder. "Can I talk to him?"

Elvin looked up at her, the redness all but gone from his eyes. He quickly stood up and allowed her his seat. She smiled at him and sat down.

"Daddy?" She reached over to him and slid her fingers into his closed hand. "Daddy?" she raised her voice a little louder.

"What is it, Cadie girl?" he asked without opening his eyes. He still looked so tired. Weak.

Cadence had always seen her father as bigger than life and full of spirit. Seeing him like this reminded her that life was short. "I...I..."

"This better not be about one of those Redbourne fellas," he said, a playful grin cracking his otherwise stoic expression. "I haven't got the energy right now to warn them about how to treat my daughter."

Cadence glanced back at Levi who looked like he was biting back a smile of his own. He winked at her and walked into the hallway.

"Do you love him?" her father asked point blank, his voice scratchy and low from nonuse.

Cadence wasn't sure how to respond. "Daddy, I have to tell you something and then I need to ask you about your mission."

Eamon turned his head and opened one eye to look at her. "Answer my question first. Do you love Levi?"

She glanced back at the doorway again. Levi, Elvin, and Rafe were all gone.

She closed her eyes and squeezed her father's hand.

Am I in love with Levi Redbourne?

Her heart swelled at the thought of him, of her hand in his, and her lips tingled with the remembrance of his kiss.

"Yes, Daddy," Cadence said quietly, "Lord help me, but I believe I do." She sat up a little taller. "I love him," she said with incredulous conviction. "I love him."

"Good." He pushed himself up from the bed. "Now, what is it you need to tell me?"

She couldn't look at him, couldn't meet his eyes.

"What is it, Cadie?"

"Mama's dead."

"What? When? What happened?"

Cadence leaned down and laid her head against her father's chest. "She got sick. It didn't take long."

Silence.

"I'm so sorry, Cadie. That I haven't been there for you." She could hear the sadness in his voice. "How's your brother?"

"He moved to Maine and got a job with a shipping company. He's doing well." She sat up, forcing a smile.

Eamon nodded. "About this assignment of ours. I'm guessing Allan sent you here to help me stop the attack on the completion ceremony." With a deep groan he eased to the edge of the bed. Avoidance was a tactic to stop from feeling the sadness overtake you. She'd used it hundreds of times over the last couple of years.

"Daddy, I can do this. I just need your help."

"And that is exactly what you are going to get."

"I just need information. It's too soon for you to be up. The doc says you need a few weeks rest."

"Nonsense."

"Dad."

"Fine, but I don't want you to go alone." He pointed at the door with his chin.

"It's my assignment, not Levi's." She held up her hand when her father motioned to protest. "But," she said with only the slightest trepidation, "Levi is already planning on being there, so he'll be with me all the way to the end."

Eamon smiled.

"Don't look so smug," she teased, leaning into him.

An exaggerated groan escaped him.

"Oh. Sorry."

He laughed, evoking a real groan.

"Serves you right," Cadence said with a laugh of her own.

"Now, listen, honey. These folks aren't fooling around. They are downright mean and will do anything they have to in order to see their goal accomplished."

"And just what is their goal?"

"To stop that railroad from being completed."

"But it'll be finished within the week. How can they possibly stop it?"

"I don't know all the details, but they have spies everywhere. I overheard the sheriff talking to a man who showed up in town a few weeks ago. He was staying at the Adwell ranch."

"The sheriff was a part of it?"

Her father nodded.

"He was part of a southern sympathizer organization that doesn't want the country to be united under one government." He stopped speaking and turned to look at her. "My little girl." He shook his head. "A lady detective. I still can't believe you went and followed your old man. And now you're headed directly into harm's way." He winced and didn't speak for a moment. "I can't help but think this is about Daniel."

It had been a while since Cadence had thought about Daniel and a twinge of guilt settled in her gut. She looked away from her father. She didn't want to admit that she'd joined the Pinkertons to learn how to distance herself from ever feeling as helpless as she had the night they'd told her that her betrothed had been killed. She'd also joined to bring justice to the man who'd killed him. She'd used everything in her power to find out what had happened to him, but by the time she'd learned what to do, the trail had gone cold.

She didn't say anything. Couldn't.

"Yeah, well, what's done is done, I suppose. If you're who Pinkerton sent, he must have a lot of faith in you."

Cadence pursed her lips.

"Don't suppose there's enough time to get Annie out here instead?"

"Dad." Cadence whispered as she shook her head. She hadn't been aware that her father knew Annie. She'd never even thought to ask if there might be a connection.

"I know I should have been home more." Her father's eyes moved to the floor, a distant expression crossing his features. "But I'm here now."

"I know you are. I have to go." Cadence cleared her throat. "Rafe is going to stay with you here in Bryan until the real Marshal arrives. He'll make sure no one strings you up in front of this town."

"Those Redbournes are quite strapping young men, don't you think?"

She inhaled deeply, willing patience to find her. "I've come to collect your information. So, enough of this runaround. Tell me what I need to know."

Hahaha.

Her father's deep, rich laughter, almost made her forget her sudden irritation with him.

"Ouch." He pulled his legs back up onto the bed and leaned against the outside wall. "All right. All right. I can tell you some of what I found, but you'll need to head out to the homestead for the rest."

Cadence scrunched her brows and squinted her eyes. "What do you mean?"

"I have a list of names. The sheriff found out that I had it and—"

"And that's why he tried to kill you. He was on that list."

Eamon nodded. "Very perceptive. There's also a journal, which I suspect is a cipher, and some sort of medal that I took off one of their operatives. These are dangerous folks, sweetheart."

"We're headed for Promontory Summit in the morning." Cadence stood up and walked to the window. She had to think for a moment. "We'll have to head out to the ranch tonight," she said more to herself than to her father. "Where did you put them?"

"In a hidden drawer. Under the desk in my study."

Cadence nodded. She turned back to her father. "Thank you," she said as she leaned down to give him an awkward sort of hug. When she started to pull away, Eamon tightened his grip on her arm.

"They killed Lincoln, Cadie."

She looked at him, concern engraved into his face. "They can't kill his dream." Cadence leaned over and kissed her father on the cheek. "I'll be careful." She walked over to the door, pulled it open, and twisted back around to look at him. "By the way, do you have any idea what might be inside of the sealed tube I'm supposed to deliver?"

"*You* have the cylinder?"

"Yes. Why? What's in it?"

"Lord, help us all."

A single light flickered in the window of the small homestead as Levi and Cadence pulled through the gate at the Walker Ranch.

Strange. With Eamon being in jail, there shouldn't be anyone inside the house. The bunkhouse was dark, but the soft nicker of horses and lowing of cattle were the only indications that the place had not been abandoned completely. Levi suspected the place had been deserted by the hired hands when their benefactor had been incapacitated by a crooked sheriff's bullet.

"Shhh," he said quietly, placing a finger to his lips. "Stay here." The sun had only just disappeared behind the horizon and the waxing moon provided scarce light. Levi placed a hand over the gun strapped to his side and gingerly made his way toward the house.

The sound of furniture scraping against the floor and cupboards being opened and closed indicated, to Levi's disbelief, that the intruder had not heard the wagon approaching.

"This is Cade Walker!" Cadence bellowed. "Be warned, I'm coming in." She held up the lantern from the wagon and drew her gun before opening the front door.

Levi shook his head. He should have known she wouldn't stay put in the buckboard. She was a detective, for heaven's sake. Of course she would be curious. He followed her inside, his gun also drawn.

"What are you doing in my father's place?" Cadence held up a lantern, her revolver pointed at the prowler.

Eddie, the foreman, stood with both hands in the air and a mess of bread and dried meat spilling from his mouth. He spit it out.

"I...I just finished feeding the livestock and...thought I'd come in and get myself a bite to eat." He took a step forward, but Cadence raised the gun with renewed focus. "I'm sorry I came in the house, Miss Walker. It's just that with all the boys taking on new positions at other ranches, I'm really the only one left to make sure your father has something to come home to."

That must have struck a chord with Cadence, because she dropped the gun to her side.

"Thank you," she said with a nod.

"Was there something I could do for you, Miss Walker? Mr. Redbourne?"

"If you could just direct me to my father's study."

Levi had been to the Walker property on several occasions over the last few months, but each time he visited something else had changed. A bunkhouse had been built. The stable housed more horses, and fences extended out across the property. In this light, however, he had no idea what else had changed since he'd last been here.

Eddie picked up his own lantern and guided them down the hall. He pointed to a room with a set of double doors just around the corner from the kitchen. "Guess I'll be on my way," he said as Cadence stepped inside the dark room with the light and walked straight over to Eamon's desk.

"Eddie?" Levi asked as the man passed by him on his way to the front door.

The man halted, held up his light, and turned to look at him.

"You staying in the bunkhouse all alone?"

"Yes, sir. I figure someone's got to feed the animals."

"How long's it been since you've been paid?"

Eddie looked down at the ground, then raised a hand and rubbed it across his chin.

"I reckon it's been a while." He looked at the floor, at the doorframe, and finally out the door.

Levi sensed there was something the foreman wasn't telling him. "Is everything all right?" he asked, taking a step toward him.

The man took a step out the door. "Why wouldn't it be?"

An odd feeling wrenched Levi's gut and he paused. A knocking sound came from Eamon's office and Levi turned toward it. He needed to get in there and help Cadence, but he felt bad for the man who'd stayed on to help Eamon on his own. He reached into his pocket and pulled out the small bundle of bills he carried. He wanted to help tide the foreman over, but when he turned back, Eddie was gone.

I'll drop it by the bunkhouse on the way out, he thought, tucking the cash back into his vest pocket.

Levi walked into the study. The faint scent of kerosene intruded on his senses and he glanced about the darkened room. He couldn't tell if the smell was coming from the lamps or somewhere else. Something was amiss, but he couldn't place it.

A light glowed from the underside of Eamon's desk, where he guessed Cadence had disappeared. The sight that greeted him as he approached evoked a chuckle that caught in his throat. Cadence lay on the floor, her head hidden by the cumbersome desk and her ankles and feet sticking out from the deflated folds of material of her skirt. Levi wondered if lying down with such bulk had been as difficult as it looked. He bent down to see what she was doing.

"It's here," she called excitedly. She moved her fingers across the flush boards, then pounded in one spot against the edge with the side of her fist. A good sized drawer popped open and Cadence quickly reached inside.

The smell was stronger here.

"Cadence," he said firmly.

"You smell it too," she said unperturbed.

"Yes."

"I'm almost done." She pulled something from the hidden compartment, but Levi could not make out the contents. When Cadence started to scooch out from below the desk, Levi stood up and extended his hand. It took a moment before she was clear enough to take it, but once she was out, she grabbed a hold and he pulled her up.

"Thank you," she whispered, looking up at him. She touched his chest momentarily before turning to reach down for the lantern. She placed it on the desktop and held out the leather-wrapped bundle she'd collected from the drawer for Levi to see. The clasp on the binding appeared to be some sort of medal, but in this light it was impossible to distinguish its markings.

"I'll take that, if you don't mind, Miss Walker."

Levi and Cadence both turned to see Eddie, aiming a pistol at them, his hand extended toward her.

"Oh, but I do mind, Eddie," Cadence said without missing a beat. Without any warning, she threw the package into the air.

Eddie followed it with his eyes and while his head was raised, Levi landed an uppercut to the man's jaw, sending him sprawling backward. His gun flew from his hand and slid across the new wooden floor toward the two large bookcases on the far end of the room.

Cadence caught the leather bundle and stomped down at precisely the right moment. Eddie's pistol halted to a stop beneath her foot.

Levi pulled the foreman to his feet. "Are we going to find your name in that book, Eddie?"

The man tried to shrug away from Levi's grasp, but Levi tightened his fist and even though he was merely a few inches taller, he lifted Eddie off the floor.

"Let go of me, Redbourne. I'm warning you."

"Or you'll what?" Levi didn't care much for traitors, especially up so close.

Cadence bent down and picked up the gun from beneath her feet. She opened the chamber and turned it upside down. It was empty. She moved behind the desk and set the wrapped bundle down in front of the lantern.

"See," Eddie exclaimed. "I didn't really want to hurt you, but if I don't deliver that book by morning…" he dropped his head. "Please. They have my wife."

"Who are *they*?" Levi asked, relaxing his hold on the man—though, he didn't remember Eddie having a family.

"I don't know exactly. I swear." Eddie said, looking directly at Cadence. "I just need the book."

"Who are you supposed to deliver it to?" Cadence asked, leaning against the desk and placing her hand over the top of it.

Levi could see the wheels turning in her head.

Eddie lunged for the package, knocking the lantern off the table and onto the floor. Cadence jumped back as the floor and desk caught on fire, spreading more quickly than usual, trapping her on the far end of the study. The kerosene. The corner of the leather book binding had flames licking at the rawhide. Cadence fell to her knees and seized it from the blaze.

Eddie turned and ran for the door.

"You all right?" Levi asked even as he turned to follow.

"Go after him," Cadence cried above the blaze, which was now nearly as high as her waist and blocking the only window in the room.

"No."

"He might have the answers we need," she tried to persuade him.

"I don't care," he shouted as he paced the new wall of flames, looking for a way to get her out.

Think, Redbourne. Think.

"I'll be right back." He darted from the study and into Eamon's bedroom. He ripped the sheets and several blankets from the bed and ran outside to the water pump with the over-sized load.

"Thought you might could use a little help." Rafe stepped forward, holding a handcuffed Eddie at his side. "Eamon's sleeping. Vinnie won't leave his side. And the deputy is keeping watch outside his door." He paused. "What is it, Levi? What's wrong?" he asked, tilting his head downward to meet Levi's face.

Please let there be water, Levi pleaded silently.

The town of Bryan was quickly diminishing in population because the water source had started to run dry. He hoped there would still be enough ground water to do what he needed. He dropped the blankets on the earth in front of the spout and started to pump.

"Fire!" he said, his jaw tight with determination.

Rafe looked at the house. The flicker of light coming from the study grew brighter with every passing moment.

"Sit!" Rafe commanded the weasel of a man who'd started this whole mess.

Eddie sat down in front of the fence and Rafe secured him to the post.

"Buckets?"

Levi shrugged. He had no idea where Eamon or his men had kept any of the supplies. After a few pumps, water finally emerged from the faucet.

Thank you, Lord.

He continued pumping until the blankets were nice and soaked. He shoved a few of them into Rafe's arms and gathered the rest into his own, allowing the water to soak into his shirt as he ran back for the house.

Rafe was right behind him.

Smoke now filled the house and Levi could hear Cadence's coughs through the haze rising above the flames. Several times he saw her try to break through the flames, but it was no use. They were just too hot. An urgency, unlike he'd ever known, filled him and he ran as fast as he could to the study. The room had become an inferno. Rafe took one of the blankets from his hands and started beating at the flames. Levi didn't know if it would be enough.

"Cadence," he yelled, trying to see her through the blaze as he also beat the floor with a wet sheet. He raised a hand in an attempt to block the heat, but to no avail. "Cadence," he called again.

Cough.

His ears perked at the quiet sound.

Thud.

He had to get to her. Levi picked up one of the remaining blankets and quickly wrapped it around himself.

"What do you think you're doing?" Rafe asked as he landed another swat to the floor.

Before his brother could stop him, Levi jumped through the fire into the smoke-filled, but flameless section of the room. He kept the blanket over his face to avoid inhaling any of the dark smoke.

Cadence lay on the floor, her propped elbows barely keeping her from collapsing completely. Her head hung low, her dark hair blanketing the wood.

"Rafe," Levi screamed, kneeling down beside her. "Toss me more of those blankets."

He only had to wait a few seconds before the heavy, sodden coverings nearly knocked him down.

Cadence wheezed.

Levi shook one of the wet blankets free and tossed it over the top of Cadence. He doused the bottom of her skirt, wrapped another around himself, and reached down for her, lifting her into his arms. Without wasting another moment, he hurled himself through the flames and didn't stop running even once they were outside in the fresh night air.

Rafe followed.

Levi ran as quickly as he could with Cadence in his arms until he was far enough away from the house that smoke did not hang on the air around him. He stopped just outside of the gate and carefully set Cadence on the ground. He tore the blankets back away from her face.

She coughed again, gasping for air.

"Breathe deeply, Cade." He brushed the hair from her soot-stained face as he sat down beside her. "Take a deep breath. The fresh air will make you feel better."

Fire and Cadence did not mix. At least this time he didn't think she'd sustained any burns.

"That was quick thinking, Levi." Rafe said, dropping down next to them both. "How's the breathing?" he asked, the doctor inside of him surfacing.

Levi looked down at her. She no longer looked like she was struggling for every breath.

"You called me Cade." She smiled at him, her hand wrapping around his forearm. "Thank you," she whispered, her voice raw and raspy, "for not dumping me in the trough."

Levi laughed in relief, pulling her upward and into his embrace. Her hair smelled of burning pine.

"Can you sit up on your own?" he asked as he pulled away

from her.

"Of course, I can," she responded even as she fell backward again.

"Whoa." Levi caught her before she hit the ground. "Come on. We need to get you back to town."

"At least we still have this." She held up the leather bound book.

Levi picked her up again, taking the small package from her hands.

"What do you want to do about the house?" Rafe asked.

"I'll head back into town and see if I can round up some men who can ride out and help extinguish the fire," Levi responded as he carried Cadence back to the wagon. "Maybe we should let the horses and cattle out into the field in case the fire jumps to the stable." He walked around the side of the buckboard, reached down into the back, and opened the small lockbox secured beneath the seat. He laid the book inside and closed the lid.

"I'll see if I can find some buckets in the meantime," Rafe told him. "Maybe I can get the yard wet enough that it won't spread."

Levi released the back latch of the wagon and set Cadence in the bed. He didn't trust her to remain upright on the buckboard seat. Luckily, there was a crate full of empty, dry potato sacks he could to use to help keep her comfortable.

The temperature had dropped significantly over the last hour and Cadence had started to shiver. He wished he could use the blaze to help keep her warm, but he was worried it might do more harm than good. He just needed to get her back to the hotel where she could get into something cozy and dry.

"Levi?" Cadence grabbed a hold of the wagon's side and pulled herself up into a sitting position. "I am fine. It's just going to take me a while to fully catch my breath." She inhaled deeply followed by an exaggerated exhale. "See?" She shrugged.

A loud crackling sound split through the air as a portion of the roof fell into the study.

Cadence turned her attention to the burning house. "We don't have time to go back to town to get help. We need to get that fire out now or everything will be gone."

"Sweetheart, it would take an act of God to get that fire out without help from town."

BOOM!

A loud crack of thunder rolled across the horizon.

Levi and Rafe both looked up as the heavens opened and an onslaught of rain dumped down on top of them. They glanced at each other and suddenly a wellspring of laughter erupted. The sound of sizzling embers played like music in Levi's ears.

Cadence smiled at him. "I guess He was listening." She swung her legs out the back of the wagon and braced herself against the wooden flap.

It was the most beautiful sight Levi had ever seen and he stared at her for a few moments, rain streaming in rivulets over his head and face.

"What's wrong?" Cadence bit her bottom lip and pulled at the sodden locks of hair just below her ear.

Levi strode over to her and delved his hands into the hair at her nape, his fingers bracing her jaw and his thumb her chin.

"You are some woman, Cade Walker." He leaned down in slow descent and paused a moment before capturing her warm, moist lips fully in his. He could not lose her. Not now. Not ever.

Her arms wove up and around his neck, her hands gripping his too-long hair, pulling him closer. The soft moan that escaped her throat was nearly his undoing and an unwitting groan formed in his own. He tore his mouth away from hers.

"Don't ever scare me like that again." He leaned his forehead against hers for a brief instant, then forced himself to take a step back. To leave the heat of her touch.

Cade's shoulders flinched, unraveling her tough façade—though she was resilient, she shivered from the cold and Levi had nothing to warm her.

"I'm not riding back here," Cadence informed him. "I'm feeling much," she slid off the back of the wagon and back into his arms, "much better." She shoved away from him and walked to the front of the buckboard, climbed up into the seat, and turned to look at him.

"Merle's going to run out of room in that little jailhouse." Rafe unlocked Eddie's cuffs and pulled the man to his feet. "Unless you want to walk back to town behind my horse, I suggest you get in the back of that wagon."

"Rafe, I don't know if that's such a good idea…unless you're going to ride back there with him."

"No need. I'll just cuff him to the latch at the back and ride behind you. He won't do anything stupid, now will you, Eddie?"

Eddie's lips crinkled into a scowl that looked as if he'd sniffed something sour, but he didn't respond.

"I can take Cade with me if you're worried she might fall."

Levi raised a skeptical eye at Rafe. "How about you drive this old cart with your prisoner in the back and I'll take Cadence with me on Lexa?"

Rafe rubbed his chin briskly with the back of his hand. "Smart man." Rafe clapped Levi on the shoulder, lifted Eddie into the back of the wagon, and clamped the cuffs to a metal casing ring, then made his way to the front of the buckboard.

Levi smiled despite himself. He climbed up into Lexa's saddle and urged her forward up alongside the wagon seat. The ride would take no more than fifteen minutes or so, but he didn't think the saddle horn would be a comfortable place for a woman for any length of time, so he maneuvered behind the saddle onto the broad backside of Rafe's enormous mare.

"Come on." He held out a hand to her. "You're with me."

Cadence blinked a couple of times against the torrents of rain that still fell. She shook her head and smiled, pushing off the toe board, and arranging her foot on the corner of the box. Her skirt looked weighted with all the excess water and she wavered slightly. Levi was afraid she might slip, so before anything else could befall her, he lifted her up and into the saddle in front of him.

The dress she wore did not allow her to straddle the horse, but he preferred her sitting sideways.

"Better?" he asked.

"Much." She leaned against his chest, her head cradling in the perfect spot beneath his chin.

Levi tightened his hold on the reins, making sure she would be secure in his arms.

"Levi?" she spoke quietly, her breath hot against the skin of his neck.

"Hmmmm?"

"Thank you…for not leaving me in there to die."

How could he tell her he wouldn't lose her? Couldn't lose her?

"You're an amazing woman, Cadence Walker." He chuckled to himself as he leaned down and placed a kiss on the top of her head. "I couldn't have left you even if I'd wanted to."

Silence passed between them for a few excruciating moments. He couldn't deny the feelings he'd developed for her any longer.

"I love you."

CHAPTER SEVENTEEN

Cadence couldn't remember ever having slept so well. She opened her eyes, the dizziness and headache gone. Soft beams of sunlight filtered in through the sheer curtains at the window.

I love you.

The words echoed in her head, each time filling her insides with a combination of gratitude and excitement splashed with fear. She'd loved one man before and she'd lost him. She didn't know if she was strong enough to ever face that kind of loss again.

"I love you too," she whispered aloud, brushing a finger across her lips, still tingling from his kiss. Though she hadn't been able to admit it last night.

The journal and list.

Cadence bolted upright and threw the covers off her legs. She hoped the leather-bound bundle would have vital information about the attack planned for the railroad. They needed to examine the list for any familiar names and see what they could figure out from the journal. The ceremony celebrating the meeting of the rails was coming quickly and she was afraid they may not be able to stop an attack before it was too late.

Would having a date and a time be too much to ask?

It didn't take long for her to get dressed and to make herself presentable. She dropped down onto the floor, lifted the quilt from the bed, and looked beneath to verify that the cylindrical package was still secured to the mattress support boards. She could not risk it or the Lincoln spike getting into the wrong hands. Today she would meet Thomas Durant and everything had to be perfect.

Cadence opened the door. An empty wooden chair had been stationed just outside of her room and a half-filled glass of water sat next to the leg. She smiled to herself. Levi had kept watch over her all night. He didn't know about the several weapons she kept within arm's reach during any assignment.

Focus!

It had been a long time since something had distracted her this much, but Levi Redbourne had certainly proven to be a troublesome diversion. One she could ill afford if she kept acting like a...well, like a female. She walked down to her father's room, but when she opened it, it was empty.

Where could he be? Her heart skipped a beat and the pounding grew stronger. She lifted the hem of her skirt and raced down the steps, careful not to catch her foot on her dress.

Once out in the street, she glanced over to the town square where a dozen or so men stood around, scratching their heads, examining a pile of neatly stacked wood. As she got closer, she realized that the gallows was gone. Each of the boards had been neatly stacked on top of one another, completely dismantled. Next to a skillfully wound rope, several small boxes full of misshapen nails were aligned in a perfect row.

Levi.

Cadence smiled to herself. The beautiful man had shared a lot with her while they'd traveled together alone across the territory. One night, just before dozing off to sleep, he'd told her about the many shenanigans he and his twin brother, Tag, had used to pull on his family and friends. When she'd first met him, she'd have never guessed him capable of such tomfooleries, but now…now she'd seen him change. She'd seen a spark reignite the light in his eyes. He'd shared with her how the war had changed him and that his days of pulling pranks were long over, but just maybe he'd remembered who he was. Remembered how to find the joy in living.

It had to have been him. Who else?

The train was scheduled to leave Bryan today at three o'clock. Cadence had no choice but to be on it. More people were going to die if she couldn't figure out how to stop these southern sympathizers from attacking the celebration at Promontory Summit. She needed to find Levi and to get that journal. They had some time to sit and try to figure out where and when the next attack would be.

Cadence marched into the sheriff's office to find Merle sitting behind the desk with his feet elevated…again. The two imposters, who had accosted her, the doc, and her father yesterday, each sat on one end of the lone bed in the cell. Eddie sat in the corner of the enclosed area on the floor, apparently sleeping with his head up against the bars.

"Have you seen my father?" she asked the deputy.

Merle scrambled to his feet, grabbed ahold of his belt, and adjusted his significant belly.

"Redbourne's got him down to the doctor's office. Guess Elvin's going to be the new town doc and he'll be setting up shop there." He shot a disdainful look at his prisoners. "Miss Walker," he said as she started back out the door, "I'm real sorry about your pa. I'm sorry I didn't…"

"It's all right, deputy. At least you found out the truth before it was too late."

He hung his head.

"Oh, and Merle," she waited until he looked up at her,

"*every* life is worth saving…if you can." She walked out the door.

Clive's face still haunted her.

If you can, she reminded herself.

Cadence knocked on the door to the doctor's office before pushing it open to find Levi, his large, dark Stetson covering his face as he leaned back in one of the three black padded chairs beneath the window. His even breathing told her that he was sleeping. Or, at least trying to sleep. It was no wonder after the night they'd had. Not to mention to then have completely disassembled the gallows.

The man must be exhausted. She almost hated to wake him, but she really needed that journal.

Voices came from the room in the back.

"He's almost back to his old self," Levi said, his hat still covering his face.

Cadence jumped. "You startled me." She swatted at his arm.

"Might as well sit for a spell. Elvin's checking his wound." He lifted the brim of his Stetson to glance at her and smiled. He nodded sideways, indicating the empty chair next to him and then returned his hat to hide his face.

"Train's leaving today, right?" she asked, taking the seat next to him.

"Mmhmmm."

"You still coming with me?"

"Mmhmmm."

"I need to get that journal from you. We have to look at that list and try to decipher the passages in the book. There has to be some information we can use to find out what is going on or a clue as to who we can confront for answers."

"Already did."

"Confront someone?"

"No. Looked at the list."

"Without me?" Cadence couldn't keep the disappointment

from her voice.

"Rafe wanted a copy of the list to give to the Marshals who should be arriving this morning from Cheyenne." Levi handed her the book with the list sticking out from the binding. "I didn't give him the journal. Just showed him the list to see if he saw anyone he knew."

"And did he? Were there any names *you* recognized?" She asked, pulling the parchment from the pages of the journal.

"I'm afraid not. Though, my brother said that one of the names sounded familiar, but he couldn't place it. A woman, I think. I figured you'd want to hold onto that book. It appears to just be a bunch of journal entries and letters." He readjusted his hat. "That's a really interesting trinket attached to the buckle there though. I've never seen anything quite like it."

Cadence looked a little closer at the small metal medallion. Molded in the center was a laurel wreath encasing a man astride a horse with a broad X marking the background of the engraving.

The Confederate States.

Cadence had been warned about a group who still believed the country was at war. But this was proof that somebody was still in the midst of the fight.

"Rafe thought that maybe if the Pinkertons and Marshals worked together, you all might be able to figure out what's in that book and, hopefully, prevent a lot of bloodshed. That *is* what you want, isn't it?"

"What?" She'd heard him, but it took a moment for his words to register in her mind. "Of course it is."

Copy the list? It was such a simple thing. She wondered why her father hadn't thought to make a dozen copies and send them to various Pinkerton's across the country. Surely, they would be able to uncover some of the spies in their network. Maybe she should wire a list back to the agency.

That is exactly what I am going to do.

Cadence determined to wire the names on the list back to

headquarters before leaving today. If this extremist group was working so hard to stop the railroad, chances were they would be conspiring to prevent other such achievements throughout the nation. She opened the journal and started to scan the names scribbled on the worn parchment.

The door to the doctor's office opened and Rafe stepped inside, followed by two other men, nearly as tall as any Redbourne she'd met. Cadence looked up, raised a brow, and leaned over to Levi. "More of your brothers?" she asked without taking her eyes off them.

Levi guffawed as he stood, his hat still in his hands. "Nope." He held out a hand to help her to her feet. "Speak of the devil," he said, turning to his brother.

Cadence clapped the book shut and stood.

"Levi. Cadence." Rafe acknowledged as he stepped aside to reveal the first man. "This is Marshal Keaton Stevens. The real one. My friend and our ally."

The Marshal extended his hand to Levi, who shook it firmly. He then looked at Cadence, bent down, reaching for the empty hand resting at her side, and took it into his. Raising it up to his mouth, he kissed the back of it. She found his touch to be more...gentle than she'd expected.

"Ma'am," he said with a deep, gravel-like voice that no doubt had gained him the favors of many a lady, "it's a pleasure to meet a woman such as yourself. Redbourne here tells us that you work for Allan Pinkerton."

Her smile froze in place and she simply dipped her head with the smallest of movements in acknowledgement, not sure whether she should openly recognize that fact. This was new territory for her as she generally worked alone and deeply undercover. If everyone found out who or what she was, she would lose any future usefulness in the field and probably land herself right out of a job.

Cadence imagined that Marshal Stevens was quite effective at keeping the peace...and she was sure he quickly gained the support of the ladies in any town. His eyes were an odd color of grey, but stood out drastically against the tanned skin of his face. Handsome, she imagined most would say—if not a little rough.

Still, she thought as she glanced over at the man next to her, *he is no comparison to Levi Redbourne*. She leaned closer to the man she feared owned her heart until their arms touched. She was surprised at how quickly she'd come to appreciate having him near.

"We came the moment we got word that you'd captured that blamed imposter." He finally released her hand and cleared his throat, rubbing his fingers together. "He's been pretending to be a lawman throughout four territories now. He's a slippery one all right. Escaped capture quite a few times. No one seems to have been able to get ahead of him. Until now." He tipped his hat. "Nice work, madam detective."

"How'd he get your badge?" She recognized that he was attempting to flatter her, but she wanted to know. It was a fair question.

"Now that's a story in and of itself." The man behind Rafe stepped forward, clapped Marshal Stevens on the back as he slid past him to the forefront, and extended his hand. "I'm Jeb."

"Well, *Jeb*, let's hear it." She'd dealt with enough men who thought they could weave a tale around the truth.

Jeb whistled. "Tough as nails."

Cadence turned to Levi. "He's definitely not the quiet one," she whispered loud enough they could hear.

The door to the back room swung open and her father wobbled into the waiting area with a groan alongside Elvin. "Thanks, Doc. You sure got the touch."

Cadence rushed forward and squatted low enough that her shoulder could snuggle up beneath Eamon's arm for support.

"Don't you have a job to do elsewhere, young lady?" he said. "Seems to me you should be headed to the end of track."

"Part of my assignment was to locate the missing agent.

You," she responded as she helped him into one of the chairs, "are the missing agent. I had to make sure that you were okay."

"And now?"

"And now, I'm headed to the end of track. I just have a few questions for you about that journal. What did you find out?"

Eamon grunted as he adjusted in the seat. "I'm afraid I did not have enough time to discover anything. I seem to have gotten shot before I had the chance to figure out the cipher, though I think the key is in a book. Not sure which one."

"Well, maybe we can figure it out together. I've got to be headed out to the end of the line, but would appreciate knowing what fire's need to be put out before I get there."

"You certainly don't mean to do it alone? Didn't Allan send any other Pinkerton agents with you?"

Cadence dropped her head. "There was a derailment. They didn't make it."

Her father shook his head. "Damn." He hit the edge of the chair with his fist. "We have got to stop them."

"We will." She placed her hand over her father's. "We just need to find the cipher key and get to Promontory before something happens."

"Without the other Pinkertons you'll need someone to be there to back you up. To be your partner."

"Agreed." Levi spoke up.

Cadence turned the playful glower on him.

"I'm a big girl, Daddy. I can take care of myself," she said to both of them in quick retort.

"No question here." Levi laughed, putting his hands up, palms out in front of him.

"So, you'll be escorting my daughter..." he looked up at Levi, then stopped as if just seeing the strangers in their midst. "Who are you?" He looked from Jeb to the Marshal.

After brief introductions and Rafe's assurance and confirmation of their identities, her father seemed satisfied.

"Eamon," the doc said, drying his wet hands on a towel, "you need to rest."

Elvin looked sober, but tired. Cadence appreciated the time and effort he had spent on her father's behalf and she made a mental note to thank him before they left. She was continually amazed at how Levi's belief in people seemed to incite a change in them. She'd experienced it herself.

"You know how it will appear," her father said, still looking at Marshal Stevens before his gaze shifted again to Levi. "I would say you should cover as brother and sister, but anyone who looks at the both of you together would see through the lie right away." He raised a brow. "You ready to marry my daughter, Redbourne?"

Cadence gasped, stealing a look at Levi. "Daddy!"

"Yes, sir," Levi said with a mischievous grin.

Cadence's mouth fell wide open. She wasn't sure what to say, so she just looked between them. When the silence became thick enough to cut, she turned to Levi. "Don't you think I should have something to say about this?"

"You wouldn't have had to say vows, Cadie," Levi smiled warmly. "Not yet anyway," he added with a wink. "We would just have needed to *appear* to be married. Unfortunately, most of the men along the track know me, but I guess it wouldn't be too strange for some of them if I showed up with a bride." His smile widened.

Heat flooded her cheeks, but she did not take her eyes from his. Of course she should have thought of that, but it was getting harder to think straight when Levi was around. That just wasn't acceptable. "I have a job to do and that doesn't involve a husband," she raised her brow. "Besides, I imagine a single woman would gain more favor with Doc Durant than a married one."

"Well, that's certainly true," Levi responded.

"Come on, Daddy," she turned to her father, "we need to get you back to the hotel."

"Allow me." Levi stepped to one side and Rafe followed suit and stood to the other side. They each took an arm and hoisted Eamon from his seat. She didn't miss the slight wince that crossed Levi's face at the effort. His shoulder had to be hurting.

"We're going to head over to the jail and collect our prisoners," Marshal Stevens said. "But, we thought you might join us for an early lunch first?" His eyes met hers with open challenge.

A part of her wanted to say 'yes' just to see how Levi would react, but the time for playing coy had long since passed. "It's a lovely offer, Marshal, but it appears I may have some courting to catch up on. Seems I may be getting married." She turned on her heel without looking at Levi and walked toward the door. She stopped, turned back and captured her 'beau's' attention. "And don't *ever* call me Cadie. Only my father can do that."

She smiled at the sound of Eamon's laughter as she stepped out of the doctor's office and into the street where she could catch her breath.

Wife?

CHAPTER EIGHTEEN

Levi stared out the window of the restaurant dining area, watching thick droplets pound against the earth with relentless fervor. "It doesn't look like it's going to let up anytime soon." The curtain swung back into place when he released it.

"Mr. Redbourne, I'm so glad I found you here. This came for you and I wanted to see it to your immediate attention." The telegraph clerk placed his hands on his knees, took a deep breath, then stood and handed Levi a small folded piece of paper.

"Trouble in Piedmont STOP Not safe for railroad STOP," Levi read the telegram aloud. "Telegraph compromised STOP."

"Do you think that is where the next attack will be?" Cadence sat forward in her seat, staring up at him.

"There's obviously something going on farther up the track. I've heard that there are a lot of grumblings amongst the graders and track layers." Levi wiped his mouth with his napkin, tossed it onto the table, and pushed his chair back to stand up. He pulled out his watch and clicked it open. Twelve o'clock. "Durant's special train is not supposed to be here for a couple more hours," he said, looking at the watch he'd pulled from his vest pocket. "He and Dodge will both be on it for the ceremony on Saturday along with a dozen or more officers and dignitaries."

"Then, we'll just have to get to Piedmont before the train." Cadence looked at Levi—no hesitation. Her unfailing courage continued to surprise him. She stood up next to him and looked down at her father.

"I couldn't agree more." Eamon gingerly pushed himself away from the table, his chair scratching the floor, and he attempted to stand.

The deputy had agreed to let Eamon go in light of the new information about the sheriff and with the Marshal's encouragement, there wasn't going to be a trial. Levi just hoped that the townsfolk who had been out for the man's blood could make peace with it. Either way, Levi doubted Bryan was a good place for Eamon to settle. Especially now that his ranch house was all but destroyed. Stevens and Jeb had already picked up Mr. Adwell, whose name had been on the list, and taken off for Cheyenne with their prisoners.

"Don't get up like you'll be coming with us, Daddy," Cadence said, placing her hands on his shoulders and guiding him back down into the chair. She pursed her lips and glowered at him playfully, a hint of a smile curving her mouth. "You're in no shape to ride for that long and I'm afraid we don't have much time."

Levi held his breath. He'd never heard anyone speak to Eamon that way. He didn't expect his friend would appreciate someone telling him he wasn't fit to travel, least of all his daughter. The old coot was as stubborn as a mule.

"Eh, I'd just slow you down anyway," Eamon responded gruffly.

Levi could hardly believe how easily his friend had given in. While the man still had a long recovery ahead of him, Levi had thought him to be back to his obstinate old self. However, he couldn't help but wonder if the emotional strain Eamon had experienced over the last few weeks had finally taken its toll.

Levi glanced over at Cadence. He could see the wheels turning in her head, then, suddenly a spark lit up her eyes. Heaven help them, but by the expression on her face it looked as if she'd come up with a plan.

"Mr. Redbourne," she turned to his brother who hadn't said much of anything all through their morning meal, "would you kindly help my father board the train when it comes through?" The lilt in her voice had undoubtedly come from much practice.

Rafe nodded, taking another bite of the potatoes he'd ordered.

She turned to Levi. "You and I can ride on ahead. It can't be more than a couple of hours from here." She turned to look at Eamon. "You can be our eyes and ears on the train. I remember how skilled you are with that Smith and Wesson revolver strapped to your side."

Eamon leaned back against his chair with a knowing smile. "My daughter's got a right smart head on her shoulders, gentlemen. I suspect this hole in my side hasn't affected my aim."

Well played.

Just as Levi had suspected. He guessed that joining Durant and the others on the train to Piedmont had been Eamon's intention all along. He'd just needed his overly protective daughter to think it had been her idea.

Smart man.

A loud boom of thunder rumbled in waves across the darkening sky and everyone looked to the window, which was now splattered with masses of fat wet droplets streaking down the pane.

"There's only one glitch to your little plan," Levi said, placing his hat atop his head, preparing to head out into the seemingly endless storm. "There's not a horse alive that can make the sixty mile trek to Piedmont in just a couple of hours. Not even Apollo. And in weather like this on top of it, we'd never make it there by nightfall, let alone before the train."

He was honestly surprised to have heard Cadence even mention a horse. After all the traveling they had done over the last couple of weeks, he didn't reckon the memory of a saddle sore hind end was easily forgotten.

Cadence's shoulders slumped, but rigid determination quickly spread through her entire stance. "It's time to go through the cipher passages in the journal and figure out what they, whoever *they* are, have planned."

"Well, you still have it, don't you?" Levi asked.

Cadence reached into the pocket sewn into the folds of her dress and produced the leather wrapped journal. She held it up with a smile, pulling out the chair next to Rafe, and sat down again at the table.

Levi removed his hat, set it down on one of the empty chairs at the table, and took the seat next to Eamon, across from Rafe. "Are you sure there is a message inside the journal?" he asked, running a hand through his limp hair. "When we looked at it earlier, it just appeared to be a collection of love letters written to a woman during the war."

Rafe looked up from his food and stopped chewing a moment. He graciously guided meat to the side of his mouth. "I always considered you and Tag experts at creating and deciphering hidden messages." He turned to look at Cadence. "Our little sister, Hannah, once stole their little book of tricks and the lot of us spent days trying to figure out what tomfoolery they were up to." He laughed. "I still remember the look on Hannah's face as she came screaming out of her room when she met Genesis, the twins new pet lizard they'd hidden in her bed."

Levi and Tag used to send coded messages to each other all the time. Mostly the missives had just been childish plans for the monkeyshines they pulled on their unsuspecting siblings, neighbors, or just about anyone else who'd cared to stop by Redbourne Ranch.

Levi smiled and chuckled to himself, surprised that he was not at all embarrassed by Rafe's retelling of the account. "What? I think he was more scared than she was."

Both Redbournes laughed.

"Never did figure out what that book said."

"And I'll never tell," Levi said with a smirk, moving to the chair next to Cadence.

She met his eyes with a raised brow, her lips curving upward on one side. "Well, then it seems you should be able to help me figure this out in no time."

"Eddie wouldn't have gone to such lengths to destroy it if there was nothing in it to hide." Cadence undid the leather straps surrounding the book and removed the list, setting it aside for a moment. "There has got to be something here." Cadence started flipping through the pages, stopping occasionally to scan the entries. Levi followed along. It only took a moment and he saw it.

"No. It can't be this easy," Cadence said as she turned another page. "We'll need some paper and a writing utensil."

Levi had already pulled a small notebook from his vest pocket along with his favorite stub of a pencil and placed them on the table in front of her. She picked up the instruments, flipped through a dozen or so more pages. "Here," she said, holding the journal open to a specific page with multiple entry dates. *May, the seventh, eighteen hundred sixty-four.* The last date on the page. Odd. It would be exactly five years ago today. It couldn't be a coincidence.

While Cadence quickly began jotting down letters that coincided with the other entries. Levi couldn't help but decipher the last of the entries on the page.

"Impressive, isn't she? My daughter?" Eamon nodded his head in approval, an encouraging smile playing with his face.

As if Levi needed any more encouragement.

"It's all here," Cadence said excitedly, still not looking up from the pages. "The derailment. The fires. Everything.

Levi looked over and read the current passage. It was short and he noticed immediately how the capital letters were slightly exaggerated.

> *My heart is full today as correspondence finally arrived from my beloved Albert. Today gave me hope that he will come back to me one day. The war continues and has taken him even farther from me at this time. 16 months is too long to be separated from my love and my fear is that it will be many more before we are reunited. 18 is too young to be left alone in times like these and it is my prayer that he will be home soon.*

> *M   A   T   T   16   18*

It had been a long time since Levi had picked up a bible, but there was no question in his mind what it could mean. The answers he needed would be found in the book of Matthew, chapter sixteen, verse eighteen.

It only took Cadence a couple seconds before she looked up and locked eyes with Levi. "We need a bible," she echoed his thoughts.

Levi glanced over at Rafe who shrugged. "Don't look at me. It's not like I carry one wherever I go."

"Is there a preacher in town?" Cadence asked her father.

Levi remembered the old parson who'd agreed to come live in Bryan.

"Pastor Nichols." Eamon nodded. "I think he and his new bride, Edna, live in the space behind the church."

"Bride? The man has got to be eighty years old," Levi said in disbelief.

"Nope. This pastor can't be much older than you." Eamon waved a hand in his direction.

It had been months since Levi had been out this way, but it was hard to believe just how quickly things changed. He wondered if the old man had simply died or if he had decided to move on up to Green River like so many of the other townsfolk.

"Well, I'm guessing you won't need my help anymore, Eamon," Rafe said, pushing his chair backward. "Since you're catching the train and all. I think it's time I head out. Unless you still need me," he added, looking at Levi with a measure of uncertainty.

Levi knew that Rafe would be collecting his bounty for the imposters from the Marshals in Cheyenne. After being left at the altar last year, his brother had refused to take any more of their parent's money and had left medical school to set out on his own to deal with his demons. Rafe had a job to do and this time it wasn't policing the railroad. "Thanks, little brother, but I think we'll manage from here."

"Thank you, Mr. Redbourne," Cadence said, leaning over and placing a kiss on his brother's cheek.

Rafe cleared his throat. "It was my pleasure, ma'am." He moved to tip his hat, but must have realized it was still hanging on the side of his chair because he simply smiled and nodded, his hand waving haplessly at the air. He stood up, placed the last bite of his food into his mouth, and reached back for his Stetson.

Levi also stood. "It's been great to see you, Rafe. You headed home anytime soon?"

"It's been a while. I reckon Mama's missing us both. She tried to make me promise to be home for Christmas, but I'm not quite sure if I'll make it this year."

Levi nodded, then pulled Rafe into a firm hug. "Take care of yourself."

"You too." He leaned in a little closer to Levi's ear. "And

don't you let that one get away." Rafe cleared his throat as they pulled apart. "I don't think this rain is going to let up anytime soon. I imagine the good preacher will be home, but if there's trouble in Piedmont, you'll want to be ready." He slapped a coin down on the table, shook Eamon's hand, and tipped his hat at Cadence. He walked over to and out the door, turning on the boardwalk toward the livery.

"He's right," Levi said, grabbing his Stetson from the chair.

"Well, what are we waiting for?" Cadence asked as she closed the journal and secured the bindings. She returned it to the folds of her skirt.

Levi wondered just how big the pockets were in that dress, but thought better than to ask.

"If it's all the same to you, I'm a bit tired. I think I'll just wait over here until the train arrives." Eamon pointed to a thickly stuffed chair in the corner of the room next to the stone fireplace. A small leather traveling case peeked out from the side. Levi smiled. The old Pinkerton hadn't planned on staying in Bryan no matter what Cadence had said. His friend's eyes looked more sunken in than usual and Levi hoped that he hadn't overdone himself. The last thing they needed was for Eamon to collapse. Or worse.

"That's hours yet. You're just going to sit here? And what? Wait?" Cadence helped her father into the chair. She must have caught sight of the bag because she bent down and grabbed a hold of the handle, pulling the bag up in front of Eamon's face. "What is this?"

Eamon attempted a laugh, but coughed in its place.

"You were planning on coming all along," she stated accusingly.

"Guilty. I might have had Doc Fister pick up a few things for me at the General Store."

She crinkled her brows and looked at Levi.

"Elvin," Levi whispered at her confusion. He didn't

remember ever having told her the man's last name.

She nodded, her lips forming an 'oh.'

Cadence eyed her father warily. "Did he pick you up something to read?"

"Nope," a voice called from behind her. Elvin stood with a big smile on his face holding a deck of cards. He set them down on a small table and pulled it over in front of Eamon, then grabbed a chair and sat down opposite him.

Levi laughed. He couldn't help it. It took a moment, but Cadence laughed too.

"Maybe you should just stay here with the doc until this whole mess is all over," she told her father.

Suddenly, all laughter was gone.

"I ain't dead yet," Eamon said seriously. "I'll be there, on that train, at three o'clock."

"We don't want to cause panic on board the train, so maybe we should just keep all this information to ourselves— except for Gren Dodge and whoever the Pinkerton is traveling with them. They'll know what to do." Levi knew enough that a Pinkerton always traveled with Durant and if Gren understood there could be trouble, he would take any necessary precautions.

It didn't take long before Cadence and Levi had collected their meager belongings. When they passed by the table where Eamon and Elvin were playing cards, she took the cylinder package from around her neck and handed it to her father. She leaned over, whispered something in his ear, and kissed him on the temple.

"Take care of him," she told the doc, then turned to Levi. "The preacher?"

Levi smiled to himself.

Cadence stared at him a moment. "You know, Mr. Redbourne, you are a very beautiful man. Anyone ever told you that? Strong. Smart. I might do well to keep you around."

Eamon nearly choked on the ale he'd just swallowed and

he started to cough, but Levi didn't take his eyes off Cadence. Heat flooded his neck and he raised an eyebrow at her, the corner of his mouth turning upward.

"Why Miss Walker, I do believe you are a first for me." It took every ounce of control he had to refrain from dropping his bags and pulling her into his arms. He doubted her father would appreciate the forward display, so he held his ground, feet planted firmly in place.

"Breathe, Daddy," Cadence said with a giggle as she turned to leave.

Levi took that advice, sucking in a large breath. "I'll be right there," he told her. He exhaled. "Elvin," he asked the doc, "can I have a moment?"

Elvin joined Cadence as they walked out onto the boardwalk under the terrace roof.

The rain seemed to keep rhythm with Levi's heart as it pounded relentlessly in his chest. His mind was made up. He smiled.

Eamon pulled a handkerchief from his pocket and wiped his face.

"What can I do for you, son?"

Cadence ducked under the church's awning while Levi closed the umbrella he'd stopped to purchase in the mercantile on the way over. With the rain coming down like this, she had to admit that she was grateful she would not be out in the storm, astride a horse, tirelessly trying to make Piedmont before the train.

What had I been thinking to even mention it?

Levi pounded on the door of the small house that had been attached to the back of the church. It wasn't long before a thin, blond man with spectacles resting at the tip of his nose appeared in front of them, a book open, and a pencil behind his ear. He looked up from what Cadence guessed was his sermon and smiled.

"Come in. Come in." He motioned them into a small parlor room adorned by a simple couch and two chairs with a low table in the center.

Levi leaned the umbrella against one of the corners in the entry and the both of them took a seat, as directed, on the couch.

"I am Pastor Nichols. I don't believe we've had the pleasure."

"My name is Levi Redbourne and this is Cadence Walker."

"Well, Mr. Redbourne. What can I do for you and Miss Walker this beautiful morning?

Cadence glanced out the window and scrunched her eyebrows together.

"Don't worry," he said with another smile, "I do know it's raining. I just find beauty in it." He clapped the book he'd been holding shut and snapped his fingers. "A wedding. You two would like to get hitched. Is that it?"

Levi cleared his throat. "Not today. We wondered if we might be able to borrow a bible."

"Is there something particular you are looking for? Maybe I can help," the pastor offered hopefully.

"It's not that kind of question, Preacher."

It was Pastor Nichols's turn to be confused.

"We just need to know what is said in Matthew, chapter sixteen, verse eighteen," Levi told him.

The preacher pushed his glasses a little higher on his nose and opened the book he'd been holding. He turned the pages until he found the appropriate section.

"Well, let's see here…And I say also unto thee, That thou art Peter, and upon this rock I will build my church; and the gates of hell shall not prevail against it."

Cadence mulled the passage over through her mind. It only took a moment. She and Levi both shot to their feet.

"Devil's Gate Bridge," they called out in unison.

"Thank you, Preacher," Levi said, shaking the man's hand enthusiastically. "You may very well have saved a lot of lives today." He retrieved the umbrella from the entry and opened the door.

"Just a moment, please." Pastor Nichols stepped over to a humble bookcase in the hallway, pulled out a small, worn copy of the Holy Bible, and handed it to Levi. "You never know when you might need to look up another verse."

Levi nodded. "That's mighty kind of you, Preacher."

Cadence waited under the awning until Levi had opened the umbrella before stepping back out into the rain. The hem of her skirt was already covered in mud, but she preferred to keep the upper half of her dry to stave off the extra chill.

"It's Devil's Gate," Cadence told her father as soon as they entered the hotel dining room.

He swung his head around to look at her. "You got all that from reading through some old journal entries? I read every blasted letter and didn't see anything about an attack."

"You were right before. It *is* a cipher. See?" Cadence pulled out the book and opened it to the appropriate entry. "Every letter that has been capitalized and every number is a part of the message."

"Well, I'll be. I guess the agency hired some of us for our brawn and others for our brains. Smarty."

"Devil's Gate Bridge was built specifically to get the trains across the river and over that deep valley." Levi placed a booted foot on one of the empty chairs next to her father and rested his arm on his leg. "Without it, the railroad cannot be completed and the train would never make it to Promontory for the ceremony. We have to stop them. Whatever is going on in Piedmont could just be a distraction. To give them enough time to damage the bridge."

Cadence looked at Levi as if for the first time. As much as he gave credit to his brothers for being the lawmen in the family, he was good at decrypting information. Enough that if he wanted to, he could fool the best of them into believing that *he* was the bounty hunter, Pinkerton, sheriff, or all three. She imagined that Levi was a man who would excel in any profession of his choosing.

"How much longer 'til the train is supposed to arrive?" she asked.

Levi pulled a fancy silver watch from his pocket. The thick chain dangled as he clicked it open. "If it's on schedule, I imagine we have another few hours or so. Why?" he asked with a wry grin. "Do you want to go for a ride?" He held up the umbrella.

Cadence couldn't help herself. What started as a light giggle erupted into a laugh she could scarce contain.

"Yes," she dared him.

A loud guffaw sounded from the card table. Her father had obviously also found amusement in their conversation.

Levi held up one finger and disappeared out into the rain. When he returned near ten minutes later, he held out a crooked arm to her. She eyed him warily from her chair next to the fireplace, but curiosity got the better of her and she stood, weaving her hand onto the little shelf made by his proffered arm.

"Make sure to stay where folks can see you, Redbourne. I wouldn't want anything to spoil my daughter's reputation."

Cadence smiled at her father and Levi nodded.

"M'lady," he almost sounded like a British Lord, "your carriage awaits."

They stepped out onto the covered boardwalk, in front of which a single seat covered carriage was hitched to two horses—Apollo and a sorrel she'd never seen before—complete with a driver. Levi took her hand from his arm, opened the umbrella, and held it up while helping her into the carriage. Before she sat down, she spotted a small bunch of wildflowers with hues of yellow, blue, and pink tied neatly with a purple ribbon on the seat. She scooped them up, sat down, and raised them to her face. Their sweet aroma filled her nostrils and brought a quick smile to her lips.

Levi climbed up next to her, reached for a folded blanket on the opposite side of the seat, and pulled the small quilt around her shoulders. She hadn't realized how chilly it had become and was surprised at and thankful for the warmth the coverlet provided. The rain still came down in a drizzle, but she was surprised that it did not make it into the carriage.

"They are lovely," Cadence said, lifting them again to her face.

The carriage started moving forward at a slow and easy pace. "I hoped you'd like them. They reminded me of you."

She glanced over at him, not daring herself to speak.

"Against some of the greatest odds, these beautiful little flowers grow in a terrain that is often harsh and ever-changing, yet they survive while still maintaining their beauty, grace, and dignity."

She met his eyes, searching them, but for what she was unsure.

"Every day you do something new that surprises me, and every day I find myself falling further. Faster. Deeper. I love you, Cadence Walker."

Cadence swallowed.

"Will you do me the honor of becoming my bride?"

Silence.

Cadence didn't know what to say. She knew she returned his sentiments, but his timing couldn't be worse. She still had a job to do and with the threat of an attack at Devil's Gate Bridge, she needed to focus.

She smiled as good a smile as she could muster and she fought back the tears that threatened. "I love you too, Mr. Redbourne."

His smile broadened.

"I just can't marry you." She pounded on the front of the

carriage and it came to a stop. She removed the quilt from her shoulders and jumped down.

"Cade?" he called after her.

CRACK! BOOM!

Streaks of lightning followed a roll of thunder across the sky.

"I'm sorry," she screamed back at him, hoping the words had not been swallowed by the new whirl of wind that danced around them.

His use of her preferred name was too much and the tears began to flow, melding with the drops of rain tapping against her face. She couldn't risk him seeing her heart breaking, so with the flowers gripped against her chest, she started to run through the mud and seemingly never-ending showers. She glanced up to gain her bearings. Luckily, the driver hadn't taken them too far from the main street and she headed back toward the hotel.

"Cade. Stop."

She should have known that Levi wouldn't just let well enough alone.

He caught up with her and in the next moment was standing in front of her, his arms encircling her. Though she tried to fight him, for fear his mere touch would change her mind, she couldn't deny that she felt safe with him, in his arms, and she buried her head into his shoulder.

"It's okay," he soothed, his hand gently stroking her sopping hair. "I understand."

How can he understand?

Cadence didn't even understand. How could she say no to a marriage with the one man who'd shown her it was possible to love again? She'd chosen a life that had given her an unfoundedly sullied reputation. A profession that forced her to keep secrets from those closest to her. He knew all of that and still he wanted her.

What can I possibly offer him?

She wasn't sure which bothered her more—the idea that she was dishonoring Daniel's memory by allowing herself to fall in love with another man or the fact that she didn't know how to be someone's wife. She'd traded her soul when she'd become a Pinkerton and now she had to live with the consequences. That didn't mean Levi should suffer because of her choices.

Levi placed a hand on each of her shoulders and set her away from him enough that she could see his eyes.

"I'll wait," he said quietly, leaning down toward her.

Cadence's heart beat so loudly, the methodic sound seemed to deafen her to her surroundings. She stood there, stock still, cursing the moment his lips would meet hers, yet anticipating it even more. When she could feel his hot breath on her face, she closed her eyes, her breathing staggered and short.

"I can't," she cried and turned away from him, resuming her retreat to the hotel.

I can't.

CHAPTER NINETEEN

Levi stomped down the main street of town as the storm grew fiercer by the moment. The Durant Three-Car Special and adjoining train cars would arrive within the next couple of hours and he wanted to be presentable. It wasn't every day a body had the opportunity to witness such a historical event and to be a part of the celebration. He'd received word that his friend and mentor, Grenville Dodge, had been detained for a short while in Salt Lake City and wouldn't be able to join them until they reached Promontory Summit. However, there would still be several other high profile politicians and businessmen on board.

Luckily, there was still a bath house in Bryan where he could clean up, then get a much needed haircut and a hot shave. After the events of the early afternoon, he couldn't wait to crawl into a tub of hot water and allow the steam to wash away some of his pent up energy and frustrations. He made his way back to the hotel to retrieve a clean shirt and trousers, and his wallet.

I can't.

Levi couldn't seem to get those words out of his head. He understood that he'd probably chosen the wrong moment to declare his intentions, but he'd never felt like this about any woman. And he wasn't about to give up without a fight. Cadence was strong and smart, and he loved that she didn't dance around her words, but said what was on her mind. Their last encounter played again through his head. He had simply wanted to kiss the tip of her nose, to reassure her that he understood her hesitation, but Cadence had retreated from his touch as if it burned.

Women.

The blaring sound of the train's whistle carried the distance to the station where Levi, Cadence, Eamon, and a few townsfolk waited to greet the approaching locomotive. Cadence had determined to keep her distance from Mr. Redbourne, but he was making that very difficult.

She almost resented the fact that he'd had the forethought to bathe before the train arrived. His clean scent and newly cut hair played havoc with her insides. His freshly shaven face displayed the firm angles of his jawline and chin, but if truth be told, she kind of missed the stubble of hair growing on his face.

Puffs of steam shot up into the storm with expressed fervor and Cadence tried to remain focused on the assignment now at hand. She was to gain favor with Mr. Durant and uncover any threats. She only hoped that they would be able to warn them about Devil's Gate Bridge in time to stop the attack.

Cadence patted her pocket, containing President Lincoln's signed spike and the cipher journal of events. She glanced over at her father who now carried the leather cylindrical case. He nodded. Once settled on the train, she would resume decoding the locations of each planned attack and finally finish looking over that list.

"Nervous?" Levi asked, probably because she couldn't stop fidgeting. She willed herself to stand still.

"Not at all," she lied. "This is what I have been trained to do." Cadence could feel Levi's eyes on her. "Fine. Of course, I'm nervous."

Levi smiled and turned back to face the tracks.

The engine finally came to a stop with an ardent release of steam. The train would only be stopping long enough to pick up the passengers and then would resume its route. The conductor hopped down off the metal step and onto the platform with a grin.

"Mr. Redbourne, sir, it's good to see you've made it all right. Miss Walker," he acknowledged while reaching out to shake Levi's hand, but Levi pulled him in for a quick hug.

"James! Last time I saw you, you were mending the crew and hauling logs. I guess everything has returned to normal?"

"Yes, sir. Can you believe we've come this far? By this time tomorrow, the Transcontinental Railroad will be complete."

Suspicion, founded or not, reared its ugly head.

James reached down to collect Cadence's bag. "I guess you are traveling a little lighter than before."

Cadence smiled and stepped to the side, revealing the large trunk they'd carried across half the country. Poor thing was held together with a few yards of rope, but she didn't have the time or means to find something equally as capable.

James smiled. Cadence didn't remember him ever doing that before.

"Where is Mr. Durant?" Cadence whispered to Levi.

"He'll be waiting down there," he pointed toward the back of the train, "in his personal coach. It'll be the fanciest of all of them. Can't miss it."

Cadence counted twelve cars in total. "It seems you don't much care for the man, Mr. Redbourne," she said, then without waiting for his response, she turned to the conductor. "I wonder if we might get someone to help my father on board. He's suffering from an injury and needs his rest." She took a step back and James saw the man about whom she'd been speaking.

"Detective Walker?" James stood up straight and looked between Cadence and her father. "Are you two…?"

"She's my daughter, James." Eamon took a step toward the metal stair. "Don't you pay her no never mind. I've done this a thousand times. I can get to a seat all by myself." He pulled himself up on the railing, but his legs had already been weakened by all the exertion of the morning. He refused any help.

"You are one stubborn man, Daddy. They're not going to think any less of you because you need help recovering from a bullet."

"You were shot, sir?" James motioned for two large men at the end of the platform to come and help. "I wondered why I haven't seen you in a while."

Cadence suspected the men he'd called to be the Pinkerton agents assigned to this train, but she didn't recognize them. While she'd heard that the Union Pacific Railroad had thousands of people on its payroll, she wondered at how her father, Levi, and the conductor all seemed quite familiar with each other. She guessed the number that actually rode the trains back and forth was much smaller.

Levi held out his hand and helped her up onto the stairs. She climbed up ahead of her father so she could help him once he boarded. Before the Pinkertons had made it to their coach, Levi heaved her father to the top step, much to Eamon's dismay, but after a few disgruntled comments, he reached out for Cadence and they made their way to a seat.

She trusted that Levi would find out which sleeping compartment belonged to each of them—hopefully, this time they each would have one of their own—and she'd be able to get her father settled for the comparatively short ride to Piedmont. She was beginning to second guess her decision to allow her father to come along. Not that she'd really have been able to stop him once his mind had been made up. He looked rather peeked and she could tell by his gait, he was getting weaker and needed some rest.

It didn't take long before everyone had boarded and the train was on the move.

"Looks like there are only luxury compartments on this train. Eamon, looks like you need to sleep for a spell. Let's get you into the next coach and you can lie down. At least until we get to Piedmont." Levi turned to Cadence. "He doesn't look well. I'm not sure we should have brought him along."

"You know my father," she said without looking up. "What would you have had me do?"

The sound of Levi's brief laughter warmed her.

"We need to go and speak with Mr. Durant about Piedmont. We have no idea what trouble awaits us there, but it will be better if the Pinkerton agents and Mr. Durant are informed."

"Colonel Levi Redbourne?"

Levi turned around and snapped a salute. "Yes, sir, Major General, sir?"

Both men broke into wide grins and greeted each other with a handshake, then pulled each other firmly into an embrace of genuine comradery.

"How the hell are ya, Levi?" the Major General asked. "Excuse me, ma'am. I forget that there are ladies aboard this train."

"Gren, this is Cadence Walker. We're..." he paused. "She's..."

Cadence raised a brow, wondering what he might say.

"I thought you were already in Utah on business." Levi changed the subject. "How...?"

"It seems my friend is having a hard time with his words

today." The man laughed. "It's quite the pleasure to meet Levi's lady friend. You are a very lucky woman, Miss Walker. The Colonel is...well," he clapped Levi on the shoulder, "a great man."

"I wish I could say she was mine, Gren, but Miss Walker and I are not together. Miss Walker, this is Grenville Dodge, and as I'm sure you can tell, we served together for quite a while during the war."

"Right alongside President Ulysses S. Grant." Grenville boasted. "Redbourne here was an invaluable asset and a reputable officer. You should be proud."

Levi hadn't talked much about his service in the war. She'd guessed it to be a difficult time for him and couldn't imagine the turmoil he must have experienced.

"That's enough of the past," Levi said modestly. "We have something far more pressing that needs to be discussed."

"Fine, but first, you wanted to how I came to be on this train. Let me introduce you to my family." Grenville turned to her. "If you'll excuse us, Miss Walker. It was a pleasure."

"I'll be right there, Gren. Just let me see them to their quarters first." Levi hunched over and pulled Eamon to his feet, draping her father's arm over his shoulders.

"Ready?"

Cadence nodded. They made their way to the sleeping compartment and Levi laid her father down on one of the beds with an ornately decorated covering. The coach was much bigger than the one she'd slept in before. It was more open and there were benches on the opposite side for looking out the window. While the room was far from private, with three other beds, it was an acceptable accommodation.

The Major General lifted a hand to Levi's shoulder, bowed slightly at Cadence, and whisked Levi off to one of the fancier coaches—which she guessed were for the railroad's important guests and dignitaries—without a word.

Cadence didn't want to wait. If Levi's friend wasn't ready

to listen, maybe Mr. Durant would be. She needed to find him and introduce herself. Levi had told her that his was the most ornamental coach of them all and if she was right, it would only be two cars down. Surely, Annie would have told the railroad officer she was coming. Cadence had expected to join up with him much sooner, but her delay couldn't have been helped. At least she would be able to warn him against the looming attack.

"I think I might just sit here for a bit, Cadie," Eamon told her as he lay back against the mattress.

Cadence tucked a pillow under his head and patted his arm. "I'll be right back." She stepped out onto the connecting platform of the next car.

"Miss Walker?" The door opened and one of the large men from the platform stepped outside. "Mr. Durant would like for you to join him in his personal compartment, ma'am."

That was easy enough.

"Of course," Cadence responded with a coy smile. "I would be delighted." She stood and brushed the wrinkles from her skirt, pinched her cheeks, and followed the man through the next couple of coaches.

When they arrived at Mr. Durant's palace car, Cadence stopped to take in the extravagance of the coach. Even the door that opened into the man's 'special' car was ornamented with overlay. Without meeting the man, Cadence already understood some of why Levi disliked him. When she stepped inside the compartment, it seemed much bigger than she could have ever suspected.

"Ah, Miss Walker. Welcome. I trust you find your accommodations on my train acceptable?" A man with a long, well-kempt beard stood from behind a delicately carved wooden desk. "Come in. Come in. Please have a seat." He motioned for her to take a seat in the leather-backed chairs in front of his desk.

Cadence made her way into his car, taking in the

extravagance of his quarters. Two matching gilded mirrors sat like windows behind him, placed against a wall of the most intricate inlaid woodwork. Couches made of the most exquisite velvet and carved timber adorned each side of the room and brilliant crystal chandeliers hung from the ceiling.

"Your coach is quite something, Mr. Durant," she said, trying not to appear too taken with the luxuries as she moved to the proffered chairs.

"Thomas, please." He stood and reached out for her hand before she could sit. "I understand we will be working together over the next couple of days." He kissed the back of her hand. "You are even lovelier than Miss Kramer here described." He waved someone into the room.

A woman in a large, overly garish hat walked in and made her way to the front of the car, an aristocratic expression painted on her face. Cadence was stunned to see Annie, her mentor, standing in Mr. Durant's car. Her elegant green dress seemed ill-fitted—the waist resting too high on her frame. Her cheeks were fuller, her face different somehow.

Why is she here?

Cadence had been chosen for this assignment. Annie had questioned the decision at first, but had ultimately agreed and had given her instructions. Cadence quickly tried to recall the conversation she'd had with the woman before she'd set out West. Annie had specifically told her that Mr. Durant had requested Cadence instead of her. Something was amiss.

"Hello, Cade." Annie's lilt was smooth and sultry, not at all like the Annie Kramer that she knew. "When Mr. Durant wired me and told me you had not yet made it to him, I was worried and came straight away. Wherever have you been?"

Cadence did her best to keep the surprise off her face and out of her voice. "It's good to see you, Annie," she acknowledged. "As I told you in my telegram, my original train derailed and—"

"Yes, yes, dear. Well, you are here now. Safe and sound."

She patted Cadence on the hand.

Cadence's eyes dropped to slits as she watched the carefully trained actions of an astute Pinkerton agent.

"Darling," Annie said to Durant, "would you mind pouring us a drink?"

"I hadn't realized that you were a part of that unfortunate incident in Laramie," Mr. Durant tsked as he pulled the crystal cork of a glass bottle of amber liquid. "It's a shame how many people were affected by that accident. I believe it claimed six lives, is that right?"

"Seven."

"Ah, yes. The engineer." He poured a small amount of brandy into the first glass and held it out for Annie.

"And it was no accide—"

"You must be exhausted with everything you have seen over the last few weeks. I imagine you're due for some much needed rest before we get into the details of what you've been doing."

She did it again.

Cadence had sent a telegram every chance she'd had along the way, explaining her delays, information she'd uncovered, and her location—the last of which was just a few days ago, never having seen a response. Was it possible Annie had never received her messages?

"I'll just have a glass of water if it's all the same," Cadence told Mr. Durant with a smile.

It seemed odd that her mentor would not have apprised their client of the delay or provided the information about Clive and the others sabotaging the train.

"As I was saying, sir, the derailment was—"

"Unfortunate," Annie filled in for her, "we all agree."

She really had to stop doing that.

"Now, you've seen that Mr. Durant is being well taken care of, so you'll understand if your services are no longer needed," Annie waved dismissively. "I'll be taking over from here."

"But I have inf—"

"I'll escort you back to your quarters, dear." Annie took a hold of Cadence's arm and pulled her into a standing position, then placed her hand at the small of her back as if to guide her from the room.

Enough.

"No, Annie!" Cadence said firmly, stopping in her tracks and ripping her arm from Annie's grasp. "This was my assignment!" She turned to Durant. "The derailment was not an accident. Neither was the explosion at the bank in Flat Plains or the fire that claimed my father's ranch just outside of Bryan. There is a conspiracy here, sir. No one on this train is safe. There is going to be an attack and we have to stop it."

"I'm sorry, Thomas. Obviously, she's had some difficulties on her way here and I think they have clouded her judgment. I will see to it right away, that she gets some rest." She took ahold of Cadence's arm again with a firmer grip.

"Let her speak, Annie. I'd like to hear what the woman has to say."

Annie glowered, but released her.

"We know there is going to be some trouble in Piedmont, but we believe the attack will be at Devil's Gate Bridge."

"We?" He asked.

"Mr. Redbourne and I."

"Ah, Levi. He's a smart fellow and very talented with a gun—or so I hear. Did you know that he can hit a target from the top of this train at more than one hundred yards? I believe the men call him The Iron Horseman." He folded his arms. "May I ask how you and Mr. Redbourne came about this information?"

Cadence wanted to ask more about Levi's nickname, but looked over at a seething Annie and changed her mind. Now was not the time for idle chatter. She reached into her pocket, her hand caressing the soft leather of the journal, her fingers tracing the contours of the medallion attached to the bindings, but something within her told her to keep it safe and she decided better than to offer it here as evidence. She needed Levi.

"Mr. Redbourne and I discovered a journal with coded messages we believe were written by a group of southern separatists who will do anything to stop the railroad from completing. They are trying to regain the Confederate States of America."

"The Confederate States of America," Annie scoffed.

"And why would halting the railroad's completion help them?"

"Because, Mr. Durant, it will fulfill President Lincoln's dream of uniting the nation," Cadence told him. "We will no longer be the North and South. We will be the United States of America."

"Bertram!" Mr. Durant yelled. His door swung open and the train's Pinkerton agent who'd escorted Cadence here stepped inside.

"Yes, sir?"

"Bring Mr. Redbourne here immediately."

"Yes, sir!"

"Thomas," Annie said, maneuvering behind the desk. She sat on the corner and ran a hand through his hair. "We are so close to seeing the end of this railroad endeavor. Why spoil it with talk of a conspiracy. I am one of Pinkerton's top agents. Don't you think that I would know if there really was something to be concerned about? Are you going to trust an agent with whom you just became acquainted—my protégé no less—or me?"

Cadence couldn't believe what she was hearing. Annie had always been very complimentary of her skills as an agent. She clenched her jaw, controlling her desire to swat her colleague.

Light filtered in between the deep burgundy tasseled curtains and glinted off Annie's bracelet—the same bracelet she always wore. Cadence had never seen her without it.

It can't be.

She took a step closer, trying to get a better look at the small dangling trinket near the clasp. The ugly bitterness of betrayal brought bile to Cade's throat. The Confederate symbol being displayed openly in front of her was the same as that on the journal's medallion. Cadence had to force herself to breathe. To refrain from reacting. Anger and indignation welled within her chest and she fought to remember her training.

"Is there really any question?" Mr. Durant responded. "Still, my dear, what if you missed something that could be important?" He stood up and tapped Annie lightly beneath the chin with the knuckles of his fingers. "Your protégé, as you call her, seems quite confident in the information she is presenting." He walked around the desk, leaned up against the front of it, his legs and arms crossed in front of him, and studied Cadence for a moment. "Tell me more of this journal you found. What else did it say?"

Screech.

The train slowed very quickly, tossing Mr. Durant off balance and nearly on top of Cadence, effectively pushing her back down into the seat. She waited for the sound of crashing mirrors, but it seemed they had been well secured to the wall. Papers flew from Mr. Durant's desk, however, and Annie had fallen to the floor.

"What in tarnation is going on out there?" Mr. Durant pushed himself away from her and took a moment to collect himself, coaxing his floppy hair back into its slicked position. "Excuse me," he said as he marched from his coach, stopping only long enough to retrieve a rifle hanging lengthwise next to the door.

Cadence drew her weapon, intent on following. Annie quickly pulled herself up from the floor, her gun already in hand. The rain was heavy. As they stepped out onto the short metal platform, Cadence leaned over in an attempt to catch a glimpse of where Durant had gone, but the small balcony offered little view of what was happening up ahead. However, conveniently, the UPs Vice President's personal palace had its own staircase. Cadence carefully, and as quietly as she could, climbed down the stairs, using her arm to block the assault of rain that seemed would never let up.

A shot rang out through the air and she stopped, hurling her back up against the train, and looked from one side to the other, but couldn't see where the shot had come from. Suddenly, swarms of yelling men surrounded the locomotive and the first few passenger and sleeping cars of the train. Not wanting to be caught in the open by a mob of angry men, Cadence crouched down and ducked beneath Durant's coach.

Within moments she was joined by Levi and Annie.

"Couldn't let you have all the fun," Levi said when Cadence turned to look at him.

Cadence shook her head, then peeked out from beneath the train in time to see several men hoist Mr. Durant up into the air onto their shoulders and head back toward his car.

"They're coming," she whispered, motioning for the others to move back toward the other side. "And they have Mr. Durant." It seemed the crowd was sticking to the front portion and south side of the train.

Thump. Someone had just jumped up onto Mr. Durant's private staircase and the hinges had squealed in protest.

"It has been near four months, Mr. Durant," a man said forcefully. "These men have worked hard for the money you promised them. So, we're going to stay right here, chained to the track, until you pay up.

"You are mad. I don't keep that kind of money just lying around. Let us go and you'll get your money."

The man chortled darkly. "We've heard enough of your promises. I'm going to stick by your side until you get the Union Pacific to pay their debt." The door to Durant's quarters opened and shut, followed by another thud. Cadence guessed Durant had been tossed to the floor. While she could still hear the man who obviously represented the disgruntled workers talking, she couldn't make out what he was saying.

Clink. Clank. Clunk. Durant's car had just been uncoupled from the rest of the train and moved a few inches. Cadence breathed deeply. There was not a lot of room under the car and she didn't think that being crushed by a train would be a very pleasant way to die. It stopped. They didn't have much time. Cadence glanced at the other two.

"Go for help. I'll stay and make sure no harm comes to Thomas," Annie proposed.

"How can I trust that you aren't a part of this? That you aren't the one who's going to kill him?" Cadence asked.

"Because," Annie said with strained tones, "he is the father of this baby. Don't pretend you didn't notice. I saw the way you looked at me up there."

Cadence whipped her head around to look at her once-friend, completely stunned. It took a moment for her to recuperate, but even then, she didn't know what to say. It certainly explained a lot.

"Annie, I…"

"Go!" Annie urged.

Cadence rolled out from beneath the train on the opposite side of the tracks and lay on her belly, hoping that the tall grasses would provide enough cover to go undetected. Moments later, Levi scrunched up next to her, looking out at the mob of angry rail workers demanding payment for their labor.

She placed a finger over her lips and Levi nodded his acknowledgement. She pushed herself backward across the grass until she was behind the station and she sat up against the side of the building to look around. Several large charcoal kilns towered over the ground with their enormous beehive shape rising what she guessed was at least thirty feet in the air.

If she and Levi could get over to them, the structures would provide cover for a short while—as long as they were not in use, but there was nothing but open prairie all the way into town. There would be no way to get horses or call for help.

Cadence edged up to the corner of the building and jutted her head around the side to catch a quick glimpse of what was happening. She watched as a large group of men pushed the palace car, along with two others that she suspected housed Durant's high profile guests—statesmen, dignitaries, and wealthy businessmen—onto a side track. She guessed they would be retained as hostages while the others would be allowed to leave.

The locomotive pulled forward with the remaining passenger and freight cars reattached.

"Levi," Cadence turned back to look at him, still slightly breathless and rain streaming down her hair and into her face, "my father is still on that train."

"I know." Levi cinched a little closer. He reached out and caressed her cheek with the back of his fingers. "It's going to be all right."

Click.

There was no mistaking that sound.

Cadence looked up to see a young man aiming his rifle at her, motioning for her to relinquish her gun. His face was covered in smudges and water poured from the brim of his hat.

"I've got a couple over here!" he yelled. "Hand it over," he said to Cadence. "Nice and easy like."

There was nothing she could do.

Blasted all.

CHAPTER TWENTY

"Mr. Redbourne is that you?"

Levi breathed out a sigh of relief that the kid's face was a familiar one.

"Billy, what is going on here?"

"We just want what's owed us, sir. We haven't been paid in near four months and we decided it was time to take matters into our own hands." He lowered his gun. "You gotta understand. This is nothing against you. You've always been real decent to all of us and we respect you, but…"

"But you still need to get paid."

"Yes, sir."

Levi cursed Thomas Durant for his many unethical and oily business practices. He reckoned the man would cheat his own mother out of her home if it would get him an extra dime.

Two bright flashes of light split the stormy sky followed by a deep rumbling that seemed all too close. Time was not on their side and neither, did it seem, was the weather.

"What's going to happen down at Devil's Gate Bridge, Billy?" Levi didn't think these workers had anything to do with the supposed attack, but he had to make sure.

"I don't know nothing about the bridge, Mr. Redbourne. Honest. We just want our fair wages. I have a wife and baby. They're hungry and I can't feed them with Mr. Durant's empty promises. As soon as he pays us, we'll let him and all of the others go."

"I understand, Billy, but what makes you think Durant will give in? You realize he's going to try to call in soldiers from Fort Bridger to come in and take control of this situation."

"Not with Jinx working the telegraph. Every unauthorized message in or out gets intercepted. Besides, Durant wants to win this race, right? Well, we figured now would be the best time to get his attention while the whole world waits on him."

Levi hated to admit it, and he certainly did not condone these tactics, but they were right. The only way to get Thomas Durant to follow through with promises that would separate him from his money was to dangle a carrot too big to ignore. His own pathetic life and the completion of the railroad were two very big carrots.

The engine whistle blew.

"It sounds like they've cleared the stack of ties off the tracks."

"Billy, you need to listen to me very carefully, all right? I need you to give Miss Walker back her gun."

Suspicion crossed the young rail worker's face, but without questioning, he reluctantly reached out and did as instructed.

"Good. There is going to be an attack at the bridge and all those people on that train are going to be in serious trouble if we can't stop it."

Billy nodded.

"We need to get back on before the engineer leaves." Levi pointed to the cars starting to pull forward on the tracks. "Now." Any longer and they would miss their opportunity.

"Can I trust you, Mr. Redbourne?"

"You have my word, Billy. I've never lied to you before.

We just need to get to that bridge before anyone gets hurt. There are a lot of innocent people on that train."

"You'd better hurry. Looks like it's pulling out."

"Thank you!" Levi said as he reached down and pulled Cadence to her feet.

Without letting go of her hand, they dashed toward the departing train. It had started picking up speed, but Levi couldn't see anywhere to grab hold that would keep both he and Cadence out of harm's way.

She grasped the hem of her dress while they ran, but the mud was deep and sticky, effectively slowing their escape. The caboose was upon them, if they weren't able to catch it, they'd lose their one chance left to board. Moving his hand to the area just above her wrist, he tightened his grip, reached for the railing, closed his fingers around one of the bars, and jumped, pulling Cadence up along with him.

His booted foot planted firmly on the platform and he immediately wrapped his arm all the way around the rail. Cadence's toe glanced off the balcony and she slipped. He squeezed tighter around her wrist and caught her before she could fall to the ground below, but now she dangled dangerously just above the track. Levi quickly glanced around for something he could use as leverage as he was losing his hold on her. The rain wasn't helping.

"The ladder," he yelled to be heard over the hum of the wheels.

There was a metal ladder that had been built into the caboose leading to the roof. If he could just swing her enough that she could use the rung to support her weight, he could crawl over the railing to gain better leverage to pull her all the way onto the train.

With all the strength he could muster, he swung Cadence high enough that the heel of her boot caught on the inside of the rung and she was able to pull herself into an upright position. She gripped ahold of one of the higher rungs and let go of Levi's hand.

"Aaaaah," he ground out in pain. He felt the stitches in his arm pop and he glanced over to see small red splotches seeping into the sleeve of his shirt.

He closed his eyes briefly in thanks that they'd made it.

Once Levi had collected his bearings, he quickly climbed over the railing, which he in turn used to ground him as he reached out for Cadence. She held out her hand and carefully moved her foot across the open space to the edge of the platform. When her foot was securely situated on the ledge, she jumped. Levi slipped his arm all the way around her waist, holding her firmly against the railing. In the next breath, he lifted her up and into his relieved embrace.

Cadence snuggled into his chest, her arms curling up around his shoulders.

"It's okay. You're going to be all right."

She pulled away from him. "All right?" she asked incredulously. "You almost dropped me," she accused, wiping sodden locks away out of her face and tucking them behind her ear.

"But I didn't," he keenly reminded her, appreciating the fire in her eyes. Even now, she was beautiful.

"No," she said with softened voice and a reluctant smile, "you didn't. Thank you."

They stared at each other for a moment without saying a word.

"You're hurt."

Levi looked down at his arm again. It was still sore, but the bleeding seemed to have stopped. "I'm sure some of my stitches just came undone. It'll be fine."

"My/Your father," they both said simultaneously.

Levi thrust open the door and waited for Cadence to pass before he entered the caboose.

They passed through each car, making sure no one had been hurt. When they reached Eamon's sleeping car, he was nowhere to be found.

"Where would he have gone?" The worry in Cadence's voice was evident by the high pitch. "Please tell me he didn't try anything in Piedmont."

"We'll find him, Cade. Don't worry. A lot of those men back there know your father too. They won't hurt him if he was left behind." Levi spoke with more confidence than he felt.

Whenever an angry group of men got together and took a stand, there was always a chance of innocent casualties. He just hoped that Eamon had not gotten off the train with fanciful ideas of being the hero—even though he was a hero in every sense of the word, he was hurt and his pride was going to get him killed.

When they approached the last of the passenger trains, the dining car, Levi spotted Eamon through the small door window sitting at a table holding a handful of cards. Relief washed over him.

Cadence strode into the car and casually made her way over to her father's table and sat down next to him. She didn't say a word, but after a moment, she laid her head on his shoulder and closed her eyes.

"Gentlemen," Eamon said to the two male passengers sitting across from him, "this is my daughter, Cade Walker."

A wide grin spread across Cadence's face. She popped her head up, kissed her father on the cheek, and stood up. "It was nice to meet you. Now, if you'll excuse us."

Eamon winked at Levi.

He knew how much it meant to Cadence for her father to see her all grown up and not as the little girl who used to follow him around the house with toy wooden pistols. Levi had heard the stories a hundred times over.

"Let's go talk to that engineer," she said, cool determination returning to her demeanor.

"Let's."

Echo City provided a junction for the train to be able to switch directions. It was also the closest town with a telegraph where word could be sent when it was time to return to Piedmont to retrieve Durant and the others. In the meantime, the passenger and freight cars would be uncoupled and left overnight. Most of the people on the train had a sleeping room and the dining car was fully stocked.

It didn't seem as if this rain would ever end, but Cadence tried to remember that there was probably a group of farmers somewhere who were grateful for the water. She stepped down off the train dry, at least for the moment, and watched from beneath the umbrella as Levi and a few of the others worked to lower the side of the livery coach. Her rifle was gripped comfortably in her hand.

"Whoa, boy," Levi called as Apollo pranced down the ramp.

She imagined that the animals were just as fidgety as the people on board. At least now, they'd be able to stretch their legs. The abandoned Pony Express station would serve as temporary shelter.

Before long, the stock car was closed back up.

"You want to rest a while before heading out?" Levi asked, guiding an already saddled Apollo and the sorrel mare toward her.

"We don't know how much time we're going to get," she told him, removing the satchel from across her shoulders and handing it to him. "For all we know, the bridge could already be out. We need to get there and the sooner, the better."

Cadence had to believe that Annie and the other two Pinkerton agents left behind in Piedmont would be able to protect the people on board those three coaches. It now fell to her and Levi to make sure that nothing bad happened at Devil's Gate. If the bridge was out, they could at least warn the engineer before it was too late. She just hoped it wouldn't come to that.

"That's what I thought you might say." He handed the sorrel mare's reins to her. Cadence slipped her rifle into the holster in the side of the saddle. Levi picked up her bag and secured it to her horse.

Devil's Gate was just under a day's ride from here. If they pushed it a little, they might even arrive before nightfall. She hoped they'd be able to find some shelter from the rain, or at least a place that would stave off the chill. She wasn't looking forward to the ride, but they just didn't have the time it would take to get there by wagon.

"Here, I thought you might want this." He handed her a buckskin jacket. "To keep out the cold for as long as possible."

Cadence pulled the jacket over her shoulders, admiring the workmanship. "Where did you get this?" she asked, pulling her hair up into a ribbon behind her. He hadn't been out of her sight since he'd started unloading the car with the livestock.

"It's mine. Rafe made it for me a long time ago. It will keep you dry, and warm…at least everywhere it covers."

So many questions invaded her mind at the revelation.

Rafe sews?

"You mean you've had this the entire time and haven't used it?"

Levi didn't respond, just lifted a large canvas bundle and draped it across Apollo's back. "Are you ready?" he asked as he cinched up the rope.

"You two be careful." Her father stepped out onto the platform at the top of the staircase.

Cadence looked up, smiled, and with the reins of the sorrel still in her hand, she closed the umbrella and quickly climbed the stairs. She knew he was worried. "You too." She stood up on her toes and placed a kiss on his cheek. "You need your rest." She squeezed his arms, then turned around. When she reached the bottom step, she pulled the reins toward her and she mounted.

"I love you, Cadie."

"I know, Dad. I love you too."

By the time the sun had started to descend behind the elevated horizon, they'd finally reached their destination. Rushing waters could be heard echoing through the canyon valley. Levi didn't dare travel any closer to the bridge in case there were unsavory eyes watching them. His time with military intelligence had taught him a lot about reconnaissance work. And right now, they would be better served with the light of day in their favor. Even if this blamed storm continued. He looked up.

Although the rain had lightened over the past couple of hours to a slight drizzle, he was soaked through. He glanced over at Cadence. The skirt of her dress clung to her horse's back and her unkempt hair, which had come loose from its ribbon, hugged her face, but she wasn't shivering.

They only had a short amount of daylight left. For days the rain had been coming down and he wondered if it would ever stop.

"We'll make camp here." Levi pulled to a halt in front of a small cluster of Juniper trees that hid an indentation in the rock of the mountain that would offer some extra protection from the elements for the horses as well as hide them all from immediate view.

This area was perfect. The vastly curved trunks of the trees provided areas to which he could secure the canvas tent top that he'd hauled along the way. It also didn't hurt that as he was prepping the area under the trees, he discovered that a flat slab of stone lay just beneath the top layer of soil. While it was wet, the surface could be dried off and hopefully, would prove to keep them drier than lying directly in the mud.

"Why aren't we heading on down to the bridge?" Cadence asked, pulling up alongside him. "I can hear the river. We can't be too far, and there's still plenty of light."

"Not enough," he said, taking the weighty bundle off his horse and hanging it up over a particularly angled part of one of the tree trunks. "We need to prepare for the night and be ready to go at dawn's first light." He doubted Cadence was familiar enough with the area to venture out on her own, but he walked over to her, his hand raised in an offer of help, just to make sure.

Reluctantly, she allowed him to help her down. They'd only taken a couple of breaks to walk around and water the horses along the way and he knew she would likely be extra sore. After he tied the horses up behind the trees in the would-be cave, he pulled out a handful of apples that he'd been saving for them until they'd arrived. Apollo nickered in approval and the sorrel snorted, her ears forward, and pawed lightly at the ground.

"You did great." He rubbed Apollo on the nose and the sorrel on the side of her head. "We'll give you both a good brushing and a dozen more apples when we're done here."

"I don't know how you cowboys do it."

"What's that?"

"Ride around on your horses all day and not want to die by day's end."

Levi laughed, but not so loudly to be heard at any sort of distance. The element of surprise was the best advantage they had.

"Come on over here and help me get this up and then you can walk a bit." He picked up one side of the canvas. "Just lift that end and we'll attempt to secure each corner to a different section of one of these trees with one end higher than the other so the rain will roll off. I think there is enough space we can make a cozy little shelter."

He chuckled to himself as Cadence gingerly bent down to

pick up her side of the material.

Poor girl.

Once they'd strung the cloth into position, Levi retrieved his rope from his saddle. It proved to be a little too short.

"Need this?" Cadence asked, holding out the knife he knew she kept just above her boot.

"Thank you."

When the shelter was as secure as it was going to get, Levi backed away to see if the white canvas was hidden enough from view. It definitely could be seen, but he didn't think it was cause for too much concern this late in the day. Especially, if the men they were looking for were down in the valley.

Levi grabbed the bedrolls he'd stuffed into a potato sack. They'd stayed mostly dry beneath the canvas and he rolled them out on the ground over the rock slab. He placed the head of one bedroll at one side of the rock and the head of the other on the opposite side.

"I'm afraid we won't be able to start a fire tonight," he told Cadence when he caught a glimpse of her stretching backward, her hand on the back of her hip. "Can't risk being seen," he added.

Cadence turned to look at him. Dark circles befell her eyes and several times he could have sworn she concealed a yawn.

"Walk," he told her. "It will help, but don't go too far. The descent into the valley is a steep one and with all this rain, I'm worried there might be a slide."

As if by his mere mention of it, a few rocks slid out of place and tumbled down into the valley. But then, the rain stopped.

Ha.

Levi hurriedly walked over to his saddle bag, retrieved a dry shirt and pair of britches, and grabbed the small knapsack of foodstuffs he'd collected from the dining car aboard the train. He was hungry and he was sure Cadence was too— though, he imagined, she'd never complain about it.

She returned after just a few minutes with a dry skirt, her rifle, and the lantern in tow. "I thought this might be helpful," she said, handing him the light, then slipping past him and ducking into the shelter. "How long do you think the rain will stay away?"

Levi turned his back to the trees, looking up at the storm clouds that still loomed over them.

"Hopefully, all night, but I think we have a couple of hours at most."

"You can come in now," she said quietly.

This oddly reminded him of a particularly cold and rainy night they'd spent in the back of a wagon on their way to Laramie. He closed his eyes to the memory. It wasn't going to be any easier this time around, sleeping so close to her.

When he stepped beneath the shelter, his eyes were drawn to the wet skirt hanging from one of the lower branches at the far side of the makeshift little room. Cadence was already snuggled deep into her bedroll.

"Thank you for all of this," she said with a deepening lilt to her voice. He noticed her hand rested on the stock of her rifle. Her eyes were already closed and he imagined she would be asleep in no time. He just prayed that the weather would hold.

At least through the night.

"Goodnight, Cade," he said quietly as he climbed beneath his own blankets.

"Mmmmhmmm."

CHAPTER TWENTY-ONE

Cadence awoke to the pungent aroma of pinewood burning and light penetrating the limbs of their makeshift shelter, warming her face. She opened her eyes and sat up straight, surprised that she had been able to sleep all through the night. She glanced over to see Levi's empty blanket already rolled and the covering overhead gone.

"I thought he said we couldn't have a fire," she mumbled to herself under her breath.

The top of the bedroll was damp from the morning dew, yet she'd slept surprisingly well. Warm even. Cadence pulled Levi's buckskin coat closer around her, reveling in the warmth it had provided both on the journey here and throughout the night. She tossed the bedding from off of her, got to her feet, and quickly rolled it up. Hopefully, they would be able to find the culprit who'd been charged with destroying this bridge and whoever was behind all of these attacks before it was too late.

The final ceremony for the achievement would undoubtedly be postponed. She only hoped all of their efforts had not been in vain. The Transcontinental Railroad was not only the completion of a dream, but the beginning to a new future.

Cadence picked up her rifle and took a step toward the break in the trees they'd used as the doorway.

"Glad you're up," Levi whispered as he stuck his head inside of the tent. His face was very close to hers. "We've got movement down below."

Cadence shrugged the jacket from her shoulders and handed it to Levi. "Thank you. I wouldn't want anything to happen to that." She smiled and swerved around him out into the morning's air. "I may need it again," she called back.

The horses had already been saddled and their camp picked up and loaded onto Apollo's back. Cadence again slid her rifle into the holster on the mare's saddle, then felt her pocket for the trinkets she'd grown accustomed to having with her at all times. For a moment she panicked at their absence, but then she quickly remembered that she had left the journal and Lincoln's spike with her father, but her pearl gripped six-shooter was still there, readily available.

Smoke rose from what looked to be a small camp below. "And here I thought you were cooking up something delicious to eat." Her focus moved to the enormous bridge that spanned the valley and a new respect for nature suddenly took root. She watched as the tremendously high waters slashed against the wooden supports of the bridge.

"And that is exactly why I said no fires," he pointed at the huge white cloud rising from the camp below. "Looks like there's just one man, but there are two tents, so there may be as many as four." Levi lifted himself into his saddle. "Well," he said after a moment, "you coming?"

"Yes, sir." She stuck her boot into the stirrup and pulled herself up.

Owwww. Her legs were still stiff and protested at the mount.

As they rode along the ridgeline, the sound of the rushing river filled her ears. It was louder than she'd expected. "Are they sure that bridge will support a whole train?"

Levi stopped at a flat area with very little vegetation and nodded toward what looked like a trail carved into the side of the mountain. "We'll head down from here."

She pulled up alongside of him. "Look at it." The bridge seemed small from their vantage point, which made her apprehension that much stronger. "I don't know that I'd even want to walk across it, let alone be on a fast moving rail car as it traversed."

"There have been multiple trains that have passed through here, but I must admit, it *is* a little unnerving whenever we cross one of these bridges. I just worry that Durant has been so focused on winning that he's allowed the men to cut corners." He clicked his tongue and started forward. "This rain has made the river swell. It looks as if some of the bents have been compromised by the high water levels."

"What can we do? That doesn't sound like sabotage or an attack." Cadence had been unprepared for such a steep hill and she leaned down as far as the saddle horn would allow, keeping only one eye open. Her horse, however, seemed more nervous than she was as the mare kept trying to back up, sending rocks and debris down the hill at Levi. When he looked back and saw her, he quickly turned his mount back up the hill. He reached out and grabbed the cheek piece of the sorrel's bridle.

"Whoa, girl," he said soothingly. "Cade, you need to lean backward as you ride down the hill to shift the weight evenly. If you lean forward, there is a good chance that both you and the horse will tumble, heads first, down this mountain. And then where would be our element of surprise?" He laughed.

Cadence immediately switched her position and leaned backward. It felt like she was more in control this way. "One way or another, Levi Redbourne, someone will be surprised."

He laughed again. "Come on."

It must have taken near an hour, Cadence suspected, for them to navigate the descent of the trail as the sun had risen a great deal in the sky since they'd begun. Storm clouds still hid its position on occasion as the light turned to shadows for short lengths of time.

Smoke from the camp they'd seen from above came into view through the scrub of trees, jagged rocks, and other foliage. Levi pulled his rifle from his holster and Cadence did the same.

Ping. A shot glanced off a rock to Levi's side. Apollo reared, squealing his protest.

"I won't miss next time," a voice shouted over the roar of the river. "Now, get down off your horses."

How did people keep getting the drop on them?

That's twice, Cadence thought. *I'm losing my touch.*

They both dismounted and carefully made their way to the camp situated just above the sloped embankment. Cadence looked up at the bridge. It was a completely different picture as now it towered over them. As the sun dipped behind the dark grey of the clouds, it grew even more ominous. No wonder it had been named Devil's Gate, for surely the devil himself had built it.

"Toss your guns next to the tent," the voice instructed.

They both did as he'd told them.

"Step away."

The river was full and seemed to be moving very quickly. Any closer and they would both be going for a swim.

Cadence squinted at the landscape, searching for any clues as to from where their attacker might be watching. The sun peeked out from behind its mask and glinted off the barrel of the man's gun. He was hiding behind a bush no more than ten feet from them.

"Did you see that?" Cadence whispered.

Levi nodded discreetly, but did not respond.

Cadence took another step toward Levi, hiding herself behind his large, muscular frame. She handed him the sorrel's reins and slowly pulled her six-shooter from the folds of her skirt. She peered around Levi's shoulder, hoping she would appear the frightened female.

The man was crouched down, his knee exposed through the shrubbery. She needed to take a shot, but did not want to kill him. They needed answers and a dead man wouldn't provide them.

"On my count," Cadence said coolly, "you need to get out of my way."

"There's no need for anyone to get shot today," Levi called out to the man. "I'm sure we can work something out."

"What are you doing?" Cadence whispered.

"Saving a man's life," he responded under his breath. "I'm sure we can make some sort of deal," he said more loudly.

A few seconds passed.

"What kind of deal?"

"The kind that makes you a rich man."

One of the horses snorted. Cadence saw movement on the ground. A shadow moved as if someone was creeping up behind them. She whirled around. A hefty bearded man approached, knife in hand. Before she could raise her gun, he lunged at her, grabbing her by the hair and pulled her backward into his arms. The hand he used to hold the knife rested on the bone just below her neck and the blade grazed her cheek.

Levi whipped around, his hands in the air, ready for a fight.

The brute had obviously not seen her pistol.

Carefully, Cadence twisted her arm behind her back and shoved the barrel of her gun as close into the man's ribs as she could get.

"If I go," she spat, "you're going with me."

"That's mighty big talk for such a little lady," the burly man challenged. "You hear that, Abe. The girl says she's going to shoot me."

Abe stood up from behind the bush. A clear target. He'd lowered his gun.

Cadence pulled back the pistol's hammer with a click. She heard the man swallow hard.

"That's right." Levi stood up straight and turned so his back was no longer to the man behind the shrubbery. "I'd listen to her if I were you."

Cadence wrapped her fingers around her attacker's wrist. She hoped Levi would recognize the move as one taught to Pinkertons and military officers for tactical combat. If she could gain the proper leverage, she would be able to twist his hand away from her and relieve him of his knife, but she would need Levi's help in neutralizing Abe.

"She is the bravest, most selfless person I know," Levi continued. He looked at her with a curt nod. He'd understood. "But she's fearless when she needs to be."

Now.

Cadence stomped on her captor's foot.

Levi threw the reins in the air, dropped to the ground, and rolled toward the rifles.

The man's hand was beefier than she'd realized, but she was still able to pull down on her unsuspecting captor's wrist while pushing her thumb firmly against the back of his hand and she jerked it hard. The knife fell. She kicked it away as she twisted away from him, reaching down for the blade in the process.

"Damned hellcat. I think you broke my hand."

Levi shot one of the branches off the shrub next to Abe, who stopped in his tracks.

"Next time, *I* won't miss," Levi said with a smirk, motioning for him to join them in camp. Once he stepped foot on the semi leveled ground, Levi flicked his wrist and the man dropped his gun.

"What are you and *Abe* doing here?" Cadence asked, her pistol pointed at the man who'd threatened her.

"It's a nice day for hunting," Abe said derisively as he looked down at the fire.

A good sized rabbit was roasting on the spit. "Now I know what smelled so good," she told Levi off-handedly as she made her way slowly back to Apollo, not taking her eyes off her prisoner. Thankfully, the horse hadn't bolted when Levi had fired the shot. "You taught him well." She rubbed the side of the horse's face and then pulled a length of rope from Levi's saddle.

Drip. Drop.

Cadence looked up into the sky.

Not again.

She tossed the rope over to Levi as the sun retreated behind another grouping of large threatening clouds. "This weather's not going to hold."

"Are there any more of you?" Levi asked, pushing Abe down into the dirt and tied him to an oversized rock, smooth on one side, jagged on the other.

"Don't take more than two of us to skin a hare," he responded, his cheeky grin revealing several blackened teeth.

"There are going to be a lot of people coming on that train," Cadence thought she'd try to appeal to their compassion. "Is that how you want to be known…just what is your name anyway?"

He met her eyes, still clutching his hand. He spit in her face.

Bile rose in Cadence's throat. Her jaw clenched and her fists tightened.

Levi handed her his handkerchief before landing a punch across the man's face. "Didn't anyone ever teach you how to treat a lady?"

She wiped the sticky mess from her nose and cheeks. "This isn't going to get us anywhere. Check the tent. There's got to be something around here that will give us a clue."

Levi agreed. "You okay?" he asked her, looking at the man whose nostrils flared and his teeth bared.

"Ol', let's see, how about Bart? Ol' Bart here and I are going to do just fine, aren't we?" she took a step back and shot at the ground in front of the man, who barely flinched, though he still cradled the hand she'd hurt. "I recognize that symbol," she said to Levi, pointing to the ring on Bart's finger. "It's the same one Annie had on her bracelet. The same as the medal on the journal."

Bart growled.

Levi glanced around the camp, then threw back the fold of the first tent. "Look at this," he said, holding the flap open to reveal a box of explosives. Six sticks were missing.

"Cade!" Levi screamed. "Look out!"

Bart lunged for her, but Levi came out of nowhere and knocked into him. Both men rolled off the embankment and down into the rushing water.

"Levi!" she called, peering over the ledge and scanning the river for any sign of the men.

Nothing.

Her heart pounded, her chest constricting. She searched the banks, then scanned the water. Still nothing.

"Levi!" she screamed again.

"Ain't nobody going to survive a fall into that river. He's hell and gone." Abe said haughtily.

Cadence refused to listen, to even consider that...that...

"Levi Redbourne!" she called out as the rains started falling in thick sheets.

Nothing. She closed her eyes and strained her ears in hopes of hearing anything that might give her a little hope.

"Here."

The voice was faint, but she'd heard something.

"Cadence."

She heard it again.

Cadence opened her eyes just as a bolt of lightning thrashed the heavens and lit a part of the river where a tree had tipped, but had not yet been completely uprooted. A splash of white appeared amongst the earthy browns and greens of the edge.

Levi. He was alive.

Thank you, Lord.

Cadence shoved her gun into her dress and carefully made her way down to the tree. Levi was not holding onto the tree itself, but hugged a large rock in the middle of the river that had somehow managed to stick out of the water's rapids.

"You need to go for help," he yelled, but she could tell his voice was strained.

The tree trunk jutted out just above him, but appeared just out of his reach. If she could just lower it enough that he could grab hold. Cadence took a step out onto the wood, testing its durability. The trunk lowered a little, and luckily, the roots seemed to hold.

"No!" Levi yelled. "It's too dangerous."

Images of the night he'd saved her from the fire flashed through Cadence's mind. She would not lose him. Couldn't. She stepped out a little farther on the trunk, though the tree was slippery. She sat down and straddled the wood, inching herself out farther, gripping fiercely onto the bark, until the tip was low enough for Levi to grab onto. When he tried to pull himself up, a cracking noise sounded behind her and the entire trunk dropped a few inches.

Levi let go.

"Don't you do this to me, Levi Redbourne. You will take ahold of that branch and pull yourself up here. Do you hear me?" Tears streamed down her face both from fear and anger. "I will stay out here all day and all night."

Levi bowed his head and shook it.

"Fool woman," he said as he reached up again and grabbed ahold of some of the broken branch nubs.

Cadence gingerly scooted backward as quickly as she could until she was able to push herself up onto the bank. She didn't take her eyes off of Levi as he placed hand over fist, his feet still fighting with the water. At last, he swung a leg up over a thick branch that allowed him to pull his weight atop the trunk of the tree.

The roots cracked again, the tip of the tree now buried just beneath the surface of the water.

Cadence couldn't breathe. He was only a few feet away, but it seemed so far. She held out her hand, leaning over as far as she dared, but it was no use. He would have to make it the rest of the way alone.

"You listen to me Levi Redbourne. I love you!" she mustered a smile when his eyes locked with hers. Rain mixed with her tears as they ran down her face. "I want to be your bride," she yelled. "To spend forever with you. To have children with you. I'll marry you, Levi, but only if you get over here and off that damn tree."

He stood up.

CRACK!

She reached out to him and his hand gripped hers. He jumped just as the remainder of the tree broke apart and fell into the flow of the river.

Levi threw his arms around her, holding her so tightly she could scarcely breathe. But she didn't care. She tightened her arms around him, pulling him closer. His hands were suddenly at her face, cupping her jaw. His tear-filled eyes met hers briefly as he lifted her chin to meet his ardent kiss. His cool lips melded with hers and joy filled her completely. Her hands grasped the side of his face, her fingers running through the short hairs at his nape.

"Tell me again," Levi said as he pulled away from her.

"I love you."

CHAPTER TWENTY-TWO

Levi and Cadence returned to the camp, hand in hand, only to find it empty. Abe had gotten free of his bindings and the horses were nowhere to be found. The rain had all but put out the fire, but the rabbit still sat on the spit. Levi threw open the tent flap. The box of dynamite was gone.

"I've seen those explosives before. At the end of the war, I saw them used more than once. They are extremely dangerous and highly unpredictable. Just one or two sticks have enough power to bring down that entire bridge." Levi ran his hands through his hair.

How could he have let this happen? He kicked at the ground and mud sizzled as it flew into the fire pit.

"He couldn't have gone far," Cadence said, spinning in slow circles as she scanned the entire valley.

"But without the horses, we'll never be able to catch him. He knows we're going to try to stop him, so he won't take any chances by waiting until the train comes through. We need to find him. Now."

"Look," Cadence said, grabbing Levi's arm and pointing to a section of the bank only a short distance from the base of the bridge.

Abe was hunched down over the crate of explosives.

"I can't let him do this." Levi started running down the bank toward him.

"Wait," Cadence called after him.

Abe looked up at them, his eyes locked with Levi's, victory written all over his face. He smiled and turned toward the bridge, a raised stick of dynamite in his hands.

Levi tried to run faster, but the mud made for a slippery terrain and the weight of his wet boots slowed him. The fuse stayed lit in the rain. Abe lifted it behind his head, ready to throw it into the bridge supports.

"Long live the Confederate States of Americ—"

BOOM!

BOOM! BOOM!

Levi was thrown backward and slammed into the rocky terrain beneath him as the entire mountainside shook. Debris of all kinds tumbled down the hillside and the bridge groaned in protest. The air had been sucked from his lungs and his ribs hurt, but he tried to push himself up off the ground. His ears rang and his head was spinning.

"Levi," Cadence whispered his name.

He rolled over onto his back and opened his eyes. She wasn't there. He forced himself into a sitting position and tried to shake his head clear. It wasn't long before everything came back into focus and he spotted Cadence lying on the ground covered in mud and debris.

Cautiously, he dragged himself to his feet and stumbled toward her.

"Cade," he said, bending down, "are you all right?" He carefully turned her onto her back.

"You should just leave me lying here all alone," she said with a whiny voice he'd never heard from her before.

"What are you talking about?"

She sat up and looked at him. "I tripped." She slammed her palms against the muddy ground. "Landed right on my face. I could have stopped this whole mess with a bullet when I had the chance. No questions. This was my assignment and I failed." She pulled a strand of grass from her muddied hair.

Levi wasn't sure whether or not it would be prudent to laugh, but he couldn't help himself. Relief, exhaustion, and wonder all combined into one. "It's over," he said, pulling her to her feet. "Both men are gone. The bridge is…well, it's still there. And, we're together."

"I wish that were true," she said, shoulders slumped. "I mean the being over part," she was quick to assure him. "There are still six sticks of dynamite unaccounted for, and in case you hadn't noticed, we're stranded here. We have no idea when or even if Durant is going to be released and we still haven't decoded the rest of that journal."

"Shhhh," Levi pulled her into his arms. "One victory at a time."

Cadence pulled away, her eyebrows knit together. "You're shivering."

It was funny. He hadn't felt cold, but as he held up his hand to examine it, a chill washed over him and he shook from the inside out.

"Come on. I won't be able to carry you back to their camp." They slowly made their way back to the tents, Levi leaning on Cadence's shoulders for support. He was tired and hungry. The smell of cooking meat on the spit didn't help with the latter.

"You sit down right here." She helped him to a rock. "We need to get that fire going again, despite the rain, and get you warmed up to the bones. It looked like there were other supplies in those tents. Blankets, maybe even some dry clothes."

Levi tried to shake the cold off, but it was just too strong.

Cadence took one look at him and her face said everything. If he didn't get warmed up soon, he was going to die out here.

Not acceptable.

She threw open the flap to the closest tent. "You need to

get out of the rain. So, you're going to wrap yourself up in one of those dry blankets or change into something of theirs, but either way, you are getting out of those wet clothes."

"Yes, ma'am." He saluted, but wasn't sure why.

"Here," she said, lifting up one of his legs and pulling at his boot, "let me help you."

Once his feet were bare, Levi pushed off the rock with every ounce of strength he could muster and fumbled with the top button of his shirt.

Cadence took a deep breath as she brushed his hands away and undid the fastening. Levi could have sworn that her hands were shaking too. One by one, she unhooked each button until his shirt fell open at the front.

Levi strained to pull the wet shirt and vest from his shoulders. Cadence slid her hands up his chest and over his arms and shoulders, pushing the clinging material from his goose fleshed skin until he was free of them. A flicker of heat started low in his belly at her touch, but he forced himself to focus.

"Trousers too," she said with a raised brow.

She wasn't making it easy.

Levi knew she had to be cold also. She may not have taken a detour in the river, but she'd been standing out in the rain all morning. He looked at her, willing his fingers to work well enough to release the fastening of his trousers. Success came quickly.

"I think I can take it from here," he said as he slowly bent down and crawled into the tent.

He tried not to think about the putrid odor that permeated the tent as he searched for some dry clothing and decided against wrapping himself in nothing but a blanket. He opened a large canvas satchel and found exactly what he needed.

It took him longer than he'd expected to rid himself of his wet britches. It didn't help that every inch of him was freezing cold, but he had to admit that donning a dry shirt and trousers took the edge off the chill. He lay back onto the haphazard bed of blankets that had yet to be rolled for the day. His eyelids grew heavy.

"I'll just rest a moment."

Cadence looked at the tent with growing satisfaction. It had taken some effort, but she'd been able to take down and re-pitch the second tent over the fire pit. She had been pleased to see that this tent had a canvas floor. She used her knife to cut a hole in the floor big enough to encompass the pit and another in the top of the tent large enough for the smoke to escape.

As Cadence fanned the coals and added one of the three large logs she'd found inside, the fire came back to life and the smoke seemed to know instinctively where to go. She needed to get Levi into the warmth as soon as possible, so she quickly changed into some clothes she'd found amongst Abe's belongings before stepping back out into the cold. Luckily, the rain had subsided for the time being.

"May I come in?" she asked.

A low rumbling sound was her only reply. Cadence flipped back the tent door and found Levi sprawled out on the blankets, snoring. She placed a hand on his face. He was still extremely cold to the touch.

"Levi," she said quietly.

"What?" he sat up. "Is everything okay?"

"Come on."

He seemed to be feeling a little better already. It took him some time, but he got to his feet and followed Cadence to the other tent, but not before she'd grabbed the pile of blankets he'd been sleeping on. She threw them toward the back of the tent with the others she'd discovered.

Cadence quickly sliced a few pieces of meat and placed them on the single tin plate she'd found.

"I thought you might be hungry," she said, not quite able to meet his eyes. She was still reeling from the feel of his sculpted chest beneath her fingertips.

He watched her. She could feel it.

"Cadence," he said in those deep rich tones that she'd grown to love. "You are an amazing woman."

Heat filled her face. She couldn't help but be pleased by his appraisal.

Silence again passed between them.

"Here," he said, holding out a piece of the meat to her, "eat."

She took a bite and smiled.

"Thank you." He reached a hand up to her face, his thumb tracing her cheek.

Suddenly, he cleared his throat. "It's going to be a long day," he said with a laugh.

Cadence held up a deck of cards. "After you sleep."

Levi couldn't sleep. He pulled back the covers of his bedroll and sat up, careful not to wake Cadence. The soft glow coming from outside the tent told him that it was almost time for the sun to rise. He slipped on his socks and boots, newly dried over the fire, picked up his rifle, and slipped out into the fresh morning air.

He'd not been able to stop thinking about the missing sticks of dynamite and thought he might know how to find them, so he lit a lantern and walked down to the edge of the river at the base of the bridge supports. He tried not to think about the life that had been lost here, rather about the ones that would be saved.

It appeared as if the water had receded significantly within the last day or so and he held up the lantern, hoping to confirm his suspicions. The lantern's light didn't seem to reach very far, but sure enough, about ten feet out into the river, the tips of three clustered dynamite sticks peeked above the water. Levi scanned the other trusses to locate the remaining sticks.

He knew from experience that dynamite would not explode when wet, but if the water continued to recede, it would only be a matter of time before they had another problem. Levi had no desire to repeat the experience of yesterday morning and thought it best to leave the removal to a crew better trained with explosives.

It also appeared that one whole section of the vertical support pilings in the framework had been washed away in the sudden torrent of rising water. They'd have to warn the engineer and he would be able to evaluate if the trestle bridge could be crossed safely.

Footsteps, accompanied by a soft nicker, brought a smile to Levi's face. Apollo's cold nose nudged his arm and he turned around to greet his old friend.

"I knew you hadn't gone far, buddy. How are you?" He scrubbed the horse's neck and leaned his face up against the side of Apollo's nose and cheek. "Come on," he said after a minute, "let's go get Cadence."

Whoo. Whoo.

The whistle of the train's engine spurred Levi to move faster.

"Was that the train?" Cadence asked as she emerged from the tent, her hair newly braided down one side. The men's clothes she wore were obviously too big for her, but Levi kind of liked seeing her in britches.

"Yep. We need to get to the other side of the tunnel before they reach it. Part of the framework has been washed away and I'm not sure the weight of the train will be able to make it across."

Apollo came up beside Levi from behind and whinnied at

Cadence in greeting.

"Where did you find him?" She asked, reaching out to stroke his nose.

"He found me."

Levi helped Cadence up into the saddle. He stopped and looked around the camp. Other than the soaked clothing, nothing else belonged to them. He slipped his rifle into the saddle holster and climbed up behind Cadence and clicked his tongue.

Once they reached the ridgeline, the steam engine came into view. It would be impossible to get down to the tracks in time for the engineer to see them and stop before entering the tunnel leading out onto the bridge. More drastic measures would be needed.

Levi nudged Apollo faster. They followed the ridge as far as they could. Luckily, the train seemed to be moving quite slowly on its approach, which should give him ample time to get down and into the train to stop it from crossing. Levi dismounted.

"I'll have to jump." He'd done it a thousand times, but never when this much was at stake. He realized he'd physically been through a lot the last couple of days, but there wasn't much of a choice. "Ride down the edge of the trail and wait for me in the meadow just on the other side."

"No!" Cadence responded firmly. "I'm coming with you." She dismounted.

Levi kissed her hard on the mouth. "Not this time, my love. I'll meet you in the meadow."

As the train approached, Levi inched his way to the edge of the ridgeline. The coach following the tender car was a passenger carriage. It would be the easiest to land on and the closest to the engine. His head bobbed up and down as he timed his descent.

Jump.

He landed on top of the car with ease, only sliding back a

few feet.

Thud.

He spun around. Cadence had jumped too. She glanced up at him looking fairly proud of herself as she gained her balance.

"And what about my horse?" he asked, unsure whether to applaud her for her bravery or scold her for stupidity. Either way, he was impressed.

Levi quickly made his way to the end of the car and dropped down onto the balcony. He helped Cadence down. "Go find your father while I speak to the engineer."

She nodded, to his relief, and opened the door, disappearing into the passenger carriage.

Climbing over the tender car and into the locomotive would have been easier without the ill fitted clothing, but Levi made it in record time. He reached out and placed his hand on an astonished engineer's shoulder. "You have to stop this train, Sam! I'm not sure the bridge is going to hold."

Without question, the engineer vigorously applied the brakes. Just as the locomotive entered the tunnel, the train stopped.

"Levi, how did you…?"

"It's a long story, but I'm glad you listened to me."

"Mr. Durant's been in a mood ever since I collected him from those workers in Piedmont. He's not going to like this one bit."

"I'll handle Mr. Durant, Sam. Just go take a look at that bridge." Levi hopped down out of the locomotive, but turned back to the engineer. "And we'll need an explosives crew." He left Sam standing there, mouth gaping open, and headed down the tracks on foot. He was joined shortly by a red-in-the-face Durant whose eyes became mere slits on realizing it was Levi.

"What in tarnation has happened now, Mr. Redbourne? I generally consider myself a very patient man, but I'm afraid I don't have much left." He twisted around, his hand wiping down his face and closing into a fist. "And where did you come from anyway? I thought you were…never mind, just tell me what is going on."

"I'm glad to see you are well, Mr. Durant, after your…extended visit in Piedmont. I presume the conflict was settled amiably." Levi knew that the Vice President had a lot of pull with the Union Pacific and was sure that to avoid any negative publicity in the newspapers the worker's demands for back pay had been met. Otherwise, Durant would not be here.

"Can we please just discuss why my train has stopped yet again?"

Levi took a few moments to explain the situation to the man. When he was finished, Durant stomped his feet and waved his hands in the air, throwing a full-on tantrum. Then, as if nothing out of the ordinary had happened, he straightened his cravat and headed up toward the locomotive.

"This train cannot go across that bridge," Sam pointed to the wooden structure spanning the distance of the deep ravine. "A whole section of the trestle supports are missing. The locomotive is just too heavy to cross."

Mr. Durant paced back and forth over the tracks before coming to a stop directly in front of the engineer. "We will be in Promontory by Monday or the only job you'll be able to find is cleaning latrines along the line!" he yelled. "Figure it out!" He stomped back down the track toward his fancy Pullman palace car, but was intercepted by a tall, curvy, red-headed woman. Annie.

"What's wrong?" Levi heard her ask.

Durant shook his head, without a word, and waved her by. A sly smile played with the corners of her mouth, and a look of satisfaction crossed her smug face. Levi had worked with enough spies in the military to know the kind who were only out for their own making. And this Annie was one of them.

"Sam," Levi said to the conductor, "the sleeping and passenger cars, are they lighter than the engines?"

"Yeah," the engineer answered warily. "Why?"

"Do you think they could get across this bridge?"

Sam scrubbed at his chin with his knuckles. "I reckon they could. With a good push." His face lit up as if realizing that would be the answer to his current job situation.

Levi nodded. "Thank you."

It wasn't long before the train crew had evacuated each car and hundreds of passengers, many of whom, including some of the troops from the Twenty-First Regiment of Infantry, carefully made their way along the foot bridge, adjacent to, but sitting lower than the rails.

The roaring torrent of the swollen Weber River crashed against the wooden trestles, and with no railing to speak of, many passengers clung to each other as they warily crossed the rickety structure, trying not to look down into the swells of what surely was the Devil's gate.

Several crew members worked tirelessly trying to shore up the bridge in these extreme conditions, while a few trained soldiers braved the water to remove the dynamite. Levi shivered at the memory of the river's chill seeping into his bones.

Brave men indeed.

"There is a siding a few miles back where we can turn around, but if we want to get a wire out to Ogden asking for a relief engine to come and collect the stranded cars and take you all into Promontory, we'll have to head all the way back into Echo City," the engineer informed the small selective group that had been invited into Durant's luxury car.

Levi guessed that he and Cadence had been invited to join the discussion as they'd been the ones to discover the problem. He was happy to sit back and observe for the time being.

"Time, Mr. Eddison," Durant said, his impatience still bubbling close to the surface. "How. Much. Time?"

"If Union Station sends a locomotive straightaway, sir, I'd imagine you can be on your way by nightfall." The nervous engineer twisted his cap in his hands, but he stood tall.

Mr. Durant rested his elbows on his desk and rubbed his temples.

"Make it happen," Durant instructed the engineer.

Sam nodded and tore from the room.

"I am not walking across that bridge, Thom," a white haired gentleman with a tight-lipped smile said from his position on one of the couches lining the walls. "Especially not in weather like this. And I doubt many of the others will either. Have you watched those newspapermen and sightseers nearly wet their drawers out of fear? No, I'll ride across if it's all the same to you."

Levi watched as several of Durant's other guests nodded their agreement. He was baffled at the idiocy and entitlement of some of the most prominent men in politics and the industry. If they thought walking across a foot bridge with only the weight of a few other passengers and a little rain was frightful, what did they think would happen when a railcar, weighing thousands of pounds, strained the trestles?

"Dodge, go inform the others," Durant told Gren with a wave of his hand. "We'll cross the bridge and wait for rescue. Again." He tilted his head as he rubbed the back of his neck.

Gren raised a brow as he passed Levi on his way out the door.

"Miss Kramer," Mr. Durant glanced up at the woman who sat on the corner of his desk, "would you be so kind as to pour me a glass?" he asked with a half-hearted smile.

Annie brushed his cheek with her hand and stood up, making her way to the liquor cabinet.

"I for one," the Union Pacific's Director looked like he'd already had his fair share as he held up his flask, "think this is quite an exciting adventure."

A sick feeling formed in Levi's gut and that always meant trouble. He placed a hand at his hip and unlatched the leather strap over his gun.

CHAPTER TWENTY-THREE

Cadence didn't care for the number of people who had been crowded into Thomas Durant's personal palace car as they headed back for Echo City. Something had felt off for the past few minutes and when Annie stepped away from the man to fetch his brandy, the tiny hairs on the back of Cadence's neck stood on end. She glanced around the car, but nothing of consequence stood out to her.

Then, in the corner of one of the twin mirrors behind Durant, Cade saw Annie open her charm and slip a powder of some sort into the glass she'd just poured and stir. She watched her old friend close the trinket, her forehead wrinkled in thought. She placed a hand over her belly and closed her eyes, swallowing hard.

Don't do it, Cadence pleaded silently.

She placed her own hand over Levi's and squeezed.

He looked down at her.

She looked over at Annie, then back at him. "Be ready," she mouthed.

Annie pulled her shoulders back and picked up the glass. She looked up and caught Cadence's stare in the mirror before turning back to Mr. Durant with a forged smile and handed him the poisoned drink. He raised it into the air.

"Gentlemen," he said in toast. "And ladies, of course."

Cadence had believed the story of her mentor's pregnancy and had felt sorry for the woman. She'd believed that Annie had loved the man who'd fathered her child, but Cadence had obviously been played the fool. Love scorned, after all, was the perfect kindling for hatred.

As Mr. Durant lifted the glass to his lips, Cadence shot up from her position on the couch and smacked the bottom of the cup with enough force that the liquid splashed everywhere. Annie sputtered vigorously, wiping her mouth free of the spilled drink.

Click.

Annie had stopped fidgeting, her demeanor now calm and collected as she held a cocked pistol on Cadence. Her theatrics had been a ploy to get the upper hand.

Levi hurriedly escorted the Senator, Director, and the other dignitaries from the coach.

"Listen, Annie, I…" Cadence took a step toward the woman.

"Annie," Durant said incredulously as he stood, still wiping the tainted liquor from his shirt, "what in heaven's name are you doing?"

She turned the gun on him. "Why couldn't you have just loved me? Accepted us." Tears had smeared the thin layer of eye paint she had applied. "We were going to spare you. Make you a king among men. And then you had to toss me aside like an old worn shoe by requesting someone else for this assignment."

"I have no idea what you are speaking of, Miss Kramer. What does that mean? *We* were going to spare you?" he imitated. "Accepted *us?* Who is this '*we*' and from what, exactly, were you going to spare me?"

The door at the back of the coach opened and Levi

slipped back inside along with the other two Pinkerton agents.

"It's over, Annie," Cadence said in a soft, gentle voice, holding her hands in front of her, palms up.

"It's not over. Not for me anyway. But you!" Annie spat. "You've ruined everything." Her voice turned to a whisper. "You always do."

It was Cadence's turn to be confused.

"Sweet little innocent Cadie Walker lost her fiancé mere weeks before the wedding." Annie bounced the gun around as she spoke.

"What does Daniel have to do with this?" Cadence's heart began to beat faster. "What aren't you telling me, Annie?"

"Oh, honey, it was nothing personal. He just worked for the wrong man. Heard too much."

"*You* killed Daniel?" Cadence stood there, staring. She could hardly believe what she'd just heard.

It can't be.

All these years, the answers had been right under her nose the whole time. A knot formed in her stomach, her hands balled into fists.

"I had no idea at the time that it would prove to be my undoing. How did you stop Abe and Milo, by the way? That bridge should have been gone a long time ago. Since it's still standing, I'm guessing you had something to do with that."

"You were my friend," she said, ignoring Annie's question. "Why do you hate me so badly?"

"Because you've taken everything from me."

"What, Annie? What have I taken from you?"

"But now, you lose."

CRACK!

Annie dropped to the ground.

"No!" Cadence screamed. She wanted answers. She ran to the floor where Annie lay heaped in a clump, her body jerking for a breath.

"What will I lose?"

"She was going to kill you, Miss Walker."

The train stopped.

Cadence looked up at Mr. Durant, gun in hand.

"She's carrying your child, you idiot. She loved you." Cadence turned back to Annie and grabbed her hand, leaning close to her.

"Tell me, Annie. What have you done?"

"You…were…" Annie smiled up at her, "so perfect. I'm…proud of you." She paused a moment. "I'm sorry." Her head turned slightly to the side, her eyes still open, a single tear slipping toward the ground.

She was gone.

Cadence bent her head over Annie's still body. Something sharp dug into Cadence's cheek. When she pulled away, she saw the confederate charm.

"My father!" she yelled, dragging herself from the floor and she threw open the door, nearly jumping to the next coach. *My father.*

Levi chased Cadence through two passenger cars and a sleeping car before she finally reached her father's quarters.

"Cade, will you tell me what's happening?"

She threw open the door as if her life depended on it. Eamon knelt on the floor next to a lifeless man. He looked up.

"I told him that stuff'd kill ya, but he wanted it anyway." Eamon pointed to the empty glass on the night table. "Annie thought it might help with the pain, but you know I never touch it. Clouds the mind."

Cadence rushed into the room and threw her arms around her father. "You're alive." She pulled away. "But you're burning up."

"I don't think I'm the one you should be concerned about." Eamon looked down at the man on the floor. "He's dead."

Levi turned the man over, but he didn't recognize him. "Did you know him?" he asked Eamon.

"I played cards with him a couple of times. Name's Felton or Belton maybe. I think he worked in the livery, though." Eamon held his nose and then waved his hand in front of it.

"That could have been you." Cadence sat down and fell back against the wall of her father's sleeping compartment.

"Ah, Cadie." Eamon sat down beside his daughter and pulled her into his arms.

"While you explain," Levi said, bending down to the dead man on the floor, "I'll take him to Bertram to deal with." He took a blanket off the bunk, laid it over the body, and heaved the heavy corpse up onto his shoulder. "I'm glad you're alive, my friend," he said before turning out into the hallway and heading for Durant's car.

After explaining what had happened to poor Felton or Belton, Bertram said they were taking the bodies of both Annie and her victim to the half-empty freight car and would deliver them to the territory Marshals once they arrived in Promontory.

Levi needed air.

He hoped there wouldn't be any more surprises tonight, but he checked to make sure his gun was at his side just in case. He opened the outer door of the palace car and stepped out onto the balcony.

He needed to think.

The train started moving again. This time, the engine was behind the first couple of cars as it pushed them down the track. Levi realized that the rain had stopped. At least for the moment, he swung around the outside of the car and climbed up the metal ladder leading to the roof. It didn't take long for him to make his way to the engine, where he perched himself on the top of the cab.

Sam blew the whistle, acknowledging he was there.

Levi smiled as the cool breeze glanced over his face. Some

of his best thinking was done up here. The Iron Horseman. Once the crew had heard the nickname his brothers had given him, there had been no turning back. They all had their reasons, and they varied amongst the bunch, but for Levi it was because he felt as at ease atop this engine as his brothers did astride a horse. It was calming. Peaceful. He rode that way until they reached the tunnel at Devil's Gate, then he swung down into the cab and hopped down onto the ground. It was time.

The first coach in line was empty, other than two brakemen who'd volunteered to be the first to cross. They were positioned on either side of the freight wagon to help direct the single coach. After the railcar had been uncoupled, Sam nodded at the front brakeman who nodded back. Slowly, the locomotive pushed the coach forward and out onto the tracks.

Levi hadn't realized he'd been holding his breath until he could hardly breathe. He forced the air out of his lungs and sucked in a lungful of the cool evening air.

Cheers erupted on the other side as the passengers welcomed the freight wagon. Several more coaches were pushed across with success and, at last, it was time for their sleeping car to travel the distance across the wide spans of the valley here in Weber Canyon. Levi climbed aboard, joining Cadence and her father at a seat by the window.

"Are you ready?" he asked, placing an arm across the top of Cadence's seat, his feet extending into the aisle way. While the seats in the luxury sleeping cars were bigger than in the passenger coaches, they were still way too small for his long Redbourne legs.

Eamon looked at him with a raised brow, nodding at his arm. He smiled.

"It's about time."

CHAPTER TWENTY-FOUR

May 10, 1869

For the first time in five days, a cloud could not be seen overhead. The sun shone brightly through the window and the morning portrayed the happiness of the day's celebrations ahead. Cadence glanced out the window as the train passed through a narrow ravine in the mountain range. Within moments, they emerged out of the canyon and into a wide valley encased round about by tall, majestic peaks.

As the train finally came to a stop, Cadence glanced over at Levi who'd taken refuge on the empty seat across the aisle from her, his feet extending across onto the bench opposite her position. She supposed they could have all retired to their beds, but after the exhausting events of yesterday, she figured they'd just been too tired to get very far.

A loud snore caused Cadence to peer over the seat in front of her. She stood up on her knees, careful not to bump Levi's feet, then reached down and placed a hand on her father's forehead. His fever had broken and he appeared to be sleeping peacefully.

Thank heaven for the small blessings, she thought. *And the big ones.* She smiled.

Like Levi, her father's legs extended across the seat and dangled off the end. She wondered why, with so many men running the railroad, the benches were scarcely big enough to accommodate children, much less a fully grown man.

"Daddy," Cadence whispered, shaking the man until he roused enough to look at her. "I need to get those items I gave you to hold onto for me."

He arduously pulled himself into a sitting position. "What?" he asked, rubbing the sleep from his eyes.

"The spike. And the journal. Where are they?"

"The spike is in the box in the drawer beneath the bed in my quarters and the journal is at the bottom of a pile of books on the shelf above the bed," he whispered

"And the case?"

"Strapped to the boards beneath the mattress."

Cadence hopped up and over to her father's unkempt bed. The trousers she wore slipped down to her hips, so she grabbed the waist band and scrunched it up in her hands before they could fall. She dropped to the floor and pulled open the drawer to retrieve the spike.

It was gone.

Maybe her father had just gotten mixed up on where he'd put it. He had still been suffering from the effects of his injury and had been running a fever. Cadence lay on her back and looked up at the under casing of the bed. The cylinder was there.

She exhaled.

The long strap secured to each end of the leather tube snagged on a protruding nail. Cadence tried to remove it, but it just wouldn't budge. She wiggled it, slid it back and forth, but only managed to shred the leather strip. Finally, she yanked on it, and it gave way, but her elbow smacked into the floor. She pursed her lips together to stop any unsavory words from escaping.

With the tube in tow, Cadence slid out from under the bed. She turned to stand up and saw something wedged just beneath the drawer. She looked closer and pried it from the wood. It was a silver heart-shaped charm.

Annie.

She shot up, knocking her head against the bed support. With clenched teeth and a suddenly throbbing head, she sat up, more carefully this time, making sure she would clear the wood.

"What are you doing?" Levi asked, now standing above her.

Her face flooded with heat and she pulled herself up off the floor, avoiding his eyes.

"Look at this?" She placed the charm in his open hand.

"A necklace?"

"Lincoln's spike is missing and that was on the floor next to the drawer where my father said he'd hidden it."

"And you think Annie took it?"

"This," Cadence picked the trinket out of his hand, "is a charm from her bracelet. Who else could have taken it, Levi? No one else knew I had it." She leaned over the bed and pulled the book from the bottom of the stack on the ledge secured to the wall above the mattress. "We have to find it."

"The ceremony starts in two hours."

"Then I guess we'd better hurry." She held up the journal to show him and strode from the sleeping car, the cylinder slung across her shoulder. As much as she hated the idea of deviating from her assignment, she had to find out what was in the case and she didn't trust Mr. Thomas Durant.

"Go away!"

Levi opened the door to Mr. Durant's palace car and stepped inside. "I need a word before the ceremony begins."

Durant lifted his head, his eyes bloodshot and squinting.

"They are uncoupling the engine and the ceremony will begin shortly, but before we head out, we just wanted you to know that we found your maps and have turned them over to the director."

"Maps? What are you talking about?" Durant asked, forcing himself into a standing position.

Cadence held up the empty cylindrical case.

"What have you done?" Durant skirted his desk, his hair oddly wild. He snatched the case from Cadence and peered inside.

"The director was very interested to learn that you were planning to sell secured railroad building locations and had illegally purchased the land surrounding the new locations," she told him.

"They are waiting for you outside, sir," Bertram said after opening the door. He looked around—the tension on the train at a peak. "Is everything all right in here?" he asked.

"Never better," Levi replied with a smile. "Enjoy the celebration, Durant," he said, turning to leave.

Cadence stepped up close to the weasel of a man and Levi unwittingly rested his hand on the butt of the gun at his hip.

"Oh, and Mr. Durant," Cadence cooed as she ran her hands up Durant's chest. "This," she said as she kneed him in the groin, "is for Annie."

He hunched over, his lips puckered and his brows ground together in the center of his forehead.

Cadence turned around, threw open the door, and walked out of the coach with nary a backward glance. Levi followed her from the car. They disembarked and climbed into the wagon waiting to take them to the ceremony.

"How did he take the news?" Eamon asked from his seated position in the back of the wagon.

"I think he's got a headache," Cadence said with a smile as she climbed up onto the tall seat.

"Among other things," Levi quipped. "Let's just say that

your daughter is not someone to be trifled with, Eamon."

They both laughed.

Levi sat up a little taller as they approached the only empty section of rails separating the two lines. The Union Pacific's Number One-Nineteen and the Central Pacific's Jupiter now sat, facing each other, preparing for their much awaited meet.

"Twenty minutes," a man with a bullhorn announced.

The news was met with cheers from the growing crowd and the engineer from each locomotive blew their whistles in acknowledgement. People gathered around the elevated podium, speaking excitedly with one another.

Levi and Cadence climbed down out of the wagon and he wrapped the reins around the metal bar next to the seat. Wagons, carts, and horses dotted the landscape while their owners assembled around the tracks for one of the pictures that would document the occasion. Levi helped Eamon from the back of the wagon and they made their way to the front, where a man sat at a small table with his telegraph, ready to send word to cities across the nation.

Chugga. Chugga. Chug. Chug.

Whoo. Whoo.

Ding. Ding. Ding.

Suddenly, it was as if the whole world had gone silent as the locomotives slowly made their way toward each other. With only a few feet between them, they stopped, waiting. The last rail, a laurel tie, had been laid and it was time for the last spike to be driven. Levi glanced around at all of the congregated onlookers, railroad workers, and a large marching band adorned in bright and colorful uniforms. A man was strapped to the top of a telegraph pole, track layers, dignitaries, crewmen, and state and city officials all awaiting the final moment when the rails would finally be joined.

Levi exhaled. Much of his work would be culminated by this moment and he reached down and took Cadence's hand in his.

"I'm sorry I lost the President's spike," Cade said quietly.

He squeezed her hand. "You didn't," Levi responded. "The Marshals found it among Annie's things and turned it over to Gren. It will have its moment and then he's going to give it to President Grant for safe-keeping."

Cadence smacked his arm. "And you couldn't have said something earlier?"

"Keep quiet," the telegrapher announced for everyone to stop talking as they were about to commence.

She met his eyes, then they both faced forward.

After a prayer by the good Reverend Todd and a few remarks from other officials, the time had come for the commencement of the blows.

Thomas Durant, representing the Union Pacific, and Mr. Stanford from the Central Pacific stepped forward. The silver maul was handed to Mr. Stanford. He lifted the sledge over his head and swung, hitting the tie. He'd missed and a huge roar of laughter exploded from the crowd. Everyone quieted again as Mr. Durant, who still looked as if his head was in a vice, took the maul and swung. He missed. More laughter ensued and one of the railroad's regular tie workers was called over to finish the job. Four spikes were driven.

Done.

Cheers erupted, photographs were taken, and the railroad was complete.

Levi searched the crowd.

"Who are you looking for?" Cadence asked.

Levi turned and took both of her hands into his. "Did you mean what you said at the river?"

Cadence stared at him, searching his eyes.

"You said that you want to be my bride. To spend forever with me. To have my children. Did you mean those things?"

The corners of her mouth upturned. "Of course I did."

"Then, let's not wait. Let's get married today. Right now."

Cadence looked at her father. Levi was glad he'd already

asked his permission. Eamon nodded his approval.

"Yes."

Levi pulled her into his arms, dipped her backward, and kissed her in front of the entire crowd, evoking whoops and hollers from many of the men. "Let's go find the reverend."

The man was hard to spot amongst the excited crowd, but finally, they found him speaking with the mayor who'd conducted the ceremony.

"Reverend Todd," Cadence said with a smile. "We'd like for you to marry us."

"Today," Levi added.

After a few minutes of speaking with them and asking them questions, the good reverend put his hand on Levi's shoulder. "What a wonderful day for marrying. The sun is shining down the Lord's blessing upon you. Come to the feast in Promontory this evening and I will do as you've asked."

The streets were filled with a torchlight procession of people laughing and dancing. The Great Hall was filled with tables upon tables of food and dance cards were being handed out to every young unmarried woman while the single men vied for their attentions.

"For you, miss," a fine young man with a fancy grey suit and clean shaven face placed a cream-colored card in Cadence's hands. 'Order of Dancing' was written on one side and 'Dances' was written on the other with a slew of named dances listed followed by a line for a potential suitor's name. Two Step, Waltz, Two Step, Two Step, Langers—

A small group of young men surrounded Cadence. She smiled, then scanned the room, searching for Levi. He was the only person she wanted to fill her card.

"May I reserve a dance, ma'am?" One of the young men in a faded blue button down stepped forward.

"I'm afraid all of the lady's dances are spoken for, gentlemen," Levi said, picking her up and twirling her about. He set her down, pulling her tightly into his chest as they moved around the dance floor.

Cadence barely noticed that anyone else was there as she stared up into Levi's eyes.

"It's about time you asked me to dance," she said, a smile spread wide across her face. She was impressed that he was able to move so gracefully—especially for a man of his size. "You are just full of surprises."

"And do you like surprises?" he asked.

"Yes," she responded.

"Then I will keep surprising you for the rest of my days." He stopped and pulled her into his arms. "I love you, Cade Walker soon-to-be Redbourne."

"I love you," she said. "But, you can call me Cadie."

THE END

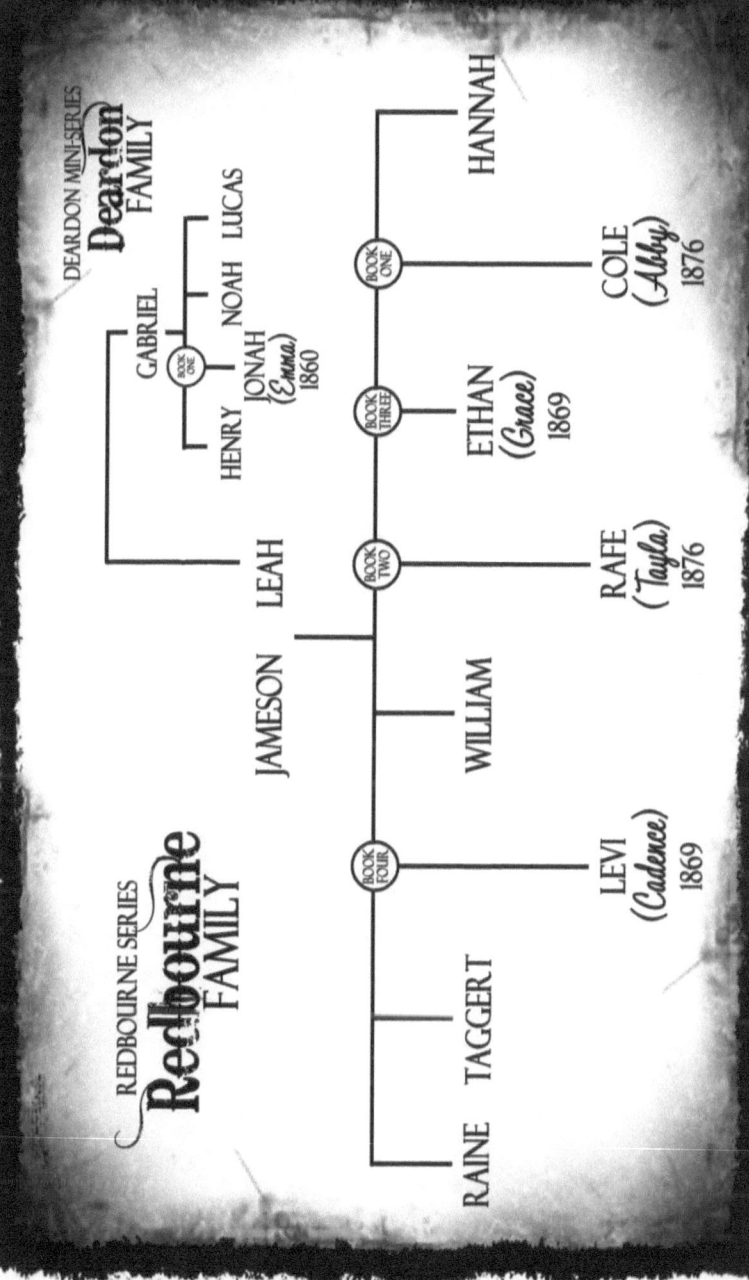

ABOUT THE AUTHOR

KELLI ANN MORGAN recognized a passion for writing at a very young age. Since that time, she has devoted herself to creativity of all sorts—moonlighting as a cover designer, photographer, jewelry designer, motivational speaker, and more.

Kelli Ann is a long-time member of the Romance Writers of America and was president of her local chapter in 2009. Her love of and talent for writing have opened many doors for her and she continues to look for new and exciting opportunities and calls to adventure. She feels very blessed to have a talented husband and son who inspire her on a consistent basis.

Her novels are on the sensual side of PG—without graphic love scenes. Great romance novels are those that make you feel the spectrum of emotion, that leave you wanting more, and it is her hope that every time you crack open one of her romance stories, that you walk away inspired, uplifted, and with a love of romance.

www.kelliannmorgan.com